# The Book of Fate's Desire

Ryan S. Hampton

Milham Books—Madison, WI
ISBN: 979-8-9885528-0-2
Library of Congress Control Number: 2023912311
Title: *The Book of Fate's Desire*
Author: Ryan S. Hampton
Digital distribution | 2023
Paperback | 2023

This is a work of fiction. The characters, names, incidents, places, and dialogue are products of the author's imagination, and are not to be construed as real.

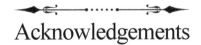

# Acknowledgements

I'd like to thank, first and foremost, my father Rick Hampton who first introduced me to the worlds of my favorite fantasy novels that inspired me to write a story of my own. Next, I have to offer my sincerest gratitude to Alex Marie Humphreys and the National Novel Writer's Month community for making the beginning of this journey possible. Without Alex's help and support, working quickly and from the goodness of her heart, this book would never have existed. If you have ever wanted to write a story, check out NaNoWriMo, it's a game-changer! I want to thank Jessica Ayers for being my very first Biggest Fan and for being so enthusiastic in her support for my work. Finally, my ever-lasting gratitude to all of the early readers of this material. It has come such a long way since some of you read it and I hope you are proud of what you helped produce: Will Fowler, Sontian Stinson, Kristen Layne, Jake Patten, and Jessi Kaasa. To everyone else who has listened to me rant about my story, vent frustrations about publishing, or asked questions about how it's going: you're the best!

# Table of Contents

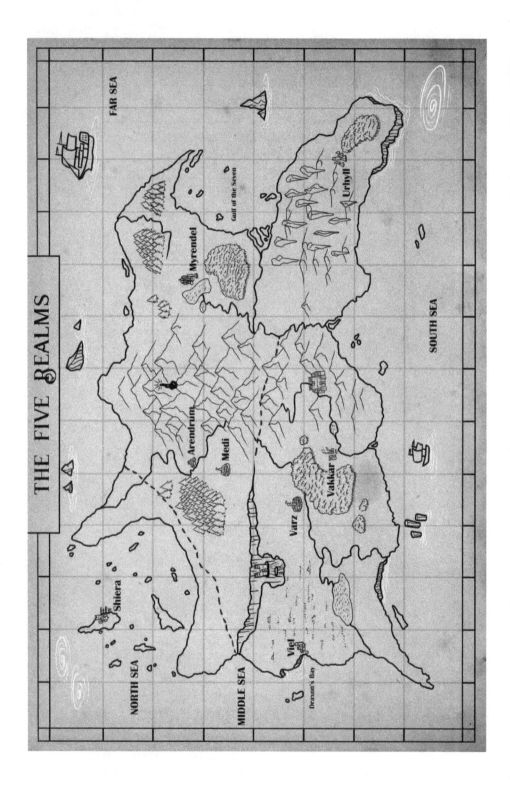

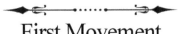

# First Movement

"It is an inescapable truth that mortals must strive relentlessly to meet their Fate, and yet in fear of what it may bring, seek to avoid its fulfillment. It is an exceedingly rare occurrence when they are successful at both."

-King Baklar of Varz

# Chapter 1
## The King of Varz

They are distinctive, the eyes of a sorcerer. Their sclerae are fully black, the irises purest white.

These are the eyes of the citizens of the Varz nation, for they are sorcerers to the last.

Two such eyes stared, unfocused, at a legion of armored men and women from within a face of gaunt pallor.

"Your assessment, my king?" A gruff, aged voice stirred the eyes and they lolled, as if awoken from a deep sleep.

"Assessment? What am I assessing today?" King Dranus VIII (DRA-nuhs) turned his head from side to side, gathering himself. Orbs of haloed night quickly scanned the helmeted faces of his troops arrayed in polished armor of painted metal, each color corresponding to their branch and each tint demarcating their division. Among this kaleidoscope of martial finery, Dranus lingered on the gray space that existed between the countless ranks.

"Have they always been this *dull*, General?" His gaze went skyward to gathering storm clouds where the gray of the dirt was reflected in the heavens.

"Dull, my king?" The old general raised a brow and shifted uneasily in his saddle. He wiped his wrinkled forehead more out of habit than anything.

"Maybe it's the...clouds..." The king said to no one in particular. "I hate clouds."

"With respect, my king, the assessment must—"

"If it rains, Armodus, I swear on my father's grave...!" Dranus's mounting fury was cut short by a staccato drip, drip, drip thumping as if from within his skull. The feeling of trickling moisture on his scalp made him cringe, his teeth grinding. "Why are we out in this, Armodus?" he asked through clenched jaw.

"The Lunar Assessment, King Dranus. You may not like it, but it is your duty, I'm afraid." General Armodus (AR-mo-duhs) brushed a

3

growing number of raindrops from the white stubble that topped his head.

Dranus slumped in his saddle as a rider approached from behind him bearing a long pole that stretched flat like rolled out dough at the wielder's behest. The light tin shield protected the king, and only the king, from the rain. Dranus's frown turned sideways, his best impression of a smile.

"King Roboris (ro-BOR-is) the Thick-Hearted thought it pertinent, Dranus. You should honor his wishes and take this seriously," a new voice called from behind him.

The young king did not need to turn to know this reprimand came from the aging lips of Commander Ven (VEN). Were it another so insolent as to refer to him by name alone, they would already have been dead, but Ven...he did not despise her so much as the rest. He hung his head, turning black eyes first to his general and then to his venerated commander before kicking his heels vengefully into his mount's sides.

"My father was a fool...wasting my time with this nonsense...time enough for a useless army but not a moment for..." Dranus muttered beneath his breath, his painted purple and black lips moving only enough that he might hear his own words and be self-vindicated.

He raised his head high as he came close to the statuesque rank and file. The constant pitter-patter that had resumed on his head made him steam in the heat of the afternoon while his shield-bearer caught up with panic in his eyes.

Dranus cast his gaze down before him to peer at the officer leading the soldiers. The little man shook. Was he cold? In this unseasonable heat? Baffling.

Irrelevant, but baffling.

"M...My king, we are ready for your assessment!" the officer shouted. Why did they always shout? Another of his father's ludicrous decrees?

"Let us be done with it." The king's lethargy made the climb down from his saddle harder than it should have been. The clouds themselves could have been balanced on his shoulders for all that he struggled.

A peculiar rug, designed in a time long before Dranus's, was rolled out in front of him. Thus, he treaded along a seemingly lush carpet that held firm its form despite the loose, wet mud beneath it.

4

In fact, the rug didn't so much as touch the mud beneath through ages-old sorcery. A royal trinket devised to keep his boots clean as so many others squished unpleasantly about him. The *wetness* of footsteps, the *plink-plink-plink* of a midday drizzle on his tin rain-shield; it was enough to drive a king to madness.

He stopped before a tall soldier, his heels clicking together as he turned to face the frozen image of a man. He could have been asleep for all the king knew. Sleeping with his eyes open! That would have been a good skill for a father to teach his son.

His face contorted to the bitter taste the thought left in his mouth.

Dranus continued down the line step by step, balancing for a moment on one foot as he thought he spotted movement in the ranks and froze, as if to mimic them. He did not waver or teeter on the floating fabric, though this was not for the surface being firm or stable, but that the king's *understanding* that he should not fall if he did not believe it possible was enough to suspend this as a version of reality for a few brief moments.

It was by a similar twisting in logic that the varying colors of the soldiers' armor turned a uniform blue to his eyes and his eyes alone. He stood still, his left foot mid-step, waiting for someone to move, begging what forces that might be to give him an outlet for his flickering rage.

After a few minutes in this realm of blue dolls standing amidst a gray backdrop, a flicker of red appeared two columns forward and eight rows back. A knee had moved to the side and the slight creaking sound emitted a mist of orange emanating from the joint. A serpent's grin took over the king's countenance.

Dranus moved with hurried steps, his vision returned to normal, towards the doomed man. Guards sprinted through the mud, kicking the stuff up on the soldiers but always in the direction away from the King of Varz himself. The ever-extending rug had a limited range but more importantly, it had to be guided. So it was that they hurried about, trying to predict the path their king would take and allowing for multiple possibilities. Oh how they scurried, like mice before the mighty hawk.

He stopped parallel to the man he had spotted and turned on his heel.

"Your name?" The king asked in a sweet, tender voice. "No. Your rank, if you please," the mockery continued.

"No, no never mind." Dranus paced back and forth by the soldier and then stopped to clear his throat. "Nameless, rankless, bodiless suit of armor," he addressed the man, "if you were to describe the Varz army in a single word, what word would you choose?" Dranus held black leather gloves to his ear, his thumb cusped so that he would not miss a word.

The young soldier's quivering eyes looked first to his commanding officer and then to the King of Varz's before darting back to look straight ahead. Of course the young man understood his predicament and it was because of that understanding that he would, doubtless, meet the end he imagined.

"Apologies Mr. Armor, I must have missed it. In one word, the Varz army?" He leaned closer towards the boy whose lip quivered. He relished that look of terror in the soldier's sorcerous eyes. He could see the thoughts racing across the boy's cheeks! Think! Say a sentence! A word! A letter! A few last words if nothing else!

"V..." the soldier started, but he would get only the letter before the king cut in.

"In-con-se-quen-tial." Every individual syllable dripped from the king's painted lips like the rain that clattered on a thousand polished helms. "Inconsequential," he repeated. "So why do we continue this charade? Why the Lunar Assessment each time the moon passes through a phase? Do you know?" He moved down the line, inquiring into each young face. "Do you? Or you? Please enlighten me." As the fear became almost an aura as real as the light fog that rose from the mud, a strong, unnamable feeling welled in his gut for a moment, but vanished as quickly as it had come.

He stopped and turned back the way he had come, tapping his chin. The edges of his lips turned down once more. "Discipline." His mouth almost touched the boy's nose as he spoke the word into the mover's face, letting him feel his warm breath, giving him at least that honor.

Without another word Dranus lifted his right hand, examining his pointer finger carefully. He considered it and its many properties, some of which it had not had mere moments before. "Hmmm..." he tilted his head as the finger came to rest on the soldier's shoulder then traced down his arm. He wondered, momentarily, if his choice were fitting for a soldier, but hardly had the attention to finish the thought before he made the slightest pinch about the gauntleted wrist of his victim. With a crunch that shattered the stillness, the armor folded and gave way so that ragged steel edges pressed like needles into the boy's skin. Dranus continued back up, tapping at points along the way, and everywhere that he tapped the armor crumpled like paper though it stabbed like steel until blood dripped out of the soldier's swollen glove.

To his credit, the boy did not so much as wince. He had some talent at sorcery, the king suspected. Perhaps this punishment would suffice.

"General," Dranus began, speaking over his shoulder, "what did my father decree as punishment for moving out of turn at the Lunar Assessment?" His apparent curiosity belied the absolute knowledge the king held of Varz's laws, both old and new.

"Expulsion, my king." Armodus was ever one to show mercy, even if that mercy was a well-placed euphemism.

"Expulsion," Dranus repeated to himself. On the one hand, he was obligated to obey the laws of Varz as were all her citizenry. On the other hand, he was presented with reason enough to spite his deceased progenitor. But this quandary, too, soon bored the King of Varz and his finger moved swiftly to the boy's head, the horror peaking in his eyes.

"Expulsion it is." His finger tapped once, altering the properties of the helm it touched, and his palm followed suit, a subtle pat that could as easily have been a mother's loving grace upon her oft-forgotten son's head. The body crumpled into the mud as Dranus turned to leave the scene.

Three-hundred and sixty-two thousand, five hundred and eighty-one rain drops had fallen within earshot since the first drips hit his head. The number came to him from some habit he had developed as a child; less so by counting, more so by sorcery he had over-practiced, alone, throughout his childhood.

Dranus hated the rain.

The king mounted his horse once more and rode back towards Armodus and Ven.

"Appropriately handled, my king," the white-haired general spoke first.

"I believe the lesson was well received," Ven echoed with a wry smile.

The King of Varz moved once more into line with his mounted

retinue.

"Well," he growled, "I do so *love* the Lunar Assessment."

Then, without another word, he headed towards his castle to change into dry clothes. He had survived the droll of the Lunar Assessment where at least he could 'expel' those that bothered him too much. Where he headed next was the realm of the truly wicked: he must hold court.

*     *     *

"Inconsequential," the king said in a mockery of the day's earlier discussion. His voice echoed through the lavishly decorated throne room of his castle. Here were the trophies of a thousand years of Varz conquest: the original golden crown of Myrendel (MEER-en-del), the last barrel of a lost brandy from Shiera (shi-ERR-uh), a four-foot tall hour glass filled with blue sand from Urhyll (yer-ill) that was said to take over a hundred years underground in cavernous lakes to attain its signature color. These trinkets stood alone or on mounting platforms between massive violet-tinted windows that stretched almost from floor to ceiling that were more like stone than a non-sorcerer might think possible. These lined the entire eastern wall of the throne room, and with every strike of lightning from the storm they cast the gathered nobles in malicious purple light.

"My king?" One of these nobles quivered in his overflowing robes, his fat cheeks reddening at the suggestion. "The army of Varz has been feared for a thousand years."

Dranus sat at the northern end of the room on a massive dais of polished black marble in a throne of midnight obsidian that was veined by streaks of gold and silver and studded with small precious gems to resemble the heavens on an empty moon. It was a gaudy thing to try and recreate the splendor of a million stars and the dust that flitted between them, but in Varz there were few ambitions too great.

From the rather uncomfortable solid throne, Dranus imagined the noble below as a hog, squealing for his slop and the vision raised his mood briefly. Compared to these nobles, Dranus was the figure of perfect fitness, and though his own skin seemed a sickly pale it was practically bronze compared to his lunar court, their hair righteous black to the last. Were it not for the duties of a king, Dranus might share their complexion, if not their skill-less frame.

"General Armodus," the king waved his hand, ivory adorned sleeves of off-white shifting in his wake, "when was the last time the Varz army waged war?" Dranus slouched in his throne, sliding this way and that, trying to get comfortable to no avail.

"In the thirty-second year of the rule of King Vulcan (VUHL-kan) the Rock, my king, amidst the Night Season at the head of Urhyll." The old general recited from memory; so complete was his knowledge.

"And the time that has passed since?" Dranus tilted his head subtly, trying to move the heavy black iron crown on his head to itch a spot near his right ear. Without thought he silently mouthed the words 'two-hundred and twelve years, eight moons, and seven days.'

"Two-hundred and twelve years, eight moons, and seven days." Armodus's voice boomed through the quiet hall.

Some of the nobles snickered while most continued staring at their fingernails, feeling the size of their guts, or otherwise dreaming of more leisurely endeavors. They were decrepit wastes of space and yet, weren't they all?

The lord who had previously spoken up retreated a few steps from the dais ashamed and found his place in the rows of nobles closed. With his spiral hog's tail between his legs, he walked to the back of the chamber.

"In. Con. Se... Quential." He repeated, being interrupted by a crack of thunder from the raging storm. There was an unpleasant moisture still lingering in the air and the king wanted nothing more than to be done with this day. "Anything else?"

The barons and lords of Varz looked up, anticipating their release from the court after so many hours of torrid rituals and tired scripts.

"Anything?" Dranus looked about him. In his mind the men and women of his court shifted into animals. A rat, a beetle, a hen, a boar, the bizarrely feathered cockatrice of the western coast. "Wonderful. Dismissed."

The king stayed seated as the others trudged out of the throne room and back towards their towers, their homes, and their huddled excuses for lives.

What had happened? Had he misread the words of the Forbidden Texts? Every tome in the King's Library depicted blood in the teeth of kings and nobles with claws, even a child without the Eyes started learning the sword before he could properly speak! If only he could ask Ven. Her family's histories were the best kept, but to share with her the secrets of the Texts would be to dig her grave...or at least to order it dug. Their sorcery was great and their technologies unmatched, but the pictures of his texts were painted in vibrant cerulean and magenta! In goldenrod and viridian! In shimmering crimson red! And yet his life felt so gray and black. It was the mud he dared not trample through or the cold unfeeling obsidian of his throne. Varz was truly great in many ways, but had it not been greater? Couldn't he, as king, be greater?

His back stiffened in his throne.

The world was moldable then, as it remained by ways of sorcery, but altogether different from the current world, he thought. It must still be now, that was obvious. But then why was it not molded? Or was it? Had the world simply changed around the people of Varz?

No. He would not accept that. A king had his pride; he would not defer responsibility to the whims of time. Who would mold the world to shape it to Varz liking if not he?

Dranus's fingers clenched the smooth arms of his throne as he gritted his teeth.

But how? What could he do? After all, Dranus was no great king. Not even as loved as his good-for-nothing father.

All that rage and anger that should have driven him to madness or to shed his king's robes and lash out at the symbols that trapped him in this title, mounted to an impressive sigh that escaped tired lips. Such emotions were, at best, inconsequential.

The rain intensified. Without seeing the flashes of lightning, he heard distant thunder.

The hall was empty save for his attendants and the lingering general. It was quiet, peaceful even. He could sit there for a while longer, he thought. He pressed his fingers to the slanted V etched into his right cheek; Queen Luna (LOO-nah) the Mad's idea if he recalled correctly.

He always did.

The feeling of the rough skin comforted him for a reason beyond his conscious mind. Deep inside he yearned for some change to come about, but he had neither the energy nor the attention necessary to effect that change.

And so sat the King of Varz, echoing the distant thunder beneath

10

his breath like a dog defending its home from the wind. His endeavor, perhaps, was equally pointless. How long had it been since he'd done something with a point? How long since Varz had? Two-hundred and twelve years, eight moons, and seven days?

A loud crash of thunder like steel on steel broke his train of thought, causing him to wince. The general silently but urgently left the room.

He hated the rain. At times he hated thunder less, at times more.

Another clash of violent sound, and shouting. Had the storm sundered a home? Struck the castle itself?

His attendants scattered to the side chambers; they were not meant as guards. Then again, why would the King of Varz need guards?

Once more: a clash and shouting.

Dranus moved to the edge of his throne, leaning as far forward as he dared without falling onto the steps of the dais. He struggled to hear a word break through the ruckus, the cacophonous clash of...what was it? Steel and bronze? Silver plating?

"Intruder!" The single dying shout of a woman's pain-stricken breath came to him, and his cheeks curled upwards as his suspicions gained footing.

It was closer then. Still closer. He was practically balancing his weight on the balls of his feet. His mind was racing with hopes that Armodus had been dodged and the intruder's way unbarred. His heart pounded heavily in his chest.

"How long has it been, I wonder," he spoke aloud, "since someone was foolish enough to challenge a King of Varz?" King Dranus's eyes narrowed, and his mind delighted in the perusal of his magical arsenal which might soon find some use for a change.

Finally, something new.

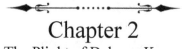

# Chapter 2
## The Plight of Deleron Kaxus

Before Dranus could decide on any real plan of action, the great doors of the hall burst open. There stood a tall, lean youth with a despicable streak of golden hair falling out from a shining conical helmet. In his two hands he held a large broadsword which dripped in the blood of the royal guards who protected the palace. While his weapon and his silver-plated armor seemed fairly typical (though he was almost certain some sorcery helped the boy carry the massive sword), there was a small rectangular buckler on the youth's arm. The outline was odd, the face was flat, and it was finished with a greening bronze plate that was now severely dented. The youth stood triumphant in the doorway breathing somewhat heavily and grinning as though he had already won.

"King Dranus!" the youth cried proudly, "I am Deleron Kaxus (DEL-err-on KAK-sus), son of Anon, the man you had executed for marrying my mother, a woman of Shiera. I will have my—"

The king stood abruptly and spoke commandingly, causing the youth to falter in his words, "You?! That is why you wear such *disgrace* on your head?" He meant the blonde streak, a sure sign that this youth was not of pure Varz blood. "You are the son of that traitor Anon?"

"My father was a great—"

"Wait, wait, wait," the king interrupted again. As abruptly as he had stood moments before, he turned about and stared at the black obsidian of his throne which seemed to pulsate with life from the glare of sputtering brands. Looking back over his shoulder as if recalcitrant, he said, "I interrupted you, you were saying?"

A smile again crept to his lips as he turned to face the youth once more.

"I will have vengeance! And take it—" Deleron tried again.

"And you will take it where? To the hills in the east? It is almost the Dusk Season! I am told that the hills are quite a sight at that time; what with all the colors of the leaves, the dancing winds..." He continued to pace about, not giving the youth the respect of his full attention as he gestured to replicate his sense of rambling detail. "Wait, wait, wait." He flicked himself on the forehead and began to pout, "you see I've done it again! I apologize Deleron, please continue and be assured I am most concerned with your plight."

Young Deleron, a bit shaken by the king's confidence and angered by his passive reaction to the death of much of his guard, took a few steps further into the room and noticed with some concern the way the torches on the walls seemed to become agitated at his presence.

"I will take it now, my king. With your tyranny removed from the throne I will guide Varz to a new future in tandem with the Lesser Folk..." He stopped abruptly, silently cursing to himself that he had used the derogative term 'Lesser Folk' when his own mother was one of those supposed Lessers.

Dranus continued to pace, hardly phased by such idealistic claims. "A union with the Lessers? You believe a single soul in Varz will follow such blasphemy?" Even with his trained gaze he could see no faltering within Deleron; his intentions were both honest and pure. The thought caused bile to rise in the king's throat.

"What you fail to see, my king, is that our folk are ripe for change! They know it not, but they beg for it with every second of their despondent days! Besides, once I am king, they will have no choice but to obey me." Deleron assumed a pose of grandeur, resting the heavy tip of his sword on the velvet covered floor where the nobles had just recently stood.

Dranus stopped then and considered these words, stroking the scar on his cheek as he often did in moments of deep thought. The consideration was, unfortunately, as fleeting as his patience for this would-be usurper.

"You will defeat me then?" The king resumed his pacing. "May I at least, before my imminent demise, inquire as to how you plan on doing so? I have the understanding of the Forbidden Texts as well as all of the finest training and knowledge Varz can offer." His nonchalant demeanor did not fade for a moment as he spoke. Dranus was all expressive arm movements and oddly convincing mummery of sadness and repentance.

"I have found power to match your knowledge and even the

13

Forbidden Texts cannot save you from that which I now wield!" The youth brandished his mighty sword, a confident grin spreading across his lips.

Dranus stopped abruptly. His look of faked interest gradually shifted to one of careful observation. What power had he acquired, he wondered. To have passed through his entire guard single-handedly was indeed an impressive feat but his sword was not immediately recognized, nor was his armor, and his shield could be nothing more than a makeshift by its shoddy design. Was it some source of physical strength he had acquired, some immunity to sorcery like he had once read about in the annals of Varz?

Turning his back briefly to the young aggressor, he walked behind his throne where, hiding within the throne's shadow, was propped the sword of his father, Fehris (FERR-ihs). Fehris was a sword with a brass hilt and a blade of black iron. He placed his hands on the back of his throne, contemplatively.

"You have found power, you say? Great power that exceeds my own? And where did you attain such great power? I might know the source of my unavoidable, catastrophic doom if I am to meet it so soon." Again, he talked down to the boy in such a matter-of-fact tone, trying to force him into an error. "Oh, and please excuse me if I appear passive. Rest assured that my demeanor is the result of sheer terror in these, my final moments."

The visibly agitated challenger began to explain but Dranus did not listen, instead he turned inward. He bent his logic at an obtuse angle then he bent it again, turning it back on itself. He warped understanding and manipulated truth as though they were simple matters of opinion. It was in this way the people of Varz controlled the power of sorcery; for them, it was the art of manipulating reality by altering one's understanding of reality and then imposing it on the world around them. His reason turned and turned again until he had completed the spell and closed his eyes only shortly, opening them again to see another image of himself crouched and looking curiously at the shield on Deleron's arm.

"This shield is of peculiar design Sir Kaxus, not very large. Is this the 'power' you mentioned?" the voice emanated now from the copy of Dranus while the true form of the Varz king took the hilt of the sword Fehris.

The worn body of Deleron Kaxus tightened as he leapt backwards and away from this apparition which had somehow manifested into thin air. The boy let out an unflattering cry of surprise; he was clearly not expecting such a spell. But then how could he without the Forbidden Texts?

The specter of Dranus, openly irritated, followed the boy with heavy steps across the wine-colored carpet and reached out to touch the buckler. The youth swung his great sword with impressive speed for its relative size and the fake Dranus withdrew his hand almost carelessly under his chin, taking a pose of deep contemplation.

"I think it is that sword of yours and your unnatural strength." At this the youth gathered himself and chuckled. "You're right King Dranus, this sword will block all of your spells and the understanding I have learned allows me to wield it as I might wield a twig. Your guard is half dead and scattered and the antechamber sealed. You cannot escape, nor can you hope to overcome me." Suddenly the clone of the king leapt to life, his eyes alight with understanding.

"Aha! It is the sword of my uncle who tried to remove my father from his place!" The clone looked at the boy dubiously. "You *do* know what happened to my uncle, don't you Sir Kaxus?" the clone began to circle the youth retelling the story of King Roboris the Thick-Hearted's brother and how he had tried to steal the power of the king.

Quiet and focused, Deleron did not take his eyes or his guard off of the ghost and he planned when he would strike, right at the last word, when the king would surely make some joke. And Deleron believed, quite logically, that the clone was a part of the king and must be dealt with first.

In truth, however, the clone was nothing more than a dancing reflection of light pulled by the king's strings and the real King Dranus, twisting thoughts and meanings again within his skull, now flickered out of sight, blending with his surroundings, Fehris in hand.

"I will not fall where your uncle fell King Dranus; of that I can assure you! Your uncle was strong, but he did not wield half the might I possess!" The clone stopped; the hidden figure stalked.

"In the end, my traitorous uncle tried to sneak upon my father while he rested and slay him in his bed...but it was his reliance on his *understanding* of my father that allowed him to be killed so easily, by my father, with nothing but a sword. And not even a sorcerous sword!" The phantom image peered at its hands and chuckled sardonically.

With these final words the young Deleron sprung into action! He raised his own sword and ran forward. The clone did not lift its gaze. He let out a loud cry and summoned all of his strength, the clone looked up quite calmly and began to speak. "And the same..." Deleron's muscles tensed, his grip tightened, and he brought the sword crashing down. "...will happen..." he felt his victory as his mind told him that now his sword had connected with flesh.

And it was a loud clash of metal on the granite floors that caused the boy to realize that his target had vanished, dispelled.

"...to you." The tone, the words, the sheer power held in that shadowed presence gripped Deleron's heart while the black blade of King Dranus, placed expertly through the exposed armpit of the challenger's armor, pierced it.

The body went limp and Dranus flicked the boy's body away like so much detritus covering his sword. Deleron Kaxus's body fell to the floor with a clatter.

It was at this point the captain of the royal guard came rushing into the throne room, all distraught in his off-white armor with a number of steel-clad warriors nipping at his heels, only to find the king now half-interestedly digging through the belongings of the boy he had just killed. The shield, which Dranus had deemed useless, had been tossed aside. The massive broadsword of his uncle's was in his hand. Fehris lay on the floor some feet away.

"My king, are you unharmed?! This rogue somehow managed to best our guard, but I will take responsibility for their incompetence, my liege." The captain fell to one knee, his eyes cast downward.

Dranus did not spare the time to look up at the guards who had come in. "This 'rogue' had quite impressive power, though he was all too young and brash to control it well." The sword of his uncle was said to have been based on a mythic sword from ancient times; it created a small area around the blade in which it was exponentially more difficult to warp reality. It was like placing a maze between the truth and one's sorcery; the path could still be made, but not quickly or easily. It's other weakness, which no one else but Dranus knew, was that the sphere of influence of the sword was smaller than a man and that when raised, it had left his uncle's feet outside its range. It had been all Roboris needed to best his brother in the climactic moment that nearly precluded Dranus's existence.

The captain stayed low, waiting for orders. In these circumstances, he could not expect that the king wouldn't take his life as well.

"Have my uncle's cursed sword melted down, reforged into cubes, and scattered in the sea with no fewer than 30 leagues between each piece. Put this shield in the armory so that I may inspect it further, and dispose of this body before it begins to foul my hall. Have Fehris thoroughly cleaned of his *tainted* blood." The now lively figure of King Dranus carried the sword to the captain who took it gingerly as he stood.

"And return soon captain, so that you may take responsibility." Dranus said in a low voice so that only the captain would hear. The voice sent shivers through the captain, a powerful warrior in his own right, so that he assumed he entertained the last few hours of his life.

"Yes, my king." He took the sword with a bow while his men levitated the lifeless corpse of Deleron Kaxus with no more than a nod of their heads and a combined alteration of how gravity affected the fallen youth.

As the limp form rose, some object fell from his chest plate to the floor with a dull thud.

Dranus glanced once at a book which now lay next to the spreading pool of blood and then to his guard, commanding them to go about their business before he lost his reserve. And this, to Dranus at least, was both a threat and a rather comical joke.

After his guard had left, he looked hard at the book that lay on the floor. The thing was rather large and of an extremely worn leather cover which had turned into a mixture of deep browns. The pages were yellowed and frayed, at some edges there were signs of burn marks, but nowhere did he find a title or any pictures giving hints as to what the book might be. Surely the boy thought it extra protection to his chest; he thought simplistically. But the book gave off an aura of something strange. It was too arcane, too peculiar to have been used simply as padding. He found himself drawn by the book and somehow disturbed by its mere presence. Cautiously, he picked the book up. He felt how the cover gave and almost resembled the texture of human skin. It was, however, bereft of any otherwise defining features. Suddenly unsure of what he might find inside, he hesitantly opened the cover to reveal the first page. There was a simple line written in the common speech understood in all the Five Realms and all the three continents.

"He who should possess this book shall be one with the desires of Fate." The line was unfamiliar, though the concept of Fate was as well-known to those of Varz as any other. Concepts like Fate and Destiny moved many facets of life in Varz, from the unbroken line of kings and queens to the farmer and his sons. It was a never-ending struggle for those of Varz to desperately seek out their destiny and yet resist the limited ends it brought.

He turned another page to see lines of speech written in many different languages, with many that he did not recognize. Each line was distinct, as if written by different hands with different pressures and senses of urgency. But what each line for tens of pages had in common was that each and every one was crossed through, like a list. Finally, he came across a page that was incomplete. As he scanned the list of more familiar languages, he raised his lip in disgust at the mention of Pyrán (pee-RAHN), his people's age-old nemesis. Below this was a line that was not crossed through.

Its message was simple: "I will kill King Dranus."

At this the King of Varz smirked and closed the book, thinking himself a fool for giving any attention to such an obvious work of nonsense. There were no records of such an item in his people's history, no mention of a magical book, not even a reference to the texts which his ancestor's had read other than the Forbidden Texts and the other books found in the King's Library. Clearly the boy had merely found some book with a list of people's fancies throughout time and had thought it auspicious. Perhaps a clever merchant had sold him the thing with promises that it would make his wishes come true! Still, he was curious as to how the young man had gotten possession of his uncle's magical sword....

The book was too thick for the king to waste his time reading so he searched his memory for a particular spell. The spell was one taught early in the childhood of all Varz youth to assist in the acquisition of what they must learn from their rigorous upbringing. A simple molding of his thoughts also required a gesture of his hand which moved concepts and truths aside as he made way for his new reality. Then, with a simple press of his palm against the cover of the book, the spell was complete, and the book attained a somewhat eerie demeanor of sentience.

"How may I inform you, master?" the words emanated from the book King Dranus held in his hands. The voice was, at first, that of a cheerful young man, but in further consideration of the tone Dranus could pick out signs of great wisdom. It was odd that a book of such apparent age and wisdom should have such a youthful voice. Normally a book's voice matched its age and contents quite accurately.

"What is your title, book?" King Dranus held control over the book, for he had given it a semblance of life and speech and thus was entitled to the information which the thing knew.

"I am a book, my master, though I do not know my title. I speculate that it might exist somewhere or at some specific time." The book's voice held an odd characteristic...it seemed almost that of a human though it mingled with the subtle rustling of pages.

He paused. The king thought hard as he stared at the book, thinking over what it had said...had he ever known a book given speech to *speculate*? Did the book not simply hold the knowledge within its pages and nothing more?

"Well then, Book, what knowledge do you hold?" The king began pacing back towards his throne, hoping to consult the pages of the Forbidden Texts for some mention of this book.

"Nearly all knowledge, sir." At this Dranus stopped dead in his tracks and stared at the book. The way the leather of the cover seemed to set...it was almost as though the book was grinning at him.

"That cannot be." He knew things no one else could know, he knew of the hidden tomb which lay beneath the city. He flipped to a random page in the book and almost felt his breath flee from his lungs, his eyes spread wide as there on the pages were drawn every detail about the hidden tombs...their location, access points, those that rested there...even details he didn't know!

"That cannot be!" He shrieked, racking his mind for something he knew that no one else could possibly have knowledge of.

Again he flipped to a random page and again he felt his heart seem to stop as the last words his father had spoken in this life were quoted on the pages. The entire castle had been vacated when his father passed, except of course, for the Son of the King. He had told the young Dranus of his love, he spoke of the shift of responsibilities that would follow his death, and he spoke of his lost wife, and then he died. Dranus had copied the words for memory, thinking some hidden wisdom lie therein. After studying it relentlessly he had burned the page and was sure no one had ever seen it. He placed the book on the throne and took several steps away from it, almost tumbling down the dais' steps.

"I'm afraid it is so my master, and my knowledge is yours to do with as you will," it said.

Did the book feel that it belonged on the throne? Dranus's thoughts were strained as he sought to understand these events. He wondered, secretly, if the book was the challenger he should fear, not the boy who had carried it.

Lightning again struck close, so close that the walls of the castle shook and the light it produced lit a face consumed at first by confusion, then by dawning appreciation for the power he now possessed. Now Dranus was sure that this book was the power that Deleron had bragged about. With this book he could do anything...with this book he could know all there was to know in the world...with this book....

King Dranus had once again taken the book in his hands when the captain reentered the hall, the loud latching of the massive doors signaling his return to the otherwise silent chamber.

"I am prepared to receive my punishment, my king." His eyes were downcast, and his arm shook slightly at his side; he knew that in Varz there was no room for such an error, no forgiveness for mistakes such as his. King Dranus, the book in one hand, walked quickly towards his captain with death in his eyes. The man in the dull white armor stood his ground and accepted his Fate with dignity.

As the king approached him, the monarch simply brushed past him with a simple order.

"Assemble the War Council."

# Chapter 3
The Council Convenes, A Star Rises in the South

Centuries had passed since the last official War Council was called in the Varz capital city of the same name. Not since King Vulcan the Rock, who completed the conquest of the Five Realms that The Ultimate began, had the general, admiral, and top commanders been called to the War Room set high in the northern tower of the castle. The room was wide but crowded with numerous tables, each with a different map sprawled across it. On cold stone walls, too, hung maps of every city of Varz, every area where they might do battle, and every detail of the landscape carefully measured and recorded by the predecessors of those proud men and women standing now in the well-lit chamber.

"The Council is convened." The dull white figure of Dranus's guard captain bowed on one knee before his king. He was overly careful as he still feared the king may take his life for the earlier mishap. This previous event was, however, quite distant from Dranus's mind.

King Dranus had spent the last hour while the war council members were being gathered to speak with the thing he now simply referred to as "Book" and to change into his war attire. He now stood at the head of the largest and most central table all clad in matte black chain mail and plated leg armor with his helmet, shaped at the crest like a proper crown, resting on the table. This was an ancient tradition, to be dressed as if for battle, when discussing war. He had been instructed that it was to remind each of them of the physical weight of war so that they would not plan idly or deploy carelessly.

Dranus had been the first to the chamber to inspect the disposition of his forces as a whole. It was, of course, his role to oversee the use of his armed forces even in peace times. He had a general sense of what each branch had been occupying their time with: the navy escorting cargo to dissuade the rare pirate, the mounted forces patrolling borders for signs of spies or invaders, or his army serving as a mostly symbolic policing force within the more populated cities. But he would rely on his Council to know how long it would take to mobilize and where they were strongest and weakest.

"Report." The king commanded to the six men and women now circling the table. Each of these were the descendants of great warriors and leaders within the people of Varz. It was not tradition, per se, that kept these roles within a family, but it was that a current general could train his child to be a better candidate than could anyone else, and thus it was fairly uncommon for the role to change families.

"My king, your father King Roboris the Thick-Hearted feared nothing more than a threat from the Western Continent and the upstart Sulvarian Empire. Because of this our naval forces are well prepared and as strong as they ever were." The figure that stood to King Dranus's right was the ever-lively Admiral O'cule (OH-kyewl), who was quite an enigma among the ilk of Varz. Nonetheless, he had proven himself an extremely competent admiral and was the closest thing Dranus had to a peer, socially. "We may set sail at your whim, sire." He was a tall, middle-aged man with medium length black hair oiled back and tied into a tail. He had a finely kept beard sprinkled with early signs of graying. His body was fit, though, and encased in the sparkling sapphire plate of a crystalline sea. He was tall and now wore a confident grin as the excitement which Dranus only half showed was fully awakened in the admiral.

"My king," a woman's voice, "the Archers Brigade is readily equipped. In the years of our peacetime our numbers have diminished but our bows have been made stronger and more accurate; our projectile and siege weapons have never been more advanced but will take time to construct in mass." Commander Kaelel (KAI-e-LEL) of the Archers Brigade was a proud woman of the same age as Dranus and in the prime of her life. She was beautiful and bold like only her sisters might one day hope to match. Her long raven hair fell to her thickly padded leather archer's armor which made her both well protected with a layer of chain and agile with the increased range of motion demanded of a skilled archer. Many times had Dranus's father tried to arrange a marriage for his son to this outstanding woman, but it had never been of any particular concern to either of the two involved. They were content with the casual intimacy they shared from time to time. Still, since his father's passing Dranus had entertained the idea that he would need an heir and that no finer a woman existed in all the Five Realms.

"My king," came the next voice. No time for lingering thoughts, not now.

"The Mounted Forces are widely dispersed throughout the kingdom. We have bred many strong war horses in recent years, but we lack riders to ride them. Lances, too, are in short supply, my lord." At the opposite end of the table stood the unimposing Commander Bourin (BOHR-in) of the Mounted Forces. For all that he was the short, stocky youth of his father, he was the most mild and soft-spoken member of the council. He was, however, a brilliant tactician and a loyal asset. He was dressed in a light riding chest-piece that was like the viridian forests of the south and thick, heavy leg plating that would protect his extremities from ground forces. Bourin was a tactician, not a lancer, but he could not expect his men to endure the strain of armor without taking it on himself.

"My king," a familiar voice started and Dranus's swirling plans and intended orders came to a rapid focus.

"I regret to report that our Mage Corps is quite small and under-trained for war on any scale. Since the decline of our military expansion there has been a greater focus on practical forms and some minor defensive spells. Only a handful, including myself, would be fit for battle." The words, though they were stained with shame, came from the wise lips of Commander Ven of the Mage Corps on the far left of the table. A woman just entering her elder years, she had sparse streaks of gray in her shoulder length hair and held herself proudly for the status she held in Varz. Ven was a master of the sorcerous arts and had been Dranus's teacher when he was younger; she bested him in all but the forbidden arts and had almost as much knowledge of Varz and its history as did the king. She, like her predecessors, was merciless and wicked when set as an enemy, but had been like a substitute mother to the young king. She was dressed in the jagged amethyst armor of a battle mage and her gauntleted hand pressed against her forehead, a sign of frustration and shame that she made sure to show to her king.

"My king..." this voice was withering and hesitant, "...why...do we go to war? And against whom?" The man who spoke then was

General Armodus, all consumed by burning crimson plate armor from top to bottom. He was the most senior both in age and rank among the Council and he was the only one in the room who might dare challenge the King of Varz on such matters.

The general looked uneasy as he carefully chose his words, his mouth shaped in a frown and his brow furrowed. "You have called this War Council, the first since King Vulcan the Rock, in the middle of the night with no pretense, no report of foreign advance, and no goal." The old general scratched at his buzzed white hair, making sure to show the proper level of deference when challenging the word of his king.

Dranus had been consumed by visualizing the spread of his forces, the targets of an outward advance, the sources of funds that would be needed to drive such a war effort, that he had almost not heard his general's words. They were words he did not want to hear so, by a close margin, he almost hadn't.

"Why?" Dranus took a moment to gaze into his general's black and white Sorcerer's Eyes that matched his own. He had not yet really thought of these questions; the call for arms had merely been a whim of the moment he had shared with the Book. Again he pressed fingers to the scar on his cheek in thought. Surely there were no political reasons, no intrusion onto their lands, no resources they were in need of, and from the sound of the reports, they were in no shape to take on such an endeavor. "Why, General?" For a moment he felt his soul reach out to his distant ancestors, trying to think of how King Vulcan may have responded, or King Valkhir (val-KEER)? Queen Tempest (TEMP-est) or Queen Luna?

"Why, indeed." Why had he even called this meeting of the War Council?

Suddenly, an oddly human sound like one clearing their throat came from the Book which was resting by the king's helmet. Seven sets of black eyes shifted to the thick leathery tome with varying levels of shock and ill-ease. A book that spoke was common in Varz, but one that attempted to clear a throat it obviously didn't have was unheard of.

"As you've all heard by now, the castle was assaulted by a lone assailant. One now deceased Deleron Kaxus." Suddenly the pieces fell into place in Dranus's mind. "There are two particular details of note from this event. One, that a citizen of Varz felt it his place, even

24

as a half-blood, to bring about change to our people before any of us did. And two, that he nearly succeeded with the help of this Book." A wave of shame washed over the faces of his council.

"Today, I have insulted our armed forces twofold." Dranus locked eyes with General Armodus. "I dubbed them inconsequential. More importantly, I allowed them to *become* inconsequential." He paused. "Has there ever been another time in our glorious history where this was true?"

None dared respond.

"There has not," the king confirmed.

Six sets of eyes went downcast.

"But young Kaxus may yet achieve his goal. This Book is no normal collection of words. It's knowledge of the world is unlimited. It is the spark we will use to reignite the roaring flame of the Varz Empire!" A wicked, twisted grin spread across the king's face.

"Limited, but vast," the Book corrected in hushed quietly.

The council silently considered this, but it took only a few moments before the wide smile spread to General Armodus who placed a heavy hand of acceptance upon the king's shoulder.

"Agreed." Ven said. "War is in the very stuff of our blood and our bones. It has always been thus." This spoken as a matter of indisputable fact.

At this reply, everyone in the room felt their spirits lifted. This was something new, something to disrupt the droll of their normal, meaningless lives. They had each of them read the stories of their ancestors since their youth and treated them almost as figures of tall tales. They had become so detached from these titans of history over the generations, but modern Varz still knew their spirit.

"Well then, we will have to make hasty preparations, my king." General Armodus stood straighter, taller than before. His finger moved deftly about the map of the city of Varz, leaving streaks like ink wherever he willed them. "Our armed forces scarcely number more than ten thousand if we draw from the entire kingdom and our most recent estimates of the armed forces of Arendrum (uh-REN-druhm) alone surpass twelve thousand. We do not have the men to conquer the remaining four realms, even with our well-equipped naval forces." Armodus was unhappy to give this news but felt this was a problem easily remedied. "If I may suggest, sire, a draft may bolster our ranks in a matter of a few short years with rigorous training."

Dranus frowned and his lip twitched.

"That will not do, general." He gritted his teeth in frustration. "How can you expect the dead to wait for *years* when they have just glimpsed life for the first time?"

"My apologies, but my estimates include all of our armed forces other than our navy...to go to war now is to march to our destruction." Again it was the old general who found the stomach to counter the king directly, but the other commanders nodded their heads in agreement.

At this Dranus felt the heavy pull of depression tug at his heart, his chest tightened, and he took a step back from the table.

An intelligent voice came from the table once more, "If I may suggest, my master...."

Dranus motioned for the Book to continue, a gesture he immediately questioned. Could this book see?

"You might increase your strength by a considerable amount if you were to reclaim the Staff of the South Star." It continued with permission granted.

The eyes of Commander Ven grew wide at once while those of the king continued to stare skeptically at the tome; the others in the room could only look questioningly between the book and the man standing over it.

Dranus sighed at this suggestion, unimpressed, "Even if we assume that the Staff still exists and that we could somehow locate it, the South Star has not been seen in our skies since the time when Queen Luna the Mad first created the staff."

The Mage Corps Commander chimed in with her own rebuttal of this suggestion with a bit of anxiety in her wizened voice, "It is said that the South Star was banished by some powerful magic gathered by all of the enemies of Varz, perhaps even from ancient Pyrán." The mere mention of the name Pyrán was enough to elicit a set of harsh stares and uncomfortable shifting among those assembled.

A condescending chuckle like the rustling of pages was all that came from the Book in response. Again King Dranus was somewhat disconcerted for he had never known a book given speech to 'chuckle' in any sense before. "No magic can banish the South Star! But like all stars it moves in and out of our view. When night comes do you lament that the sun has been banished?" Again the chuckling like agitated paper emitted from the motionless book and all present were made all the more uneasy.

"King Dranus, what is this Staff of the South Star that this book speaks of?" It was Admiral O'cule this time who spoke up with genuine interest. Naturally he could only assume such knowledge lie in the Forbidden Texts, else he would surely know of such an item. It was with this thought in mind that he glanced briefly at Commander Ven with suspicion.

Again Dranus paused, considering how much information he should divulge. "The Staff of the South Star is one of three ancient Relics of Power..."

"Four ancient Relics of Power, master." The Book interrupted politely.

The king clenched his fist in irritation before he continued, "Four ancient Relics of Power created by our ancestors and used in the Great Wars over the Five Realms. The identity of these items, save the Staff, is known by the King of Varz alone." He looked first to his council then back to the Book, "And by this Book, apparently."

It was by no accident that Dranus did not consider that the book made mention of a fourth Relic which was not kept in the Forbidden Texts.

"How would the Staff help our cause?" Now it was Commander Bourin who asked, struggling to grasp how this relic might play in to his half-formulated strategy.

"The journal of Jahnas (JAH-nuhs), Husband to Queen Luna, has been passed down through my family for generations." Ven was now composed, remembering all she had read from the journal. "The Staff was embedded with a magical four-sided gem which held great energies that were harnessed by Queen Luna. During the First Great War, and after an important loss, the Mad Queen punished the remaining 20,000 soldiers of her armed forces with death, imprisoning their souls within the Staff of the South Star. It was a special property of the jewel that the light of the South Star, when focused through the jewel, released the souls to fight once more on this plane." All in the council save Dranus seemed entranced by the story, by the wicked might of their ancestors, and suddenly felt personally ashamed that they had done so little in their respective lifetimes.

"With the Staff we could potentially increase our forces by

20,000, but the castle in which Luna barricaded herself was drowned beneath the South Sea and the Staff went with it. Not even the Forbidden Texts mark where the remains might be found." Dranus was becoming bored again by idle talk of some stratagem that was beyond their ability to employ. He felt depression dragging him back into his former demeanor with every contrarian thought.

"You will find, I think, that my knowledge more than solves this problem, my master." The Book had again taken a respectful tone and split open, flipping through the pages until it found the one it searched for. On this page was a map that mirrored the large one on the table that showed the Five Realms but with different landmarks and different names. One major discrepancy presented itself, however, in the existence of a stretch of land with a castle on it near the southern border. "The Castle Beneath the Waves, as it is called in certain lore, is easily found with my assistance, master."

Everyone at the table gawked openly at the map. It showed with such detail the realms as they had once been and identified castles that only King Dranus himself had knowledge of and, once more, some he did not.

Dranus slammed the book shut with contempt, an action which seemed to awaken the others from a trance. They looked to their king, puzzled.

"Even if the Staff could be found, it is useless without the South Star! If the South Star does not rise, the gem cannot be awakened, and if the gem cannot be awakened then the Army of the South Star will continue to sleep. The South Star will not rise simply because we possess the Staff." This was trying his patience. If his plans were foiled, then let them be foiled in a moment. Do not make him recount how foolish his ideas were over and over!

The Book seemed a bit hurt at the gesture. "I hope that you will come to trust my advice with haste King Dranus." Again the settled leather resembled the slightest grin.

A strange quiet overtook the chamber. In this quiet, Dranus began to observe his surroundings more closely. Individual tables were lit with their own lamps but still something was off. He had stood in this chamber pouring over maps at night before. Was it brighter in the room than it should have been? Not greatly brighter; not even to not need the lamps but.... Had the stones at the far end of the room taken a reddish hue to them?

Heralded by the raucous clatter of armor up stone steps, a guard burst into the chamber. Out of breath and hunched over from his exertion, the man attempted to recover with a wild look in his eyes.

"How dare you enter this chamber! Only the War Council may step foot in this place!" The poise of the white armored captain was one of intent as he unsheathed his sword and moved to punish his guard. Without warning he was stopped by a quick motion from the king, his body paralyzed by the overwhelming presence of the king's sorcery.

"Wait! Why have you come in such a hurry, guard? Is there another intrusion into my castle?" As he spoke these words, the king glimpsed a shimmer of light from behind the wooden shutters that covered the southern window of the tower.

"My king..." the guard panted heavily, "...something has risen in the southern sky!"

"Impossible!" Armodus shouted, quite agitated by all of this talk. He stomped over to the window and threw the shutters open. Though it was still a few hours until the sun would rise to bring about the next day, a dim red light poured in through the scattering rain clouds. A gasp escaped all but the guard and the king.

The focused eyes of Dranus stared off into the distance where hung a burning red orb not seen for centuries in these lands.

"The South Star has risen." He spoke to himself, his frustration dissipating and his countenance returning to that of triumphant confidence.

"Impossible! My king, this thing cannot be of natural make! It has foreseen the future; no creation of man should have this power!" Armodus raised his voice further, his mustache bristling beneath flared nostrils.

"It was, as a matter of fact, a contemporary of Queen Luna who predicted its return. I merely have access to the records he made." What the Book said was true, but it made the fact that it had *known* it would return that night no less true.

Dranus recalled the words at the front of the Book, 'one with the desire of Fate,' it had said. One could interpret this as meaning that you had control over the desires of Fate, but one could just as easily presume that the desires of Fate would consume the host. Was this war his idea? Or was it the Book's? Perhaps it was simply that his desire and Fate's had serendipitously aligned. It was comforting to think that the inexorable progression of time may be his ally in this.

Putting such thoughts from his mind for the moment, the king's gaze returned to the map now stained in scarlet light and his eyes scanned the terrain, carefully assessing the Five Realms. In the south and to the west within their continent was Varz which expanded to the east through the lower hills where it stopped at the large Trias River. Farther to the east was the desert realm of Urhyll, a great peninsula bordered in the north by the Trias (TREE-ahs) River's return to the ocean in the east. To the north of Varz was the Discidia (dih-SIH-dee-uh) Rift and the mountainous realm of Arendrum. This was separated at the east by an unnamed mountain range and to the west by an unmarked border which separated it from the northwestern Isles of Shiera. Shiera had once been a series of port towns in a river basin consisting of many winding rivers. It had, however, been flooded by Varz before the First Great War so that it was now a series of medium sized islands all separated and disjointed. In the North East was the final realm of Myrendel, ancient rival of Varz. Myrendel contained the great Lake of Hyacinthus which was named for their first Primarch who first gained the enmity of Varz. Thus the Five Realms were divided, an alliance maintained between the so-called Lesser Folk which was in place in case the wicked nation of Varz might ever try to rise in conquest again.

"We will need to increase our defenses to the north where the Discidia Rift ends." He pointed to where the canyons shrunk to nothing more than a small, bridgeable gap directly north of the capital city of Varz which stood at the center of the realm. East of the rift was their only open point on ingress as the mountains further east made a good natural border. "Increase the men at outposts in the east, tell them only to keep watch and let any invaders pass into the mountains. If we are lucky, they will tire themselves with the march and we may dispose of them deep in our own territory." Armodus and Bourin nodded in agreement with this strategy.

Dranus was expecting that once the other Realms heard of their war path, they would band together and try to make the first move, it would be this first move that they would have to defend most vehemently against. "O'cule, contact the Magemaster in Viél (vee-EL) and have him ready all available vessels. Set up a series of light scouting ships disguised as traders to gather information about the island towns of Shiera and their naval strength. Shiera will be our first offensive target." At this Commander Bourin smiled at his king's wisdom, for he had planned the same thing just moments before.

"My king, I will send word to the west immediately and follow within the week!" Admiral O'cule was full of excitement and glowing an eerie shade of purple from the red rays of the South Star reflecting off his armor. He bowed to the king and took his leave with his orders. The Magemaster was the only missing member of the War Council and would need to be informed of these recent developments.

"Commander Ven, it is time to turn our band of idle magic-makers into warrior mages. You have my permission to use any form of teaching you see fit to have at least 200 ready for battle. Our defenses are our weak point, have them focus on the Stronghold Texts and punish those who fail." The graying woman smiled a devious smile and bowed gracefully, accepting her charge with some enthusiasm. Dranus knew her potential to be cruel and to turn novices into masters by pure force of will; moreover, he depended on it.

"Bourin, make the call to rally the mounted forces in Varz. Leave a unit to each of the outposts to the east and north but otherwise withdraw the rest. Send an order to Vakkar (vuh-KARR) and have the smiths forge lances, promise them a spot of land for every lance they can produce within the next month and see that it happens. Promote the breeders and stable boys fit for battle to mounted cavalry, they know the horses best and need only be taught the basics of war to be effective." Vakkar was known for crafts of all sorts and it was inhabited by the greatest smiths in the Five Realms. For the glory of their nation they would surely not fail him.

"To the skies, my king" the short young man replied, quoting the motto of the Mounted Forces and quickly following his colleagues from the chamber.

"General Armodus, instate the draft. Draw from all corners of the realm if you must, bring our forces to twelve thousand and see that they are well equipped." The old general approached the king slowly, "It will be done." The man sounded confident and Dranus considered, while the general exited, that he might see his army rise to fifteen thousand by the time of his return.

31

"Captain." The warrior by the door stood straight when addressed by his king, as did the guard who had delivered the message. "Your men were overcome by powerful magic, educate them but show leniency. You and yours will be left to guard the capital when we march." The captain needed no more words to understand what his king implied. "My king!" the duo replied in unison and bowed low before rushing out.

The Commander of the Archers Brigade was the only other human soul left in the room and she moved with intent towards Dranus with some contour to her lips, some sparkle in her eyes. Dranus had been studying the map once more, hardly concerned with the well-prepared Archer's Brigade when he felt the soft touch of Kaelel's hand on the back of his exposed neck. He turned to her swiftly, not expecting the touch.

"I've never seen this side of you Dranus..." She stared, dazed, at the figure before her, "...it is very befitting of a true King of Varz." The sultry qualities of the woman's voice were not wasted on Dranus's well-trained senses, but his focus was now on war and their past of relative intimacy was far from his mind.

"Kaelel, you may make whatever preparations you desire." He turned his attention back to the map, but his face was taken by the cold fingers of the woman he had often thought of as the best his realm had to offer.

"Whatever I desire?" came the seductive response and she moved in swiftly pressing her lips against Dranus's and kissed him with all of the passion she could muster.

Dranus did not respond.

Kaelel pulled away, still smiling.

"You are dismissed, commander." The terse words did nothing to dissuade her intent.

With the same smile which the king somehow could not avert his eyes from, she left the chamber, ever the daunting idol of womanhood.

Finding himself annoyingly...distracted, he returned to the Book which had lain silently since the South Star had been revealed. "We have much to discuss this coming day, Book. Tell me everything you know about the three Relics of Power."

The Book heaved a sigh.

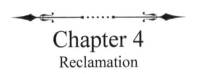

# Chapter 4
## Reclamation

The well-kept brick streets of Varz thundered under the feet of its people in a rare frenzy; its wide alleys and causeways echoed with talk of the previous night. Knowledge and understanding held the greatest worth in Varz and information was quick to travel from the lips of one to the ears of another. Thoughts aflutter with speculation at what had transpired in the castle gripped the folk of Varz in a state of agitation. Rumors spread that one of the lords had pushed a matter at court and ended up dying at the king's hand. Others heard that a coup had been attempted by the castle guard and that they had been slaughtered without mercy by the black sword Fehris.

There were others still, with a keener eye, that concluded an intruder had entered the castle and challenged the king. But surely that was not the end of the story. The castle built of dark stones from deep within the Discidia Rift breathed with life of its own as soldiers ran through the tall iron gates and into the city. The people could not possibly miss the constant comings and goings of messengers by foot and by wing throughout the day. Some claimed they'd seen that the castle had not slept a moment through the entire night!

Now that a new day was upon them, an unseasonably hot yellow sun hovered high in the afternoon sky over the winding towers of nobles and the uneven step-like structure of homes sprawling across the city. More important, however, was the twin red orb in the south that bathed the low-lying line of humble houses in crimson unrest.

A second sun!

What portent did this celestial body bring to the folk of Varz? Why did it glow with such eerie light? From whence had it come and for what purpose? Of course, the common man or lady couldn't possibly know that the South Star had graced their world hundreds of years prior. To them, this was completely unprecedented.

In the main sector of Varz, lining the causeway leading to the castle complex in the south from the city center, there were shops and businesses of every kind, with the best the realm had to offer trading their wares. On a day with such pleasant weather it would be normal to see silks hovering on display, constantly shifting their color and shape to match the favors of the customer. Bread and pastries would bake in ovens stacked two stories high and moved by the subtle practice of master bakers' magic. Bankers, jurists, and every sort of personal messenger would walk or ride around town or, if they were wealthy enough, enlist one of the horse-less carriages that moved by the will of drivers who specialized in gravity manipulation. There would be, at least in the main sector, only a few stalls practically bursting with local produce that self-sorted by color, firmness, or liquid content. These were the sights one would expect on such a fine day, but they were not the sights of that day.

Instead, dotted throughout the twisting roads and walkways, the town's Dens filled, overflowing into the bothersome heat. The capital was well known for its masterful Dens, best in the realm, where the citizenry flocked to engage with the great ideas of the day. Seated in lavish chairs or standing propped against the wafting scent of richly scented wooden walls they would argue and debate the worthiness of particular reasonings both natural and unnatural.

They drank strong proprietary brews of herbs and wine which assisted their thoughts, opening imagination and reality to new, bizarre truths. Every Den claimed to have the best formula or the oldest or the one closest to that which might have been drunk in the time of The Ultimate. But that was the beauty of Varz. Each of these places could be truth-tellers one day and liars the next; such was the fundamental law of the sorcerous folk. For the Dens, it ranged from the mundane, perhaps the brew master had forgotten a key ingredient in that day's brew, to the magical. The latter was obvious to the people of Varz who practiced the art of infinite possibilities and meaningless conundrums since they first unlocked the Eyes of a sorcerer.

There was, however, one specific Den that was closest to the castle complex (and was thus assumed closest in power) that welcomed a select few that could accurately speak on the events of the previous night.

"That which the Red Star brings is reclamation!" Commander Bourin stood crouched on a deerskin sofa, sporting the more practical garb of a tradesperson, which he had been before rising to the status of commander.

"Reclamation of what? What have we of Varz to desire from the world? What have we lost that we might even pretend to wish for?" Though he stood with nothing more than modest clothes and a half portion of the powerful brew, the farmer who spoke was an equal to even the Commander of the Mounted Forces in a Den, just as was any man or woman worth their understanding of Varz ways. In the Dens, one's worth was gauged by the strength of their understanding and the precision of their argument and nothing more. Here in this haven of the intelligentsia, all were seen as equal by default...except for the king, of course, who could not be matched even by the brightest of minds.

"It matters not for what we might reclaim!" The Varz admiral, still dressed in his padded doublet with his ocean blue armor stacked carefully behind the bar, could hardly contain his excitement. He had already had two of the thick brews that smelled cloyingly of brine and grass mingled with the smell of caramelized sugar to keep the beverage balanced. "It could be a personal reclamation for each of us or perhaps the reclamation of truth!" Admiral O'cule gesticulated wildly, tossing his third brew into the air from his mug where it hung, held by one of the attentive Den Maidens before settling back into his cup. The woman made sure to add that to the admiral's tab.

After the immediate disaster had been averted, the Den was in an uproar at the admiral's outlandish claim and people all around them clanked their spoons against their mugs, vying for a chance to express their opinions.

"The reclamation of truth!" The Den Master shouted from behind the bar. "What nonsense could any number of us agree on as 'truth'?" It was obvious that the Master could interject at any time he or she pleased, and this was perhaps one of the greatest measures of how favorably a Den was seen by the public. A quiet or uneducated Den Master would never fill his Den in the Varz capital.

"I submit to you a truth! That our brew is the finest in all the Five Realms!" A cheer erupted in response to the Maiden's claim; cups, mugs, and goblets were raised in jubilant consent. Only the most intelligent and bold of Varz's women could dream to work as a Den Maiden, and they were among the fiercest minds in the city. Thus, as this Maiden's words were a simple caress to the livened thoughts of

35

her patrons, the power in her eyes was more responsible for the united reply than the worth of the brew. This was enough to quell the uproar for the time and bring order back to the discussion.

Commander Kaelel of the Archer's Brigade stood quietly in the corner wearing a silk dress to celebrate the momentary return of the Day Season. Unlike most, she had abstained from conversation while she sipped on her beverage. Every now and then she would fix her gaze on the cooling brew and shortly thereafter it would stir and begin to steam with renewed warmth. Kaelel had enough excitement within her already without the heady high of the brews coursing through her veins. She had never craved another like she craved Dranus, then. For most of her life, sex had been all fleeting impulses and frustration-fueled whims. But the visage of Dranus standing tall, commanding his War Council, asserting his dominance as King of Varz had consumed her thoughts throughout the night and dwelt within her still.

It had been her idea among the others to come to the Den to recharge their minds. O'cule and Bourin had agreed readily but Armodus and Ven had far too much to do to even take an hour. Not a one of them had slept the previous night and not purely out of necessity. In the moments that Ven could spare from preparing a new curriculum for training war mages, she had a number of books floating around her head, all speaking in different tones, recounting every bit of information about the South Star that her family kept in their records as descendants of Queen Luna's husband Jahnas. The woman had not protested to Kaelel sitting in so long as she was silent. It had been a perfect opportunity for her to gain tactical insights about the South Star and Ven had seen the value in that without a word. That old crow would probably kill her for what she was about to do, but the secrets would spread through the city eventually.

"What purpose is it, then, that the Star rises in the south?" Bourin shakily set down his empty mug on a fine oak table and signaled that he'd had enough to the Maiden. His peculiar stance, crouching with boots dirtying the Den's couch, should have been enough of a sign that he'd had enough but then again, the energy bursting in him had to be let out somehow before he started throwing drinks around like O'cule.

Suddenly the room diminished to a low rumbling as various

philosophies were tested for fit with this conundrum. Several smaller conversations broke out in the main area and the Maidens took this time to top off drinks and suggest specific herb blends to match the current topic.

Kaelel found the moment perfect and gestured at the Den Master; it was not terribly long ago that she had worked as a Maiden in this very Den and the Master respected her even more than the average citizen. With a simple clearing of his throat, the room went silent, and all eyes focused on the Commander as chairs creaked across polished floors and cups jostled on tables moving themselves out of her path.

When Kaelel reached the center, replacing the oak table between Bourin and O'cule, she extended a single hand palm up. With a smirk she gave everyone a moment to appreciate her stunning beauty wrapped in deep violet silk accentuated with a perfectly matched tone of red that laced the front and back together at her sides. The archer was known for carefully treading the line of disrupting protocol when she showed skin like this but just the soft skin of her sides left plenty to the imagination, just the way she wanted.

In her hand was a golden shaded apple that began to hover just off her palm. She flicked a crumb at the apple, and it began to circle the apple in a slow elliptical pattern.

"This is us, our home in the vastness of the sky with our normal sun," Kaelel said. "At least this is the best model we have been able to divine."

She took a large serving platter off of a nearby table and suspended it in the corner where she had stood, with a wave of her hand, that large platter shone crimson.

"This," she pointed at the relatively massive red platter. "This is the South Star." The name was meaningless to most of the unknowing ears around her. Only her fellow council members knew this name and they looked on in horror at this breach of intelligence.

The nobles, merchants, farmers, and all else in the Den looked on in confusion at the star that simply dwarfed even their own sun but was, by comparison, a seemingly infinite distance away. If their home world was the width of a thumb and it would take months to sail around its width under perfect conditions, what could possibly cross such an immense distance as this? How large must it be to be seen from what felt like another plane of reality!

"The South Star has come before, in the time of Queen Luna the Mad and the First Great War. She used it to crush the mountainous realm of Arendrum. It is a birthright to the people of Varz; our ally, our weapon." With this proclamation Kaelel let the objects slowly fall and return to their normal features, taking a nonchalant bite of the apple as she sat down next to the wild-eyed Commander Bourin. She crossed her legs and took a small sip from her drink as if nothing had happened. The short man glared at her questioningly for a moment, but when all he received in return was a shrug, he shouted to another Maiden, his mug held high, and ordered a spiced wine made to loosen the natural insistence of the mind to disbelieve things it could not ordinarily understand.

The Den had burst into fervent dialogs at this new information. A crowd of well-dressed men bolted out of the Den, leaving far more than their fair share for what they'd consumed. Those would be the vessels of this information spreading across the city and eventually, the whole of Varz. The criers had no doubt rushed over when they heard that Varz officials had joined one of the local Dens, hoping to be the first to spread news from a reputable source in the city. They would go out and scout densely populated areas, or maybe seek to sell the information to another Den Master, before using a well-practiced spell that would make their voices boom for people to hear far into the distance. Information was a valuable asset in Varz, and those that traded in it were rewarded handsomely.

Admiral O'cule leaned over the table that had shuffled back to its original place and whispered to the commander with a twinkle in his eye, "Did Ven approve of this?"

Kaelel shook her head, her eyes closed and her smile wide.

"King Dranus, then?" the man continued.

Once more Kaelel shook her head.

"Clever," The admiral replied. "Or foolish."

"Probably both," Bourin interjected with a laugh.

Kaelel cracked one eye open to look between the two men. She breathed in deeply of the strong-smelling herbs and breathed out evenly.

"Wouldn't be fun without both."

Before the South Star set, receding a few hours before the yellowish sun, the name "South Star" had made occasion on the lips of every man and woman of Varz. This night it would be the rest of the city's turn to go sleepless as the very stones and timbers of the Dens roared with wonder, affecting the people with virulent intrigue the likes of which they had not known in the whole of their lives.

# Chapter 5
## A Few Peculiarities

King Dranus had slept very little after the War Council adjourned and had awoken to a number of peculiarities.

Firstly, instead of the general milieu of complacence and routine in the castle, there was the hustle and bustle of a city in war time. Outside his room, guards ran past, and messages were shouted through the corridors from one man to the next. Outside of his shuttered window there were officers in formation, practicing maneuvers with a level of precision and grit they'd not had the day before. These officers would then take their experience and transmit every detail to their squads. It made Dranus feel as though the Lunar Assessment he'd conducted not even a day before had been all for show.

It was, of course, but that didn't change the fact it felt more performative now compared to then.

Watching them now gave the impression that the army was learning everything from scratch. But perhaps that was the intentional strategy of the old general at work: master the basics until you can conduct them in your sleep and the rest will come with experience.

As the king stared out over the courtyard, internally critiquing the soldiers' movements, a translucent green bubble surrounded the city for a few moments, flickered, and then disappeared.

"Commander Ven has wasted no time," the king said to his new companion.

The second peculiarity was the sentient article of literature which appeared to contain some incredible properties. It was peculiar not that the book had been given speech, for this was fairly common in Varz, but that the book was quite talkative and had a certain wit about it that Dranus had never experienced from a book before. Despite the unsettling foresight the Book had shown and the seeming discretion with which it shared certain types of information, Dranus had learned to appreciate having someone to talk with about anything and everything. It was both amusing and distressing that such an item had gone without his notice for so long.

"There is no time to waste, master!" the Book fluttered open on his nightstand in a show of activity.

There it was again.

Sometimes the Book spoke twice with single phrases. Of course, with the urgency that Dranus had instilled in his War Council, it might seem obvious to insist that there was little time to waste. Still, something itched at the back of his mind; it was not quite a magical sense, but a wealth of experience in dealing with double-speak in his court of sycophants that told him the Book meant something else. Something it did not *want* to share. That was certainly peculiar.

And then there was the....

"Plot the angle of descent for the South Star. We need to know exactly when it will rise and when it will set." A voice trickled into the king's chamber, and he stopped midway through dressing.

This peculiarity was *supposed* to be a well-guarded secret. That was apparently no longer the case. Certainly the presence of a red sun floating low on the southern horizon was no secret, but the name had not left the War Council chamber. Had it been just a coincidence? The name was rather descriptive and unimaginative; it could just happen that people began calling a star that rose in the southern sky the South Star....

Said star added just a tint of red hue to the city in the midday hours. The South Star was only very prominent in the parts of the night when it appeared; otherwise the rays of the true sun dominated the land and diluted the tint the Star provided. Still, the overlap in their times of ascension were not perfect. The South Star would rise in the early morning hours of night and set a short time after midday. Strategically, it was perfect timing for war: rising early enough for an ambush by night but setting late enough that a battle starting at daybreak would be won or lost before its disappearance.

Moments later, Dranus had dressed and stepped outside his chambers, catching the Captain of the Guard as he directed the castle from within a few paces of the king's bedchamber. He had already been embarrassed once in the last day; he would not suffer a second failure to protect his king.

"Captain, a word," Dranus commanded. The man approached on

light feet and knelt low. As he did, Dranus felt as though he heard the creak of the soldier's armor shifting for the first time. Everything, even the tone and timbre of voices seemed richer. That was certainly....

"My king, somehow word has spread throughout the city's Dens about the identity of the South Star! They are in uproar about its portents!" The captain had intuited the king's question accurately, but his news was not reassuring.

Wait, had he said the people of the city were in an *uproar?* His folk hardly left their homes without the explicit need for something, and even then they usually did so quietly and with ever waning interest. To think of them as a population being uproarious about anything was shocking.

"Any word on who let slip the identity?"

"My king, Admiral O'cule reported earlier than it was none other than the Commander of the Archer's Brigade."

He should have known. Kaelel was ever the unknown variable. It made her an unrivaled sorceress and a compelling lover, but it also meant that sometimes she impulsively let slip state secrets. This, however, seemed less impulsive and more planned for the brilliant woman, but divining the difference between the two when it came to her was a task in and of itself.

"Thank you, captain. You are dismissed." Watching the captain hurry away brought a thought to the king and he weighed the man's back foot down hard enough to signal that he should stop, which he obediently did with an unperturbed spin. "Captain, call a general assembly for this evening. It would not do to have rumors abound at a time like this."

Without question the Captain saluted and moved that much faster down the decorated halls to relay his messages.

For the majority of the afternoon Dranus found himself going through his normal routine, lightened only slightly by the comments and speculations of the Book. Ignoring his first meal, he first locked himself in the King's Library with the Book and sought every ounce of information he thought might be relevant for the Varz war effort. The Book was indeed knowledgeable about nearly all things; it could tell him the last order for standing military forces each of the other realms had made so that he had attained good estimates of his enemies' forces. All things that might have once been written, drawn, or made official on paper could be perfectly replicated by the Book. It was frustrating, all the more, that the Book could not give information about current events. For instance, the Book could not tell him the current location of the Myrendel Primarch, nor could it be sure that the Relics of Power still stood where it knew they had last stood. The locations of the three Relics, and three was all the Book mentioned at the moment, seemed to the king to be inaccessible enough to have not been disturbed. Each was a castle, a former capital of Varz throughout its long history, and was either lost, well-guarded, or beyond impassible terrain. Thus he decided to move forward with his expedition.

In the early evening Dranus took his first meal of the day, having been sustained thus far on the particular brew that all his subjects had sipped incessantly in the Dens that day. After his meal, all of the officials, all of the officers, and important family representatives of Varz gathered in the Great Hall where they were addressed by their king. Dranus told them nothing of the Book, but of their desires for war and their necessary plans he spoke at length. He gave the name of the South Star and preached the blessing of strength it brought to their people. He raved of a reclamation by advice from his contacts around the city. He recounted some of the most infamous military moments in Varz history, highlighting the strength and fervor of the monarchs that led the way. The gathered assembly seemed skeptical at first, but Dranus knew how to rouse them from destitution when he needed to and this night, he found it easier than ever before.

If nothing else, Deleron Kaxus had been right about one thing: his people were ripe for change.

The king spent the remainder of the evening scribbling out orders to various members of his court, various members of the military, and many others, so that they may prepare during the two-month journey that he had planned ostensibly to survey the state of their forces around the realm. Only the War Council knew that he quested for the mythic Staff of the South Star.

An important topic of discussion was the line of leadership that would follow in his absence. Laws had already been set in place for these kinds of situations in war time. General Armodus and Commander Ven, being of the personal council to the king, would primarily serve in matters of war and state governance, respectively, but could either preside over both matters in the absence of the other.

Admiral O'cule, being of the next highest rank would take command if both Armodus and Ven were away. And the remaining two commanders would split whatever duties remained if all of the rest were away. It is for this reason that a separate law was instated that no more than three members of the War Council may be absent from the capital at any time other than when they marched for battle. During this time, regency was decided by the king while independent cities became self-governing and fell back on the ancient traditions long since set and practiced by the warlike people of Varz.

The news that Varz was on the war path again was like a pebble dropped in a still lake. In a matter of days ripples would spread to every ear in Varz and beyond. For the first time in centuries the cities soared through the night without rest, without even the want for rest. The promise of greatness awakened something deep within every soul and that greatness forbade them rest while they labored at the anvil, stocked goods for the march, and cheered for the reclamation at hand.

As night settled in, the city was still so alight by torchlight that it cast its own radiance through the windows of the staircase leading to the king's bedchamber.

King Dranus himself tread wearily, exhausted from the day's exertions. In some ways he missed the sedentary life he had lived up until that point, dealing with trivial matters of state and mastering various arts and forms of knowledge. His body and his spirit were not used to the kind of stress he had put himself under. As the day ended and both the sun and the South Star set, the tired king made his way to his chambers. Through quiet hallways he trudged with half-open eyes, making his way without falling from pure memory of having taken this route so often.

He reached the door and placed his forehead lazily against the hard wood door with a muffled thud. For a moment he contemplated the consequences of falling asleep right there, standing outside his own room like a statue. His eventual conclusion was that the extra few steps would likely save him a comparable amount of trouble.

Turning the handle, he pressed his head against the door harder, swinging it in and moving swiftly past it so that it closed behind him with an effortless drifting of his thoughts. He was quite confused at

44

what he saw in his room and at once attributed it to a delusion of exhaustion, nodded, and continued into the room.

Standing tall and magnificent in the center of his bed chamber was Commander Kaelel, dressed in a lustrous lavender and red dress, a heady sway to her stance and her siren's stare. A river of jet-black hair cascaded down her features, accentuating her tanned skin. She stared at the king, brimming with desire, and brandished that same secret smile she had shown the night before.

"I have made my preparations, my king." The words seeped from her luscious lips like so many soothing breezes.

Dranus, in his delirium, glanced once at the sorcerous eyes of this phantasm of his mind and strode with seeming indifference past this picture of feminine beauty. At this, Kaelel was reasonably upset...for all that they had never been married or ever considered themselves a couple, they had, from time to time, been intimate when it suited one or the other. It was not in her experience to be so ignored by a man.

At a high table near the far-left corner of the room Dranus placed the Book and began to remove the layers of his ceremonial robes. The sultry form of the Archer's Brigade Commander followed her prey and stood close, not wanting to disrupt him in an action that was clearly to her benefit. "Allow me, my lord."

The king ignored what he presumed to be some utterance of the Book and dropped each piece of his robes behind him where they were caught by Kaelel. She made to the closet on the left of the chamber, hoping to enter her king's sight and be noticed again; to be sought after. It was, however, that as she reached that side of the room to hang the garments, Dranus turned to his bed as though he expected something would be there and it was not.

Nude and mumbling to himself about some matter of horses and their ability to complain about different saddle types, he was somewhat surprised to see all of his clothes gone from the floor where he had thought he dropped them. But he just raised his eyes and assumed he had forgotten.

Kaelel could no longer keep quiet at this blatant disregard. "Dranus! You will not ignore me like this! Say something!"

With a squint and a clear disregard about his current nudity he stared at the commander, thinking hard about whether he was hallucinating or not. "Kaelel, what are you doing here? Weren't you making preparations or something?" and he turned again to approach

45

his bed, sitting among the scrambled silks and furs. He eyed her intently, clearly debating something in his mind.

Kaelel saw this as her chance to persuade her king and once again donned the guise of the temptress. "Preparations for you, my king." She sauntered over to the bed, untying the knots that held the intertwining red strands that kept the dress pressed against her skin. Though Dranus was tired and quite distracted by his current uncharacteristic need to take over the world, he was still a man and he felt that his eyes could not be swayed to look away from the exquisite beauty before him.

He did, despite this feeling, do just that. He let out a long sigh and when he looked back at her, it was with a stern countenance.

"Kaelel, I'm told you are responsible for spreading the name of the South Star," he started.

At this she grinned the grin of a disobedient child excited to see the final outcome of some prank they had pulled.

"That's true, my king." She stood a few feet in front of him, and her dress fell to the floor, exposing her naked form. "Perhaps I'm due some sort of...punishment?" As she whispered this, the crimson lace of her dress floated up and tied itself tightly around her wrists. She looked at him questioningly, heat radiating from her in excitement.

Dranus recalled this game they had played on numerous occasions, though usually she preferred to do the tying. Still, he recalled this information as he might recall what he'd eaten for dinner: passionless and detached. It was a piece of information that clarified the things his eyes saw and nothing more.

"I don't think that's necessary, commander. I did not expressly forbid it and ultimately, its history serves our current purposes. In retrospect, it was wise of you to disseminate that information in such a way." His uncommon leniency was punctuated by the way his eyes glazed as he recited something he'd clearly memorized earlier in preparation for just this sort of confrontation.

With some barely conflicting thoughts, the king rolled onto the bed and covered himself with the fine silks and warm furs provided him. Then it was Kaelel who sat on the edge of the bed with her chin in her bound hands, her body filled with tension and frustration. Accepting that Dranus was far too deliriously tired to be any good at love-making anyway, she waved her hands in a determined motion at the lights scattered about the room, extinguishing them one by one. She joined him beneath the covers and pressed her body against his, becoming somewhat concerned with the apathy of her king. Where the night before he had been all fire and passion, he was now script and sloth. Then again, as she sidled up close to her king, she began to feel the sleepless day catch up with her rapidly as well.

Dranus, though he felt too weary to make any talk with the woman who so desperately sought his attention, did not object to her presence in his bed. In many ways it was comforting to him to be held by someone who had at least some caring for him. He pictured all of the times they had shared a similar embrace and sought out this feeling in his past, but he found nothing. What was different this time? Usually this part didn't come until after intercourse when their sense of touch would be heightened from sorcery, but it wasn't the touch on his skin that was different. No matter all the frustrations and hurdles he had met that day, he felt at peace.

And though he had never given much thought to the importance of partnership and uniting more than his body with another, he wondered, just before nodding off to sleep, if this was what his soul was missing.

They made love later in the night, but with no restraints, no reversal of their normal power dynamics, nothing more than his body and hers and their eyes locking as if for the first time. He could not remember clearly how it had started or how long it had lasted, but he felt as though it encompassed the whole of the night. In its wake, he slept the most peaceful sleep he'd had since his father's passing.

He awoke the next morning to one final peculiarity: Kaelel was still there, resting peacefully next to him. Typically she would choose to wake before him and leave to avoid whatever consequences might arise. But that morning there was none of that cold utilitarianism in her features. Hers was a fierce beauty, but in the early morning light she was serene and smiled gently in her sleep.

She had awoken by the time the morning meal Dranus had sent for arrived and they sat together in the center of his room enjoying the warm food, strong drink, and familiar company. It was, in fact, the first meal they had shared together and it was riveting. For an hour they talked of the past, both of them had lost their parents already, and bonded over the secret weakness they had felt in those times. They talked of war and strategy and the commander fell comfortably into her routine of reporting on the strengths of the forces she oversaw. The energy that coursed through her as she spoke of the siege weapons her teams had been developing brought him life like no brew could. In the moments before duty would call them each away, they laughed about the events of the previous night.

When she left, they did not kiss and she bowed to her king as was his due, but she did so with a soft smile. Dranus had rarely seen her smile like that before that day and he realized at once that each moment he'd seen it before was a cherished memory. The first time he'd seen her at work as a Den Maiden. The day she'd been promoted to Commander of the Archer's Brigade. They'd known each other for a long time, it turned out, and had often been present for each other's most important moments.

"Well, that certainly went well!" The Book piped in a cheerful voice from the side table.

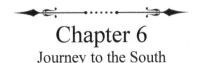

# Chapter 6
## Journey to the South

K ing Dranus's departure from the city had no cavalcade, no safe wishes from the people, no procession which might see him to the gates; it was as simple as him saddling the fastest horse they could spare with his gear and the Book and riding out of the south gate with not so much as a glance at the gate guards. He wore light armor for riding over a white shirt and black breeks tucked into riding boots, his chest armor was covered by a black jerkin and a cloak which he would need for the coming of the Dusk Season. For arms he had the sword Fehris, a bow with enough arrows to last him at his side, and a simple shield of strong steel. He did not expect to be attacked on his way, but he would not take the chance of being caught off guard; that was not the way of Varz.

On his way into the plains surrounding the city he caught sight of the shimmering gold of the Archer's Brigade practicing formation at sunrise. The king subconsciously felt for the presence of the commander, finding her in almost no time and locking eyes with her at once. It was a warm feeling of annoyance like a flock of gulls flapping about in his chest that brought an odd smile to his face. Kaelel returned the smile then stuck out her tongue playfully and barked an order at a slacking new inductee. He had no doubt she would have them in shape by the time he returned.

He would miss her; he decided in that moment. It was a strange realization, like realizing in a single moment that everything his life had ever been as a prince or as a king was about to change with the coming of war and reclamation. It was a small part. Not less important, but a wedge of his shifting circle of reality. A warm, shining wedge that filled him with emotional vertigo. Happiness and sadness. Anticipation and dread. Pleasant memories and the cold truth that memories sprang forth in her absence to fill the void.

It wasn't so bad, though.

As the Day Season gave way to the Dusk Season, Dranus rode for more than a week, taking only enough time to rest at night at the various outposts and towns along the way or pitching his own tent and making light conversation with his horse. Whenever he stopped, he made no impositions as King of Varz and tried to keep as many people in the dark about his intentions as possible. At any military outpost he was expected by precisely one member and that member would forget the king's having been there as soon as Dranus departed. In towns he used his secret knowledge of forbidden magic to alter his appearance and paid for inns like any normal person. It was these new but brief interruptions between long days of riding and resting that helped him keep his sanity. He was seeing something of a revival of Varz culture even so shortly after his proclamation to the general public. Of course, the people were almost riotous over the presence of the South Star. As it turned out, almost every town had at least one person whose family history was well-kept, and stories of the Star had been passed down. Word moved almost as quickly as the king did!

Seeing the people of Varz blossom was a new type of pride for Dranus to experience. Of course he had been proud of himself. He had been proud of his people for all that they had done in their storied past. He had been supremely proud of his residence at the top of the hierarchy of such a superior folk. But he had never felt pride for the *current* citizenry of Varz. He had inherited a great legacy, but he had not felt this new welling of glee and wonder at the creativity and hard work that the people alive right then showed in their pre-war frenzy.

But then, as he passed the final Varz outpost, resting to regain his strength (and to cherish a real bed and a hot bath), he entered the wild southern plains with their rocky steppes and sparse forests. Not only was he far from assistance here, but he was most vulnerable here in the open terrain. But even beyond that, the worst part by far was the boredom of riding day in and day out, looking at the same scenery hour by hour, day after day. Since rising euphorically into his blooming state of being, going back the dull and drab, the wet and cold of the Dusk Season, was a cruel kind of death to him.

Fortunately, Dranus's mood could be lifted reliably by the talkative tome he kept with him at all times.

At first, he had been very strict with the Book, insisting that it address him with respect as the King of Varz. But as they spent time together on the road he had started forgetting about the formalities of the court and started enjoying the straightforward and bold speech of the Book. He had hardly ever had someone who would so openly speak with him and eventually his only insistence was that the thing continued to call him master or lord but otherwise he treated the Book like he would a close friend. Perhaps the first he had ever had, strangely enough.

"Three weeks it's been now, hasn't it?" King Dranus said to the open air. He was particularly missing the comforts of his castle after a downpour had caused his tent to cave in during the night, soaking him through.

"Yes master, three weeks of tireless travel and peerless adventure, wouldn't you agree?" The Book was in an unreasonably good mood, something Dranus had come to accept as a normalcy.

"Don't make me burn you, tome." Unreasonable and inappropriate. He could be quite the annoyance.

"Oh, master, you can't burn me!" It pled.

Dranus peered at it, opened and balanced on the heel of his saddle.

"You need my knowledge!" It concluded.

Dranus glared at its open pages where a child's drawing was being replicated, all innocence and simple motives. These were not attributes of the Book. He thought, with some reason, the Book had meant its first retort in total. The thing was not a normal book in the slightest and the sorcery required to make it would be immense, likely indestructible with simple fire.

"I don't *need* anything from you. I am your master, I *demand* things of you and if your use should come to an end, then I would cast you aside easily."

The image blurred and was replaced by an enlarged drawing of a smiling face, as if to say to Dranus 'I could say the same thing to you.'

"Stop with those drawings!" Irritation suffused his attitude that day but as much as he hated to admit it, it was pleasant to express his frustrations with someone...something. Poor precedent to set, that.

After several moments of awkward silence, Dranus noticed a reliable landmark in the distance.

"We should reach the shore soon," he said to the Book. "You have yet to divulge how we might gain access to a castle flooded for so long beneath the sea. How do you know the tides have not shifted the castle or destroyed it entirely?" He pulled on the reigns, signaling his horse to pick up a little speed.

"Are you aware of the circumstances under which the castle that was Queen Luna's came to be the Castle Beneath the Waves?" There was a leading tone to the papery voice now as though it prepared to tell a story.

"It was legend that when the South Star fled, it wrought vengeance on the Queen of Varz who tried to make use of its power," the king began, "but past Varz monarchs have suggested that it was natural shifts in the tides and that a whole portion of our land slid slowly into the sea." It was as he had read in his texts since he had learned about his nation's history; he had never suspected anything more of it.

"And yet you tell a different story about a similar sinking in the north, do you not?"

Dranus had not ever considered that the loss of their historical castle might be similar to the sinking of Shiera. In the First Great War, his ancestors had used powerful magic to bring the oceans into the basin and not just flood the land but drown the towns beneath the sea where they remained to that very moment.

"Are you suggesting that the castle was sunk by magic?" The sorcery required to sink the nation of Shiera had only been seen a handful of times in this world. Besides, who would cast such sorcery against the very seat of Varz power?

"I wouldn't dare!" It said with feigned indignance.

"Well, we will see soon enough." Dranus cocked a grin. He had to remind himself often to not get baited by the foul tome. Whatever the Book hinted at, Dranus would learn of it in due time, but he would not beg the thing for information. "In the meantime, tell me something about the West."

"Indeed, master." The pages fluttered to a specific page, as if one of the blank pages that could recreate any written text were any different from any other, and settled on a foreign looking crest.

"As you know, the Western Continent is ruled primarily by the Sulvarian Empire, known for their mercenaries and well-governed trade routes. Ruled by a long line of Emperor Sulvas, the empire's patron God is Entna the Sun God."

"Wait," Dranus interrupted. "Sun God?"

"Yes, the Sun God, Entna. It is recorded that Entna is chief among the Gods of the West." The Book answered matter-of-factly.

"But surely these are fictitious accounts? Exaggerations? Legends made grandiose by the needs of story-tellers?" Dranus was intrigued, though he thought of it only as a thought exercise.

"They are not written as fictitious accounts, my lord. There are many texts, ancient though they may be, suggesting that individuals went so far as to meet face to face with some of the Gods and to have witnessed their immense powers."

"Ah, powerful sorcerers then, in the time before The Ultimate. There are even those among Varz's history who have been revered as so-called Gods before. I believe King Faust (f-OW-st) was sometimes called the God of Death." King Faust had been a brutal sorcerer during the relative peace between the First and Second Great Wars and had obsessively studied the properties of death and shadow. His creation, the Shade Cloak, would have been a Relic of Power had he not explicitly forbidden any of his descendants from using it. It was said that he was buried with the thing and that a later Varz monarch had attempted to dig up the corpse and retrieve the Cloak...only to find both missing. No doubt this had contributed to his legend like the 'Gods' the Book spoke of.

"I don't believe so. References to Entna and his kind have been consistent for well over a thousand years. Some of the first written records describe a being physically similar to the statue that stands in Sulva's courtyard to this day." The Book sounded genuinely lost in thought, as though it poured over thousands if not millions of texts from every era of time. It was possible it did just that.

"Coincidence. Or some smart upstart using a well-kept legend to ride on the achievements of someone great that came before him. Legends have a way of growing even in the absence of reality. Let us speak no more of this." King Dranus dismissed the idea of actual Gods outright. If there were some sort of divine presence on this world, he doubted they would have stood by idly while Varz conquered far and wide without so much as a prayer to these would-be deities.

Dranus pressed his mount to some exertion as he saw wavering light reflected in the sky just up ahead. The Book could not be moved from the heel of the saddle by anything other than the king's touch, but it amused him to watch the cover and pages flapping from the gallop.

Finally, after long weeks, they reached the shore of the South Sea. They had made good time this day; there were still plenty of daylight hours left.

Dranus checked the map he had copied from the Book, noting the landmarks he had added from his own collection. They should be at the point where the castle would have been, and yet the shifting currents of the sea showed nothing but a few rocks pointing out of the surf.

"We have reached the spot on the map, but I see no signs of a castle. Am I to dredge the thing up from the depths?" He dismounted and approached the shore. The southern coast of Varz was known for its sheer cliffs, this had made it seem natural that the castle would have sunk due to natural changes dragging a cliff into the uncaring ocean. As he stared from the safety of damp rock, he could see that here was no different. There was no gradual slope, just the natural progression of the steppe and then nothing that wasn't hundreds of feet below the surface.

"No, no, master. The castle is here! Or rather, there!" it said as if pointing.

"Where?" Dranus looked about, shifting his gaze through spectra of light or collapsing across dimensions.

"Theeeeere!" The Book continued. "Look! No, to the left. A little more! See that?"

"The rock...?" Even as he said it, he caught himself. If the ledge went down hundreds of feet immediately, how was there a stray rock protruding up so high?

"The tall tower." The Book corrected with some satisfaction.

With dawning understanding, Dranus began to gain some level of appreciation about the nature of the castle they sought.

"So we have found the castle, now how do we reach it?" The Castle Beneath the Waves. He had thought it a moniker referring to its resultant state after some natural disaster, an odd instance to name the thing for. But no, it was *even now* a Varz stronghold hidden just out of view.

"As you have no doubt concluded, master, the Castle Beneath the Waves was not drowned in such a sense. It was, in fact, cast beneath the sea by sorcerous means. And by Queen Luna herself."

It all made sense--when the South Star vanished, the queen must

54

have feared her enemies would take advantage of her weakness since she was then without an army to protect her. But she would not kill herself, she would not lock herself away with no chance to escape. No matter how mad she was, she was still a Queen of Varz. It came to Dranus then, that the castle was still very much intact and kept beneath the waves, not flooded like he had suspected. The tall tower provided an entrance and exit to the castle but there must be some way to reach the tower.

"I understand. So then how do we access the tall tower, I wonder." He opened the book with a certain suspicion in mind, flipping as always to a random page where he might find the answer he was searching for.

His assumption had been correct. Scribbled quite hastily and frequently blurred with signs of water damage shifting the ink, was a crude map of winding pathways that were like a random maze from the shore to the tower. Written next to each pathway that connected small dots were a series of numbers drawn in the old symbols and an arrow pointing one direction or another.

At the moment when he looked up from the page, he was convinced he saw a bit of land rise from out of the water at roughly the same location where the directions of the map changed. But just as quickly as it had risen above the crest of the water, it fell back beneath.

Suddenly the numbers gained a sobering significance.

"The map shows the rise and fall of an unnatural bridge to the tower which only lasts for the times set on the map."

The Book hummed in agreement.

"Indeed master, but I might point out that the map is only a rough sketch, and the paths are quite narrow. The horse will have to stay behind, I'm afraid. Just as well, you must do all that you can to keep from falling off the path." The Book seemed overly serious about this last bit of advice and Dranus worried that some unseen obstacle might still be lurking in the depths.

"And why is that?"

"Why?! I am a book, my lord! As much as you might crave a dip I must protest! It would ruin my pages!"

The king pressed his hand against his forehead and resisted the budding urge to cast the thing which had started this all into the water.

"I must observe the pattern and the nature of this bridge and then we will take the tower." He began to pace the line of the coast, peering off as he saw pieces of land come and go. In some places he expected to see land but saw none and yet other times he saw land where there should have been none and he began to look inward, doubting his competence. The map was drawn in such a way that it was clearly meant to be a personal reminder, but a monarch of Varz would not leave such information unencrypted. Still, no matter how he searched there was no matching cipher to divulge the secret of the path. It would be, he thought, that some paths were the true path and others were dead ends. Some rise and fell in regular intervals while at least one came up only rarely. This could take time. It would certainly take concentration.

"Once we reach the tall tower, what might we expect within?" He asked the Book, still perched on the saddle.

The thing flipped rapidly through its pages, going from one cover to the other, then back again....

"I-I do not know, master...I do not know."

To which the King of Varz felt something he likened to fear well within him.

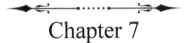

# Chapter 7
## The Castle Beneath the Waves

D ranus took his time inspecting the hastily made map, the movements of the water, and the rise and fall of the land. He tried to picture the progression in his mind and then laid that progression out as a mirage overlapping the real world. There were parts where the land bridges were too far to see the connecting paths, so he couldn't be certain all of the paths he predicted would be present would actually be there. This was most troublesome, as he was sure there was only one correct path. Perhaps what worried him most was the unknown cost of failure. At a glance it appeared that if he chose a wrong path, he could simply swim back to shore and try again. That would be too simple. A Queen of Varz, especially a mad one, would not be so lenient to failure. The Book had no record of what would happen if he were to lose his footing and tumble into the water. Despite what the tome said, he was sure it would survive a little water if it had lasted this long already. But then there was the less known parts of Varz history, like their military taming and breeding of creatures. His people had bred massive war birds for flight, dire wolves with teeth as sharp as steel, and many manners of sea beast meant to clean up the messes of a sinking enemy vessel.

It was the latter that he feared; some sentinel of a forgotten age left here to stop would-be intruders. Still, he could not stop here. Perhaps the beast would recognize him as a Varz monarch; they had always been well trained.

A glare from the South Star reminded him of the time; he needed to go now.

He slowly approached the shore and stared intently at a spot a few paces in front of him where the land gave way to the sea. Carefully counting the minutes until his first approach would be possible, he marveled at how inconspicuous the tower was; had the Book not told him its true identity he never would have suspected it of being anything more than a rock in the ocean. It was this natural camouflage, no doubt, that had kept the secret of this place for generations.

Dranus looked to the horizon. He had only a few more hours before the sun would begin to set and he could not be caught trying to get back across the bridge in the black of night.

"15 more seconds." He whispered to himself; his heart was pounding against his chest in anticipation. In his hands was the Book opened to the map which he had been studying, memorizing the times to perfection. He considered that sorcery might be invoked in a dire situation, but he also knew that careless sorcery could drain him of strength and focus he could not afford to part with. He decided to try and navigate the maze on his own. All in all he had about three minutes to cross from the shore to the tower. Were it a straight dash it would be an easy run, but with the numerous cutbacks and tangents he wondered if it would be enough.

Staring down into the water as he counted down the last remaining seconds, he could see something floating up to the surface from deep below. The first step.

"Now!" He leapt forward, gaining some distance but sinking in the soft mud. Hoping to gain some extra time by starting while it was not all the way up, he now found himself thigh deep in icy cold water as the first pathway rose. He trudged across the longest stretch with little difficulty, sighting the first little island with uncomfortable ease.

"23...24..." He continued to travel the passages presented to him as quickly as he could. Here were two branching paths, the one to the left was his choice.

"37...38..." He felt that he was falling behind, somehow. Searching frantically for the next ledge, his own foothold began to sink. The frigid bone-chill made it hard for him to focus, but he shook his head and continued on.

"52...53..." His legs became heavy as he felt himself being dragged under with the descending path. Just before he felt he would fall he made a leap and landed on one knee, his other legging dangling precariously over the abyss. Struggling, he was just able to pull himself up without getting the book wet. Here was a cut-back that took him towards shore again, costing him several seconds in time to find, but he had nearly reached the center of the maze.

"74...75..." At this point he was a decent distance away from the shore and on a relatively large island that stuck out of the water completely. If it had not been for this halfway point, he didn't think his energy would have held out. Sprinting was one thing but sprinting through cold waters in armor he couldn't afford to part with was another.

According to his calculations he had 2 minutes on the haven from soggy pages and drenched clothes. Already his bottom half was completely soaked and the water he had kicked up from running had splashed onto his upper half. A bit of focus, some snaking logic, and a few deep breathes later his clothes were dry and a pool of water melted into the obviously carved rock island.

If he had studied the maps and the pattern of the land correctly, and he had, the next half would be much more difficult. And much more dangerous.

He resumed counting, waiting for the appearance of the next bridge when he noticed a leaf blown from a distant cliff land on the surface of the seemingly calm water. Within a second it was dragged down, spun about, and plunged out of sight in the wicked currents. The danger was not from some beast or monster, as he had speculated...the waves themselves would be his undoing if he failed.

"You made no mention that the currents here could still drag a man down to the depths!" With the adrenaline and surprise he could not help but be startled at the Book's lack of information.

"I told you to do all you could to avoid falling off! What more explanation do you need?!" The Book replied somewhat playfully, as if it enjoyed the king's plight.

"Again!" The time had come, and he sprinted over the bridge, dodging a hole and jumping over a small gap to get to the next mass with decent pace.

"62...61..." He counted down the time that remained.

The next pass had appeared to be straight from the shore, but he was now finding that it turned rapidly, snaking from left to right so that he was tempted to jump across rather than go around. The time he had expected for this would not be enough...not with all this turning. But the turns had spread, he could no longer risk cutting across, so he took some risk in increasing his speed.

"47...46...No!" The island ahead of him was already sinking, but it was straight now and would continue straight...if only he could reach it! He stepped onto the patch of descending mud as the water touched his thighs...he made it...and he stepped up to the rising patch with a great deal of effort. The continued exertion was taking its toll.

"32...What?! Where?!" His eyes searched frantically, panic overwhelming him, for that path that should be laid out in front of him was nowhere to be seen! He looked all around to his left and to his right; had it come up behind him? Was it still far in the distance? He could see it nowhere and the small patch beneath him was vanishing rapidly. His thoughts were frenzied, his mind searched for some way out, some piece of him lamenting that his death should come so soon after he finally started living. Then, by some fundamental memory, some training that had been so ingrained that it came to him naturally, his mind began to corrupt the reality of the world about him.

In a sharp snap of water on water, the surf immediately around him became solid like a stone that flowed at its core, confused at what state it should adopt. Dranus stepped onto this makeshift pass and sped with the agility the more solid grounding gave him.

"19...18..." The bridge was convenient, but a sorcerer could only pervert the powerful states of matter for so long before reality would take hold again.

As the water insisted upon him that it was, in fact, liquid, Dranus jumped and landed on one hand and his knees. He held the Book before him, panting once then standing.

He had time now. The path ahead was straight and visible, leading directly to the tall tower, though thin. Behind him the tides crested and shifted like normal. Here he had to take his time. This was the final test.

"7...6..." With arms spread, he balanced along the beam; the window of the tower was almost within his grasp.

"5...4..." A shift in the sands made him teeter dangerously to his left but the Book in his right helped him balance.

"3...2..." His heart felt as though it would erupt from his chest and seek the comfort of the tower just before him.

"1...."

King Dranus sat, breathing heavily, on the ledge of a window set into the tall tower just peaking above the waves. Finally, he thought, he had reached the real danger.

"Well that was riveting, wouldn't you say, my lord?" The Book spoke again and it brought to mind the thing's motivations once more. It claimed before to know of no consequence, but Dranus had asked of *intended* consequences. The currents may be a natural barrier, or even a coincidence. But then, had it not fully warned him because it knew he was not meant to be felled here? Was that the reason for its lightheartedness? The king tried to gather his strength as he silently considered the true relationship between himself and the sorcerous tome. Was he master or servant?

Again Dranus felt the urge to toss the Book into the vacillating waves. But he had neither the energy for such an act nor for some response which might secure his relative status over the Book. Instead, he pivoted on the ledge and stood on a stone platform at the top of circling stairs. With the movement of his hand, as one might wipe dirt off of their clothes, he pushed at the water, and it willingly came free, with a bit of magical persuasion.

"Oh no, I'm fine! You only managed to get *half* of my pages wet. Thank you for your concern!" Again the king ignored the Book's complaints and focused on the task ahead. He was immediately wary of the window which mirrored the one he had entered but that was set in the south side. This window let in the dull scarlet rays of the South Star and reflected them, or so it seemed, throughout the castle. His eyes followed the gleaming beams to one reflector and then another and yet another until he could only assume that they populated the entire castle. Dranus presumed their purpose was to illuminate the castle which was indeed fundamental to his descent; he had no way to generate light in the dark depths.

Making his way down the spiraling stairs, Dranus was alert to anything which might attempt to impede his quest, and more than a few times did he quickly move to his side only to find the reflected image of himself bathed in crimson staring back at him. The stone walls creaked and ached, though whether from movement of the water or from some magical irritation he was unsure. The masonry was such that the castle could not possibly be impermeable to the pressure from outside. Had Luna conducted some final sorcery that had been strain enough to kill her? No, this was the work of many talented sorcerers. Queen Luna's legendary Black Mages, perhaps.

"Do you have any understanding of how the castle is laid out or where we might find the Staff?" He spoke in whispers to the Book as though he suspected he was watched by the other versions of himself residing within the mirrors.

"The design is likely very similar to that of your own castle, as yours was based on the design of this one."

"Really? I did feel like I recognized that tall tower..." The brief time of relative silence and absence of mishap had, paranoia aside, somehow relaxed Dranus. Perhaps it was the familiar sights and layout of his home.

"Why do you think the tall tower in Varz is so tall?"

"Well, it *is* the tall tower. It wouldn't make much sense for it to be short." He navigated the chambers now on the upper floors as he might navigate his own castle. Though the obvious purpose of each area was different from his own castle, the overall layout was nearly identical.

"Wouldn't make much sense at all..." the Book agreed.

Their voices seemed to be consumed by the water without so much as an echo to mark their presence. Being deep beneath the ocean and yet still in a pocket of air made for a disorienting experience of the senses. The rumble of the ocean outside the walls unsettled him, as though they were circled still by some great beast. The air was thick with the sickly smell of brine and fish and decay. The image of a ship graveyard, haunted by dismembered sea-folk swam to his thoughts and he shivered. But his shivering didn't stop there. If he had thought the water cold, the inside of the castle was freezing. His breath steamed out in front of him as the warmth of his exertion met the unkind frost of the dead place. It didn't help that moisture stuck to his skin, cloying at his flesh and trickling upward as if trying to escape this hellish place. The king's footsteps upset dust which hadn't been thus disturbed in several centuries.

Where were the dead? Everything about the place seemed to be well preserved, but there were no bodies marking the dead. Had the castle been abandoned before Luna sank it?

He could not know, but he did know that the longer he stayed in this place, the looser his grip on his sanity became.

"Would the queen not likely be in the Great Hall?" The Book's speculation startled Dranus. After carefully untightening his fist, shoulders, and every other muscle in his body, he noted the import of this speculation.

"Why would we want to find the queen?" He was very suspicious of the Book still; had it withheld something important again?

"The Staff of the South Star belonged to Queen Luna, so it would only stand to reason that it still be with her." This speculation was slightly less genuine than the former to the king's sharp mind and he chose only to agree and not press the topic. No doubt it knew this as fact.

Indeed, it seemed that following the spectral red beam of light from the South Star would lead them directly to the Great Hall. Descending a final set of stairs they parted from the light as it strayed upwards in the same direction they were headed. Dranus held for a moment at the door, expecting that if they would find some danger, they would find it here.

Unslinging his shield from his back and unsheathing the sword Fehris, he took a deep breath to calm himself. The frigid brine choked him, and he spat upon the stone.

"Let us be on with it." He pressed a gauntleted fist against the door and felt the aged wood give a little; it was of the same material as the door in his castle yet held a disturbing similarity to his people's flesh tone. Hesitantly he pushed the great door and it slowly creaked open with some force.

The Great Hall appeared empty.

The emptiness contrasted sharply with the dense, moving sea outside the walls. Here he saw the true power of the spell over this castle as many of the tall windows of the hall had shattered, and yet the water dare not tread beyond the threshold. He stepped towards a window and reached his hand out to touch the water. He met no resistance and brought his finger back wet with no consequence. This was truly a separate class of magic than what his contemporaries practiced.

Unlike his own Great Hall which was decorated with banners and drapes, rugs and lamps, trophies from foreign lands, the large dais and the throne, this hall had only a solitary throne at the other end of room, swathed in the blood-red light of the South Star reflected from a mirror set high behind the seat of power.

Dranus approached the center of the room carefully and stopped abruptly as something changed. There was something.... There was still the salty smell of the sea flooding his nostrils, but there was another scent. Pine? An evergreen fern? This far south? Even on land that would be peculiar! Nothing in the chamber seemed to be set up to give off a scent like a censer, and yet the smell was strong enough that he knew he must not imagine it.

Thinking it part of the spell, he continued to the throne carefully, still cautious that something might be lurking in the shadows, waiting for his guard to drop. But as he came closer and closer to the dark throne his eyes widened in a maddening stupor.

Sitting still in her throne, slouched and decayed, was the corpse of Queen Luna the Mad, the Staff of the South Star clutched firmly in her hand.

"Queen Luna..." He breathed respectfully. Dranus was in awe of this figure still sitting regally on her throne, preserved in death. The site was both terrifying and majestic, it awakened some feeling within him that he could not hope to identify. And with the contrasted silence which followed his words he knew that this feeling was dangerous in itself.

He proceeded still closer, his eyes on the Staff as this was his goal. As much as he hated to rob the dead queen of her last possession, it was for the current state of Varz, and such a purpose was noble enough for this desecration.

He was just a few yards from the throne now. With his shield up and his sword ready, he looked around the hall as best as he could. It was dark save for the light from the South Star and many corners hid in shadows.

He looked back to the staff...had it moved slightly? His eyes were then drawn to a bony skull still laced with rotted flesh that rested on a curled fist. In the skull were two sorcerous eyes staring directly at the King of Varz. Dranus froze and locked eyes with the thing which sat in that throne. Could it *see* him?

"You come for the Staff of the South Star?" The raspy feminine voice was cold, devoid of all emotion but hate; lonely, vengeful hate. It echoed from the skull of Queen Luna the Mad. With slow, methodical creaks, the corpse came to life and pressed on the sturdy staff, rising in all the shredded remains of a gown fit for a Queen of Varz.

"You are King of Varz, are you not?" The imperious voice was harsh, accusing him of his own proud identity.

Dranus could hardly focus, hardly comprehend the scene that played out before him. Had his body not frozen in shear tension, he would have fallen backward with fright. That he spoke now with Queen Luna the Mad, who died so long ago, was truth, but even with all the knowledge in the Forbidden Texts and the King's Library he had known of only one way that death might be reversed in a sense, and it was in no way like this. To pervert Death was a sorcery unknown to this world. Death was the great absolute. His specter stood over all and the folk of Varz had known his realm to be beyond their reach since time immemorial!

"I...I am." He stammered, his guard still up.

"Then why do you cower like a Lesser? You are a master of our arts, no doubt? You must accept that what you see is the reality that has been imposed." She sneered at him as best she could with what remained of her flesh, pointing a bony finger at him in disgust.

This was the basic logic by which all the people of Varz tapped their sorcerous power and thus, lived their lives. It was a strange comfort that his emotions could not refuse, and he steadied himself outwardly. He visibly relaxed, dropping his shield to his side but keeping his sword in hand and standing up straighter.

"I am the King of Varz," he projected in his most kingly voice, "and I have come to reclaim the Staff of the South Star for our people, for they have need of it once again." His confidence had returned and he found himself now speaking as though he were talking to an equal, an experience he could not have in Varz otherwise.

Queen Luna then appeared to notice the crimson light of the South Star she stood in for the first time. A smile spread across her face, and she caressed the open air as she might caress a lover.

"I see. Then if you are to take the Staff, you must prove yourself worthy by answering one question."

Dranus glanced at the Book, did it not hold all answers? "I accept Queen Luna."

The ragged remains displayed a grin and placed a ring-covered hand to its hip, turning the Staff so that Dranus looked upon a red stone near the head of the shaft.

"What must you, a king, do for the people of Varz?" The voice echoed unnaturally throughout the room and the sick smell of pine came back to him. Could this really be the test? Was it so simple?

"The King of Varz must provide for the needs of the people; he must ensure their safety. He provides the structure necessary for the people to flourish, in peace or in war. He must be a standard for all to aspire to." It was as his father had taught him, though it was clearly not to the queen's liking.

"Incorrect." She scowled and tapped the brass base of the Staff against the stone. Its rich tone filled the room and rang in his head.

"A king must provide for the protection of the lands; he must guard their interests. Succeeding in such, he should spread these interests to the furthest they can be sustained. It is his responsibility to represent Varz potential in all forms." He quoted a line directly from his childhood teachers. Had this not been the role he had been trained for his entire life? He could think of a thousand lessons and quote them perfectly, but this still did not seem to be the subject of the queen's question.

"Incorrect." The Staff clanged again, louder this time, sending a sharp pain through the king's ears.

Dranus was becoming irritated and opened the Book, thinking it best not to express the distinct properties the Book held. He thought hard of the queens' memoirs, hoping to find some clue. Reading through some brief notes scribbled almost illegibly he shut the Book in anger.

"I am king now, Luna! By my right you must obey my order and I am ordering you to provide me with the Staff!" The queen still seemed unamused by this outburst.

"Incorrect." Another tap. A splintering pain in his head.

By his memory of time, his window for returning to the surface with light was shrinking; he had no time for these riddles.

"Then I will take the Staff by force!" Brandishing his black-bladed sword and raising his shield again, he closed the gap with powerful strides. The Book, held by the arm to which the shield was strapped made a noise of slight protest and the queen's countenance changed from annoyed to offended.

The Staff slammed hard into the stone without an echo. Suddenly their stood two ghostly warriors made of red light, brandishing archaic curved shields and swords between the monarchs. He realized at that moment that the previous hits of the Staff had set a number of these warriors behind him, covering his exit. She did not intend for him to leave if his answer didn't meet her wants.

"You will do no such thing." The voice was as destitute and spiteful as it had ever been.

He had used a great deal of strength getting to the castle and exploring. Realizing his inability to fight an army of 20,000 he lowered his weapons and searched his mind...she was the Mad

Queen, perhaps her thoughts were too twisted for normal responses.

"A king must be secure, must hide away when threatened!" Another sharp noise sounded, and another ethereal soldier appeared.

"A king must fight wars and never lose battles, must keep his army in line!" Now the soldiers numbered four.

"A king must murder his people, chain their souls to sorcerous strength and flee, dying alone beneath the sea!" He railed at the corpse, slashing at the air with Fehris.

The queen's sense of humor had remained dead, but her sense of irony had not. A tilt of the Staff and a whole squad of twenty or more soldiers stood before him.

"Damn this test, Luna! I will rip the Staff from your twice dead grip!" With a dash and a shove of his shield he knocked back several of the ghostly warriors, concluding quickly that they could be interacted with. He side-stepped a downward strike and ripped the sword Fehris through the stomach of one warrior, his shield covering the back side of his swing so that he left no openings. Two others charged at him, swords posed to stab, but their points were deflected away by a sweep of the round shield. He took them each in the shoulder so that they grasped their arms in disbelief. Moving and slashing one way and another he fought, each warrior injured showing noticeable surprise as though they had speculated that after such a long life of imprisonment, they might never feel pain again and never truly die. That, or something far more powerful and unlikely in equal measure.

Dranus was struggling not to deal any fatal blows to his future forces but even the injuries he doled out seemed to hardly deter the warriors. His strength would not hold out much longer. In the back of his mind he puzzled through the pages of the Forbidden Texts until he found that which he sought. A quick ceremonial stab into the ground and the warriors around him slumped, the weight of their armor doubling and doubling again. He was learning very quickly about the many properties of his enemies and was thankful that his sorcery still affected them.

He caught a glimpse of the Mad Queen's snickering grin. Raining blows on the exposed necks of soldier after soldier the king darted for the proud figure of the queen. Believing he had achieved the unachievable, he was dumbfounded to feel the pressure of several overly heavy bodies taking him to the ground. He was pinned by the glowing soldiers; pinned, ironically, by his own magic. Queen Luna had not so much as moved an atrophied muscle to stop him.

A warrior stood overhead, the point of his sword hovering over the king's throat. Before he delivered the killing blow he stopped and looked to the former Queen of Varz.

"Will you take one last guess, King of Varz?"

Dranus, filled with adrenaline and the fury of battle refused to give the Mad Queen the satisfaction of patronizing him in the moment of his death. He wrested his arm free and threw his sword at the dead queen in defiance, nearly grazing her delicate arm.

A bony grin of a different character came to what remained of Queen Luna's lips.

"Correct."

With a light rap of the Staff, the Army of the South Star vanished. The queen approached the downed king maintaining all the elegant stature of Varz nobility.

"A king must be strong, even in the face of certain defeat. He must be powerful and unafraid to wield his power. He must be ready to do *whatever* is necessary not just to protect his people...but to make them great...even if it is against impossible odds." Luna helped Dranus to his feet with unexpected strength and returned to her throne.

"They thought me mad to imprison my army within the Staff, but at that time it was my only choice to ensure my own strength as queen against usurpers and coups. Not a single man or woman of the 20,000 who now reside in this Staff had their lives taken from them...they were given out of loyalty. And when I sunk my castle to retain my right they thought me mad, but is this not an impregnable fortress?" The anger that had first characterized the queen gave way to underlying sadness and despair. There were secrets in her eyes, and all of them were sad. Hers had been a tumultuous time as Queen of Varz. It was still early in their nation's history and rites of succession were not well established yet. No doubt she had made many an impossible choice in her lifetime. She was preparing him to do the same....

Dranus felt not pity, but commiseration with the dead queen.

He could not know the extent of her despair.

Dranus recovered his sword, ignoring the muffled mutterings of the Book in his grasp.

"Your story has not been told well, my queen." Dranus admitted reluctantly, standing once again before the corpse in the throne.

"Take the Staff, my king, and show the people of Varz your power. Show all the Five Realms and the Three Continents your power. But know the limitations of this weapon: the Army of the South Star are not immortal, but they are mighty hard to kill. They do not feel pain or fatigue but share the same vital points of mortality. They are of a finite existence, once they have all been slain in this form, you will have nothing remaining but a staff and a handful of gems. Use the Staff wisely." He respected the queen much more now than he had ever thought he might.

"Master, you should listen..." The Book struggled to get in a word, but Dranus still paid no attention to it.

He took the Staff of the South Star from the undead queen and returned to a respectable distance, giving a bow. "Thank you, Queen Luna. I will see to it that our people know that you were not mad at all."

The corpse then resumed the pose of her chin resting on her fist, but the remains of the lips were twisted, contorted, in some sign of deranged thought. The last words he heard from the queen were simple.

"Was I not?"

The figure was limp again. Maniacal, raving laughter rang throughout the Great Hall, delighting only in insanity, chilling the very existence of King Dranus. But it was not the laughter that caused him the most distress, for with every passing moment the laughter was being overtaken by the sound of rushing water.

A puddle of water touched his boot and he looked at the door. The whole castle shifted and some terrible noise of splitting timbers and stone sliding on stone set his heart again to beat with frantic fear.

He decided at once that he had no liking for these emotions he had felt of late.

"Master, I tried to warn you..." the Book began.

"How do we escape? Where can we exit?" His tone was flat and hurried as he dashed for the great doors, the Staff in hand, his shield abandoned.

"As you saw, the only safe way is through the tall tower, and it is quite tall...any attempt to exit beneath the waves will see you dragged to the bottom." The Book, too, seemed to show hints of fear and hesitation in its voice, a trait which was both uncharacteristic of books in general, and this particular Book more so.

He ran up the stairs they had come down, moving against a stream of water cascading off the stone steps. He ran past chambers that let in water through the now unprotected windows. He ran through halls growing more and more flooded with the salty brine as it leaked into every crack and crevice in the walls. He ascended floor by floor but felt he was taking too long. The freezing water began to surge against his legs and his progress slowed. His mind raced and his body ached. Everything was dark; the red light nowhere to be found. Were it not for the king's sorcerous eyes and his familiarity with the halls he would have been lost to the maze-like corridors and stairs.

He came to the spiral stairwell of the tall tower, but the flow of the current was strong. Desperately he pressed against the waves that came down with the force of oppressive furies, but the wall of water was irrepressible.

No matter how many times he tried to send his weight against the current, even with his sword and sorcery to divert the flow, he could not gain any ground. He contemplated using the Staff, but the light of the South Star had been diffused by all the moving water. He consulted the Book, flipping through pages with a frenzied pace, searching for some answer. The water was at his stomach, and he froze, stopping to listen closely to the slow monstrous groan of the beast that was the castle.

The world stopped around him. The wall to his left shifted, the stones dislodged, the side gave, and he was swept with the Book and the Staff down through the waters to the bottom. To his grave.

The current pushed and pulled his body back and forth, his limbs jerking to the whims of the tides. Dranus fought to swim upwards, holding his breath for all he could, but his efforts were futile. The freezing water pulled at his grip around his sword and the Staff of the South Star. Above him in the water the tall tower was falling and breaking apart, the polished metal mirrors drifted lazily, and glass fluttered down. He turned to stare down into the blackness, the castle to his side. As he stopped shifting side to side and was pulled inexorably downward, the king considered the ironies implied in this ignoble death after so narrowly escaping it only a short time before.

His eyes played tricks on him as he struggled to contain his breath. He saw some giant mass of blues deep below, blending with the water but somehow sticking out from the backdrop below him. Had his initial suspicions been correct? Was there some creature sucking him down into its gaping maw? Was he to be food for some brutish beast forgotten by man?!

    Then, King Dranus's breath ran out.

# Chapter 8
## The South Star Fleet

T hin ribbons of scarlet trickled through the clear water, reflected by the mirrors of the falling tower in a kaleidoscopic array of red. Like a morbid celebration of the king's passing they rained down through the sea passing over the sinking body of King Dranus as he struggled to hang on to his life.

A ray of crimson light caught once on the mirror of the tall tower, shot true into the glimmering head of the Staff of the South Star and the four-sided gem glowed a radiant blue, the same blue that had outlined the large object Dranus had seen rising to meet him.

The mass continued to rise quickly, urging forward in hopes that it might reach the surface. As the king's last breath left him, he was convinced he saw the outline of a sail, of a deck, and even...a massive ship in that deep blue disturbance.

The impact of something huge and solid against him shot every last bit of oxygen from his lungs and pressed him against something firm as he rose and rose from the depths. It was all he could do just to keep his mouth closed so that his lungs would not flood with water! But there was light! Blessed light!

With a massive explosion of mist and spray a large vessel burst out of the water, sending waves about in every direction and gaining buoyancy with unnatural efficiency. The vessel was clearly a military vessel, and it was of the same relative design as a naval ship from the current Varz military though the style was something only seen in the annals of the King's Library. More shockingly, the boat was of that dark blue hue from before and was ghostly, as though it only half existed in this reality.

As soon as the air hit the king's skin he gasped and his lungs heaved. He breathed heavily on the sweet air and spat out the sea water he'd ingested with hacking coughs. His vision blurred and his head spinning, Dranus rested on one knee, his body frantically seeking to recover. From pure instinct he had held onto the Book through everything and now it lay beside him, soaked through, but this was of little concern to the man who had nearly met his end only seconds before.

Still struggling for breath he looked around him...what was this thing he stood on and where had it come from? Surely it seemed like a boat for all that it appeared to be made of some unearthly wood and iron, but it had certain characteristics that reminded him of the Army of the South Star.

Staggering to his feet, he left the Book, focusing his attention now on the translucent cerulean man that sauntered towards him from the high deck.

With a proud salute and a grim expression, the man addressed the king.

"My king, I am Admiral Burgiss (BER-jihs), captain of this vessel and chief of the queen's navy. How may we address you, Highness?"

Suddenly the glow from the Staff caught his attention and he stared intently at the sapphire face of the gem. Even as he continued to look around in amazement, he saw more and more of the blue apparitions appear and go about typical duties of men-at-sea. His brooding eyes finally settled on the man called Burgiss.

"I am King Dranus VIII, son of King Roboris the Thick-Hearted, inheritor of the power of The Ultimate. You are an admiral, then, in the Army of the South Star?"

"Aye King Dranus, for centuries we have served Queen Luna. Now we serve you." His voice was gruff, as though every word were a waste of precious time.

Dranus stared at the admiral...he had not expected the ghouls to be so *human*. Somehow, he had assumed they had lost their minds with their souls and lived only in a sense, tied to the will of the one who held the Staff and fighting like berserkers. Contrarily, this man was surely Admiral Burgiss, likely ancestor to Admiral O'cule, in all of his presence, exactly as he was when his soul had been ensnared.

He turned the staff in his hand so that the back of the gem, which was of rich amber, absorbed the rays of the fading South Star which thus shined out of the blue face of sapphire. He had only seen Queen Luna use the staff a few times, but he had a suspicion of how it worked.

Raising the staff he brought it down with a dull thud against the deck and the sapphire poured out its radiance like flowing water. The open sea then found another vessel like the one he now rode on. Gazing at the thing in wonder, he weighed the staff with his hand, testing the balance, admiring the sharp spikes which formed a kind of crown atop the four-sided gem.

He was interrupted by the sound of agitated pages as though they were caught ruffling in a strong gale.

"No no, I am just fine. No need to dry me off, no need to do anything. Not like I led you to the Staff or helped you in any way. No, I'll just lay here and rot." The Book protested loudly.

The king smirked a bit at the Book's dramatic humor. Though he had initially suspected a book could not employ such humor as sarcasm, he had come to appreciate this companion slightly more after this ordeal.

"Have your men dry and mend the book as needed Admiral, it is possibly of greater use than the Staff." The Book remained and basked in the recognition as several well armored crew members picked up the Book and cast simple spells to dry and mend the book.

"So you remain with your basic sorcerous skills? The power of the Staff continues to impress me. I must also thank you for saving my life," the king said to the admiral.

"We merely do your bidding, my king."

"Of course. Bring us to shore; the South Star sets."

Admiral Burgiss gave the order and the ship quickly headed back towards land where his horse grazed lazily. Dranus, retrieving the Book and verifying what supplies had been lost, found himself with an unexpected appreciation for his own existence which he had never quite considered before. Perhaps it had been the near-death experience; perhaps it had been that in seeking the Staff he had actually lived just a bit.

"How is the Staff controlled Book? Surely this cannot be all that remains of the naval forces."

"The Staff is connected to its wielder my lord, it will obey your will, as it likely did to save your life."

"I see." His interest was piqued. This was an instrument of legend, told in stories at bedtime and containing uncountable rumors and mysteries. He had to know more of it, even with the waning light of its patron Star.

Again the Staff rose and again it let out a strong thud. But this time a ship did not immediately appear, and this time the gem released some melancholy sound, some dirge that echoed over the open sea. Then, as if after building up strength, the Staff gushed sapphire light and Dranus's view became overwhelmed by a force of some hundred ships sailing as far as the dimming light could show. The dirge was silenced by a bright cry as the South Star Fleet rallied beneath a newly raised banner, one of King Dranus VIII, reclaimer of the Staff. Once again, they could conquer and kill; they could spread the pride of Varz to the corners of the Five Realms; they could live again!

Their power and their passion brought back to Dranus that despicable grin; that twisted curvature of the lips that could only be a contorted expression of chaotic glee.

*    *    *

That night, the king consulted the Book and attempted to learn the basics of the Staff of the South Star. Of course, this was all done in theory as the Star would not rise again until early the next morning. But with it now firmly in his grasp and the immediate danger avoided, he planned his return to Varz and the integration of the Army of the South Star into all of his battle strategies. From his conversations with the Book, he had learned that the armed forces of Queen Luna the Mad had been structured almost identically to his own. The gem focused the light from the South Star and whatever side faced forward released its division of the Army: the sapphire released the navy, the ruby released the footed soldiers, the emerald released the mounted forces, and the amber face released the archers. The Book had no reason why there was no battle mage division, but the king assumed that this was because the warriors of Varz had originally all been battle mages to varying degrees. Although this diversity was a welcome surprise, it also meant that he did not have an expected 20,000 foot soldiers and the Book had confirmed that no record of multiple factions of the staff being present at a battle at once existed. He could have the foot soldiers out on the field, but that meant if he needed a cavalry charge, he would have to withdraw his mass of troops to do so. There was some stratagem he could devise to make use of this feature, but at current it was a slight worry.

"Tomorrow we will begin our trip back to Varz. We can resupply at the outpost we visited last within a few days and make haste for the capital." He thumbed through different pages of the Book, examining maps of varying detail and of varying areas, trying to grasp which path back might be quickest. While the direct route seemed most obvious, it exposed him to the greatest risk of being discovered and the illusion that he had somehow fabricated the Staff out of thin air was important to his image. Still, the king was anxious to see how his people had fared in preparing for war in his absence.

"There is an alternate plan I might advise, my master. With the South Star Fleet we could quickly skirt the southern coast and make it to the low hills near the border in equal time." Dranus closed the book, tending to look at its cover whenever he engaged it in direct conversation.

"But that takes us in the wrong direction. Is there some invasion plotted already?"

"None lord, but the sword of King Vulcan the Rock might be found in the time we have remaining." Dranus furrowed his brow, considering the amount of time it would take to make it to the east.

"The Sword of Righted Guard...where in the low hills does it lie?"

"Where it must, lord, in the Castle Surrounded by Stone."

Dranus was skeptical. "It cannot lie there, I'm afraid. As well protected as the castle of King Vulcan is, it has been searched by our people many times over. Such a thing as the Sword could not have been so easily overlooked in such a small castle. And would it not still be held by King Vulcan as the Staff was by Luna?"

The Book was momentarily silent, as though considering its choice of words carefully.

"You are a strategist, are you not? Trained in the mastery of tactics?"

"I am King of Varz! I paint masterpieces with the art of war." He declared boldly, with some indignation at having to say it at all.

"Then you are familiar with the strategic value of the Castle Surrounded by Stone."

Dranus considered these words, and a sudden understanding grasped him again: much like the Castle Beneath the Waves, his knowledge had been shown to be insufficient.

"The Sword of Righted Guard still rests in the Rock's hand, of this, I am quite sure." The Book had no way to tell things about current events, but it held a distinct certainty in its tone. "You might guess why."

In a flash of realization, he did.

"Then we head to the east upon the first morning's light."

Exhausted both mentally and physically, King Dranus lay in his tent, trying hard to ignore the howling winds of the Dusk Season. This had clearly been no coincidental announcement by the Book. Then again, the thing had promised him the three Relics of Power...or had it been four? Either way, King Vulcan's sorcerous sword was one such Relic, thought to have been hidden by Vulcan after his final victory in a secret location so that if need for it ever arose again, he could seize it and become the master of battle he had once been again. As it turned out, he had done just that, but in the last place a non-invader would think to look.

In his fading thoughts before sleep, he considered what difficulties he might find at the Castle Surrounded by Stone. If the events of the day gave any portent, he dreaded the excursion, though the ringing voice of Queen Luna gave him strength.

"Even against impossible odds." Dranus whispered to himself and drifted off to sleep.

*    *    *

Aboard the flagship of the South Star, *The Dawn's Fury,* they made good time sailing the southern coast. The vibrant vessel had properties which were not at once noticeable, but once noticed, sent the king back into a deep pondering and for a whole day he sat on the fore-deck considering the sails and their nature. Most noticeably, the sails of these ships did not seem to depend on the violent and rapidly shifting winds of the Dusk Season. Though the wind blew Dranus's raven hair about his head, wiping and flicking at his face with the salt-laden air, the sails were full of wind in the opposite direction and the single ship seemed unaffected.

After hours of consideration, deep sorcerous thought, bending the logic implicit in how boats normally sailed on the seas, he could come up with no answer. He had, however, frequently lost interest in the topic for periods of time, only to have the billowing blue banner of the South Star Fleet catch his eye and bring his attention running back.

Out of nothing short of stubbornness he refused to consult the Book on this matter, insisting to himself that the King of Varz should be able to understand so simple a working as some magical sail. And yet the people of Varz had long since lost the ability to manipulate the elements; though some legends of the Lesser Folk insisted that the power might yet resurface if the right conditions were met.

Watching the South Star set from the shore and seeing the ship disappear for the night, Dranus concluded that the wind that moved the crafts of the South Star must be provided from the plane of time and space when the ships were taken into the Staff. He toyed with the thought that the admiral may still know how to manipulate the winds, but the thought of this admiral, no matter his level of deadness, commanding some power which he could not himself command was not one he gladly entertained.

In the early morning of the next day, four days out from the now truly sunken Castle Beneath the Waves, King Dranus set to shore with the Book on the western side of the bay. Though it may have been faster to sail towards the center of the bay and travel up the Trias River, he would not risk being seen by some Urhyllian passerby who might then alert his people of a threat renewed at their border.

No, he took the route through the lower hills towards an outpost which sat atop a prominent hill. Every evening his horse had shown obvious relief at the touch of firm ground beneath its hooves, and every morning it hesitated before taking its first step on the ghostly gangway. The mare seemed pleased to be able to run with some freedom again and the king let the beast gallop herself tired for a ways.

Along the way Dranus speculated what challenge, what riddle or rhyme the king of the Castle Surrounded by Stone could have in store for him. There was of course the possibility that Luna had been unique and that no such trial would await him, but better to be prepared for the worst.

But then what was the import of such challenges surrounding the Relics...were they to test a Varz monarch's worth? Could only a ruler of Varz lay claim to these relics? No word had ever been mentioned of this in the Forbidden Texts. Was it possible that this was the reason the Sword of Righted Guard had never been recovered? Perhaps some soldier had stumbled across it and been deemed unworthy by King Vulcan and slain. Would he find a graveyard of failed attempts at the feet of the king's corpse?

Upon reaching an outpost, his stop for the night, he was welcomed by the captain and had his supplies refreshed. He took a couple of days to recover to his full strength and discuss battle strengths with some of the South Star's officers. Early one evening he was informed that an Urhyllian spy had been captured, and he demanded to speak with the man directly. Within a matter of moments he stood in a small chamber which smelt strongly of blood and fear.

"You are a spy of Urhyll?" King Dranus, in borrowed finery suitable for the King of Varz, stared down at a bleeding man, beaten half to death, lying on the cold stone floor of the keep.

"I am not a spy, dear king!" he begged and groveled, these Lessers had no pride, no refinement like the men of Varz.

"If you are not a spy then why are you in our lands?"

"I was captured, great king! Taken by pirates on the Trias River and abandoned in these hills." He pleaded through gaps in his teeth. It was easy to spot a foreigner in the lands of Varz: as soon as Dranus saw the whites of the man's eyes, his Fate was already sealed.

Dranus made sharp eye contact with the captain of the fort and the soldier relayed the message to his group, "Patrol for pirates."

"By pirates, you say? And of what realm where these pirates who so wrongfully stole from you."

The man was unnerved by the king's seemingly sincere concern and proactive response to the pirate threat.

"They appeared to be of my own realm of Urhyll..." he was moving back then, expecting some ploy.

"Now now, do not fear good man. You have been wronged and I am nothing if not a reasonable king." With a contrived smile and a lowered hand he helped the poor soul to his feet, towering over his small, hunched figure.

"I am not a spy, lord!" Some hope had entered the man's voice as though he might still escape this predicament.

"Oh, and I believe you, of course! But I must ask, where are we now?" Dranus smiled with all the charm of a serpent distracting its prey with a flick of the tail.

The man became hesitant, glancing about the room, to the dark eyes of the king before him, who rested a slender hand on the hilt of the sword, Fehris.

"In the lord's fortress, I suppose." His normal eyes pleaded with the guards in the room, begging for some sign as to the truth of his situation. The king was maddeningly inconsistent...though he spoke pleasantly there was a wicked aura about him, something that no man could explain, nor resist fearing.

"Ah...well sir, that presents a problem." A whirl of black robes obscured the man's vision and not until he felt the sharp steel of the king's sword in his chest did he realize what had happened.

He had died.

"Increase surveillance, if you see a Lesser in our lands, kill him on the spot. Ask no questions. Make no exceptions." Dranus stormed from the room, barely acknowledging the captain's acceptance of this task. The guards were speechless at this display of cruelty. They had only heard rumors about this king who sat on his throne staring into space and dismissing his courtiers as having trivial interests in the welfare of their nation. They had only just heard of the sudden war effort. To see this man so possessed of malicious ferocity, playing with his victim ever so delicately before dealing cold death; it was like seeing a story from their histories come to life.

That evening, after the South Star had set, Dranus took a fresh horse and headed for the Castle Surrounded by Stone. Riding at a blistering pace, a sense of urgency returning after the lazy days at sea, he and the Book reached the valley just as the sun went to bed behind the hills.

"We've made excellent time. I'd suggest a stop in Pyrán, but you seem in a hurry to return." The Book rested on a makeshift table formed of the king's newly acquired shield.

Dranus shot a maddened glare at the Book. "You will not speak of that place around me!" The king could look past many things the sorcerous tome said, but such blasphemies as those of Pyrán would never be tolerated.

"There is a great deal to be done." Dranus was terse, his mind was focused on the routine practice of his thought and a rhythmic flick of his fingers as his tent erected itself.

"Are you *sure* that's all that hastens you, master?" The thing teased like a jackal, poking and prodding for signs of life within the king. Dranus pictured a wide grin spreading across the cover of the

Book.

"Of course! A realm without its king right at the onset of wartime? Were it not a task only I could accomplish I would have never done it!" He had a notion of what the thing hinted at but refused to play along.

"Oh come now, master! You must miss Commander Kaelel, do you not?"

Dranus paused while he was stacking logs over a pit. Miss her? His body felt cold at night no matter the furs he slept with. His body ached for her touch and his eyes sought her form in the passing clouds of the daytime...but surely he didn't *miss* her.

"I don't know." His eyes wandered in thought as his inner mind pictured the rolling black hair and the luscious curves. There again! That incessant flutter in his chest! Had she spread some sickness to him in his bed?

"Maybe this is what my father felt..." His feelings shifted between shades of longing; from that of a pleasant return to his bed and the one who waited there, to the longing of a son who had only ever known pitied acceptance from a father who had to die for him to take the throne.

He stared at the budding flame beneath the logs he had started with some contraption of oils and flint, a device standard to the militant forces of Varz but alien to a king who had, until his journey, never even seen the thing. Perhaps he was his father's son after all.

"I believe it is what he wanted you to feel."

The Book showed sympathy too! What an odd thing he had discovered.

Instinctively he wanted to retort that the Book knew nothing of his father but given its source of knowledge it was possible the Book knew more of his father than he had. Holding a second-hand token of his father's blessing was a source of comfort to the king as he sat back against a fallen tree trunk. He stared at the multitude of stars in the sky and rested his mind from confusing thoughts of Kaelel and sad memories of his father.

Tomorrow would be another danger that he could not expect. He moved to an overlook from atop the hill where they camped and felt the cool night breeze against his skin. He stared down into a wide valley dominated by what appeared to be a single massive slab of stone. Like some natural monolith it held the air of an indomitable monster. But this was far from a normal occurrence, and though Dranus had seen this place many times before, he could not help but stand in awe of this testament to Varz's former might. This place was the stuff of legends; the last great stronghold of Varz.

They had reached the Castle Surrounded by Stone.

# Chapter 9
## What Lies Within the Stone

The next morning saw the king's hope of getting a better view of the stone foiled by rolling fog that lay low in the valley. It crept and clung to the stone like a sheath, revealing nothing more than the silhouette of the fortress.

In all honesty, Dranus had not thought he would gain much by staring at the complex structure from above. The Castle Surrounded by Stone was a marvel of architecture from the world of his forefathers. Though it appeared to be a single solid slab of stone from any angle one might take from the surrounding hills, it was actually a complex maze of high stone walls. The illusion was generated by the intricate layout of the maze and the 20-to-30-foot walls of stone which left no sign of space between to be seen. At the very center of the maze was the castle fortress of King Vulcan the Rock, last great conqueror of Varz.

Seven times the castle had been sieged, seven times enemy forces had entered the maze hoping to crack the impenetrable stronghold, and not once had those forces returned from the unforgiving labyrinth. The castle at the center was not particularly well fortified or even large, in fact it could barely hold a couple hundred soldiers in tight quarters. It was the delirium that came over enemies who dared enter the stone walls that brought them doom.

To the Lesser Folk it was a place of haunted misery, a place protected by unimaginable sorcery which wreaked havoc on the very hearts, minds, and souls of those who entered it. The maze turned friend into foe, masterful leaders into cowering buffoons, and even the most stalwart soldier into frenzied prey.

To a King of Varz it was a brilliant series of stratagems and well-timed tricks of the eye. The key to the maze was not that the castle sat at its center, as the castle was often empty, but that the maze was actually *two mazes*. One started at the main gate and led to the castle at the center; the other started at the castle and was interwoven with

83

the first maze. The soldiers protecting the fortress could run by the side and underneath the trails which invaders took. In some places, using sorcery to manipulate weight and friction, whole sections of wall could be moved to isolate portions of the enemy forces. An enemy army might find themselves attacked from below as if by demons, stabbed at random from unseeable slits in the walls, or suddenly cut off from their commanders and reinforcements. From there, superstition and paranoia would bring out the worst in them. Anarchy was the greatest weapon those walls supplied, for without a leader and without direction, an army was nothing more than a pack of men waiting to be slaughtered.

Dranus considered all of this as he tried to peer through the mist. What the Book had said before had held some meaning that the king now fully grasped. King Vulcan would not be found in the Castle itself, but in the second maze...that uncharted space with untold secrets. Of course, Varz historians had mapped the path from the maze to the castle and the significant paths used in countering invasions (though this information was accessible only by the members of the War Council and the king himself), but the grand half of the maze which held purpose only for making would-be intruders helplessly lost was relatively unknown. The second maze held two purposes: it was both the staging area for the first maze, and a continuation of the first maze. If an enemy managed to make it all the way to the castle, as only two had done before, they would eventually discover that they needed to travel deeper and thus the second maze was also lain with traps, though decidedly more practical ones.

"Do you have some map which shows the full layout of the mazes?" Dressed in fine gear, his sword Fehris at his side and the Staff of the South Star in his hand, he addressed the Book laid out on his makeshift table.

"Only those which were made after the death of King Vulcan, master. All indications suggest that he knew the maze by memory and thus the information was lost with him."

"Wonderful." The king rolled his eyes and stared still harder at the mist, hoping he could somehow glint some piece of information which might help him.

"I could fill the maze with the Army of the South Star, they might find it quickly or even have some knowledge of the place's design."

84

"Doubtful sir, and would they not be subject to the same miseries that have befallen so many other armies who entered the stone walls?"

The Book made a decent point, they were indeed soldiers of Varz, but they were of a much earlier age, and they were just as human in mind now as they had been centuries before. Though all of the manned traps of the mind would be ineffective, many more basic traps were likely still active in the remaining area of the maze, and he would rather not sacrifice the men's lives just to save time. Just because they were ghosts of long-dead souls did not mean they were any less citizens of Varz.

The pair made their way down into the valley, leaving their camp concealed in some brush. As a matter of course, Dranus could walk the maze from entrance to the castle blindfolded and so took little time in reaching the center while evading some of the more obvious pitfalls. It was good fortune that previous kings and queens had elected to keep the fortress armed, though uninhabited. On top of keeping out would-be bandits in the meantime, the castle might become a key fixture in the war on Varz's eastern front, just as it had been hundreds of years before. Unfortunately, keeping the small castle supplied through the maze was an expensive endeavor and the underground passages that used to supply the castle in secret had been caved in thoroughly by previous generations.

Finally, towering in solid splendor, the Castle Surrounded by Stone signaled some eerie sense of foreboding within the king. Though he had first visited the place as a child and knew it well, he had always felt uneasy there. On mentioning this to the Book, it replied that it maintained similar notions and that they were likely due to the place's reputation. Still, he couldn't help but feel that the place had been enchanted in some way similar to that of the Castle Beneath the Waves, but in this case it did not keep water out, it kept madness in. The fear of every man and woman who had died within the maze seemed to hang over them perpetually, watching and waiting for them to meet a similar Fate.

Pushing the ill omen aside, Dranus set foot into the second maze, having concluded from half-finished maps that the most likely route to the back of the maze was by a branch three turns away. Standing tall and examining the path which lay before him he considered this plan of action. The least explored area of the maze was the back, if there was some place he might find the dead King of Varz it would be there.

In his sorcerous eyes lay near infinite ways to view the world around him and as king he was privy to more of these vantage points than the average man of Varz.

Looking without focus at the first of many tall walls he began to see the world change, the wall became varying shades of green, then rippling blue, it flickered red like fire, sometimes highlighted edges, sometimes outlined certain aspects which he could not directly identify. Finally, he settled on a particular view; one that colored the world the same but showed things in layers. With this he could see walls and the walls behind those walls, and the traps beneath some patch of dirt, all possibilities that the inhabitants once knew. With this vision he could avoid the more mundane perils of the maze, but it was a taxing sense: sorting the layers by distance was not something that happened automatically and determining the depth was a rough sort of skill.

After nothing more than a few steps in, he stopped and stared at the ground, shifting the layers he could perceive, noting the changes in density. A trap which had not yet been tripped...he had indeed chosen a good path. The trap was subtle, though the dirt looked solid and like any other bit of earth scattered about, it was set to sink very gradually. As more and more would enter the area, they would sink more and eventually be stuck. On the other side of these walls he expected he would find ladders and tall stools so that archers and spearmen could rain steel on the encumbered raiders.

Edging along the side of this area, staying close to the wall, he avoided being sucked down, but his progress was slow. The Book, which was normally rather talkative, seemed hushed for some reason and this set the king to uncomfortable introspective thought.

The maze had lost some of its efficacy without soldiers to man the traps. Indeed, the most ingenious and effective traps were not simple tricks of the earth but of the mind. Walls scattered about were made so that they could be forced in one direction but not in the other unless a separate mechanism was unlocked. In this way an army might find itself divided and later be reunited with Varz defenders dressed as allies, not to ambush them, but to spread dissent and unrest.

After what seemed hours of aimless wandering, Dranus reached a

86

long straight path at what he speculated was the far west wall. The wall was different, though. It had words and pictures drawn along its length. As Dranus walked he considered the meaning of the words which formed complex paradoxes and riddles, promoted fearsome imagery, and accentuated the pictures of death. Were these to unnerve the enemy just from the confusing nature of the words?

Dranus thought on this as he continued to tread the forgotten ground. He read every word of the familiar questions and rhymes. Then, with a slighted breath he halted as he felt the faintest of pressure against his ankle. He looked down, staring at a string that was like an infant's breath. Had it not been for the pressure against his breeches he would not have even been able to perceive such a thing!

Paralyzed, he scanned all the area in front of and beside him. There was nothing! Below him? Nothing! Through layers and layers of the walls he searched but found no trap to connect to this string. Alert and prepared for any result, he let his weight bare forward and the string snapped.

Instantly the sound of disturbed earth sounded behind him. He spun to behold three-foot-long spikes stabbing out of the ground for as far back down the pathway as he could see. What devastation this might have caused the South Star Army! Even he, the King of Varz, had been distracted by the cryptic words of the wall to miss the odd quality of the dirt and patches of grass! Only the leading officers, their unit eviscerated, would survive the trap at the head where Dranus stood. What merciless ingenuity!

Now more alert than ever, Dranus continued around a corner. He would not be caught off guard again.

"Have you thought, my lord, how we are to escape upon retrieving the Sword?"

Dranus stopped dead in his tracks.

"I had not." Suddenly he was being caught unprepared left and right.

"Shall I continue to track our progress then?" The Book's tone was rather humorous, seemingly making fun of the king.

"You shall," he replied with no implication of admitting folly to the Book. So it had been keeping track of their position the whole time, good, if he had been required to command the Book to do so then he might not respect its power as he did.

A slight inconsistency caught the king's attention shortly after. Even with his sorcerous eyes it seemed that the left wall was solid, complete, and continuous but there was something wrong with the layers. Approaching the section of the wall he stretched out his hand only to find it seemingly go through the solid stone. Stepping forward he entered a new branch of the maze, one hidden by the perfect illusion of the other walls, so that one could not perceive the depth unless seen with special sight. It was artistically blended as if to appear as one solid wall!

This passage was different, this was clearly one meant to be used by the defenders of the castle. The ground was not the mulled dirt of well-traveled paths as in the first maze, nor the sporadic patches of dirt and grass that served to further distract those in the second maze. This area was well-kept, if now overgrown, grass and stone fixtures that were arranged by design. This area was linear, though he traced his hand on the right wall for more unseen passages, he continued to follow the winding path until he stopped at an intersection. Of the three new paths available to him, the one leading to the right was sealed by a massive granite slab inscribed with the curved V, the royal crest of Varz. Just as well, Dranus felt pulled toward that path.

He stared at the wall; stared *through* the wall. Inside the stone were small pockets of space. He thanked the knowledge left behind in the King's Library and pressed at a space beneath the Varz crest. The design was familiar to him and a few swift movements of stone within the slab saw it fall with great speed, swallowed by a secret compartment in the ground under its own massive weight.

With a proud smile and a burgeoning hope that his search neared its end, the king moved on.

It was not long before Dranus entered a covered area, and around a turn, led only by the light from behind him, he came into an abnormally large, open area. Standing at the cusp of the area he tried to look about, to make some distinction of the space. Was this a large trap? Or was it, like he suspected, the courtyard where King Vulcan the Rock had directed his forces?

There was too little light from behind to see into the depths of the place. However, the feeling of unrest he'd felt in the castle was completely subdued here which, somehow, made him all the more uneasy.

"Have you any record of this place, Book?"

"None specifically, sire, but I have seen mention of a camp where the high officials would rest and plot their actions. I know nothing of its physical characteristics, however."

"You are helpful as ever, my friend." Knowing that he could not rely on the Book's knowledge, he crammed the large tome into his breastplate much like the young Deleron Kaxus had done before meeting his end. With his newly freed hand he drew the sword Fehris and cautiously proceeded into the void.

It was wide as far as he could tell and the fact that he could not see the far wall made him think it was also quite deep. This was likely the reason there was a ceiling in place; such a large open area would ruin the illusion of it being a single mass of rock.

After pacing a few steps inward, letting his eyes slowly adjust to the relative darkness, he came to a stop and let out a long breath as the hair on his whole body stood on end. There was a new scent on the air...the scent of pine. Just like his experience in Queen Luna's castle, the smell could not be naturally occurring here, nor did it seem to be produced by any visible means.

Vulcan must be close.

When he reached what he expected was close to the center he became confused by what could only be a trick of the eye. Before him seemed to be a brand burning...but surely there could not still be a brand burning, it must be some distortion of the maze funneling in light from outside. He took another step forward and in an instant the area exploded with light, brands all around the outside of the courtyard alive and dancing. Some yards ahead of him was a tentative throne and seated in this throne in his massive black armor was the corpse of King Vulcan the Rock.

The body was rigid and the back was straight, two gauntleted hands rested on the pommel of a sword stabbed into the ground before him. Again he found his eyes drawn to the unhelmeted face. Two sorcerous eyes of great strength and resolve stared back at him. The face, however deteriorated, was handsome but scarred, showing the years of battle the king had faced.

"King Vulcan the Rock." Dranus whispered as he approached the man with calm determination.

The body sprung to life just as the flames had and with some energy it leapt up from the seat and sheathed its sword. It made a satisfied clink of metal as it fit into its place within the scabbard.

"Ahhh! A King of Varz! My own flesh and blood has come to rouse me from my slumber! What luck, what sport!"

King Dranus was surprised by the energy of the dead king who now walked around, stretching his atrophied muscles and inspecting Dranus's sword from a distance.

"You have a fine sword, king! And the Staff of the South Star! I thought it to be nothing more than a legend; but then surely the Shield of Second Life must also be real, however strange a device it seems."

"You seem to be in good spirits, King Vulcan, for a dead man. Will you give me the Sword of Righted Guard, or must I answer some riddle again?" Out of respect, Dranus had also sheathed his sword once his forefather king had pointed out its quality.

"Riddle?! Of course not! I am a king and a general, a warrior has no time for such trivialities!"

Dranus sighed both in relief but also some in regret that his people had once been the proud warrior race of King Vulcan and had now become the pensive and painfully passive race most personified by their king; by him.

"Then you will relinquish it? I pledge it shall be used for the might of Varz, Undaunted King, for we go to war once again!" Though the undead king's countenance seemed pleased by this sentiment, his posture did not mirror that and his drawing once again of the sword at his waist distressed King Dranus.

"Unfortunately, dark descendant of mine, I cannot. The Sword of Righted Guard belongs to the strongest of the warriors of Varz, and that title belongs to me. If you wish to have the Sword, then you must take it from me." The smile cast then was one of some secret intelligence, but its meaning was unknown to Dranus who now drew his own sword and readied the Staff of the South Star for battle.

Once the sword of King Vulcan was drawn it pointed at the ground, but as soon as the dead king took his stance, the blade seemed to vanish! He could see the king's hand and some of the hilt and guard, but the blade appeared only as a thin sliver aimed upwards at Dranus's eyes so that he could barely tell it was there at all! Dranus paced to the right and tilted his head this way and that, but no matter where his view drifted the sword remained a single thin slit in Vulcan's moving grip.

"So this is the Sword of Righted Guard, it will be difficult to defeat." Dranus frowned.

"You should not worry about the sword, son, but its wielder!" Vulcan lunged forward, stabbing straight at Dranus's chest.

Dranus brought the Staff about to swipe the blow to his left and followed with that motion, bringing his sword around to slash at the exposed head. Yet somehow, though the Sword had been deflected to the left, it whirled about unreasonably fast and knocked Dranus's strike away with the flat of the blade.

After this brief test of strength, Dranus stood back and tried to grasp what had happened. The properties that he had known about were that the Sword had perfect guard; it could deflect any attack, apparently even if it had just been deflected itself. What this meant particularly was unclear though he worried at his chances of besting the greatest swordsman in the history of Varz wielding one of the most powerful weapons it had ever crafted.

Deciding to adopt a new strategy, Dranus used the length of the Staff and the sharpened crown at its end to stab at his opponent in repeated strikes. But every strike was met by such a slight rotation of the wrist, such a brief movement of the arm, that his stabs were deflected powerfully and yet the Sword seemed to have not even moved! There were no openings and again The Rock brought the fight to him, showing such mastery of movement, extending his reach through the sword rather than simply swinging it around.

He was too slow to match Vulcan, and the serpent-like movements of the Sword of Righted Guard were impossible to predict. Fehris was meant to be held with two hands and could not be easily used with just one, even when Dranus was reinforced by sorcery.

Taking yet another step back from the fight, Dranus stabbed the pointed bottom of the Staff into some loose ground and the thing let out something akin to a groan as it had no light from the South Star to feed on. Then, Dranus took the sword of his father in both hands, matching the stance of King Vulcan, and rushed the resurrected king with an upward swing. The blow connected squarely with the smaller sword of his opponent, and yet his strike was stopped as though he had hit one of the thick walls of the maze. Vulcan's block was followed quickly by swiping Dranus's sword to his left, leaving his side open. He was forced to dive to the ground to avoid being impaled through his side. That gave him some knowledge: Vulcan

91

was fighting to disarm, not to kill.

Getting to his feet with some speed, Dranus defended himself from a hurricane of blows. For the relatively small size of Vulcan's Sword, it hit with incredible strength and even when Dranus could successfully glance the blow to his side and step into the opposing king's guard, the Sword had already righted itself and was there to deflect the next blow.

King Vulcan seemed to be enjoying himself greatly in this exchange; he brandished a broad smile beneath a bristling mustache lined with the filth of the dead. Vulcan dashed forward and brought his sword down over his head in a great arch. Dranus raised Fehris and braced for a heavy impact but felt only the soft tap of the dead king's steel against his own black iron blade. Instead of striking, Vulcan turned and spun with his forward momentum, slapping the side of his sorcerous blade against Dranus's knee then his shoulder. He moved like the wind while Dranus was but a tree shaking in its wake. The move finished with an almost gentle touch to the plate of his back armor that normally could have sent him flying to the ground.

King Vulcan was just playing with him! A few light taps to Dranus's armor while he stood frozen in a pose that blocked a mere feint!

This was getting him nowhere. He could not fairly defeat such a weapon, nor such a veteran warrior. If he were to best King Vulcan, it would be the only way a King of Varz could claim true dominance: sorcery.

It was to a recently utilized spell that Dranus turned in his mind, performing the same mutilations of space and rationality until standing beside him was a separate image which circled around to the back of King Vulcan. The dead king, however, gave it no notice...even when the image came in to strike from behind, he did not move. The image went right through the black armor and again stood next to the real Dranus.

"A good trick, young one, but it lacks a certain something from the original." Accompanying his belittling chuckle was the appearance of a second King Vulcan, seeming to step forward from the king's back and moving to the side wall where it took down an old, rusted sword. "You see, my prowess in battle is unmatched. You may leave with your life good king, but you may not have the Sword of Righted Guard. Retreat. Sharpen your skills. In a decade's time or more you may pose a challenge." The copy came and stood next to the original, clanging his sword against his armor to show that he was as solid as the original.

Dranus had no time for thoughts of retreat, only for some way to overcome this. He had started a plan but was interrupted by the charge of the two challengers. He was barely able to hold his own and was being constantly pushed back. He blocked thrust after thrust, slash after slash. The strong sword of The Rock bit into his left arm, the rusted sword of the copy hit against his leather greaves and though it did not break the skin, he felt the power of the blow weaken his stance.

Losing energy quickly, he struggled to think of some plan. The Staff could not help him without the light of the South Star! The Book could not fight with him! He could not hope to defeat this weapon of immense power or the two who fought him!

He brought up his black sword weakly to block a strong downward strike. As metal struck metal, Dranus's knees buckled, and he was brought to a kneel. With the intense pressure of the King of the Rock he struggled, but Fehris's resolve was weaker than that of its wielder. In an instant, Vulcan's sword shore right through the black iron and rested its tip at Dranus's throat.

"Surrender, king! You have fought valiantly and you are quite skilled, but you are no match for me. I would rather not kill one of my own, but if it is death you desire then it is death I shall grant you!" The lofty form of King Vulcan looked down on Dranus and suddenly an idea had formed.

"I concede King Vulcan, you have bested me fairly. Allow me my life and I shall leave this place." Carefully and slowly he sheathed what remained of his sword and held his hands out in front of him.

"You have sense, good king, and you will serve our people well, I am sure. As I said, train yourself and return and I will be more than happy to fight you again!" In triumph and jubilance, King Vulcan the Rock returned his treasured sword into its sheath and reached a strong gloved hand down to help up the defeated King Dranus.

At the exact moment that Vulcan's hand left the hilt, Dranus, who was already in a set position, dove forward and took the hilt of the sword, dragging it from the scabbard and rolling to the side. He stood as victor, feeling the relative weightlessness of the Sword of

Righted Guard and staring menacingly at the king who was the greatest fighter in Varz history.

"Well done, king! Well done! I did say that you had to take the Sword from me, and you have done just that." Vulcan bellowed a laugh, and the shambling corpse approached him with no ill intent, resting a proud hand on his shoulder. The Sword of Righted Guard was aimed at his throat. "You have discovered the Sword's only weakness in such a short time! Truly you are a worthy opponent!" Some bright emotion, some thing Dranus could not understand emanated from the dead king.

He had been tricked and deceived! He had his victory stolen from him by dishonest methods and yet he was happy! Such happiness at that! Who were these ancestors of such strange emotional timbre? Had they all been mad in their own ways, taking such joy from such defeat?

"I did not gauge its weakness, I simply surmised that if I could not defeat it, I must take it through deception," Dranus replied.

"And a clever deception it was! Though I feel foolish for letting my guard down, let this be an important lesson to you, king. The Sword of Righted Guard will defend you from any attack, so long as your hand rests on the hilt. In battle you will be undefeatable, but the moment you let your guard down is the moment you will meet your end. Take heed, clever king, learn from mistakes already made or you will find your end too soon."

The cryptic wording of King Vulcan further muddled Dranus's thoughts, but he felt pride to receive such praise from his worthy ancestor.

"Before I return to my sleep, tell me your name." Vulcan was still all smiles and beaming pride.

"I am King Dranus VIII, son of King Roboris the Thick-Hearted."

"Ahh, King Dranus." The great king smiled and returned to his seat. "My son's name was Dranus; I hope he was fully as good a king as you are. I am proud that you do his name an honor." King Vulcan discarded his sheath and returned to his throne, folding his hands in his lap.

"Lead our people to battle King Dranus, and may valor always find you." With these last words the life left his eyes, the brands burned out, and Dranus was again alone in the dark. The scent of pine had gone with the old king's reprise.

94

"A clever ploy master. I was worried for a moment that you might lose your life." The Book's voice was a mix of calm and feigned stricken concern.

"You were worried about my safety?" Dranus asked skeptically.

"Quite the contrary! About my own! What should I do if you were to fall here in this maze where no one would ever find me! What a terrible existence!"

Dranus smiled a bit at the irony the Book represented. A living thing that should not live.

"What, indeed."

He picked up the discarded sheath and replaced the one at his waist with it, the single torch in the back of the area providing him with enough sight. He left the remains of the sword Fehris at Vulcan's feet as a tribute, bowing low before the mighty warrior. In going to retrieve the Staff of the South Star, he looked back at the motionless body of King Vulcan the Rock.

"It was an honor and a pleasure, King Vulcan." He whispered solemnly to himself. He had never met a character such as that of King Vulcan. So full of life and energy, similar to O'cule, but in a way that exuded like heat from his body. The man had been a strong warrior and a noble swordsman, relying only on his own strength unlike Dranus. He was everything that Dranus was not. How was it that Vulcan seemed so fulfilled in his death and his defeat while Dranus, alive with victory in hand, felt so empty?

Brooding on this encounter, Dranus exited the maze by the Book's guidance. Though now the Book was lively and talkative, Dranus did not respond. Instead he contemplated, as he had often done, if he had ever lived a day in his life like Vulcan had lived even in death.

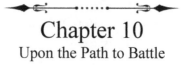

# Chapter 10
## Upon the Path to Battle

The final leg of the king's journey was mostly uneventful, and for this Dranus was quite grateful. He spent the hours of travel in silent planning and consideration of all he had gained recently. Of all that was new in his life, he thought of Kaelel most. He found, in the quiet of night, that his leather-bound companion had more than a few stories to tell. Tales lost to the degradation of time that ranged from comedies to wild epics concerning his sorcerous ancestors. There were a select few he made sure to commit to memory. The stories it could share from other parts of the world were most interesting because it opened him up to perspectives he had never considered before. Whether or not the Book could convince him of the existence of literal Gods, the way that this belief had shaped the West was incredible. Architectural wonders and feats of engineering were talked about as being collaborations with these Gods as a means of bridging the gap between mortal and immortal worlds. Moreover, the people from the distant past wielded sorcery as his folk did! He had known that others used sorcery before the time of The Ultimate, but somehow he had never thought this might apply to other parts of the world! There was one such sorcerer-warrior that had nearly as many legends about him as all of the Monarchs of Varz *combined*; his name was Tullern.

A brief stop in the industrial center of Vakkar brought the king to the foot of a towering pile of lances tied and bundled neatly in the city square. It was just as he had expected of the smiths of Vakkar! But when he heard that this was only that which remained after the main shipment was sent to Varz on caravan, he was stunned. Where had this productivity been in previous years? In the last two-hundred years, smithing had stagnated behind tradition. Then, in a matter of weeks, they had reinvented the production of weapons by working in organized teams specializing in one or more part of the process! What hidden potential did the folk of Varz hold if they could produce such amazing feats! Was this truly the same people?

Feeling energized with each first fresh breath of the day, Dranus returned to Varz within two weeks of leaving the Castle Surrounded by Stone. Wasting no time, he called every officer and influential noble in Varz to the city walls and summoned the massive South Star Army in its luminous crimson splendor. Their united battle cry shook the very stones of the city! With this display, the few detractors and old crones addicted to their former way of life were thoroughly convinced.

Dranus's next display brought all the folk of Varz who could manage into the wide city center. The citizens piled in on top of one another, climbing to rooftops, and hanging out windows to catch a glimpse of their magnificent king. At the center of the square was the king in his royal finery, seated in a makeshift throne, an odd-looking sword lay across his lap. Opposite him was General Armodus and two of his finest warriors. The people looked on in bated breath as the three great swordsmen attacked the king with all their might, as was their order. Yet every strike and blow, no matter the force behind it, was glanced away by the dancing blade of the seated king who feigned a yawn and examined the finish on the freshly painted nails of his free hand. It was in this way that the Sword of Righted Guard returned every thrust, parried every slash, and eventually disarmed all of the attackers one by one.

The silence that had gripped the audience erupted into a fury of cheers and whistles. Flags and banners waved above the crowd and the people of Varz felt as though they had lost their sanity with the pride and fervor that had overcome them! Their king had done the impossible; he had dug up the stuff of myths as though it were an afterthought of some leisurely Dusk Season vacation!

The elation of the capital spread as word of Dranus's recent exploits quickly became the stuff of legend, traveling between the towns. With the simple demonstrations he had given, the storyteller's embellishments often *underestimated* the power he had gained. Flocks of messenger birds came and went every hour of every day until, as if overnight, King Dranus was revered almost as a God himself!

Meanwhile, the War Council had met every night since Dranus returned to the city. They considered numbers, both their own and those of the enemy according to their most recent records. As suggested, they had declared war on Arendrum officially while the king was absent, and forces from around the continent were mobilizing. This was well expected and within their agreed upon strategy. In the council room, filled with maps of every favorable battlefield, they considered tactics and strategy and how it must change in response to the Staff of the South Star. They considered the morale and the general feeling of Varz. All of these things were good, better than could have been expected; the conditions were perfect.

"My king, while you were away, we received a declaration from the forces of Arendrum that we desist in our military actions lest we face the 'might' of the Four Realms." General Armodus let out a derisive chuckle, thinking it preposterous even as he uttered the words.

Standing sharp-witted with his War Council, King Dranus breathed a whisper of subtle anticipation. A devilish grin spread across his lips and his eyes glared wicked glee at the map laid before him.

"Let them come. We will remind them of the invincible strength of Varz!" A look to the large man at his left signaled the start of the council for that evening.

"Today's report counts our total forces at well over 13,000. Hearing of your lust for battle, the whole nation has been moved to fight for Varz! We have many young, strong men and many bright minds that have come from all around and they practice diligently to learn our formations. We will be ready to march in a few weeks' time!" General Armodus was more animated than Dranus had ever seen him, his old warrior's spirit finding purpose again.

"All other preparations have been made as you ordered my king," echoed Commander Ven, showing some fatigue from the intense training but clearly proud of the work she had done. The lines of gray in her hair had once been a sign of her age and declining strength but now they struck him as fierce streaks of power overflowing from her will.

"Excellent. With the Army of the South Star our forces will stand roughly 33,000 strong. However, I must remind you that only one division of the Staff may be present on the field at one time. This will, I think, bring exceptional diversity in our field tactics." The king was confident and better rested since returning to his bed which had been warmed by his renewed lover Kaelel. Much in the way she had regained passion for him after seeing him take charge, he had found passion for her after his educating journey to the south and the east.

"My king, if I may suggest our strategy." Commander Bourin now spoke and by the look of the carved figures on the large map they stood around, he had some complex plan in mind.

"Proceed."

"From our scouts and the intelligence you have given us we estimate that the enemy force numbers near 20,000. They are composed mainly of Arendrum troops with a group from Myrendel and Urhyll each showing some 4,000 as reserves while their primary forces continue to prepare in their respective realms. Although Arendrum has maintained a standing ground force, it appears that the other realms are far less ready for battle. We project it will take them at least another two months to put a full force into the field. The navy of Shiera, however, has sailed and waits at the border to attack from the west."

"My king, per your orders we have refrained from engaging the enemy." Admiral O'cule interjected, looking as gleeful as ever in his dazzling sapphire armor.

"Good, maintain position. After repelling the land invasion we will deal with Shiera."

"My king," Kaelel's sweet song-like voice gripped his chest, "we have successfully leaked false reports of our numbers and, playing on your former reputation, we've been slowly spreading the rumor that you have committed us to war against our communitive will out of boredom. It appears that our inactivity in the last centuries has given them a sense of security, they might believe this now to be their time to wipe us out completely."

Bourin began moving pieces around on the map. "Indeed, the enemy already moves as to invade with a preemptive strike. The enemy will have to cross the Discidia Rift here, where the gap is nothing more than a thin split which a man can easily cross on his own." The commander pointed to a point on the map where a massive chasm stretching east to west formed a natural border with their northern neighbor. "Therefore, we should position our archers to the west of this position, where the Rift widens. From this point our archers can attack their back lines while our front contains the charge."

Dranus watched the movement of the figures around the board, his training in strategy allowed him to see the movements like an actual battle, developing one way or another.

"We should deploy the Army of the South Star's footed soldiers at the head..." Bourin continued.

The explanation continued for some hours, going over possible developments until Dranus was satisfied with the plan, the contingencies for certain likelihoods, and the plan of retreat if the worst were to happen. Just as the South Star was about to rise, they began to adjourn for the night.

"Before we retire, Highness." The smooth voice of Commander Kaelel caught his face like the delicate hand of a lover who wanted one last kiss before parting.

"The Council has met many times in your absence. Though morale has never been higher and all in Varz praise your leadership, we thought there could be more to give them." Dranus was confused by this, not predicting that such a thing as morale had become an issue...though he supposed he should have.

General Armodus cleared his throat uncomfortably.

"My king, your father King Roboris the Thick-Hearted truly wished for your happiness and had often suggested a marriage between yourself and Commander Kaelel. We believe that this gesture would further unite our people under the King and his Royal Wife like they had been united under your great ancestors." Armodus had come to be the wise voice of suggestion, being the only one brave enough to readily suggest such a thing right before a war began.

Dranus thought on this for several moments. He left the table and paced about the room. Despite his recent feelings, he was not sure what it was to love a woman, but then neither had many of his married ancestors. As the Council suggested, all of the great kings and queens, even Luna the Mad had Royal Husbands and Wives, symbols of the unity of Varz. It would surely unite his people and politically it was a sensible marriage with a powerful and well-respected family. Kaelel would produce unmatched heirs, of that he was sure. In truth, the only reason they had not been wed before was a lack of enough reason or motivation.

"Are you all of the same mind?" Dranus asked and they replied one after the other, "Yes, my king."

Dranus looked hard at Commander Kaelel across the table. "Comma...." He stopped. "Kaelel? You want this?"

Kaelel softened momentarily, her posture easing and her sharp grin resolving into a loving smile. "I do."

For a moment everything around her faded as the words washed over him. He remembered, as if for the first time, all of the memories they shared. He knew, then, that not only was this wedding right for Varz, it was right for him.

"Then we will be wed! Captain, have all of the necessary preparations made. Send word to the nobles from around the realm that the wedding will be held in two weeks' time here in Varz. General Armodus, have the armed forces ready to leave immediately after, with whatever strength you can feasibly field. We will have the wedding at the camp, and they will be moved by our union, then they will head to the front with that vigor and unleash it upon our enemies." He turned, resuming the powerful guise of the ruler.

"Commander Ven, see to it that all of Varz knows of the wedding, assist the captain in orchestrating preparations for a space large enough for the whole city if need be." The white-armored Captain of the Guard, who had remained silent throughout, bowed and exited the room quietly. A royal wedding was a thing of great tradition and the preparations to be made were all but completely set in stone.

General Armodus, too, bowed and exited swiftly. The other commanders followed suit; all but Kaelel. She left hand in hand with the king, for within the next cycle of the moon, they would be wed.

*       *       *

The spreading news of the royal wedding coupled with the recent display of power the king had given found the city of Varz moving like a finely tuned machine. The folk could not do enough to please their king; they could not be bothered with rest until all had been accomplished!

The once empty streets surged with frantic movement pouring over the worn stones. Smoke spewed from the chimneys of every smith in the city throughout the day. Every manner of fine stone or precious gem was given by the people of Varz to the jewelers and smiths so that theirs would be a royal wedding that would put to shame even their great ancestors! Their armor would outshine even the wealthiest palace of the Lesser Realms!

And so the people toiled day and night, relinquishing the lazy practices of sorcerous craft in lieu of the masterful diligence of a sharpened mind with a purpose. For the first time they felt the arduous aches and pains of sore muscles. For the first time they bathed in the sweat of their brow. And for the first time since the Third Great War, the mantle of Varz was supported by the arched backs of its folk.

The Dens became places of healing and respite for the weary. There they took brews to heal in body and mind. Though many of the Den Maidens had been recruited by Commander Ven, the Master's made use of skills they had nearly forgotten they had. Every day a new brew was developed, stronger or longer lasting than any other before, and spread throughout the city. In these Dens the folk of Varz celebrated this unrivaled period of vivacity.

"To our invincible king!" A mug raised in cheer brought others to its cause.

"To King Dranus!" A heavily bandaged hand raised a goblet filled with ache-suppressing vitality.

Some lay in makeshift beds around the Den, passed out from their exertions and assisted in their sleep.

The Den Master juggled more spells, more complex twists of reality, than he had thought he could. Moment by moment his understanding of everything around him was jarred from truth. But what was truth if not his own workings? Warped thought to warped thought led men slowly to madness in their efforts. It was in this way that the efforts of the city slowed as the day of the Heavens' Union approached. The folk of Varz were not prepared either in body or mind to keep this pace for very long and what had begun as intoxicating revelation turned quickly to a descent into chaos.

It had gotten so bad that Dranus decided to instate a mandatory day of rest to the city the day before the wedding. Only the city's guard patrolled this day, making sure that even the most adamant of the king's followers gathered their strength.

Even Dranus, himself, took this day for rest. His presence was the symbol of motivation to every man and woman in Varz and thus he had spent nearly every waking moment over the last two weeks in preparation for the war. But on this day, he would spend some much-needed time with his bride-to-be in their chambers, warming himself by a crackling fire against the drafty cold of the night.

"But if there were once Gods among the Five Realms and the Three Continents, why would they not still be present?" Kaelel had forsaken the mental comfort of her armor for the physical comfort of a beautiful but simple robe with a pattern like snow-powdered evergreens. The robe itself was infused with the smell, making their chamber like a thriving forest in the Night Season. When she first entered, Dranus had blanched at the smell, but then explained his odd experience in the castles of their ancestors.

"How could one know if they are still present or not?" The Book retorted with a bit of leading wit.

"If what you say is true, these Gods were once a powerful force on our planet, directing the flow of events! Why would they give up such influence willingly?" Black eyes stared at the worn pages depicting fantastical scenes of Gods and their ilk. Kaelel sat at a small table near the hearth, having her own showdown with the Book.

"Cannot the same be asked of the people of Varz?"

She could not refute this point directly.

"But we are just mortals! Surely Gods are not so fallible as we?" The Book flipped its pages in response to such a claim until it showed a sketch of a towering mountain peak among a smaller range. It was capped in snow though a mist was drawn circling the summit.

"Hah! Perhaps it was our ancestors who drove the Gods from these lands!" A smile of pride graced her luscious lips, and the sorcerous tome emitted a sound that was like the agitated rustling of pages in the wind. It was foreign to the commander's ears but the king, watching in amusement from his spot at the hearth, knew it well as the patronizing laughter of a secret intelligence far greater than theirs. He had watched his fiancée in her intellectual duel with the Book in silence until that moment.

"That's enough Book, you tried and failed to convince me of such fantasy, I'll not have you try and turn my future wife against me." Dranus stood and took her strong ivory hands in his, leaving the Book on the table.

"What are you doing, Dranus? I was winning!" Her calm turned to playful consternation without warning as she stood. "I may soon be your wife, but I don't need you to fight my battles for me!"

Dranus smirked and took her in his arms, holding her close like he had become accustomed to in the past few weeks. "Believe me, you were not as far ahead as you thought." The Book's philosophical musings were rarely that. Normally they were fact posed as thoughts, but Dranus knew the thing better. Still, he had come to believe in many things he had once thought untrue since gaining possession of the Book, but he could not possibly be convinced that all-powerful Gods had or still continued to exist in this world. It simply didn't make sense.

"Oh really?"

He felt sharp nails drag down the center of his bare back while a wicked twist of his lover's mouth formed. "You may have that fancy staff and sword but without those I bet I could beat you in a fight." She attempted to push off of him, but his hold kept.

Dranus raised a brow, his smile matching hers. "Really? You, defeat me?" He pulled his arms tight around her and lifted her light form in the air. Her arms and feet struggled in his grasp as he brought her to the bed and playfully threw her onto the soft furs, a giddy laugh escaping her as she landed.

But Kaelel was a trained warrior, and she regained her balance with a speed the king had not expected and before he could register what was happening, he felt the hard press of a heel in his gut.

Still, she was not the only one trained to be a fighter from childhood. His stomach muscles relaxed and let the blow lose its force before he took the foot of his lover and twisted her.

Nimble like a cat she landed on her hands and knees and rolled away to the far side of the bed. Dranus's heart raced and his muscles were tense. He burned with desire for her like the sun itself. He could see it in her smoldering eyes, her pride too strong to let her inner emotions seep to the surface.

Kaelel herself was conflicted with the myriad emotions and feelings that rippled through her heart and mind. Like Dranus, she too had been struggling with the odd range of inclinations and needs that had arisen recently. She had nearly lost her mind when he was gone for so long! She had many lovers in her past but never one that demanded her attention like Dranus. Was it weakness that had manifested somehow?

104

She shook the thought from her mind. Weakness or not, she had never felt like the world around her was alive; not like she felt at that very moment. All she knew was that Dranus caused this.

The two of them feinted one way and then the other, trying to anticipate each other's moves as though they were in a battle for their lives.

Learning from a recent conversation he had with the Book, Dranus moved his hand almost automatically and the Book rose from the table and receded into his study, the door closing behind it. From the far side of the bed Kaelel, aggressively pulled loose the band of her robe and jumped naked onto the bed on all fours. With every predatory motion she made towards the king, torches went out one by one until all that was left was the flicking light of the hearth playing off their bare skin, making her look a Devil in the contrast of shadows and he an ambitious warrior, ready to make an unbreakable deal.

They wrestled playfully, claws turning to caresses, gnashing teeth turning to kisses like tasting fresh water after a month in the desert. For the last time they lay together as simple lovers; upon the next evening they would unite as King and Wife.

# Chapter 11
## The Heaven's Union

The next morning the city was an overwhelming orchestra of manic preparations. Through every means available the entire city of Varz was alerted to the wedding and now everyone was scrambling to finish preparations for it. This was a moment for people to move their families up in the hierarchy, to gain a centuries-long reputation, to show off some skill or ware they might possess to the whole city. The people fought over the privilege of preparing even the smallest detail for the royal wedding that there was an overabundance of every necessity.

That King Dranus, who had been secretly styled as 'the Bored,' had finally taken a wife was like sorcery itself. This increased support for the wedding tenfold, and his pairing with the beautiful and powerful Kaelel, Commander of the Archer's Brigade, enfrenzied them even further. Scarcely a finer pairing had ever been made throughout the history of Varz!

By the evening the grounds outside the city walls had been set. There was no other place large enough or grand enough to hold this momentous wedding and all its attendants besides the very land of Varz itself. Looking down from the battlements of Varz one would hardly see the elegant stage built for this occasion. Its sides were painted to closely match the color of the ground and the surface was a special material, treated with sorcery to reflect the colors of the Dusk Season's foliage as it floated on a cool, crisp wind.

Intermingling with the trees in their different states of beautiful death were the folk of Varz, with the nobles and wealthy sitting near the stage in a ring. After a small barrier lined with guards there were the masses, wearing their most lavish finery as far as one could see from the stage. At regular intervals there were large bonfires for warmth and splendor, both. Children climbed the branches of the trees to get a view above the heads of adults, shaking red and brown and gold leaves loose to float over the shifting stage.

The armed forces, fully prepared for war, held a special section of the circle of the crowd around the stage and from this slice rang cheers and ancient songs of victory, old battle ballads, and chants of unity. A number of songs were old favorites, included portions of calls and response in which a cheer of men and women pierced the afternoon silence and was followed by an earth-shaking roar from every citizen of Varz. It was a spectacle that had not been seen for some time; not for centuries had a royal wedding carried such import.

The mandatory day of rest had given back the strength and clarity of thought to the people of Varz, so they drugged it away again with ales and wines and all manner of haze. The royal wedding was the purest of Varz celebrations, and it was not only for the monarch and their spouse, it was to be shared equally among all citizens of Varz. It was, after all, a blessing upon them all.

Finally, as the sun reached its zenith, a hush took the crowd; not all at once, but one by one as raucous cheers turned to stunned silence.

Down a wide causeway from the north came the first procession: a carriage and a team of bulls, styled in the colors of the Varz royal family. The carriage itself was all obsidian shine and silver trim with the curving lines of the royal V painted in too-smooth strokes of purple. The six bulls pulling the carriage were black as midnight with jingling reins of silver finery and studded with ovals of the deepest sapphire blue. Standing atop the carriage, reins in his hands, wild elation on his features, was King Dranus VIII. He had donned his most valuable king's robes sewn with diamond threads and decorated gemstones from honored houses to show that he was master of them all. The robe, too, sported the shimmering, almost undulating black of Varz whipping behind him in the wind with silver tassels cascading in his wake. The mesmerizing contrast of the high noon sun reflecting off a hundred precious stones set against the black backdrop made him into a figure of the Sun itself, the source of all light and thus life in the world. An insensate cheer of revel and amazement followed in a wave behind the king's carriage.

When Dranus reached his halfway mark to the stage, a gasp of awe radiated from the outer rim of the circle, following a new carriage painted every color of pearl and shining beams of heavenly light. Pulling the carriage was a team of six pure white mares, adorned with saddles bearing the likeness of wings abreast, and reined by strengthened silk inlaid with the same gems as the king's. Soon, all the nobles' houses would be beneath her status as well. But even these sights of beauty were not the cause of breathless gasps. It was Kaelel, standing atop her own carriage, silk reins in hand, wrapped in a wedding gown that sang the purest gold. Ribbons and lace of fire-tinted fabric fluttered in her wake like real flame. She wore a golden helmet-crown and raised a hand in valiant triumph, her long shout overwhelming the hushed silence of the crowd and igniting them into a frenzy. Her raven hair fluttered in the wind, snapping sparks behind her with a little trick of magic and strands of flint braided into her hair.

The two met at the center, Dranus looking on in a feeling almost like a battle fever, but of pride and joy, not bloodlust. What had started as a wedding of political and moral importance had avalanched into the greatest celebration in recent history and he, just as every other man, woman, and child of Varz, had been swept entirely into its weight. Watching his bride to be slap aside a helping hand and leap from the top of the carriage onto the stage sent shivers through his spine. Kaelel reached him and he took her hand, fighting hard against his desire to kiss her then and there.

Tradition, Dranus, do this right!

Kaelel had that same confident smile that steeled his resolve, but it was somehow softer as it had become in the last few weeks. She looked happy. He was, as far as he could tell from his limited experience, happy too! Though the marriage was mostly a valuable political move, his attraction to Kaelel had blossomed into something new that he could not place. Something that he could not wait to let out in front of every single person present.

Dranus returned her warm smile then turned to address his people, his voice booming by magical aid to even the furthest of the onlookers. He looked first to his armed forces in their splendid war attire.

"Soldiers! Warriors! Mages! We leave for war against the enemies of Varz." To this the armored ranks let out a violent war cry.

"And my beloved citizens of Varz, we will depend on your strength!" he turned to regard the rest of the crowd. "We are more than the Lesser Folk of the Four Realms! We are men and women of Varz! They believe they can overcome our wit and our sorcery through brute force and superior numbers, but we have reclaimed the Staff of the South Star, and with it, the greatest military force the world has ever known! We will be victorious. We will take this battle to their lands, to the walls of their cities and remind them why they once feared the name 'Varz' like Death himself!" Another roar was his earned reply.

"With this unity between myself and my beloved, we will show that our bonds are strong; that they cannot be broken. We will stand against anyone with those bonds and we will stand proud! They may pull and tear at our resolve, cut down our strength, and plot to take from us all that should be ours! They will certainly try. But ours is the strength of an entire people united. Our soldiers go to war, but they have the strength of every man and woman of Varz, each of their hearts and souls bristling with life. There is nothing we cannot accomplish, as our noble ancestors have shown time and time again. We are strong! We are right! We are destined!" Dranus paused to look at the beaming faces of the masses cheering and waving in exultation. There was only one way to describe the frenzied delight of his people.

"We! Are! Varz!"

The crowd was like a sea of rabid beasts, clawing and screaming even as they celebrated this momentous occasion.

Kaelel turned to her soon to be husband and smiled, speaking so that only Dranus would hear. "You must've been practicing that for some time."

"Practically all day," he said with a smile. "To get the best from our folk, we must give them the best." He felt her squeeze his hand tight and he smirked. What could have been a trite manipulation of the masses became something just as powerful, but all the more genuine. That was what made them a great pair: together they were greater than the sum of their parts. But then, that was the purpose of the Heaven's Union.

"Witness now the union!" Commander Ven, being the keeper of Varz's sacred traditions, presided over the wedding and performed the rites and rituals alongside the pair. She approached solemnly, her head bowed and her sorceress robes billowing in the wind as the dancing leaves were reflected on their platform. Carefully, and with great respect, she moved the forms of the king and wife to be into specific poses.

Their hands remained together, but their bodies mirrored one another, their free hands flared out as if preparing for a dance. Ven prepared to speak.

"The Heaven's Union is a sacred oath, passed down in our history since before there was a Varz. It is a binding pact with one another between our ruler and the one they have chosen to share life with. As such, it cannot be broken, except by the inviable twin forces of Time and Death. But certainly not by man," Ven shook her head solemnly, "nor by woman."

She looked up sharply to Kaelel, a fierce glare in her eyes, and spoke just to the two of them, "Kaelel, your love for Dranus is as binding as your service to Varz. Do you accept this pact?"

Without hesitation, Kaelel shook her head up and down quickly. "I do."

Then it was Dranus's turn. "My king, Dranus VIII, my sweet one." Tears brimmed in her eyes, a motherly joy overwhelming her even as she tried to maintain her professional air. "Your love for Kaelel is as binding as your service to Varz. Do you accept this pact?"

Dranus looked first to his wife to be, then to Ven. "I do," he said as firmly as he could manage. There was so much more he wanted to say. He wanted to yell how much he wanted this, to tell Kaelel everything he admired in her, and how thankful he was for Ven's guidance. But there was tradition. And there was time. There was time aplenty for all of that.

Dranus's lips curled as a jagged rune was carved into each of their thumbs where they lay side by side in their grip. This was the bond of the Heaven's Union; ancient blood magic that tied them together. This magic bound one to their word, and if they broke it before one or the other died, the victim of such a betrayal would gain control over that part of the other's body. In the distant past, it had been used for things like hands or arms to guarantee deals, but today it was used on the lowly thumb as more a reminder than a threat.

Ven took several careful steps away from the couple and then projected her voice as loudly as she could manage.

"Unite!" she yelled.

At this call and the following heavy impact of a hundred drums, they began a symbiotic dance in concert with a choir of Varz's best. The dance was a feast for the eyes: obsidian black mingling with gold in large sweeping motions to make it seem as though the sun was concealed for a moment only to have it erupt upon the scene again. They span and dipped together; every movement designed so that a specific flow of their dress would be achieved to stunning effect. Like the pitch and yaw of a great ship the flowing mass of contrasting colors reflected light off a thousand gems.

A powerful wind stirred and fallen leaves of crimson and rose and sunlight ascended, doubly reflected by the stage. They were entranced by the dance, just as the folk of Varz were, and then moved in great sweeping motions with the rise of the king's hand and the sparking whip of Kaelel's hair. A cyclone of wind and illumination surrounded them, and it moved in unnatural directions at the behest of their dance. Some leaves burned up in the fires of Kaelel's dress while others disappeared into the abyss of Dranus's robes. The crowd was hushed in awe of the scene; the promenade of color was unlike anything they had ever witnessed or hoped to witness again. Truly, whatever ancestors watched over the ritual must have been delighted at the event.

As the drums beat faster and the voices of the choir rose to a fevered pitch, they danced with more passion; leaping and dashing together, but never letting go of the other's hand. It was a saga of The Heavens' Union, and it told the tale of strength, unity, and unbridled love. It was romance and adventure and it was trouble and strife, and it was every moment big and small that they would face. It was a union of all disparate things, of the heavens and the earth and of the light and the dark, all in the presence of the king and his wife.

Then, all in a crashing instant the dance had finished. The leaves settled back to the ground as if they had only wished to show their elation. And so King Dranus and Kaelel, Wife to the King, stood together and embraced one another, completing the ceremony with their kiss.

Despite expectations of cheers, the onlookers stood in stunned silence for some time.

This silence was broken by Ven who proclaimed them, "Dranus and Kaelel! King and Wife!"

Then followed the expectant cheers and shouts as the crowd roared themselves hoarse and expended every last bit of energy they could. This was a moment that would happen only once in their lifetimes, they could hold nothing back!

Dranus and Kaelel walked back southward to the city walls where a new carriage would await them. Their journey back to the castle was the signal that everyone was to return, and the people hurried to pack up their chairs and wrangle their wild children back into the city.

They had a war to win.

Though the ceremony had been beautiful, and the entire realm was alive with the passion of this occasion, of the second rise of Varz, it seemed almost over in an instant. An instant of glory and beauty frozen in time, but an instant, nonetheless.

The armed forces were to deploy directly from the Union and practically sprinted off to the front with all their pride and energy welling and spilling over.

Kaelel had chosen to go ahead with the armed forces that night, but before that, they'd gotten a single moment to themselves. They sat together in the carriage, sharing the same bench despite the crowded enclosure stuffed tight with the excess of their clothes. For that moment, everything else went quiet. He could hear only the clatter of the wheels on cobbles and feel only the warmth of his wife's skin against his, her pulse beating through her hand and into him. He had never thought much of the Union, even when his council had suggested it. He had thought it bold and smart, but not something to *change him* as dramatically as this had. He was entirely full of her and she, with him. They didn't need to share any more words, despite his earlier want. They belonged solely to one another and now all of Varz knew it. It was carved into their skin, burned into their blood.

When they reached the castle, they had to go their separate ways to prepare for battle. Kissing her goodbye and good journey, he felt some odd regret filling him as she turned away from him. Was this feeling love? He could not stand to watch her go and so turned his back from her, looking inward instead.

He wondered if he had missed the opportune moment to tell her the words his heart shouted into his ear but his mind reared back from. Was it not what a husband should say to his wife upon their separation? He had no time to dwell on this, however, as he had preparations of his own to make. Such was the duty of a king of Varz, a duty he had also sworn to uphold this day. But he knew it then, that the very instant he saw her upon their victory he would tell her.

"I love you."

*     *     *

The Dusk Season was in its peak, the trees all shedding their leaves in preparation for the cold sleep of the Night Season. As King Dranus rode at the center of a wide ring of guards, he seemed to notice the range of colors in the leaves as they fell all around him, as if for the first time. Somehow he had never noticed the falling leaves or their astounding colors before. Everywhere in this thin forest were trees of bright red, of burning oranges, rich greens, and even deep blues. There were trees that were tall and seemed to house clouds of pure gold, the leaves sparkling in the morning sunlight.

It was several days after the wedding of King Dranus and Kaelel, Wife of the King. Though he had hoped to leave the next day he was held by the responsibilities he must fulfill in preparing the city for leadership without any of the commanding officers or the king. Though this was of some importance, Varz had rules for wartime; the few decisions that those left in charge would have to make would have clear precedents and any other problems could be handled with little worry. So he had left two days after the wedding and was now coming near the battlefield.

Dranus did not regret that he could not make the journey with his new bride since she had decided to leave immediately after the wedding to be with her forces. They had spent lots of time together since he returned and he knew that soon they would be reunited, perhaps atop the walls of Arendrum! Besides, he had gotten quite used to just being alone with the Book. Indeed, he found that while he and his guard proceeded at a rapid pace, he was surprisingly relaxed. His guards, however, blanketed the area both for protection and because they found the odd characteristics of the Book to be more unsettling than the king who had gotten used to them.

"My people have ever been poets, you know." Dranus spoke to the Book which was tucked in his arm.

"Poets, my lord?"

"Poets indeed, though they created subtle ironies and complex meanings with their minds in ways that words could not express."

"I see, they were ever the masterful sorcerers, the folk of Varz. Their most beautiful masterpieces were painted with the blood of their enemies, especially those of Queen Tempest the Undying."

Dranus flipped through his memories for recollections of Queen Tempest the Undying. Her kind of sorcery was perhaps the most fearful to have ever come from a Varz monarch. It was legend among the royalty of Varz that Queen Tempest had actually once bested Death in a duel. It was her profuse understanding of mortality that spawned some of the most twisted texts in the King's Library.

"Have you any of her work not found in my library?"

"Only the results of her exploits, I'm afraid. Letters of defeat, of atrocities they could hardly speak of, and of a blissful comprehension of the shadow of Death." The book spoke cheerfully as though these were normal issues to write home about.

"Ah, you are a bit of a poet yourself, are you not?"

"I don't know how many times I have to tell you master: I am a book!" Some ruffling of the pages signed the nature in which the Book joked.

"Yes yes, a book I know...a simple tome and yet you create do you not? Unlike any other book I've ever seen!"

The book was silent for a moment.

"I create only from what I have already gathered."

"But are we humans not the same? Do we not create war because it is all we have known?"

At this the book made a combination of sounds that the king took as a sardonic laugh.

"No, not at all master! Think about the courtyard where you found King Vulcan the Rock. Based on the maps I have collected I had a reasonable estimate of where it was located, but you...you followed your instinct as King of Varz and this is something I could never hope to do!"

Dranus blinked rapidly, thinking to himself if he had heard the Book correctly before pulling it in front of him and threatening to hurl it from his mount.

"You knew where to find King Vulcan?! And you didn't tell me? How many hours did we waste searching for nothing?! I asked you if you knew where he was!"

"Oh no, King! You asked if I had a map of the full layout of the maze! You never asked if I had an idea as to where the Undaunted

King might be!"

The king was full of flooding rage and of anger towards the Book, but in the pleasant weather of the morning he quickly turned to smiling at memories of the escapade they had gone through.

"We did find it, I suppose...but should you not be trying to help me? You were the one complaining about what would've happened to you if I had died." He had calmed down with ease and was thinking about the Sword of Righted Guard.

"Help you, no. It is my duty to answer your questions, among other things." Dranus shrugged, uninterested in the seeming whims of the Book he had discovered. No matter how irritating it had been, it had brought him great power.

Dranus looked down at the Staff of the South Star strapped to his mount and then he unsheathed the Sword of Righted Guard. He held it in his free hand, holding the Book and the reins with his other, and tested the balance, the weight of such a fine sword. It was perfect.

The Sword was not of the properties he had expected. It was much shorter than his sword Fehris, which still lay with King Vulcan, but was still longer than a short sword. It was sharp and relatively thick, a sword of tremendous power and mobility. The guard was also somewhat different, instead of being flat it had a prong on each side of the blade that came up several inches. Dranus assumed that this was for some defensive mechanism of breaking other swords but had not tested it. All in all the sword seemed entirely defensive, when testing it he found it acted on its own to deflect attacks but had no such volition in attacking.

The king's thoughts were interrupted by a thunderous boom in the distance. Dranus's eyes squinted, and he wondered, with great hesitation, what the sound might be. A great wind blew from ahead of him and his mind raced to possible causes, and one made him tighten his grip on the reins and stare ahead, waiting for something more.

His fears were realized when one of his forward guard came riding up quickly from the north.

"My king! The battle has begun!"

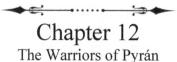

# Chapter 12
## The Warriors of Pyrán

King Dranus and his guard raced at full gallop through the remainder of the forest, heading for the cliff that would overlook the plains surrounding the Discidia Rift. Once more the leaves and the surroundings were a blur, the air lacked scent, and he no longer felt the cool breeze on his skin. Instead, he felt the weight of his stiff black armor, the tense muscles of his horse, and the firm brass of the Staff of the South Star in his free hand. Their entire strategy had been built around the Staff, but they had not expected the enemy to aggress so soon...had Armodus not feigned hopes of peace like they had planned? Whatever the reason, Dranus recognized the disciplined shouts amplified through sorcery to send orders to form up ranks for an advance. Armodus was a decisive general, he would already be thinking of a new strategy.

Fortunately, the group of horsemen burst through the tree line and looked down to see that the battle had not yet been joined. Instead, a large green bubble, flowing like a lake pressed by a gentle breeze, encompassed the forces of Varz as huge flaming projectiles crashed into it and exploded against the raw power of the shield.

The battlefield was neat and composed like the pieces on his war boards in Varz. Armodus had not, as he thought, initiated a different strategy, but had gone ahead with their extant one and believed that Dranus would arrive in time.

"I'm here, old man." He said under his breath as his heart thumped in his chest.

At the base of the cliff there was a large detachment of Varz troops facing the north and a force estimated to be twice that size opposed them. Both sides of the Rift had cliffs at their rear with the Rift itself closing to a flat plain that stretched between them. Either force could retreat along the gaping Rift to the west safely whereas the east stretched into rolling hills.

It was clear that neither force had committed their full numbers as that would leave their other borders undefended, but those present would provide enough advantage to decide the pace of this front of the war.

"Commander Ven has done well." The Mage Corps was nestled away near the base of the cliff in their amethyst robes and armor. Commander Ven stood on a tall construct, acting as the locus for the shifting green shield that protected their forces. So long as she was at the helm and their forces were unperturbed, the enemies could hurl stones and flame until nightfall and get nowhere.

Dranus sighed but pressed down his relief; there was still a battle to be had.

"Herald, give the call." Dranus dismounted, preparing to take up his position.

A loud horn split the air and a sudden roar erupted from the colorful masses formed below him. King Dranus grinned at the thought of battle, of the power he held, and the men and women that were willing to give their lives for Varz. A certain wicked pride crawled over him like growing vines. In the days leading to this battle he had felt some doubt and anxiety about how they would perform...Varz had not been to war in centuries and Dranus had never lead an army or participated in a campaign like this. But now, there, looking down at the scene, the blood of Sorcerer Kings took over and the years and years of grueling training that made war second-hand to him guided every movement of his hand and every breath of his voice.

The massive green shield roiled and lurched in preparation for the next bombardment. But Dranus saw his chance to announce himself formally and in the only manner a Varz Monarch knew how.

From the hilltop burst a ray of orange light which trailed overhead, colliding with the burning projectiles and devouring them, nullifying it as though the two could not exist in the same space. There, left hanging in its place was the symbol of Varz, the curved V, sign of the royal family. It was the tip of this symbol which aimed itself like a spearhead at the enemy. It was the prophecy of their doom. The blade at their throats.

The Varz warriors rallied their approval, letting out a guttural battle cry their warrior's hearts knew better than their conscious minds. The heat of his men's passion warmed the king and in his state of elation he slammed the Staff of the South Star into the ground. As before an unearthly dirge played about him and brought a sense of malicious foreboding to the field, humming like an echo of the warriors' wrath.

With the South Star near its zenith and the ruby gem facing forward, an undulating crimson behemoth formed in the space that existed between the two forces. But this behemoth was neither beast nor monster, it was the Army of the South Star, and its cry shook the very dirt that scuffed their boots.

On the cliff opposite the Rift from where Dranus stood, the long-range weapons of the enemy were being rolled away and legions of archers replaced them. Their arrows would rain from the high cliffs in the east, and the western side of the battlefield was separated by the massive rent in the earth. The enemy forces had chosen a perfect place to invade; they could not be flanked on either side and their archers could not easily be reached. However, the Varz forces also made use of the Rift and stationed their archers in the west where they could not be harassed over the wide gap of the Rift unless the enemy archers moved to match them. Only by approaching on foot and by passing the Varz army could their exposed flank be reached. Dranus inspected the battle formations as the giant single enemy mass began to show signs of movement.

The enemy's strategy was clear: they had positioned themselves in such a way that flanking force could not easily decide the outcome of the battle, leaving them to a straightforward brawl. The Arendrum forces, believing they heavily outnumbered the Varz soldiery, had chosen an aged offensive formation in which a central mass of foot soldiers formed the charging front and on each flank was a pillar of horsemen. This formation allowed the front to move as one and either collide with the enemy foot soldiers and use the flanking cavalry to threaten the sides or could quickly send the cavalry ahead for a charge to break lines with their troops following in tightly to take advantage of the chaos. It was an old formation, but in such narrow ground and with such large armies, it would prove quite effective.

The Varz forces were in a much more complex formation, integrating both their long-range weapons and the Mage Corps into the bulk. At the front was the massive crimson Army of the South Star which now posed like statues, their martial poise more intimidating than the loudest shout.

Even as Dranus stared at the moving enemy force he could see the disarray. The sudden appearance of such an enormous contingency of things the Lessers could not explain was their first stratagem. Some of the enemy generals would likely want to try and withdraw, to recalculate their efforts. They would not be used to relaying orders over such a vast force in a short time. Still, the Superior of Arendrum was hot-headed and had already moved out so far and made such bold claims against the fallen realm of Varz that he would not turn back now and see the pride of their realm dragged behind them.

Behind the glowing red army was half a line of horsemen to the west, split into two sections, and a seeming hole in the east where a mirrored cavalry formation should be. Behind this line was the Varz Army in their red-tinged magically treated armor which made them almost as spectacular as the haunting Army of the South Star. At the back center of this force was the Mage Corps. From this position they could erect massive shields, cast auras of rejuvenation or protection, and even go on the offensive with Commander Ven's guidance. Farthest in the rear were the long-range weapons which, as Commander Kaelel had boasted, were more advanced than ever before. Somewhere near the center would be General Armodus, waiting to give out tactical orders as the battle went on.

On the cliff at the most south point of the battlefield was King Dranus and his Staff, his guard, and the Book which had garnered him such power. There was a tension in the air almost as real and tactile as the dissolving magical shield above his forces. From his vantage point, the battle would seem to move almost in slow motion and yet his every muscle was taut in preparation as if his army were itself his body and he prepared to engage in a life-or-death duel against a much larger enemy.

A low, heavy rumbling of drums broke the momentary stillness; apparently the enemy had decided to stay more quickly than he had given them credit for. The army of Arendrum charged with impressive speed, quickly leaping the tiny crack in the ground where the Rift sealed shut. Now the battle had begun in earnest and a king who wielded unknown might would be put to the test. His actions there would soon become the stuff of war ballads, sang until the end of time—or so he dreamt.

As expected, the enemy was deploying their cavalry swiftly into a wedge formation. The wedge's point was off-center towards the west; likely they expected to break the Varz front and charge the Archer's Brigade while their own foot soldiers clashed with the crimson ghost army. It was a surprisingly good tactical decision on their part, given that they had no idea what properties the South Star Army possessed. Did the enemy generals think them nothing more than illusions?

Dranus swallowed hard as he watched the formation take action, impressed with the order that the enemy maintained. Still, this was basic strategy and the King of Varz had prepared for this, too.

With a wave of his hand, he bid his herald blow a high note, signaling the third of four strategies the Council had decided on previously. Below, the Army of the South Star was still, holding their curved shields to brace for the initial charge. Behind them, however, there was a great hustle of men as the Mounted Forces unraveled large woolen bundles and distributed short green lances that seemed to pulse and glow in their hands.

The enemy cried with righteous fury, their cavalry charging at speed, hoping they still caught the Varz front off guard with their efficiency.

The point of the enemy horsemen formed and as the first enemy blade sought the iridescent red skin of their grinning foes...the Army of the South Star vanished! The enemy charged full force into a barrage of green lances borne from the Mounted Forces. With terrifying speed and accuracy the lances flew until each one had planted itself firmly in the chest of an enemy rider; utilizing an ancient magic developed in the First Great War.

That otherworldly music belched again from the cliff top and Dranus imagined he heard some type of chanting while the hole in his own cavalry formation was filled by glimmering viridian soldiers and their mounts. These were the riders that lead the Varz charge into the disoriented ranks of Arendrum forces struggling to comprehend where their foes had gone and recovering from the pile-up of corpses and riderless mounts in their formation. Having the tip of their wedge formation broken, the enemy cavalry split into two sections. The Mounted Forces took one and the South Star Cavalry took the other.

The skill and practiced efficiency that the South Star Cavalry possessed was stark against the hastily bolstered ranks of the Varz

Mounted Forces. While the current Varz mounts held themselves proudly and moved in a steady mass, the celestial warriors had perfected their form and moved with unrivaled speed and unity. Instead of pride, these warriors held an insatiable thirst for battle; a burning desire to hack and slash and murder those which they had known as Lessers for as long as they had lived. They had surrounded the enemy and corralled them like livestock before Dranus's own horsemen had even reached their quarries.

Dranus's horse moved and whinnied as it seemed unsettled by the wailing of the Staff. This was a trained war horse, of the finest they had! It was certainly bizarre to see it so unnerved, but he could not be distracted by such things. The entire strategy they had chosen revolved around his precise timing and use of the Staff.

Now the waves of ghostly riders had pierced into the slowly advancing foot soldiers like an unforged blade pierces the waters of its creation. The boiling devastation of the enemy ranks was on a scale that sent soldier and officer alike sprawling back in fear. But that would not be enough to end this battle. No matter the ferocity of his forces, they were still few against many. The enemy's numbers would make up for their lack of skill and discipline.

As expected, the South Star Cavalry, having cut deep into enemy ranks, were surrounded on all sides. A tightening noose of fresh troops and rejoined cavalry pressed in on them until, with a rapid thud of brass on rock, the dull voice of the Staff was silenced and just as suddenly the South Star Cavalry vanished! Again the enemy was left bewildered by an enemy that had at once been there, then merely ceased to exist without warning!

Confusion and discord ran rampant within the enemy ranks as they fought to regain order, hacking hesitantly at their allies in belief that their eyes had merely been tricked momentarily. The Arendrum army fought not only the might of Varz, but chaos incarnate. How could one strategize against an army that could deploy and retreat in an instant?!

But the battle's tempo did not wane; there was no time to let them recover.

The Varz Mounted Forces retreated swiftly in favor of the Varz Army, bowing to the west to further cover the Archer's Brigade which had yet to strike.

Dranus watched carefully, speculating what the enemies next

move might be. They appeared to be trying to rally their forces and regain some order before the Varz Army hit, but they were cautious while the presence of that otherworldly army was absent.

"We cannot let them regain their footing! Sound the Archer's Brigade!" Another tone blasted from the war horn and the unit to the west, safe behind the Discidia Rift and the Mounted Forces, spread themselves quickly, pulling back bows of staggered lengths. A flash of rippling gold moved across the formation as armor flexed and gilded bows stretched. The sound of crackling fire could be heard below the cliff where seething balls of black flame were loaded into enormous launchers and even Dranus, high above, felt the itching heat.

With the faintest crack of the wind, a thousand arrows chased the western flank of the enemy back across the Rift in retreat. Massive eruptions of oozing, viscous flame lay waste to the back ranks as the Varz artillery spit its hell breath with precision.

Despite all this, the enemy was keeping a rough order and had managed to isolate the disarray in their ranks. There was something disconcerting about how they managed this. The barrage of arrows should have done more damage; the fires from their projectiles should still be raging. Yet somehow order had been restored while the Varz Armed Forces clashed with the disorganized front of the enemy formation. Had some genius tactician been born in Arendrum in recent years? Had his plots been so thin as to be seen through so easily?

Dranus frowned; they were resilient if nothing else. He considered if the Army of the South Star could be deployed at the enemies rear but when he tried to summon them at that distance they would not come.

"Limitations...no matter," but his confident words belied the growing unease in his chest. Something was not right, but he couldn't tell what.

The Army of Varz was pushing across the rift while the enemy seemed to be slowly retreating. The united twang of bows sounded over the melee and arrows came raining down from the far eastern enemy cliff. But the Mage Corps had been waiting for just this and the green barrier reappeared, though in limited expanse. Unfortunatley, this barrier would block their own projectiles just as easily as it blocked the enemies.

The enemy was moving with discipline, retreating slowly back towards the wall of the cliff. Not towards their path of retreat? Did they hope to pressure their forces to fight doubly hard with the threat of annihilation looming? Certainly Dranus would prefer a route here, but what cost would his forces pay with the enemy having nowhere to flee?

At the moment, these thoughts were abstract as the enemy was holding. Something else was strange, though. Even though the Staff was silent, his horse still seemed disturbed. Its eyes were wide and its nostrils flared; it stamped at the ground and shook its head as if it yearned to flee from some unseen danger. As his horse paced, Dranus now scanned the horizon, searching among the enemy ranks for something out of place. It was a simple, tight formation. He had a perfect vantage point...there was no flanking maneuver waiting as if hidden inside the walls of the cave.

He fingered the V-shaped scar on his face as his conviction wavered. In his sorcerer's soul he felt a disturbance which he could not readily identify. Was this another of the many feelings he had come to experience recently? No, he was certain that something was approaching, but he had no inclination as to whether it would show to be friend or foe. As much as he wanted to, he wouldn't dare take his eyes off the battle long enough to consult the Book.

Trying to shake the feeling of unease, the king tried to focus on the tactics of the battle and the things he could control. The unseasoned warriors of both sides were a mess of flesh and blood pushing back and forth over the shallow split of the Discidia Rift. That kind of front-to-front battle favored the enemy heavily. What could he do to secure his victory? Would he deploy the South Star Army next? The battlefield was so cluttered with fighting such that deploying them to the Varz eastern flank would do no good....

He caught sight of a golden flare from the West and watched his new wife riding among her warriors, encouraging them and letting loose a few glowing arrows of her own. She was a strong woman and beautiful. She was, he thought, the picture of elegance among the roughness of battle.

"That's it!" The vision of Kaelel had given him the stratagem he needed. If the archers were out of range because the army had crossed the Rift...then he need only deploy more archers on the other side of the Rift.

He turned the Staff of the South Star in his hand and slammed it against the ground. Amber light poured from the gem like a beacon on a rocky shore. Where the crooning of the Staff had been muddled before, Dranus now clearly heard the sound of voices at varying pitches chanting in unison. They chanted a dirge for the enemy, heralding the appearance of a small unit of golden archers on the enemy's western flank.

Then suddenly, as if echoing the call of the Staff, Dranus could just barely make out the sound of a chorus of horns from atop the opposing cliff which set the enemy to delirious cheering. He stared hard, using every twist of reality he could to see what figures stood on the other side.

There were six warriors, each with their own banner representing a force of the elements, and all clad in blinding silver armor.

"What?! Who?! Who are these warriors that bear the standards of the elements?!" Dranus was frantic at this development. It must be a ruse! What could six more soldiers do where thousands had failed?

The Book, which had been placed in the king's chest plate as before, made a sound of fluttering pages and banged against the inside of Dranus's black armor.

"Aha! The Warriors of Pyrán! I had begun to wonder if they would appear here or not!" The voice echoed from within his armor, alight with apparent glee at this development.

The name of Pyrán set the king's spine to straighten, his head to spin, and his chest to tighten with trepidation. Bewildered and wishing desperately that his earlier premonition had not predicted this arrival, he drew the Book out with haste.

"You know these six warriors? What connection do they have with Pyrán?!"

"When the empire of Varz began to decline, a prophecy was told that if the they should ever rise to power and go to conquer again, that the Holy Knights of the Mountain, the Warriors of Pyrán, would appear to smite them. Though I had not expected them so soon."

The Book's tone of nonchalance drove the king to madness.

Between the pressure of the battle and the information he had just received, Dranus was struggling to contain his rage; a rage which had never existed within him before that moment.

"You knew of this power and yet you said nothing?! This is beyond a lack of help you wretched thing! You have lured me and my folk to our doom! You have brought about our greatest enemies!"

"In my defense, master, I had not expected them to come for many more years..." the Book tried to speak but it was cast into the dirt by the king's furied hysteria.

King Dranus had already remounted and was racing down a narrow path to the base of the cliff.

As the Book settled in the dust it flipped between a few pages, letting out soft sighs and murmurs of curiosity. "Strange. Did he say *six* Warriors? There should be seven..."

Dranus raced with all speed towards the area in the rear where he'd spotted General Armodus. He knew nothing of these Warriors, but that they were of Pyrán, the most ancient of Varz's enemies, was all too much reason to worry.

A wave of arrows had risen again from the Archers of the South Star, but they would not reach their targets.

The king's mouth hung agape as he witnessed an impossible thing, pulling his mount to a stop to make sure he wasn't seeing things. In a matter of moments, a wall of earth hundreds of feet tall rose between the enemy army and the amber archers. Up on the cliff one of the figures radiated a bright aura of shining emerald and Dranus felt the weight of incredible sorcery bear down on the battlefield. Was this the strength of just *one* of these Warriors?

He looked on with horror as the giant slab of earth fell forward towards his forces. Clutching the Staff tight, he slammed the base of it into the ground and the amber light faded just in time to be spared from no less than complete destruction.

"How could something like this have avoided my sight?! How can *they* have this power?! That power was extinguished in full by The Ultimate, I know it was! This is impossible, it cannot be!" But if they were of Pyrán in truth, then Dranus knew all too well that this power was not strictly beyond them.

He pushed down his fears and resumed his descent. The battle was not yet lost, but he needed to consult with his general.

A sudden flash of brilliant sunlight forced him to look away momentarily. When the king looked back at the cliffs, there remained only one figure silhouetted by waves of scarlet light like a massive pyre had been lit behind him.

He saw a single arrow loosed from the figure, massive and burning as though made purely of flame. It soared like a phoenix through the sky. Its path was set.

Dranus mouthed the single word "no" as the target of the strike became apparent. He begged with whatever forces he believed might side with his cause. He streaked magic through the sky to intercept it, but the flame pierced his magic like a stray leaf on the wind. There was no stopping it. No changing its trajectory. The single arrow plunged into the ground at the center of the gold-clad archers who could do nothing but stare, mesmerized, as their Fate rushed rapidly toward them.

The arrow disappeared among the ranks. Nothing. Had his magic worked? Had it been extinguished in the final moment?

For a single second he dared hope that his prayers had been answered. But there was no forgiveness for the damned.

An ear-splitting crack like a whip ripped through the sounds of distant battle and the rush of hooves. The front half of the Archer's Brigade flared into towering flames that threatened to caress the very heavens! Those of the archers not immediately consumed by the explosion were flung in every direction, some even being cast into the Rift.

"Kaelel! You must live! You have to live!" Dranus screamed his desperate fury over and over again as though she might hear his command and know that he cared; know that he could not lose her so soon. Tears bristled to his lashes as any notion of control he had once entertained fled like the scattering Archer's Brigade.

Another round of rattling ropes shook the air as his own artillery fired balls of black flame launched at the enemy, only to be tossed aside casually by a wild wind that came from a hazy white radiance amidst the enemy's troops. Earth, fire, and wind already....

Finally Dranus had reached the camp that was most southward, at the rear of all the Armed Forces. Here were all the commanding officers and strategists who tried to adapt to the battle. And here General Armodus, in his burning crimson armor, rushed to meet him. The normally composed general's hollow gaze was that of a man who saw Death bearing down on his soul.

"My king, what is this sorcery that controls the elements with such potency?! I thought this...how is this possible?" His hands shook feverishly as he took the king's reins. .

126

"They are the Warriors of Pyrán, as I am told, prophetic heroes of some sort. But they are only six! We must overpower them!" Dranus had to put the desperate thoughts of his wife out of his mind if he could. If he did not lead his forces with a level head he would lose everything even before his war could begin.

He dismounted and unsheathed the Sword of Righted Guard in his right hand, remembering King Vulcan's warning.

"Your Highness, we risk much in this course." The old general reasoned.

"Do not speak of risk General, speak only of how it may be overcome!"

But what Dranus had not seen was that his forces were falling back in mass from the destruction brought by these warriors. From the ground burst hills of spikes and barbs! From the sky rained lightning like the furious hand of the divine.

King Dranus had his pride to consider...he could not let such a battle be won by only six warriors! He rode to a man-made mound where Armodus had overlooked the battle and from here he saw the gap he needed. A clash of bronze against rock and the haunting chant of the Staff came forth in accompaniment with the Army of the South Star.

"Army of the South Star! Your king needs you! Destroy these would-be heroes!" The Army, though still mad with battle rage, were visibly hesitant by how the tide had turned since they left the field.

Dranus was alight with emotion, with fury and rage, a sense of impotency, and a hanging cloud of frenzying fear.

"Armodus! Draw up the back ranks, order the Archer's Brigade to full retreat and have the Mage Corps cast the Aura of Valor!"

A series of blasts which coded complicated messages sounded from around him. In return came codified horns of confirmation. The Archer's Brigade responded...and did not announce a shift in leadership. Kaelel was alive!

His heart lightened for a moment; he was distracted by a small shining figure in the distance. One of the Warriors was advancing alone but...they did not run, nor did they ride, but somehow appeared closer and closer every time he spotted them, similar to how the Staff could deploy and withdraw instantly. The Warrior would at once be running low and hunched to his right, then kicking off the back of a soldier to his left, and then running on helmeted heads like stones in a river coming right towards him! Then gone again!

Just as suddenly as the figure had disappeared, a silver Warrior burst from the bright rays of the sun, flying down towards him and brandishing two large daggers which she clearly intended to drive into his throat. The Sword of Righted Guard, acting faster than could its master, swiped from the side and with supernatural power knocked the warrior from the air.

He looked to where the body should have fallen but there was nothing! No trace remained! A sudden realization overcame him as he noticed some border, some moving outline on the ground. A cloud! A cloud had passed over him! But what of the warrior? Had it not been but a young girl unhelmeted and grinning like a child? Where had she gone?! This was sorcery beyond even the wilds of his own imagination!

Before Dranus could speculate further, the Warrior reappeared crouched on his horse's saddle, lunging at him with the mass of her armor. Again the Sword reacted first, but it could only sweep her arms upward with god-like speed before her weight fell against him. The girl's weight lifted from him suddenly and he struggled to his feet, waiting for another blow.

No follow-up came, however. He was hesitant at first, but then eyed once more the outline of a cloud's shadow cast on the ground. This was an element his folk had hardly understood even before The Ultimate: *Sun magic.*

A thin red light stole King Dranus's attention at the center of his ranks, and he was more than pleased to see that it was the Mage Corps casting the Aura of Valor and not some new disaster. He was even more pleased to feel the energy which filled him and swarmed like a red mist around his armor.

But this was not sufficient. The enemy had the blind audacity to attack him directly, had even taken him to ground! His Varz pride could not stand for such disrespect!

Dashing through a few ranks of men, he reached the dancing figure of Commander Ven. Unlike the shaken General, Ven thrived in the sea of chaos. The recent changes had only brought a wild grin to her aging features.

Dranus placed a hand on her shoulder, and she stopped instantly, awaiting any order.

"Link me, Ven." Witch-like cackling was her response and it

echoed through the minds of the Mage Corps and soon, the mind of the king.

Dranus dipped deep into the recesses of the Forbidden Texts and there he found the words that quickly trickled into the minds of the violet soldiers. It was a reasoning which could not be known, for it was a twist to an already extant untruth. It overcame any understanding which even Ven might suppose or permit with the lavish contortions of an ever-changing reality she was familiar with.

With this, the red aura that flooded the field became thick and coarse. To the enemy soldiers it was as if they drowned in an ocean of blood; to those of Varz, it was a luxurious bath. The Aura of Vampiric Valor drained the strength from the enemy and fed it in large portions to his forces. It was a spell meant for Monarchs and Monarchs alone; it had never been intended to be used en masse like this and to do so was somewhat of a breach of etiquette, but etiquette be damned! Surely Vulcan had not become the legend of his day without breaking an ancient rule or two!

The scene of swirling reds, of crimson, scarlet, ruby, and every hue of the color imaginable was the palette of unchained havoc and death. This was no longer a battle of opposing sides on roughly equal footing. This was a slaughter of men born from every corner of the Five Realms. It was a picture of the past reenacted on the plains of the Rift.

The yelling of his army began to overpower all other sounds, but this was not because they were regaining their form, as the king had hoped.

It was because they were being flanked.

From the west came impossible legions of Urhyllian swordsmen who were unaffected by the spell which Dranus had cast. As he ran back to the rear he could only surmise that they must have crossed the Rift farther down and now hoped to cut off the head of the Varz beast. He arrived next to General Armodus while a few more officers and guardsmen from the back ranks made a makeshift formation, a layered semicircle facing the enemy with Dranus at the epicenter.

Empowered by the Aura of Vampiric Valor, Dranus had lost all restraint and every reasonable thought from his mind. Once more he dug deep into the chasm of his thoughts for the forbidden spells which he had learned since his adolescence. In his rage he was filled with magical might and his throat strained from the complex syllables of the old speech which guided his mental acrobatics. The king's sword flashed and all in the party of barely thirty began to titter with cackling laughter, waving about swords of steel which burned a molten orange and gave off a heat that blackened the sparse greenery of the plain about them.

Now the enemy swordsmen met the elite of Varz, the greatest swordsmen and most masterful sorcerers in the world, and almost as soon as they had rushed the small group they regretted such haste like the trees regret the passing of the Dusk Season. As wild as reavers and bandits drunk on their own strength the warriors of Varz moved fluidly with practiced ease through the enemy and when their glowing swords met armor, sword, or flesh they slipped through with delicate ease. All around limbs wore shorn, whole torsos separated, and the black-armored king relished the sport. The scene of death was oddly punctuated with the complete absence of blood as wounds cauterized closed instantly from the immense heat of their blades.

Dranus rapidly moved to the head and took on a whole band of enemies who sought the head of the king. To his right three men hesitated at the serpent-like movements of the Sword of Righted Guard. At any one moment only two of them could see the glowing blade and they feared its sting like the desert serpents of their homelands. More terrifying than that, was that the king seemed to not even pay attention to that side of his body and yet the sword tracked their movements perfectly. A rash young warrior dashed in and had his sword cut clean off near the guard. When Dranus felt the movement he instinctively brought the sword down, relieving the boy of his sword hand.

On the king's left he stabbed and blocked with the Staff of the South Star. Between his two sorcerous weapons he kept five men at bay at once. A small feat for a King of Varz.

Focusing on his sword hand, he stepped forward between the two men and with a shredding twist of his body halved first the man on the right and then the man on the left at the waist. Turning, he chased the remaining two soldiers as they fled. Their hearts gripped first by the king's howling cry and second by his thirsty blade.

All about were signs of a massacre. The elite of Varz had shown as much mercy as they expected, and they had further shown that they were ever the battle-hungry descendants of the fierce folk of Varz. They were like reapers of men's souls come to take their due!

"My king! We must retreat and regroup! This battle is lost!" Armodus, blood trickling from a shallow cut above his eye, yelled to Dranus over all of the other sounds. Despite the strength of their army over the other, whenever a force met with one of the shining Warriors of Pyrán it spelled unavoidable defeat. Already the Archer's Brigade had retreated, and the Mounted Forces were scattered, heading for the forest to their rear.

"Call the retreat!" Dranus ran back to his horse, leaping into the saddle and racing along the length of his forces. The words burned in his throat as he forced them to leave his lips. This was a loss, but this war would be far from over.

"Retreat my brothers and sisters! We must regroup!" A loud blast from the south cliff sounded the retreat and the red aura dissipated like morning mist.

The near hysterical laughter of Commander Ven whispered in the back of his mind suddenly. He heard the insanity on her breath and the sorcery that forced her to see it as sanity echoing behind it until it faded to a soft unsettling murmur. Then, with an eruption of white light Ven's voice found weight and volume, echoing through his mind. A pillar of pearly white formed from Ven's position surrounded by a few of the Mage Corps. Higher and higher it climbed until Dranus could no longer arch his neck to see it.

"Ven...I hope you know what you're doing." Dranus removed the chorus of Ven's voices from his mind to save himself from the spell and retreated towards the cliff where he had started the battle. He hoped that Commander Ven was not willfully sacrificing her own life, she would be needed in the future. But that was not what alarmed him most.

Another eruption of flame lit the retreating Archer's Brigade as though it sought a vendetta against them. Kaelel had survived the first, she would survive the second! She was Commander of the Archer's Brigade; she would have already retreated to a safe distance surely. He couldn't spare the thoughts. He simply had to keep faith in his wife.

The vivid beacon of blinding white light crowned in the space above the Varz forces and came down like a tent, splitting the two forces not entangled with the enemy. Those enemies who were too unknowing found their reckless charges met by a flash of searing white and a quick death that left nothing but ashes in its wake. This was as close to fire magic as one could get and the cost for this violation of reality was heavy, but its effect could not be argued with. Unfortunately, his own forces on the other side could only meet their end with nowhere left to retreat.

Under this protection the remaining forces of Varz retreated at full speed towards the capital of Varz, demoralized and beaten. The appearance of the Warriors of Pyrán had been a development that cost them dearly. Dranus searched the corners of his knowledge for a way he could possibly hope to overcome these prophetic Warriors who controlled the most forbidden of sorcery.

He would need the Book, that much was certain.

After reaching the cliff top, he recovered the Book from the feet of a guard loyally watching over it but not daring to touch it. Those of his guard that had stayed to herald the movements relayed from below had done well, those that had followed Dranus had died.

The King of Varz stuffed the Book into his chest plate without a word and rode for the rendezvous point deep in their own territory. His mind was numb and as the adrenaline began to wane, his body ached. That was a dull pain indeed compared to the chasm of fear that stretched deep into his soul.

*       *       *

That evening, as the forces of Varz gathered in the cold night and the commanders and captains entered the king's tent one by one to give their reports, Dranus's heart pounded with anticipation, hoping that the next figure to enter the tent would be his wife. But as the night grew longer and the sun threatened to rise, his heart sank lower and lower.

She was injured, maybe even direly, but she was alive and recovering and it was against tradition to send someone to report for her in the immediate aftermath of a major battle. Ven had not submitted her report either and yet he saw her stumbling through camp earlier. This was no time for paranoia, he needed to focus on these reports, the future of the war may very well depend on it.

Finally, General Armodus and Commander Bourin entered once more, having given their initial reports early in the night. Their normally regal posture sagged, and their eyes looked to anything but their king.

"My king..." Armodus spoke first, his eyes staring at the colorful mixture of leaves next to Dranus's makeshift throne and his fist clenched tightly. "...we could not have known of the existence of such warriors as those from Pyrán."

Still the mention of Pyrán was like daggers in his heart.

"What is the total count, General?" Dranus let no emotion tinge his words, despite his heart sitting firmly in his throat.

"We have no definite numbers for the Army of the South Star, but we expect large losses from their rank and file. However, the South Star Archers and Cavalry appeared to suffer few to no losses overall. Our own casualties are reasonably minimal. The Mage Corps is nearly untouched, but the Mounted Forces sustained heavy casualties from some sort of lightning magic, their mounts have been mostly recovered."

Commander Bourin had not dared to say a single word, he simply stood in his shame. He had not cleaned himself or removed his armor since the battle and was caked in dried blood: his own and that of his men.

"What of Commander Ven? That spell...."

"She will live but is greatly weakened. All those who assisted her in the casting perished."

Dranus nodded, the only sign of his relief.

He could not bear to ask the next question on his mind. They had not spoken of the Archer's Brigade. His body shook, his chest felt as though it would burst with the pounding of his heart. He could not force the words to his lips, so they sat in uncomfortable silence for many long moments.

"My king, other than artillery units the Archer's Brigade was near completely annihilated and..." Armodus's breath caught in his throat. The old man approached the temporary throne where the king sat and placed a hand on that of the young man who could barely contain his shaking.

"I'm sorry, Dranus. The Wife of the King has passed."

The lump in his throat descended quickly to his guts where it swelled with red hot rage. Everything he had felt these last few months began to boil over, threatening to drive him insane! He would level everyone and everything around him and then he would go to the enemy and he would kill every last one of them personally! His magic would overflow and corrupt this world! The vengeance he

133

would wreak would be a permanent stain on history, he would see to it personally!

But that flame inside of him sputtered and died quietly in his chest as the reality washed over him slowly. Kaelel was dead. Because of him. He had led his best friend, his lover, his wife to battle for what? For glory? What did glory mean to he who had nothing left?

He would never see her face again. He would never hear her voice, never touch her skin, or taste her lips. The one person he could talk to as equals, the only person who understood even one single iota of his true self...was gone forever.

# Second Movement

"When night turns crimson and Chaos is reclaimed, the Just will find not mercy from the swords of the reborn.

All things to the past shall march without rest; relentless. And from the past all things shall come.

The Warriors' bane and tainted light of their father; they shall gather at the crest of thine sacred mount.

The guilty shall know despair; their icy hearts enviced, their black blood spilt to refresh the tarnished land.

Sun, Moon, Fire, Wind, Lightning, Earth, and Water. The Seven will bear with them a divine labor.

And upon the dawn, the fallen shall lie faceless in the ashes; the memory erased, their deeds undone.

And the world will be as it will..."

-Prophecy of the Warriors of Pyrán, author unknown

# Chapter 13
## Heroes of Light

Five figures sat huddled around a crackling fire. Ten eyes stared calmly at the flickering flames which kept them warm from the cold, hard winds of the Dusk Season in a foreign land. Each one of them was exhausted from all they had been through recently, in mind and in body. Their shining silver armor rested next to their tents in all their splendor.

All their strife and struggling, the hard training and grueling conditions, had culminated in a battle like which the Five Realms had not seen in hundreds of years. The aftermath found the Arendrum Allies with a strong but cautious foothold into Varz territory. Their tentative cavalry was greatly hewn, and their soldiers were worn by the sorcerous dealings of the Varz army, but *their* presence had made all the difference. They had won the day and morale was high.

An owl made its presence known. Some small rodents skittered by.

The figures made no notice of them. All around them was darkness; their allies had given them more than enough space and they had sought out the solitude greedily. The night was thick around their small camp; signal fires relaying messages in the distance increased the feeling of isolation.

Only the single flame at their center cast them in dancing light.

A sixth figure approached from the south, a tall muscular boy no older than seventeen with short hair of light brown and a bit of fuzz around his jaw. He carried with him a massive sword which was longer and wider than any sword one might easily wield. This fact seemed to go unnoticed by the Warrior who carried it like a branch on his shoulder.

This was Leon (LEE-on), the Warrior of Wind, fourth Warrior of Pyrán. He rested his sword on the ground, coming to stand behind a young girl of the same age who was half asleep sitting on a downed tree. Her frame was small and her tan skin was freckled. Her hair was a sandy blond and cut short but messily kept. Leon placed a comforting hand on the girl's shoulder and then sat down next to her. She nuzzled up to him, taking his arm and closing her eyes, her head resting against his strong chest.

This was Olette (oh-LET), the Warrior of the Sun, third Warrior of Pyrán.

"The general says we will wait to see if Varz surrenders. Their forces were injured greatly in the battle at the Rift but those were mostly of that ghost army, and we have little information on their properties. For all we know, they might all come back to life before the next battle." Leon gave his report, trying to keep it as informal as he could. Having been the only actual soldier before this ordeal had all started, he was generally the only one who interacted with the military leaders on their behalf, but this alienated him somewhat. He had been trying to act more like a teenage boy around his friends and less like his rank dictated.

A solemn figure from across the fire raised his eyes from the blaze and stared at the couple. He sneered at the pair and at the report. This youth had pale skin and long, coarse black hair which occasionally caused people to mistake him for a child of Varz, but his eyes were plain and his parents...well, had he known his parents, he would have known them to be proud citizens of Myrendel. He was of medium height and held a few lengths of black chain in his hands.

This was Voradore (VOHR-uh-dohr), the Warrior of Lightning, fifth Warrior of Pyrán.

"We shouldn't be just waiting around. They're in retreat and their morale is broken! We should press our advantage to their capital. We were *born* to destroy those bastards, let's just get it over with!" Voradore made no effort in hiding his contempt for the general's command; besides, he had been the most willing to take on his prophetic responsibility and he hungered to spill Varz blood.

"We can't be too headstrong, Voradore! We haven't had these powers for long and we don't know what other tricks that King of Varz might have. We're strong but we are *not* invincible!" A short and stocky youth with rather jolly features and dark brown hair tried to reason with Voradore. On his back was strapped a massive shield made of gray rock that gave him the look of a tortoise.

This was Teego (TEE-goh), the Warrior of the Earth, sixth

Warrior of Pyrán.

"Besides, we are not trying to take over Varz, we are just trying to keep them from becoming violent again!" Teego stood, taking a position of dominance over Voradore.

From two other positions across the fire a boy and a girl's eyes met and then shifted to Teego and Voradore.

"And that's *exactly* why they'll eventually defeat us if we don't take them out first! What about our 'divine labor'? What about spilling their black blood?" Voradore stood to match the stance of the other Warrior and marched to face him. Normally it was Leon and Voradore who argued incessantly; warring as wind and lightning might for dominance of the skies. Then again, it was Teego who constantly kept Voradore grounded.

"They are blood-thirsty demons and they won't stop until we kill them, or they kill us! Might as well be the former!" Voradore was vehement, having some personal motivation for his enthusiasm. Like most of the Warriors, he had been an orphan at birth, but the couple that had raised him had met their end at the hands of Varz bandits. The Warriors had uncommonly similar pasts; they were all seventeen years old and had a shroud of mystery around the circumstances of their birth. Not least of these was that all but Raven had been wronged by Varz sorcery in horrendous ways.

The boy and the girl locked eyes again. Finally, the boy took initiative and stood, coming between the other two adolescents whose tempers had flared.

"Stop you two! Save your energy! Regardless of what we think, we can only do what the general tells us." The one who had broken them up was of medium height but was rather skinny and unfit compared to the rest of them. His expression was somber and weary as he took his seat again. This youth had medium length hair of a dark brown similar to that of Teego's but flowed upward with volume like flame.

This was Keine (KAYN), the Warrior of Fire, first Warrior of Pyrán and rightful leader of the group, though he lacked most of the necessary attributes of someone in such a position.

"You think the Guide would tell us that?" Voradore spat back. Teego shied away at this. They hadn't heard word from the mysterious man that had brought them together and trained them in a long time. Without him, they all felt a little less certain of what they

139

should be doing but they had no idea who he was or how to contact him. Most of the time he seemed to appear and disappear suddenly as if out of thin air.

With a huff, Voradore returned to his stump and resumed staring at the fire.

"The Guide made Keine our leader. Keine's word is his word." Teego said with a distinct lack of conviction and sat down. Teego was Keine's adopted brother and was always defending the smaller boy. Although the mysterious Guide had made Keine their leader, Teego had mostly acted in this role, though he tried his hardest to not embarrass his brother. Usually he failed.

Keine sat silently, the smell of the fire filling his nostrils and its warmth seeping into him like air into his lungs.

After sitting he had noticed something off about the girl across from him. This girl had fair ivory skin which glowed in the light of the fire. Her black hair ran down her back, tied in a long braid.

"Is something wrong, Raven?" Keine asked.

The girl glanced at the long, intimidating trident stabbed into the earth next to her and then back to Keine, averting her eyes almost instantly.

"I just feel uneasy about all of this. And I miss my home, I miss Shiera. Didn't we win this battle too easily? What if they attack us from behind?" Her face was troubled, and a deep concern showed through the sheen of fatigue on her features.

This was Raven (RAY-vuhn), the Warrior of Water, the seventh Warrior of Pyrán.

"Shiera has the strongest navy in the Five Realms! Don't worry Raven, I'm sure your people are ready for anything." Keine tried to reassure her.

But the sentiment spread quickly. They all, even the cross Warrior of Lightning, nodded subtle agreement to this concern. It had been months since the first of them had left their homes behind. They had left homes, friends, and some of them families and had been forbidden to send word to them since, lest they give away their presence to the enemy.

An uneasy silence fell over the group and the crackling of the fire, the soft howl of the winds, the consistent chirping of the crickets set a mood of gloom. It was a new moon that night and none of them had missed the importance of such a detail.

"Keine," Leon started, "has the Guide sent word about the Second yet?" The focus of all the Warriors turned quickly to their leader. Even the sleepy gaze of Olette piqued at this topic.

"Last I heard, there was still no sign. The Guide seemed to know exactly where to find the rest of us, but he thinks the seventh warrior may have died young or may have not even been born." The Warrior of Fire unraveled the parchment tied to his bow and scanned it again. 'The Seven,' it said. At the bottom of the yellowed page were the symbols of their strength in a row and in the second position was the crescent moon. "But she could still be out there...supposedly the Warrior of the Moon is supposed to be elusive by nature."

It was sobering to the group to think they may have lost a comrade before they even knew their identity. The somber mood returned as each sat with their own thoughts; recent memories playing out like pictures by the lolling flames reflected in their empty stares.

This time the silence was broken by Teego, ignoring the toes of his brother he was about to trample on.

"If we are not needed here," he began without lifting his eyes, "then we should go back to our homes and make sure they are secure." Now his eyes met Keine's. "The Guide wanted us to remain secret for this battle in particular. We've done everything he asked of us so far, I think that gives us the right to see our homes. Besides, now that those of Varz have seen what we can do, they won't try a frontal assault like that again."

Leon mulled this logic over and tried not to disrupt the dozing girl at his side to whisper over the sounds of the night. "You're not wrong, Teego, but we are under orders to hold our position until told where to go next. This war is bigger than just us...."

"So?! Are we their saviors or their servants? It's our destiny to stop Varz, shouldn't our way be best no matter what? I say we give our own orders!" A bright, confident smile stretched across the boy's face. Had it not been for Teego's constant cheeriness, they may not have made it that far.

For once, Voradore did not challenge Teego, even if it might have only been to disagree with Leon.

"I agree." Raven latched onto the opportunity like a drowning woman to a raft. "Many of our forces are focused here, if our hometowns are attacked they may be unprepared for battle. Especially without knowing about that ghost army we fought."

Raven's mood was lifting as she thought of her home town of Shiera; the docks and boardwalks massing out over the calm waters...her place on the beach where she had lived before joining the others on their journey. Unlike the others, she had never really wanted to take on this responsibility, though she had never voiced that to the others. She was a fisherwoman, spearing fish and fixing nets for a living! She had never had a family and had never been wronged by Varz. Of all the Warriors of Pyrán, she had ultimately taken the longest to recruit and felt most out of place among them.

Olette roused and pumped a small fist in the air, sounding her approval with a light, whimsical "Wooo..." which faded like the owl's call as her energy waned.

"It's your call to make Keine, you are our leader and we'll follow what you say." Leon was conflicted. As much as he wanted to go home and visit his family, he felt duty-bound to stay at the front until told otherwise.

Keine deliberated, staring at the fire and trying to weigh the options like he thought a good leader should do. He and Teego were from Arendrum. If they needed to return to the front, they could do so quickly. Then again, was it not his responsibility most of all to see the prophecy to its conclusion? And didn't he seek revenge as avidly as did Voradore?

His blood boiled as thoughts of that bitter night came to mind. A centuries old trap. A raging inferno. The faces of his orphan brothers and sisters twisted in agony as their flesh burned. He would let no further harm come to the innocent of Arendrum.

With these thoughts, he made his decision.

"I agree. I will tell the generals in the morning, and we will split up for a set amount of time. We will need to come back together, likely in the capital city of Arendrum, at a moment's notice though. It is our responsibility to guard the people of these realms from those of Varz and for that we must make sacrifices." Keine didn't need to remind them all about the necessary sacrifices required of the Warriors of Pyrán, but to remind them of their charge was worthwhile. Though none had known this would be their Fate, they had all eventually accepted that it must be and that they had to fight to save the people from the terrible nightmares of Varz. Even though they were still just adolescents, all without families save Leon's adopted family, they had to shoulder such burdens and wield such unimaginable power.

And they had...they had killed people. They had taken the lives of the enemy soldiers with their awesome powers, as simple as it had seemed at the time. Keine could still picture all of the burning bodies he had set aflame with his arrow. The horror he had felt stuck with him as memories of his own tragedy resonated with those of the one he had created. All but Voradore, who had killed to stay alive most of his life, were shaken by the murders they had committed. Even Leon, who had been a soldier before, was shaken; after all, this was the first war in the Five Realms for several centuries. Before, his position as a soldier was more for keeping peace within the city.

None had the energy to consider the moral consequences of their deeds at that time, however. All they knew was that the world needed them and their power and that wielding such power had its perks.

With the prospect of returning to their homes giving them hope, they stayed up for another hour or so going back and forth retelling their greatest feats and triumphs in the previous battle. Still, none but Voradore mentioned the conclusion of each great action...and the black-haired youth's familiarity with death continued to unsettle the rest.

Mirrored by the festive movements of the long shadows playing against their tents, they told stories of the happier times of their lives. They had already shared enough about their own personal tragedies.

They would almost all sleep well that night, knowing their homes and some semblance of temporary normalcy awaited them. All but the snoring Olette who had nightmares of the black-armored King Dranus and his lightning-fast sword which blocked even her attacks. But it was not the sword she feared most, it was those eyes. The hellish black eyes of a demon staring back with fierce defiance and evil. He had to be stopped.

He *had* to be stopped.

# Chapter 14
### A King in Darkness

King Dranus VIII sat alone in his bed chambers at a table in the dark corner of his room.

The rain outside was heavy. It was constant, never-ending. It was familiar if nothing else. Like the familiar weight he felt in his chest as if the corpses his ignorance had produced sat piled upon him.

The rain would not lift its burden.

Though Dranus had lit every light in his room, hoping to chase away the shadows tucked deep in his thoughts, no light could reach him in that corner. It did not reach him. It did not dare.

He stared towards a chair opposite his own where once had sat his wife, Kaelel. In the brief time they had spent impassioned together they had often sat at this table and talked and joked. They spoke of philosophy, of war-making, and even of the ever-elusive feelings of admiration they had for each other. For hours they could pass the time as if such a thing as time held no power over them. Now it was as if time stood still, unmoved even as the rain relentlessly crashed down.

His mind, his whole life had been a puzzle; a riddle he had picked at and turned every which way to no avail. But Kaelel, she was the answer. She was the single light amidst his darkness. Now he felt there was no light in his life. He was forsaken and all the worse, it was only his own choices he could blame.

On the table was the Book on which he had tried to lay fault for all of this misfortune. Before he had wanted to burn a hole in it with his spiteful glare. He had sat thus for many hours since returning to Varz...glowering at the wretched thing which had so upset his normal life, which had given him purpose only to strike it from him. He had purely hated the thing with everything he was.

But those hot, burning feelings were those of the king he had briefly become. Now was his time to recede into the man he had been. Unattached and aloof; safe.

The truth was that he could not bring himself to harbor such hate for the Book for too long. The Book had been the closest thing he had ever had to a friend who was equal to him and their relationship, though frustrating at times, was valued. The Book had brought him power to rival even his great ancestors' and for this he had to be thankful.

Idly, he thought it may be neither the loss of his wife nor his mixed feelings for the Book which had him in such a state.

It was this pain, this ache in his chest like some bottomless hole that set him to searching his own soul for answers. How had he never known such feelings like this? Was it not tragic when his father died? But then again, had he ever been very close to King Roboris the Thick-Hearted? As endearing a father as he had been, most of his favor had gone to his wife while his son was trained in the traditional arts of a monarch of Varz. If anything, Ven and Armodus had been more parent to him than either of his biological parents.

Dranus had not known his father like he had known Kaelel. In some ways, he always knew that his father would pass; it was the only way he would ever become king. Somehow he had never quite accepted that the same might happen to others he cared about. But maybe that was the problem. Before the Book, there were no others he cared about, not really.

So he came to avert his eyes from the Book and ponder, as he had often done, of its true nature. Was this thing to be used towards his ambitions? Or was it he who danced like a marionette to the invisible strings of the Book's whims? More than once it had withheld information from him that led to outcomes not aligned with his own. But then again, he had directed the Book in discovering the Relics of Power.

Or had he? Had his thoughts been twisted, seized by the unknown powers of the Book? The South Star's rising had been motive to seek the Staff of the same name, but the Book had known it would rise. The Book had recommended the detour to see King Vulcan too.

Doubt hung around him like a sodden cloak.

Dranus's eyes hardened as he snapped back to the Book, considering how it had infected him so with such unnecessary feelings and how he might best cast off these moral chains.

"What have you done to me Book? What sorcery do you cast on my mind that corrupts me?" His fist clenched tight, waiting for an answer which did not come.

"Speak wicked tome!" He shouted. "I have addressed you with a question and you must answer it!" Dranus slammed his fist against the table and the Book rattled softly against the wood.

"I have cast no spell on your thoughts, master, for I have no such powers. I presume you feel this way because you cared about your wife." The Book indeed could not avoid a direct question for long as it was a binding principle of the spell which gave it life.

"I cared about my father! I have cared about many who have passed but none like this!" Low rumbling thunder echoed the booming voice of King Dranus in his agony.

"Did you?" The Book challenged. "Is this not proof that you have never truly cared about anything in your entire life? Have I not provided you with purpose and means to fulfilling said purpose?"

"But you have withheld! You have brought doom upon my people by tricking me into summoning the Warriors of Pyrán! I begin to suspect that you serve your own purpose...or...or...that you were created to destroy my nation and all of my folk." Dranus blatantly ignored the first two questions asked of him.

"I do not know the reason for my creation, but I do not seek to destroy you, master. It is my duty to answer your questions and provide my knowledge to you when I can. It is your own oversight and lack of clarity which has led to your current state of affairs." The Book spoke calmly, unfeeling towards the situation.

But Dranus would take this insolence no more.

"You will not speak to me this way!" He stood abruptly and swatted the Book from the table. "I am King of Varz! I am your master! I gave you life! Your meaning *is* my meaning, as you seem to have forgotten! You have life only so far as it serves my purpose and if you wish to keep it then you will learn your place! Else you will find a new place as a pile of ashes!"

Dranus paced around the room in a baffled rage, 'if you wish to keep it'? What madness had overcome him to treat a book this way? It was nothing but pages, as easily dispatched as so many dried leaves, how did its existence influence him so heavily?

A light knock came at his door.

"Leave." Dranus roared.

"My king, please allow me a word." The weak voice was quickly recognized as that of Commander Ven and the king snapped his attention to the door.

He took a moment to compose and quiet himself.

"Enter." If nothing else, he owed Ven an audience for what she had done at the Battle of the Rift.

His door creaked open and Ven, a patch over her left eye, entered slowly and with some effort. Dranus sat at the end of his bed, ignoring the Book which lay silent on the floor.

"Commander, I am relieved that you are still of this world, though you seem to have paid a high price." He looked once at the eye patch and then to the ground.

"Not at all. A single eye for the safety of Varz is a price I would gladly pay. Those who assisted me gave far more." Her voice was strained and interrupted by spasms of coughing. Her frame shook simply from the breaths she so carefully took.

"And you, my king, how fair your wounds?" Ven was hesitant to approach despite her history with the young king.

"I received no wounds from the battle, my armor was hardly touched." Dranus retorted still staring at the floor.

"I did not mean wounds of the flesh, my king. You have lost your wife, and so soon after finally making her yours. I cannot imagine the suffering you must feel." Slowly she made her way towards the sad figure staring into loneliness. "You two had always made an exemplary pairing. Your love awakened something within the people of Varz. Within all of us." She attempted a smile, though he did not see it.

Dranus could not find words. He only felt a thick lump form in his throat as she spoke, thinking back to the wedding and his beautiful bride. How full of life they had both seemed at that time. Now one was dead and the other might as well be.

"Dranus, our people have become quite stoic with our decline from power. What you feel is not sorcery or some trick on the mind, I promise. This is what our ancestors once felt deep in their hearts. Passion, joy, love, loss, and yes, despair. All of these things we once knew, they suffused our lives and brought us color, that is why we were the Bright Empire." Ven lowered her voice. "But we have forgotten. What you have done and what you have become has brought these back to us. You should not fight these feelings. Accept

147

them. Conquer them. And you will become stronger!" She sat next to him on his bed, assuming a level of intimacy and lack of decorum only she would get away with.

Dranus looked up to the wizened face as tears began to trickle down his cheeks. No matter what Ven said, he could not bear the pain that welled within him any longer. He was certain that he was not strong enough. He was no King Vulcan or Queen Tempest. He was no Valkhir the Rageborn. He was not a fraction of the seven Dranus who came before him. He knew that this pain and his inadequacy would kill him soon and that there was nothing he could do to stop it. No amount of soldiers or sorcery, no ancient Relics of Power, nothing could stave off this pain. He buried his face in Ven's embrace and softly wept.

"We will honor Kaelel as a hero and we will exact vengeance for her death. The Lesser Folk have everything to fear from us. We can still show them why." Ven held the tearful King like she had held him as a boy. Though she had always been very strict with Dranus and was very much a warrior of Varz, she too had succumbed to the changes brought about by Dranus's exploits.

Dranus could not tell how much time passed but he let it pass without worry. Slowly, his breathing stilled and a calm like a warm, dry blanket fell over his aching soul.

Remembering his pride as a King of Varz, he stood and collected himself. Ven looked at him softly, without judgment, in some version of the way Kaelel had looked at him. Surprisingly, that healed him some small bit.

"We cannot match the power of the Warriors of Pyrán as we are now. Even if we massed all of our forces against them, their power combined is too great." He had not yet considered how those heroes might be bested but he had taken Commander Ven's words to heart. He would accomplish nothing by sitting in his room venting steam at a book.

"What about that book you carry? Can it not guide us to some solution?" Ven's eyes traced to the spot on the floor where the Book lay and guessed the events that had led to its current position.

"I am loathe to rely on the Book. Though it has brought us great power, it knew of the Warriors and spoke nothing of them. It is a tool, but it is not an ally, I think." Dranus still did not go to pick up the Book and Ven dared not touch it.

"Then we should use it as a tool and be more careful in the future of the consequences of our actions." Ven commented, looking away.

She held a dark secret that she struggled to hide in her weakened state. The truth was that she had long since known of the legend of the Warriors of Pyrán but, assuming it to be nothing more than a myth, had made no mention of it. It was she who deserved the king's enmity even more than the Book. She felt guilty and partially responsible for the death of the Wife of the King, but in the end she could not bring herself to admit this to Dranus. He had lost enough recently, hadn't he?

The king stomped over to the Book and reluctantly picked it up, wiping some dust from its cover.

"Book, can the Warriors of Pyrán be overcome?" The Book hesitated for a moment as it had done many times before, ostensibly searching for the correct answer, though Dranus felt that it was more looking for the right words to say.

"They can, master." Its voice seemed almost to shake, though it could have been that the Book was just as upset with the king as the king was with it.

"How?"

"First, you should seek the Shield of Second Life from Queen Tempest the Undying. Then you must obtain the fourth Relic of Power."

Commander Ven could not hide her surprise and interest. As much as she was a historian of Varz, she had limited to no knowledge of the Relics other than the Staff of the South Star.

"You have spoken many times of a fourth Relic but there are no records of such a thing in the Forbidden Texts. What is this last relic?" Dranus too had his interest piqued, though it struggled to wade through the hatred he bore for the object in his hands.

"I cannot speak of its identity now, master, but I can assure you that it will defeat the Warriors of Pyrán."

"You *cannot* speak of it, or you *will not*?" Again he considered who it was that directed his Fate.

"I will not, master." The Book was resolute in its statement. It was the furthest of oddities about the thing, as it directly refuted the power of the spell which he had cast upon it. Whatever magic fueled the thing, it was likely ancient, beyond even the power of a monarch of Varz.

149

"But you will lead me to it? Where does it lie?" So long as he could attain it, he would know of its truth at some point. And as long as it would defeat the Warriors he would make it his.

"I will lead you to it, yes...though you will not be fond of its location." The Book stopped again, this time it seemed as though it was deciding on whether or not to divulge this information.

"Speak the name tome or I will have you burned here and now."

The book made a nervous rustling of its pages.

"It lies in the ruins of Pyrán, master...."

"Pyrán?!" He snarled the name. "To go there is of the highest order of blasphemies in Varz!" Simply mentioning the name almost made him rabid with disgust. His skin crawled just thinking of stepping a single foot on that holy soil.

Dranus turned swiftly to Ven, his eyes piercing like a hawk. "Commander Ven, you would do best to forget all you have heard here."

Ven had been too shocked by the news even to show her disdain. Now she stood, doing her best to control her trembling limbs. With a less than graceful bow, she headed for the door.

"It is forgotten, Highness." And so, in truth, it was.

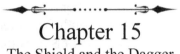

# Chapter 15
## The Shield and the Dagger

Ven's words had soothed him for the night, but only the night. The next several days were filled with zombie-like attendance to meetings and catching up on his kingly duties. The times passed by somehow both slowly and quickly. He was as a corpse moved by sorcery: his body simply going through prescribed motions while his mind suffered the eternal rumination of all that he had lost. Fortunately, his years of training and the assistance of his War Council ensured that all was right in the kingdom and with the continuing war front. Unfortunately, Dranus could no longer lay in bed most of the day hiding from the world.

So it was with great reluctance and a heavy sigh of exhaustion that King Dranus started off from the relative safety of Varz. Again he insisted on traveling alone, reassuring his guards that the Staff of the South Star would provide him with more than enough protection from unexpected threats. Though he was still wary of the magical Book he possessed, its knowledge was the key to his nation's success.

Still, he had realized he had treated the Book with too much familiarity before, so it was tucked into a saddle bag with open contempt.

General Armodus had reported that the shining Warriors of Pyrán had not been seen on the field in several days, but Dranus suspected a ruse. Instead, King Dranus decided that the enemy must be forced back not by confrontation, but by the threat of confrontation. He had Armodus send commands to gather the armies of the east at the Urhyllian border and for the people of Vakkar and the other cities near the Arendrum border to erect huge camps in plain sight and to fill them with fires every night so that it appeared the full strength of Varz was preparing to invade from the high ground of the mountains.

Meanwhile, Armodus would hold the front outside of Varz and

hope that the strategy would work. Dranus would go to Viél in the west where Admiral O'cule waited with the Varz navy. If they could draw the Shieran armada to the border in a stand-off, a small detachment including the hidden South Star Fleet could circumvent the enemy and attack the home ports of Shiera then move in to attack their forces from both sides. The plan was to draw the allied forces apart, to separate the Warriors of Pyrán, and to eliminate them one by one through superior strategy until the fourth Relic of Power could be recovered.

Messengers were sent ahead of Dranus in every direction to relay the orders. Like Varz, the other nations would not be accustomed to war-making after such a long period of peace and though they had at first united to meet them at the Rift, he suspected that loyalties would split as soon as the others' home territories faced real threat. Besides, so long as Armodus and Ven remained in Varz, he had no worries that the city would hold against even a lengthy siege.

For now, Dranus had to focus on a task only he could accomplish. To the west and then north across desolate desert he would reach the monstrous canyons and chasms that made up the bulk of the Discidia Rift. From there, the castle of Queen Tempest the Undying nestled away and forgotten by Time.

The trip was filled to the brim with silence, interrupted only by the howling of the wind and incessant canter of his horse's stride. Dranus only addressed the Book when he needed something from it, and the Book only spoke when spoken to. For some time Dranus had even considered rescinding the spell that gave the tome the ability to speak, but he could not risk that something important might need to be brought to his attention with speed. They were in war and had already realized that, if Armodus addressed a letter to Dranus, the Book could show it to the king as it was being written. The thing had strict instructions to share such messages with him no matter the circumstance.

It was thus that Dranus slipped back into his dull character of mind, staring at the binding Rune of Union on his thumb, and trapping himself in deep contemplations about life and death and about the meaning in either. He ate his bread around the fire out of habit only, knowing that no amount of food would fill him. Occasionally he would spot a desert vermin or a bird in flight and wonder what his life might have been had he been born a simpler creature. A short, uncomplicated life of managing survival, heartless reproduction, and then a satisfying death. At least then the meaninglessness of his existence would be expected, if not justified.

In what could have been a day, could have been a year, he began to see signs of the Rift; rocky, barren terrain where magically excavated rock had been deposited after removing it from what was currently the Discidia Rift. The Night Season was fully upon them now. The great sorrow of the sky fell in a constant stream. He was there, alone, not another living soul within a day's ride. In this isolated safety, Dranus let loose his own sorrows.

*    *    *

The morning found the king awakened by the annoying scarlet light of the South Star mixed in with the pure rays of the sun. That day he would reach the Eastern Cross.

The Discidia Rift was another of the great scars on the world that Dranus's ancestors had left. It was carved into the earth by incredible sorcery from east to west to both clearly delineate the borders between Varz and Arendrum, and to create an impassable blockade for any would-be aggressors. To further this second cause, it had been carved southward into Varz in the shape of a figure eight so that two islands of land were isolated from the rest by deep rents in the rock. On the northern most edge of the northern island was a large castle that had once been connected to the territory of Arendrum by a strong bridge which only allowed limited numbers to cross at a time. In this way the castle had become a veritable gauntlet of death for those who so much as considered that they could attack it. The irony, then, was that it had been so well guarded that none had ever made efforts against it.

It was because of this invincibility that Queen Tempest the Undying, who had a self-proclaimed rivalry with Death himself, had made the place her home. However, since most historians knew the immutability of Death to be beyond the powers of Varz sorcery, most considered this a metaphorical rivalry in which she prioritized self-preservation over all. Then again, none of these historians had access to the King's Library or the Forbidden Texts.

By the time the sun had reached its zenith, the soft humming of wind across these deserted plains had begun shifting to the harrowing moans of the Rift. The canyon to the east of the northern island seemed almost to be pooling with the waning ruby light of the South Star. To unfamiliar eyes it might have seemed as nothing more than a natural illusion made by dust and heat haze in the canyon, but Dranus knew better. There was a good reason that the main Rift to the north of his position didn't swim with the same almost-solid light, and it was a secret only a monarch of Varz could truly grasp.

Stopping his mount with a healthy respect for the edge of the canyon, the king glared at one of his saddlebags with precisely practiced disdain. Nonetheless, he fetched the Book with rough handling, no longer treating it with reverence and regard he thought befit the magical item.

"Book, does the Shield of Second Life lie in the Castle Above the Canyon?" The Book had made reference to the castle of Queen Tempest by this name; supposedly it was what the leaders in Arendrum had named it. Unimaginative bunch as they were.

"The last written record explicitly specifying its location points to the castle, yes."

Dranus was unconvinced. "But...?"

"But, other later records suggest its presence elsewhere. One of your ancestral monarchs predating King Vulcan references having returned 'it' to its rightful place in the castle decades later. This is the last likely reference to the Shield. As you already know, I cannot divine current events and it may have been moved without written record of the occasion." The Book spoke as if it struggled to keep the tickled irony out of its words. It was trying to be serious even though Dranus had easily guessed at the thing's game.

It was inconclusive evidence at worst, but the fact that a former monarch of Varz had mentioned returning something they would not name to this castle was as good as he could hope for. Still, the Book was right, hundreds of years had passed since then, and it was unlikely that if some daring looter had found it that they would write about it. Or even know how to write at all, for that matter.

"I suppose that's as clear an answer as I could hope for." The next words hung on his lips as he tried to force them out.

"Thank you," he muttered silently. "But can the legends of the thing really be true? A simple shield that can undo death? Even maintain youth if some of the wilder tales are to be believed? Our sorcery is powerful, especially that of a Varz monarch, but we have our limitations as well." It was something that had bothered him about this item. The South Star was not of this world and its power hung in the endless sky unknowably far away. King Vulcan's sword actually operated on fairly simple logic, though its execution was far beyond what other imitations had attempted. The Shield, however, violated simple laws of Varz sorcery: much of reality was theirs to alter, but not all of it. And when one attempted to change what they should not, they paid direly, as Ven and her mages had been reminded so recently.

"They are true master!" The cheery tone of the Book interrupted Dranus's musings. "If you die while wearing the Shield, your body will stay dead for the day and then you will simply awake the next morning as you were the moment you first donned the Shield. I've seen much speculation that the precise timings of when your corpse vanishes and your body reappears correspond to Queen Tempest's own sleep cycle, interestingly enough!"

Dranus believed that, actually. He had read the queen's account of how the Shield had been crafted and that seemed to be a likely artifact of the process given the rules of Varz sorcery.

"However, it is not entirely as you've read."

Dranus snapped his attention down to the Book from where he had been staring off in thought. Works on the Relics had been fairly well preserved in the Forbidden Texts. The idea that the Book knew something of the Shield that he did not was hardly a welcome one, but one he must consider.

"Explain," he commanded.

"There is a condition for attaining the shield." While the Book had been somewhat more direct since their...disagreement, it spoke more hesitantly now.

"What? Another riddle? Another challenge set by the undead queen, I presume?" He had nearly lost his life to both of the previous tasks. Had he anything further to fear than the threat of nearly certain death?

"In a sense..." As it often did, the tome seemed to flush through its pages searching for the correct wording it needed. "The Shield does not operate quite in the way as the Sword or the Staff. Although I admit to some extrapolation from events occurring after one of the queen's more permanent 'deaths,' I understand that it is an inescapable characteristic of the Shield that the potential bearer of the thing must first...die...to tame its powers."

Dranus thought on this, pursing his lips considering all he knew. Finally, something clicked. He recalled that as Queen Tempest had developed the spell, she had referred to the shield as offering three opportunities at life. It was only after the Shield had actually been crafted that the name changed to the Shield of *Second* Life, and not third.

An irony worthy of one of the greatest Queens of Varz.

"I see." He paused, considering that he was potentially about to reveal secrets from the Forbidden Texts, but then remembered that the Book already knew everything in their pages! "Tempest's telling of creating the Shield includes the otherworldly draw she felt after completing the sorcery to end her own life. The way she tells it in her journal makes it seem that she was testing the mechanism, as an academic might, but perhaps it was just her justification for that necessary condition of the magic."

That, at least, made his trial all too clear.

"Then Queen Tempest's trial will be for me to use the Shield..." His mind immediately returned to ruminations about the death of his beloved. What could he learn of life and death from such a thing? Could he dissect its workings in such a way to return Kaelel from beyond her unmarked grave? Suddenly the thought of her ashes blowing across the Rift and settling in a foreign land washed over him and a wave of nausea almost caused him to collapse from his horse.

With great effort he siphoned away these thoughts as he had practiced, sealing them in an empty wineskin to be disposed of at a later time. This was not the time to be distracted. His questions would be answered soon enough.

"Precisely, master. But fear not, the Shield most certainly works."

Normally, Dranus might have sought some loophole to circumvent the trial so that he might use the Shield at its fullest potential, but this was no common sorcery. Not only could he not afford to meddle with such magic beyond even his comprehension, but as one who so pondered the implications of death, this was a firsthand opportunity he could not miss.

"The Shield is a thing of dark sorcery born from the madness and speculations of King Faust, the Reaper. It is a thing which should not exist on this plane but must never leave." The Book held a solemn tone which Dranus had hardly ever heard from the tome. Normally inappropriately jovial, it was strange how the thing seemed to *feel* the malice or import of the Shield.

The king took a moment from his thoughts to consider the Book in his hands.

"Why are you telling me all of this? I did not ask you of such information." His brow furrowed and his gaze hardened, he could not help but suspect some ulterior motive from the Book.

The Book was silent for a few long moments.

"I am sorry that you have lost your wife, master...and that you blame this loss on me. It is not, in an exact sense, my responsibility to help you further than you ask of me, but I would like to do so, nonetheless, as far as I am able." The fact that the Book seemed to be feeling the kinds of sadness that he felt and that it voiced some volition to mend their relationship resonated within the king, no matter how impossible it should be.

And it was quite impossible.

Regardless, he did not fully trust the Book and would not any time soon.

"I think you will find that this is to your advantage as well." Dranus replied stoically, his callous features drifting away from the flesh-like leather cover.

"I think you are right." It said softly; the sound of a single page turning carefully.

Wishing to move on from this tenuous reconciliation, Dranus dismounted and brought his horse carefully closer to the edge. A strong, moaning wind blew, and he almost instinctively brought an excess weight to his boots and an excess of friction to their bottom surface.

"I do not need your help in this Book, we Kings and Queens of Varz know well the secret paths to the castle since the main bridge to the north was destroyed." Dranus led his horse up and down the edge thinking of the markers he had memorized from his books. The cliffs were sheer, carved with unassailability in mind, and dropped further than one could see through the thick red light.

"Ah, then you will use the Eastern Cross?" The Book seemed somewhat cheered, likely happy that the king was speaking with a little less tension again.

"Of course, if it is in the Forbidden Texts then you know of it as well." Dranus rolled his eyes but smiled a little, briefly slipping back into the familiar relationship he had once had with the Book. "Yes, we will take the invisible bridge to the island and proceed to the castle from the south."

Twisting and snaking his logic through loops of contradictions and discrepancies his vision shifted repeatedly until he locked into the one he was looking for. Now an effervescent glow of white light could be seen hanging over the maw of the canyon, backlit by the scarlet glow of the South Star. Ironically, the canyon had been filled with this highly reflective gas so that when in this view the bridge would glow and stand out in sharp contrast. The unexpected presence of the South Star similarly took advantage of this property and made the Eastern Cross even more distinct. This was one of three invisible bridges that connected the central islands to the mainland which only the kings and queens of Varz...and the Book...knew existed and could locate.

Unfortunately, whereas Dranus could see the bridge, he could not force his well-trained horse to step out into the abyss as easily. With some frustration, he walked out onto the invisible walkway and tried to motion to his horse that he was safe and that it could follow.

His horse pawed at the ground in frustration and confusion and Dranus's shoulders slumped.

After a few more attempts to convince the beast to not trust its own senses, Dranus sighed and resorted to using his sand-cloak to blind the steed. Still whinnying nervously, the horse followed the pull of the reins. Once it gained its footing on the solid stone of the bridge it calmed down somewhat but would not be mounted and had to be held tightly until they reached the other side.

Another hour of riding through the somehow *more* desolate wasteland and Dranus spotted the tall spires of the Castle Above the Canyon in the distance. Now there could be seen some signs that vegetation had once grown here. The castle had held a great number of peoples and there had even once been a small castletown to the south. Dranus mused at the magical means by which they likely were able to sustain the land despite the lack of water and the arid climate.

Once they were closer, however, Dranus pulled his horse to a stop and tensed his muscles, straining his sight. He stared in shock and in fear at what remained of the castle sloping dangerously into the gaping maw of the canyon! Only half of the Castle Above the Canyon actually *remained* above the canyon! He looked to the Book with hurried pulse.

"Was the Shield in the west or east wing of the castle?!" A clear desperation was in the king's voice which contrasted with the comfortable ease of the Book's.

"Do not fret, sire, the Shield was kept in the far west, it was not lost in the landslide." With the reassuring words of the Book it hardly even crossed the king's mind that the tome could not see and yet somehow knew about which half of the castle had fallen. Then again, an Arendrum scouting report was likely to exist of the event in some detail since it had always been a place where their Lesser neighbors to the north had forever been paranoid of a surprise invasion. As if the armies of Varz would need something like the element of surprise to conquer them.

Dranus released a breath of palpable relief. Then he thought again, trying to ask every question which might have relevance.

"What about now? Do you have any inclination that the castle might further collapse into the canyon after I claim the Shield like the Castle Beneath the Waves?"

The Book rustled its pages mimicking the sound of laughter.

"No no master, to gain the Shield you must die so that once you have it, dying again would be a bit redundant! There is no purpose for traps or schemes when Tempest's trial already requires your life!"

There was a certain logic to that, and with the Book's recent claim to actively try and help him, he chose to believe this was true. In the worst case, Tempest's trial was to die as the castle fell into the abyss and he would already be prepared to meet this trial.

They approached from the south, entering into some area that looked like the remains of a kitchen. A beam of light shown in through a hole in the ceiling revealing a ring of rusted cookware hidden in layer upon layer of sand and dust. As he had learned from the Castle Beneath the Waves, nearly all Varz royal castles were laid out in a similar fashion. The most obvious difference at first glance was that the castle seemed almost built directly out of the earth. Had they even used the excavated rock of the Rift in constructing the castle? Or had they grown it from the stone with some since-lost sorcery?

Though he suspected there was little threat in a place so clearly abandoned, he had become accustomed to holding his hand on the hilt of the Sword of Righted Guard as King Vulcan had suggested.

Unfortunately, the nature of the castle's construction was by far the most mundane of the differences between his own castle and this one. Though it maintained similar types of areas for related types of purposes, the general layout of the place was truly perplexing, almost nonsensical. More than once did the king enter a room of oddly decorated hallways that grew narrow at eye height so that he had to crouch between walls that bent like a wave and crawl over areas pinched so tight as to be impassible by any other means. Once reaching the end of this hallway, he would often find that it eventually turned back on itself, leading him back into the same area he'd just left! Even as he tried to hold a generally westward advance, he found himself turning around multiple right corners just to make a simple left or ascending staircase after staircase only to reach an overlook with no way back down but to turn around! He once descended an ornately decorated flight of steps that snaked into an indoor courtyard thinking he needed to descend to the first floor but was bewildered to find that the only way to proceed was back up an almost exactly mirrored set of steps!

"Why was this castle built in such a way? These hallways make no sense!" Dranus spoke in quiet but terse words, lest he upset the constantly crumbling stone beneath his feet.

"It does not make sense to you, my lord, but you must recall that this castle is left over from the Second Great War, a time generally known for its esoteric design. Even the Shield of Second Life has an odd rectangular shape and a seemingly random pattern on it."

Dranus accepted this as memories of his books in the King's Library came to him. The time of the Second Great War was a time of incredible prosperity for Varz and having such extra resources, the people of Varz set out to differentiate themselves, even from each other, in any way that they could. Many of the signs of this time—huge obelisks of contrasting colors, statues of the most insignificant creatures, even castles such as this one—had since been demolished or abandoned. They were often seen as grotesque and antithetical to the theme of loyalty and cohesion among the current peoples of Varz.

"Do you know where we might find Queen Tempest?" He had not thought to directly ask this question yet, suspecting that she would be found in a similar place as Queen Luna.

"She can be found in the Main Hall as far west as one can go in the castle." The Book confirmed. "If you stay near the north wall of the outer court you will find the fastest route there. I would have told you sir, but you do so seem to be enjoying the search." At this little

160

joke the Book chuckled with the sound of moving pages.

"Not as much as I will enjoy commissioning this place's demolition upon returning to Varz." Dranus's tone remained serious. He had not quite gotten back to the relationship of joking with this tool of his. Indeed, he now reflected that the informal relationship they had previously had may have been too tolerant for the King of Varz.

Taking the Book's instructions, he stayed close to the north where many windows and slits gave him sight of the enemy territory across the gap. The place frustrated him such that he half hoped there would be some interesting challenge waiting around the next corner. Each footfall that sent rocks scattering down some unseen cliffside put him on edge but nothing ever came of it. Instead, he entered what appeared to be a natural waiting room with faded murals of a night's sky, but where he supposed prominent constellations should be (given their relative position to the moon painted overhead) there were clouds painted in such a way to mask the constellation without giving away the overall shape. What was the purpose of this?! Why paint the night sky, make pains to map it closely to a specific time of year, and then *cover* the signs of your work with clouds like bloated buffoons lazing about?!

Perhaps the strangest thing he had seen in his life was a massive statue of a simple sheep in the center of the room, reaching up to the ceiling. It was, clearly by design, missing its left ear but, in a way Dranus could not clearly state in words, seemed happy about it? He shook his head of the image and moved on.

It was not until Dranus reached the large iron door leading to the Main Hall that he noticed something was off. He had been so focused on the abnormalities of the place and their import to the history and culture of his people that he had failed to see something that should have been the first thing on his mind. This place had been sitting here stagnant on a dusty windy plain for centuries and a sheen of dust so thick it was practically a crusted shell had settled everywhere, even on the floors.

But here and there were places where the crust had been broken and a more shallow collection of dust had accumulated. Footprints. Recent ones.

Dranus's jaw clenched and his heart sank into his stomach. Finding the massive door rusted in place, he just barely managed to squeeze into the Main Hall while keeping his sword hand on the

Sword of Righted Guard.

What struck him at once was that the place was filled with all manner of junk! Unlike the barren hall of Queen Luna, this place was full of old armor, tables, weapon racks, chairs, and all in a random, meaningless order. There were tables with no chairs, there were groups of chairs all facing away from each other...it occurred to Dranus that perhaps Queen Tempest might have earned the title of the Mad if Queen Luna had not already taken it.

This was but a nuisance as Dranus moved carefully through the dusty, rusty mess and towards the back of the great hall. He followed the same path as another.

Dranus drew his sword as he approached what could only be the corpse of Queen Tempest the Undying, lying prostrate on the floor in front of her throne.

Hesitantly he approached it, expecting it to burst to life like the others had. Would it lock its sorcerous eyes with his like Luna? Would it jump up and take his life before he could register the challenge?

But even as he loomed over the dusty pile of bones and tattered cloth it did not stir. He called the queen's name, even gave the bones a little nudge with his sword and yet there was no response.

"Ah, it is as I feared!" The Book sighed, as if reading his mind. "It seems I was wrong, and the Shield of Second Life has not returned! Without it, there is no magic to wake the dead queen! I am sorry master, but I fear that our quest has been for naught!"

King Dranus was not quite convinced that was the case, however. As much as the Shield was certainly gone, as he had expected upon seeing the footprints, something else caught his eye. In the queen's hand was a ceremonial dagger, the likes of which were still used to that day for blood pacts such as his Union's pact with Kaelel. Most importantly, it showed signs of dried blood on it, and not centuries old blood by his guess. Someone must have come and taken the queen's trial, obtaining the Shield of Second Life...but who could possibly do so? From what he had gathered, only one with Varz blood could claim these items or have any hope of utilizing them. Who from Varz would seek such a thing as this or even have knowledge of it? It was information kept in the Forbidden Texts which only the king could know. It was possible another previous king or queen in recent times had taken the Shield, but then wouldn't they still be alive and ruling? Could a Varz-born bandit have stumbled upon one of the Crosses and unknowingly claimed the Relic? That seemed too many coincidences to consider.

It could not have been his father. He had watched his father die, prepared the body the next day, and seen it buried. No, it could not have been his father. Had his traitorous uncle found the thing, he certainly would have tried again to take the throne, so that seemed unlikely. No matter how untraditional, Dranus concluded that the secret of the Shield must have been shared outside of the Forbidden Texts and that information had made it into the hands of someone who either simply wanted to live a peaceful life for longer, or who had not yet sprung their ambitions in any recognizable way.

King Dranus sheathed his sword and wretched the dagger free from the dead queen's bony hand, still paranoid that the corpse may animate without a moment's notice and try to kill him. As he retraced his steps to leave he was deep in thought as to who might now possess the Shield of Second Life. The Warriors of Pyrán were both mystical and powerful; was it possible one of them had obtained it somehow?

Then, a new thought arose.

"As you say, Book, there is no way to avoid the trial?"

"No. He who desires the power of the Shield will, one way or another, die to attain it."

"What if they take it but *do not* desire its power?"

The Book was unsure. There was only one clear example of someone using the Shield openly and that was Tempest herself.

Consumed by speculation, Dranus approached an outward facing wall and blasted apart a section of stone so to avoid the obnoxious maze upon exiting. It wasn't until he left the still air of the hall and laid eyes on the setting sun in the distance that he noticed another thing that was wrong, or rather, missing.

Upon reaching both Queen Luna and King Vulcan, he had been overcome by the wafting scent of unnatural pine. He retraced his steps only a few feet back into the Main Hall before knowing with certainty: there was no such scent here.

# Chapter 16
## Difficult to Score

Dranus longed for the fanfare of a welcoming entourage as he entered the outskirts of Viél, walking his horse through the curiously abandoned streets. His whereabouts were completely secret and even the messenger who had brought notice of his coming to the admiral didn't recall having come to Viél with a message. So, despite the sharp feeling that he was being withheld of something that was his birthright and his due as king, Dranus wandered the streets in disguise.

A bit of makeup to hide his trademark scar, a change of clothes to alter his body proportions, and a bit of illusion work to cover the seams of his new image and he looked to be a simple messenger. In these times of war, such messengers would be coming and going like a leaf caught in a current.

It was this fact, however, that brought his attention to closed up shops and homes without the smoke of a hearth to warm the residents from the Night Season chill. Where were the people? Had they somehow caught wind of his arrival and prepared something in spite of the necessary secrecy?

For a moment Dranus grinned widely at the thought of a surprise welcome. Men, women, and children of Viél lining the streets cheering his name. A choir singing praise of his recent deeds, perhaps? Viél was a port city so...an offering of the sea's bounty would not go without praise. Traveling rations, even for a king, were hardly a delicacy and Viél was known for its flavorful shellfish in a creamy, buttery sauce with fresh herbs and spice and....

Dranus's daydreaming almost made him miss the steadily increasing sound of cheering crowds roaring in the distance.

He stopped, cautiously, assessing his surroundings more carefully. Among the din of raised voices he could hear the staccato of steel on steel punctuating the roars of the crowd. A battle? No, this was not the sound of war being made. These shouts were joyous, even enraptured, not the sounds of men and women fighting for their lives.

"Book," he began after surveying his immediate surroundings for onlookers, "is there record of some event in Viél today?" Dranus hardly knew what day it was after his sojourn through the wasteland surrounding the Rift. Somewhere in the thick marsh of his depression he'd lost sight of the coming and going of the sun as he sank deeper into the emotional muck of his mind.

"One moment, master. Your kind are not the best at time keeping." The Book's pages flipped against one another in the cramped confines of his travel sack, a motion he'd learned was more for his benefit than a strict necessity of whatever method the Book used to peruse its vast knowledge. "Ah! Here is a flier posted about a week ago for something called the 'Monarch Candidate Festival?'"

"The Monarch Candidate Festival! That's today?!" Dranus reeled, how could he have forgotten?! "That's right, it is already mid-Night Season. The Mask of the Monarch will be in just a few months from now!"

It wasn't quite the festive welcome that he had day-dreamed of, but a Varz festival, and especially a military one, was something no one would willfully miss. He hadn't had the chance to enjoy one up close since becoming king!

With the knowledge that the streets would be completely empty until he reached the festival, Dranus remounted and sped through the dust to the ever-quickening shouts of the festival and the games taking place therein. Soon the brine and salt-tinged wind of the bay filled his nostrils, and a familiar lightness forced its way into his chest, pushing back the dull darkness that had holed up there since leaving Varz.

He found that the local marketplace, typically filled with stalls and booths of all sorts selling wares and fresh fish and even some specialized spell work, had been completely emptied out and the broad space was now brimming with every citizen of Viél in their colorful festival attire, each trying to outshine their neighbors in support of their chosen Candidate. Indeed, the specialist artistry mages would have had their busiest morning of the year sharpening colors of banners and washing out contrasts between nearly matching shades to create glorious flowing artworks that blended their Candidate's colors in a stylish display. Many of the women wore bright, overly pronounced make-up of their colors on their face and nails, and some weaved dyed shreds of fabric into their hair with bells and noise-makers to match. Young men, hopeful to show off their toughness and dedication, were painted nearly head to toe in their colors. Despite the frigid wind of the season, they brandished every bit of skin as was decent for an event like this (which is to say nearly all of it).

This was a side of his people's culture he had so dearly missed participating in. He had almost even forgotten that festivals like this took place. Typically in Varz he would make an appearance to congratulate winners and deliver awards (such as his presence for them to bask in) but miss the festival itself!

Finding himself quickly pressed against a nearly impenetrable wall of festival-goers frantically trying to catch glimpses of the mounted javelin throw, Dranus regrettably dismounted and tied his horse up near several others on the outskirts. Traversing the crowd on horseback would be fine for the king, but not for a messenger.

Instead, he waded forcefully through the crowd brandishing the Varz capital flag and shouting, "Message for the admiral! Make way! By authority of King Dranus VIII, make way!" in a gruff tone that was even alien to his own ears.

The crowd was not as receptive as it should be with a royal messenger making his way through, but they parted reasonably enough for him to reach a raised platform where nobles were seated, watching the games from their privileged comfort. Here he stopped to look about.

Closest to him still was the mounted javelin throw and a young girl, probably 13 years in age, herself nearly covered head to toe in her own colors, held the reigns of her mount in one hand and a long, thin javelin in the other. Her eyes still showed the clear white sclera and dark brown irises of one who had not yet unlocked the constancy of Varz sorcery. Here in the forge of martial excellence and combat, she would devote her entire self to change that before the Mask of the Monarch later in the year.

He watched as the crowd watched, with breath held hushed, as the girl stared hard at the ring hanging more than 20 feet away, just barely wide enough for the javelin to pass through. A soldier more than twice her age would rarely be able to make such a throw while mounted if using skill alone. She would need to recruit her budding sorcerous powers to assist.

Dranus watched closely with the carefully trained will of a Sorcerer King. He could see, or rather, *sense* the subtle warping of reality that amateur magicians created along with their rough spell-making. So far she was dull, focusing her muscle movements and trying to steady her mount.

Suddenly, a spark! A wave wafted around her, and she launched the javelin with a wild shout. The lance went true, spinning in the air and flying in a too straight path! The point of the javelin was dead accurate, but the javelin caught in the hoop!

The crowd erupted into cries and jeers, all aimed at a lavishly dressed woman who sat in a prominent location down the platform from where the king stood. This referee had watched much in the same way as Dranus had, but not for skill coming from the Candidate.

After a moment searching through colored paddles at her side, she raised one showing a vertical stripe of yellow next to a vertical stripe of almost psychedelic blue; the same colors the girl wore like clothes. The girl grinned and the crowd burst into shouts of approval! But then, the referee raised another paddle that held an off-center red cross trimmed with gold on a green background. Cheers and boos alike echoed this motion, and they were all aimed at a boy dressed in the same colors at the edge of the arena. His eyes were as black as the lightless depths of the ocean.

"That was well-played," a noble nearby said softly to his companion. "Varis earned a point of his own without directly making an enemy of the girl."

It was an astute observation. The Monarch Candidate Festival was a test of young members of Varz society's magical prowess, but it was not restricted solely to the games themselves. They were being judged from the moment the sun rose to the moment it set. And although it was strictly forbidden for anyone who had already passed the Mask of the Monarch to interfere in any way, it was encouraged for the Candidates. Obviously, this meant that Candidates who had already unlocked The Eyes since last year's Mask festival held a distinct advantage. Still, the girl had mustered enough magic to guide a difficult shot. It was admirable for someone who was still working towards The Eyes and had this Varis made her miss, the judges may have scored this as disrespectful...or as particularly cunning. One had to know the disposition of the referees for each contest, another important aspect of Varz society.

"Oi, messenger! If you've a message to deliver, be about it, otherwise take off!" A noble shouted at him from nearby. Dranus resisted the immediate impulse to skewer the man where he sat and laugh in the faces of the others while he dripped the noble's fresh, warm blood from his fingertips.

"Pardon, d'y'know where Admiral O'cule watches from?" Dranus imitated a strong accent from the eastern province of Vakkar, holding his rage at bay through strength of will alone.

"The duels will start soon by the shore; the admiral will likely be about there." The noble changed his tone when Dranus showed the Varz crest he held by his side. A messenger bearing a message from the king himself demanded much greater respect than a common messenger. Were Dranus actually the person he portrayed, the noble may have just ruined his entire house in a moment of drunken rudeness. Fortunately for him, Dranus did not immediately recognize the man and was in a hurry to enjoy the festival.

"Gratitude," Dranus said.

"With apologies," the man replied, bowing his head.

The duels would be the most hotly contested and closely watched game of the day. Sure, some young ones already had goals to go into the Archer's Brigade and would spend all of their time practicing for those events, or the same for the Mounted Forces, but most wanted the glory associated with rising through the ranks of the Armed Forces. To do this, they would need to be masters of a type of one-on-one combat that honed Varz warriors into efficient killers.

Dranus made his way to the shore and then skirted the outside of the gathered crowd to where several armed guards, sober and frustrated, stood next to a ramp leading up some scaffolding that had been erected for the day.

With little more than a flash of the Varz crest, Dranus was let through and ascended the zigzagging ramps to where the high officers of the Varz navy sat in conversation around a famous Den brew prepared specially for them and specially for this day.

Before approaching the lively Admiral O'cule, who stood, leaning precariously against a guard rail of bamboo, Dranus stayed out of sight to survey the duels.

Opposite the ring where Candidates would soon do battle from him was a tall, broad-shouldered teenage boy with wickedly sharp Sorcerous Eyes. Dranus vaguely recognized the crimson swordfish insignia on the teal flag that flapped above the boy. He had heard mention of a once in a generation genius of magic that had also, by pure chance, emerged into adulthood ahead of his cohort. At just 12 years or so he had the built body of a 16-year-old that had trained every day of his teenage years. Word had made it to the capital that the boy had even started his training later than most, going from novice to unlocking The Eyes in just three years! He would be favorite for this Candidate festival by far and potentially have an honored seat at this year's Mask festival.

Shockingly, the boy, announcing his name as Vikra (VIHK-rah), entered the ring first. Hadn't he a pass for the first rounds as favorite? Maybe he just wanted the warm-up. That could be a tactical move that might earn him a point in the eyes of the right referee. A warrior of Varz knew to never underestimate any opponent, no matter how strong they might think themselves.

From down the scaffolding he heard O'cule jumping in place, making the whole structure shake uncomfortably.

"Make him fight Rafe (RAYF)! Make him fight Rafe!" O'cule shouted through cupped hands at the organizers below.

Although the schedule was mostly predetermined, someone in O'cule's position could certainly demand an alteration. He was technically High Referee, after all.

Following the admiral's order, a massive young man emerged from just below Dranus, draped in a cloak of pea green teardrop shapes emanating outward from a white sun on a black background. Rafe was an oddity at first sight. This boy was clearly older than the rest, maybe even aged into early adulthood, but his eyes were still the normal white and hazel of his birth. In a sense, he would be dubbed either a fraud, hiding his potential for years, or a failure, lacking the skill or dedication to unlock The Eyes even so late in his adolescence. But what he lacked in sorcerous prowess, he more than made up for in physical form.

As Rafe tore off his cloak to be fitted with padded armor for the duel, the body of a seasoned war veteran stood where that of a greenhorn boy should be. He was all glistening musculature, obviously oiled for spectacle, and his height was astounding. He might be upward of a foot taller than his opponent!

169

O'cule had been clever in deciding on this match. This would pit one extreme, a genius sorcerer with an inferior body, against the opposite extreme. Although unlocking The Eyes was a prerequisite for consideration in the Varz military, Rafe looked as though he could have been inducted that day. This would be an excellent test for the young sorcerer and a chance at glorious redemption for the older brute.

Dranus grinned wildly to himself, his heart beginning to rush with excitement.

Noticing the flag Dranus carried, a servant quietly offered him a drink and the king took it without thinking.

In just a few moments, the two boys met in the center of the ring with all signs of sport gone from their expressions. To them, this was a battle to the death in practice. In reality, it was a battle that could very well decide their futures in Varz. Further, they both knew the rules and how many of the other Candidates would be watching.

And how many would be *more than watching*.

Along with their provided padded armor, each boy wielded a buckler shield and a dulled sword with a cap on the tip. As soon as the ring of metal on metal from their swords touching sounded, they would fight within these confines until either one could fight no more, or one had secured a 'killing blow.'

The two approached each other near the center of the ring carefully. Vikra held his sword out at length, trying to keep as much distance between him and the larger boy as possible. Rafe, on the other hand, kept his sword close. When he was in range and could tell the younger boy wouldn't get any closer, they locked eyes and Rafe nodded, extending his sword slowly.

A clink of the blade flats and the battle swung wildly into the ruckus of cheering and intense focus.

Rafe thrust straight from the meeting of their blades; an unconventional start that was frowned upon but not against the rules. Vikra seemed to have expected this as a possibility and swept the incoming thrust to the side with his wooden buckler, an unexpected metallic clack resonating from the collision.

Both boys swept outward, putting space between them and regaining their posture.

Dranus could see that, while potentially scoring Rafe negative points, that move was his best shot at winning this duel. From even footing he was at a great disadvantage.

They circled one another slowly in a battle pose. Vikra had the distinct advantage magically, but instead of using this, he closed in slowly testing the strength of his grip against that of his opponents. Their blades came together gingerly multiple times and each time Vikra's was the one knocked away. He clearly couldn't match the larger boy in pure strength.

Then, a dull clunk sounded, and Rafe's blade flew away from the collision while Vikra's remained motionless. Both boys expressed quick shock, but Vikra took advantage first. He pushed off his back foot, spinning into a backhand slash at the off-foot Rafe, but the bigger boy dove out of the way, scrambling quickly to his feet. His eyes shifted around the arena quickly then settled again on his opponent.

Standing up a little straighter, Rafe tore off his buckler and took his sword in both hands.

True, Rafe's large frame and strength made a two-handed broadsword the most suitable weapon for him, but that was not the weapon he held. At least, it hadn't been when they started.

Suddenly Rafe was hefting a sword nearly as tall as Vikra with both hands, wrapping a leather thong around his right wrist.

This was advanced sorcery, Dranus thought. This couldn't be achieved by someone of Rafe's level. He must have forged an agreement with others that assisted him in tandem. That was only natural, because while Rafe could not offer magical assistance in return, if he eliminated Vikra from the tournament then everyone else's chance at coming out on top increased substantially.

The king scanned the crowd carefully. One boy with The Eyes had increased the density of the metal. A teenage girl was pressing that metal into a larger blade. A third with The Eyes balanced the two, no small task for a novice.

However, this pause gave Vikra ample time to prepare as well, and he was nearly the equal of the other three in the crowd combined. Subtly, almost imperceptibly, Vikra's sword *changed,* and he too cast aside his buckler and took a wide stance.

In the king's estimation, Rafe had two paths to victory: to dominate with his overwhelming strength, or to take advantage of sorcery's main weakness. Unfortunately, one could not do both. Building his strength took time and stillness, the two things an

171

inferior sorcerer should try and rob from their opponent. Also unfortunately, it appeared that Rafe chose incorrectly.

Perhaps in realization of this fact, Rafe leapt forward with a massive overhead swing of his great sword, howling like a gust of wind through a tunnel.

Vikra dodged to the side, knowing he could not parry the blow, but tapped his sword against the side of Rafe's as he did so.

Rafe continued his barrage, swinging the full might of his sword expertly so that Vikra must leap out of the way and thus lose any chance at counterattack.

From the vantage point of the stands above, Dranus could see that he was trying to corner him and was at least proficient at doing so. However, each time Vikra dodged, he made increasingly perilous attempts to touch his blade against that of his opponents.

Finally, Vikra was cornered in a tight space, both of the boys panting from exertion. Rafe's wide stance and far-reaching blade made the tight space inescapable, and he prepared for another crushing blow.

This time, instead of moving to dodge, Vikra took an offensive posture and swung his sword with all his might against the larger boy and the larger sword. But incredibly, Rafe's sword broke in two where Vikra's made contact near the guard! The detached piece of the sword spun off dangerously, spewing shards of steel like spittle from the swords roar.

Suddenly, everything was stopped.

The edge of Rafe's detached blade hovered an almost immeasurable distance from Vikra's head, threatening to split his skull with just another moment of freedom. The larger boy, too, was frozen, the capped tip of Vikra's sword expertly positioned at his throat following the disorienting blow he had made.

Dranus looked to the referee, who looked up at Admiral O'cule. The man's hands gripped the banister tightly, his knuckles bleached white with strain. Then he sighed and both swords fell to the ground, set free but altered.

"Th-thank you, admiral!" The referee stammered. It was his job to prevent potential catastrophes such as this, but he had apparently not quite figured out what Vikra was planning and hadn't anticipated that this might happen. The man motioned that the match was over.

Admiral O'cule nodded and smiled, then whispered to a

messenger who would go and explain what had happened to the judges who hadn't noticed.

Dranus smirked at the young man that was the leader of his navy. Anticipating what Vikra had done, increasing the carbon content of Vikra's magically unstable sword so it would break, was not necessarily exemplary for someone of O'cule's standing. That said, stopping the ensuing danger in such a small fraction of time was certainly impressive.

The same could be said of Vikra. The boy had quickly surmised what was happening to Rafe's sword and identified a weakness. Rafe's sword was being balanced in an unnatural state with sorcery, but only a few features of it were being altered. With the added pressure needed to make the blade physically larger, Vikra's best chance at overcoming it was to physically compromise the sword itself and he had chosen likely the most reliable way to do so in slowly raising the levels of carbon in the metal.

Rafe's fractured sword snapped back to its real state, carbon levels and all, and the girl who had balanced the other two spells fainted in the crowd.

This would be a difficult duel to score for all involved, but it would likely set the tone for the rest of the day.

A light tap on his shoulder made Dranus turn abruptly, almost slamming his elbow into the shorter admiral's chest.

"Woah! Peace, messenger." O'cule smirked in recognition. "I can take your message upon my ship, if you please."

Resisting the urge to make a flashy appearance and create spectacle to add to the festival, Dranus stayed in character, nodding apologetically and following O'cule down the ramp from the scaffolding.

After weaving easily through the crowds, the people parting for the admiral in his shining cerulean armor, they came to a complex system of interconnected docks and boarded the Varz flagship, *The Dawn's Fury*.

Once on board, Dranus dropped his guise, but held O'cule back from descending below decks for privacy.

"My king? Do you not wish to rest after your long journey? Perhaps a brew to help you recover?" O'cule raised a brow and his lips frowned.

"The festival has invigorated me! Our minds are primed for battle and strategy, we should use that." Dranus lectured calmly, feeling his heart still pounding. His blood still surged with the ultra-focus of a sorcerer in battle: perceiving every minute detail from moment to moment, understanding it all, and bending it to his will.

In short order, a few soldiers had retrieved the king's belongings from his mount and Dranus picked out a long, wrapped bundle. The thick wool fell away with little effort and revealed the polished bronze and sparkling gems of the Staff of the South Star.

Wasting no time, the thud of staff against wooden planks broke the din of gull caws and creaking timbers. A ghastly blue man appeared in a somewhat rustic version of the armor that Admiral O'cule wore. O'cule, having never been up close with the astral warriors, was overtly amazed by this sight and shook the man's hand first with great caution, as if he expected the specter to be intangible, and then with great fervor when he felt the very real texture of the man's rough hand.

"Aha! It is as the king said! You are my distant ancestor Admiral Burgiss! It is a great honor to meet you, sir! A great honor indeed!" Dranus marveled to himself how even a man such as O'cule, who was one of the liveliest men he knew, had changed since his discovery of the Book.

Burgiss, who was much more formal than his distant descendant, took the compliment but made little of it. He had been summoned by his master once more and could sense that this time his services would be needed.

Just as O'cule appeared to load himself with a barrage of questions, the Magemaster, Captain of Naval Sorcery, crossed a gangway and boarded the flagship. With him there, they formed a makeshift Naval Council, and the agitated admiral withheld his curiosity with some effort, like swallowing a difficult medicine he knew was good for him but hated. He replaced questions with thoughts of the future and ready-making plans.

The war table had been brought up by a few sailors in sparkling blue and placed on the high poop deck, which was abandoned save for the council and two of O'cule's trusted guards at the stairways.

The Magemaster was the first to speak up as he approached the table covered in maps of the Middle Sea.

"The Shieran forces have set up a loose military blockade

perpendicular to the shore where our lands meet those of Arendrum. They are set up in a single dense line of battle that will be well prepared for engagements. Unfortunately, the line extends out into deep waters so that taking our navy that far out would leave us at the mercy of the unpredictable tides of the north. Even then we might be spotted."

Admiral O'cule was looking hard at a map which showed the location of the blockade. The line of ships started just far enough away from the coast so that the horizon hid their leading ships, but the resulting gap was not enough space to sneak a navy through. The other end was no better; it was said that in the ancient sinking of Shiera, the tides of the north had been disturbed and now flowed in unpredictable directions, steering more than a few daring ships to a grave at sea.

"This may actually play to our advantage," O'cule began. "Our best course of action is to sneak to the Shieran capital city and take it unaware. A blockade that long means that their forces back home must be very thin." King Dranus also studied the map, already concocting a plan.

"The South Star Fleet can be taken by any means my king, even by land, until you reach the capital." Admiral Burgiss voiced what the others didn't dare. Despite the difference in rules of decorum in a war council, Dranus rather appreciated that others voiced their opinions instead of simply leading Dranus to the point himself and waiting for him to make it.

"An approach by land will take time that we don't have. Rather, we should send the king with a light crew on a disguised fishing vessel, sail her close to shore to avoid the blockade and fly Arendrum colors. This will allow us to use a fast ship and transport the South Star Fleet safely by sea so that they may be deployed in defense or in taking the capital." Admiral O'cule moved figures on the map deftly, displaying his unusual cunning at naval strategy. Could any naval commander ever predict that an entire fleet would be smuggled past their blockade aboard a single ship? Even Admiral Burgiss, despite his earlier annoyance, had to acknowledge the quick thinking of his progeny.

"Ah, you really are my descendant...for a moment I had begun to question it." The stern blue features of the ancient admiral cracked briefly into a smile.

"It's settled then." Dranus was impatient to begin. "Offer twice the value of the fastest vessel and crew her by the end of the week. I'll leave after a brief rest." Though the trip there had been secured, Dranus was still considering what should be done with the blockade in the back of his mind. Once they heard that the capital was sacked they would rush back to give aid. Were the ships and sailors of the South Star not contingent on the light of the South Star, he could hold such a position with ease. But the South Star Navy could not hold ground; at certain times of the day it would just be Dranus against every man and woman of Shiera.

"I'll give the order sire, but I don't think they'll be very keen to take our money! People have been trying to offer their vessels for our use since hearing of the war effort! All of the captains in the harbor are trying to join our forces." The Magemaster had been in Viél since the war began. If anyone were to know of the fastest ship in the harbor, he would.

Dranus smiled a little at this news.

"Well, we don't need any civilian ships holding us back, but we will take the fastest ship we can find. Give the order."

The Magemaster nodded and left to speak with whatever sailors he could find not at the festival about opinions on the fastest ship in the port, though he had an idea already.

Admiral Burgiss made a stern salute and bowed. "My king, I would speak with you on the capabilities and limitations of my fleet when it suits you." To which Dranus nodded, matching the stern expression the man made before tapping the Staff again to recall the admiral.

Finally, Admiral O'cule turned and smirked, appreciating his king and the efficiency with which they had settled on a course of action.

"Now," Dranus smiled back as night gradually approached and with it a cold wind from the sea, "about that drink."

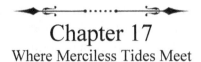

# Chapter 17
## Where Merciless Tides Meet

By the end of the young month, all of the necessary preparations were made and the king set sail early one morning with a small crew of thirty men aboard a light merchant ship, graciously donated by one of the richest traders in the city. The trader had requested only that his deed be remembered by the people of Varz, and Dranus saw it done.

Dranus stood at the bow, sniffing at the briny wind, as they left sight of the inlet where Viél lay. Shortly after, they passed by the major bulk of the Varz navy at anchor, resting like a nautical beast just peaking above the crest of waves. Beneath was not the unthinkable mass of sea giants and mythical creatures, as this was not where the Varz navy's strength hid. It was far from the size of the Shieran navy, which boasted the largest armada in the eastern world, but it was extremely well equipped for a military so deep into the swaddled warmth of peacetime. If worse came to worst, they could hold off the Shieran navy until their plan was set in motion.

Keeping close to the shore meant their journey would be long, but keeping incognito was their primary objective. To this purpose they had outfitted the vessel with forged flags and drapes of Arendrum forest green and all the normal trappings of an Arendrum trading vessel: long booms with grapplers on the end typically used to brace ships at anchor against the cliffsides of Arendrum's shores and a large rock, supposedly from their favorite stretch of land. By late afternoon they had reached the border between Varz and Shiera where to the east could be seen the closing point of the Discidia Rift and to the west was the Shieran blockade. Smaller scouting ships patrolled the area and approached them as they knew would happen. Sorcery would hide their distinctive features, but their guile would decide if they succeeded here or had to force their way through.

With Dranus pretending to be too sick to wake below decks, his crew explained how they had been caught in Draxon's Bay at the sudden onset of the war. They had been in hiding in a sheltered cove for weeks before they grew desperate enough to try a mad dash to the border. After receiving some supplies in exchange for a wildly inaccurate report of the state of the Varz navy, they were released, but not without a scout following them until it had to turn back to join the blockade.

Once they were comfortably away from the blockade, King Dranus emerged from below deck with the Staff of the South Star in his left hand and the Sword of Righted Guard at his hip. He left the Book below in his chambers because, like it had always done, its odd form of speech and near human characteristics made the men uneasy. It was inconsequential, however, for what came next was something he had prepared for since he was a child. The Book contained great knowledge, but it had not the instincts of the merciless monarchs of Varz.

The small ship certainly proved to be one of great speed and by nightfall they had reached a safe anchorage on the other side of the blockade.

Now there was only to wait.

They would not be advancing towards the Shieran capital as planned, but instead had come up with an altogether different strategy. For the time being there would be only the tension of looming bloodshed, the mindless repetition of plans and contingencies committed to the deepest part of Dranus's consciousness, and the regular moan and creak of a ship waiting to return to motion.

\*       \*       \*

At the center of the massive blockade was the Shieran flagship, the *Fire's Folly*, which was on a much different scale from almost any other ship in the world. To say it was large would be to say the ocean was deep or the sky wide; it was true but wholly inadequate. The ship was a fully man-made, that is to say without the assistance of sorcery, dreadnaught of several layered decks which rose high out of the water like an inverted ziggurat but oblong instead of square. It was well armed with pivoting catapults and shielded by interlocking plates of light metal and treated wooden planks that resisted fire, earning it its name. The highest deck was such that no other ship in the world could look down on it and thus taking such a ship had to start from the bottom up...a difficult task even for the crew of multiple ships. With all of the archers and sailors on board next to the engineers and support crew, it was almost a small city drifting through the sea. It was the pride of Shiera and was feared even by Varz navymen.

Standing above the forecastle towards the starboard rail was a single guard, as there was one above the poop deck at the stern, as there were in the crow's nests, and as there were on every ship along the blockade. As the Night Season had all but fully arrived in the Five Realms, the man was shivering, huddled next to a struggling open flame.

"Cold night like this... 'sa real shame I have guard duty...real pain, it is." He mumbled to no one in particular.

The man rubbed his hands together and stared at the fire, hoping if he looked at it long enough he would be warm like it was. From the corner of his eye he thought he caught a glimpse of a light to the north. Reinforcements? Someone come to send a message to the flagship? The faint glimmer disappeared but somehow it seemed there was something that remained. The sailor stared hard at the black horizon, walking closer to the starboard rail and squinting, trying to make out any faint outlines. Staring at the flame had ruined his night vision and as he tried to will his pupils to dilate he could do nothing but look dumbly into the darkness.

"What's out there?" The sailor grimaced; it was too early for anything less than an urgent message...had someone gotten around the blockade? Impossible! Theirs was the greatest navy in the world!

Turning his back to the north, a strong cold wind took his breath away from the south. He braved the gale with eyes clenched shut, but when he opened his eyes something had changed.

The South Star began to peak above the horizon. Its scarlet light rippled across the surface of the sea like a velvet runway laid out to welcome the false dawn. It was always disconcerting...a new sun in the sky after a lifetime of just one. Not to mention the reports from the Rift of the ghostly army it seemed to animate.

He jumped suddenly as he heard the loud splash of something big landing in the water. He whirled and reached for his bell to sound for man overboard but instead froze at the sight of another glimmer of light in the darkness.

This time he could see better in the pre-dawn light but still had to squint. The line of crimson raced towards the distant light and revealed, for a moment, a single ship. Then, as if bouncing off the line of the horizon, a sheet of blue light rippled back towards them...but this light was in the shape of ships. Dozens of ships!

Another barely visible object fell into the water some fifty yards away; closer than the last.

"No...can't be...." He stumbled as fear rose up along the surface of his skin, raising every hair on his head.

Practically falling on himself, the guard moved to a different, much larger bell and took the rope in both hands. The last thing he saw before bowing to ring the bell as hard as he could, he saw a burning rain of hellfire, all pulsing cerulean and purple in the mixing lights of the false dawn. And it came from the north...from the direction of their homeland.

They were doomed, he thought.

"All hands!! To stations! Alert! Alert! Battle Stations!" The bell *dong*-ed loud and deep, carrying over the open water and on every ship in a wave from the center a similar bell rang, heralding the coming battle.

In unison the balls of fire came down, striking ships all around the *Fire's Folly* though most still missed their targets. All around the ships heeled from the impact and burst into hungry flames fed by the south wind.

In the lull between volleys all of the crews had awakened. Fortunately for them, this was an active war zone and as a standing order the sailors had been fully dressed for just such an emergency. Within minutes the blockade was alive with light and panicking sailors, captains, and even the admiral of the Shieran Navy trying to surmise what could possibly be happening.

"How have they got around us? Is it Varz?!" The admiral barked orders left and right as he reached the top deck of the *Fire's Folly*, trying to get a hold on the situation. With the dawning light of the South Star the dim outlines of two wide ranks of glowing blue ships could be seen in the distance, all alight with ghoulish, unnatural flame as they prepared their next barrage.

"Just like the soldiers at the battle of the Rift...it must be that unnatural army again! But how did they skirt our blockade?!" His hesitations aside, the admiral chose swiftness rather than caution.

"We have the windward gage; outer ranks hold position! Divisions three through seven to the Cup Formation, don't let them spread out and surround them." The orders traveled up the crow's nest where flags relayed information between ships along the blockade. From their position upwind they could initiate easily, closing the gap with their enemies quickly. In the experienced admiral's eye it appeared the enemy was small and comprised mainly of long-range ships, though they likely housed a number of marines for anti-boarding maneuvers as well.

"Admiral! To the South!" A sailor pointed to the south where now several more torches were being lit and the mass of the Varz navy came into view. The blockade, thinly spread and caught unawares, was surrounded by both the windward naval forces of Varz and a flanking force of unknown properties!

"We must act as we can! All ships advance towards those at the north, use the wind to wrap westward and contain the front while moving to take the enemy flagship! We must break their line of battle and regroup before we can be caught from the south. Board and capture as many of those ghost ships as you can, we may be able to use them to our advantage!"

Aboard *The Night's Wrath*, the flagship of the South Star Fleet, King Dranus watched the blockade's movements. The coordination he had set up with Admiral O'cule was perfectly executed. The enemy would likely separate into two lines: a larger force to hold the Varz navy at bay, using the brute power of the enemy's flagship to hold, and a smaller force thinking they could rush the artillery quickly and overpower them with the wind at their backs. They would not be entirely mistaken. The South Star Fleet consisted of old, outdated vessels and the winds were strong this morning in their favor. His vessels were large and cumbersome, meant for siege rather than battle on the open sea, and unable to maneuver quickly. They were of a fair number but were scant compared to the behemoth of the Shieran navy with their ships estimated to be nearing one hundred; more than the Varz navy and South Star Fleet combined.

"My king," Admiral Burgiss stood next to him, watching closely through a looking glass as ephemeral as his body, "the enemy line is separating but their center is headed this way."

The battle-worn admiral was a sight to behold. It was as if he returned to his days in the First Great War, his grin wide and his eyes alive. In between reports he joined in on a song to the old Gods of the sea which echoed from the lips of every man aboard the South Star ships. The Staff itself seemed occasionally to join in the battle song though the dark chanting that emitted from the pulsating gem gave the merry cheer a more solemn harmony.

"Within expectation. Take your lead, admiral." Dranus gave the man free reign over his own navy. He knew them best and would use them most efficiently.

The songs the South Star sailors sang lulled in regular intervals for changes in the tune. Admiral Burgiss took advantage of one such lull and shouted: "Queen, lay me down!"

His ship echoed the call and the song changed to a slower, lolling tune with the call of 'Queen, lay me down!' and response of 'Lay me down, queen!' Responding to the song, the entire astral fleet shifted at once, lowering catapults and raising sails that billowed towards the south, ignoring the winds of this plane.

In the south, the Varz forces advanced in an attacking formation. With a strong back line furthest south, *The Dawn's Fury* held the center flanked by ships on each side. Ahead of these lines were the main spearhead of the Varz navy, the Titan Ships. Spread like three wide-stretched prongs of a trident they advanced quickly. With the wind in their two short sails and the rowing power of the men inside the boats they were bearing down on the enemy with great speed.

The Titan Ships were a marvel of Varz engineering and had not been seen by an enemy before this time. They were shallow and simple: a bottom deck for rowers and ballast, a middle deck where the artillery was held, and a top deck that was not a deck at all. Instead they were roofed with hard iron plates and jagged spikes painted as though they dripped with enemy blood. These were ships made for battle and battle alone.

The Titan artillery was not like those of other ships; instead of launching projectiles in the air, they had catapults which spun on a vertical axis and launched heavy lead balls horizontally as broadside fire. For this reason they were built small for quick movement and intricate formations to get between enemy ships and into raking positions.

These were willed by Admiral O'cule who led from *The Dawn's*

*Fury* as it surged in behind the Titan Ships, a hungry shark behind its tortoise vanguard.

Upon *The Night's Wrath* King Dranus tried to keep a frown from his face. The enemy was acting out of line with his expectations and they were doing so with impressive speed. Impressive for Lessers, anyway. The South Star Fleet would be decimated by a full-frontal attack of the enemy, and he could not afford to sustain so many casualties. Admiral Burgiss had confirmed that the ships were like any other, except that they could not be repaired. Whatever ships sank here were lost to him like any other.

Remaining calm, he glanced at the admiral who held an almost tangible presence of battle lust in an aura around his person. His brow was more furrowed now; he had not commented on the massive Shieran flagship. In another lull he continued the song 'Queen, lay me down' which had become more of a hum as the wind drowned out the voices, but changed the key of the song.

Some ships sped up and some slowed down until the ranks of ships formed a triangle with the long edge facing the oncoming enemy to the south and *The Night's Wrath* at the northern corner. At first they had moved to meet the enemy, engaging them as closely to the Varz navy as possible, but now they lowered sails and turned to meet the enemy. Glowing sapphire armor phased onto the bodies of the sailors and archaic curved shields and swords appeared in their hands. Their song had changed into a simple repetitive call and response, cleverly bolstered by the sorcery of every man and woman in the fleet to sound as if thousands upon thousands sang along.

"Call the isles!" a few select voices called first.

"SINK THE ISLES!" thundered across the water, almost deafening even to Dranus's ears.

The King of Varz knew of this call and grinned at the cruel irony. The Shieran forces would likely not know this, but this battle cry referenced the ancient sinking of Shiera, which some of these revived sailors may have actually *seen* firsthand!

There was a tense stillness that hung in the air in between calls. Without the sound of men preparing catapults and clambering about to change sails, a sort of readied calm spread.

Dranus stood on the upper deck looking out at the battle and the movement of the ships. From his experience in strategy he saw everything in formations, movements, and common tactics from books he had studied a hundred times over. Everywhere were patterns that he recognized. It was as though he could see various outcomes before they happened, calculating the likelihood of each one independently and deciding moment by moment what would happen. Like well carved pieces on a table, he could see every opening, every opportunity, every chance for victory. And as the game changed, so too did the king's mindset.

Just as he prepared his mind to spread a strengthening spell with the admiral's assistance, he stopped. What they needed on this front was not victory, but time.

The enemy was closing in rapidly and the king had to make a decision.

"You're sure this will work?" He checked with the South Star admiral, as he had done time and time again.

The admiral was stern and decisive. "The Staff will respond to your will, whatever that may be."

When the king looked back out to the water his forces were holding steady, allowing more and more enemy ships to enter their formation and spreading to create ample room. As he had expected, the Shieran admiral knew better than to ram and become entangled in the generally larger ships and simply moved swiftly, raking ships with fire arrows and capsules of oil. Fortunately for him, it appeared the admiral hoped to take at least a few ships captive for study so the damage was less than it could have been.

The ranks of Shieran ships suffused their formation, the enemy flagship dwarfing the South Star ships which barely reached the middle deck. While glowering archers returned fire at the passing ships while the South Star Fleet held firm, they depended on their large size and sturdiness to not simply collapse at the doubling to their lower decks.

Soldiers and marines raised shields and put out fires as efficiently as they could, their song quieted. But as the enemy launched their hooks and laid their planks to board, the ghost soldiers retreated to the innards of their ships. In a matter of minutes, most of the glowing ships were crawling with Shieran soldiers in their sea-green armor like rusted copper. They covered all the weather decks, entered the lower depths, and filled the ships with their number. Some of them cheered as though they had captured a ship abandoned by its crew.

But other areas of the formation were disquieted by this. Why posture? Why sing songs of battle and then retreat? And more importantly, how?!

King Dranus judged the timing to be right from the merchant ship he had retreated to and focused his mind on the task at hand; already he had used the Staff in an abnormal way, he could do so again.

With a wild howl the King of Varz slammed the Staff of the South Star to the deck with both hands and the South Star Fleet vanished in an instant!

As if in such disbelief to defy nature the enemy soldiers hung in the air over the water, bewildered by something their minds could not comprehend.

And then they fell into the freezing waters of the Middle Sea, armor and all.

The sea was suddenly darker, missing the blueish light mixing with the red of the South Star.

The sea was suddenly louder, now filled with the shouts of drowning sailors and the crews that watched on in horror.

Nearly a fifth of the Shieran Navy had set ships to board and now they were reduced to mere skeleton crews who struggled just to maintain order and the keeling of their vessels as the waves reacted to the sudden absence of ships that were once there.

By this time the Titan Ships had caught up with the enemy rear and wove between the back ranks, taking advantage of the heel which revealed the enemy undersides to blast holes in ships in quick succession. A rain of arrows and oil slicked off the solid rounded tops of the Titans. A few of the smaller vessels were forced into the larger ships and were quickly submerged, sinking under their own weight and inability to dredge water. Still they kept moving forward, seeking to relieve the merchant ship that housed their defenseless king as the Shieran flagship threated to crush it almost in passing.

The Varz navy moved through that of the Shierans quickly, but their focus on the center of the massive formation made it so that many enemy ships broke to the west and east, seeking to avoid the deadly Titan Ships. *The Night's Wrath* surged forward to find the small merchant vessel almost visibly pulsating with the combined magic of the king and a few ethereal sailors on the deck. It moved with unnatural speed with the wind in its sails and the force of rowers. It kept a healthy distance from the lumbering Shieran flagship and the few ships that trailed behind it.

Just as suddenly as the South Star Fleet had vanished, a portion of it reappeared between the king's ship and the enemy flagship. Dozens of Shieran vessels had escaped, but they left behind their greatest treasure and a few ships with it. Those were surrounded on all sides by Varz ships from two different eras.

The slower Varz forces that trailed in behind the Titan Ships made short work of the crippled ships left in the battle's wake. Not a soul was saved, no ship was left unsunk. A few managed to ram their own ships into those of Varz but even if a ship or two was lost here and there, the crews were easily rescued and the Varz fleet sustained very few casualties.

Rather than chase down the surviving ships, the two fleets consolidated around the captured flagship.

But the behemoth would not die without bearing its fangs.

The Shieran flagship had dropped several massive anchors and, before it could be reached, let fly a deluge of metal shod stones and guttering fireballs in every direction. Many ships were struck and immediately stopped to deal with the damages. Some Varz ships simply burst into flame and were consumed by the greedy ocean in a matter of moments. Approaching the thing directly was suicide for any normal ship and many of the zealous Varz navy learned this the hard way.

However, the Titan Ships took the fireballs and heavy stones as hardly more than an inconvenience as they bounced harmlessly off of the iron roofing. Swiftly, they surrounded the *Fire's Folly* and were tearing into the protected hull with all they had, using what magic they had to try and peel away the protective plating or weaken it from afar. But the pride of the Shieran Navy was incredibly strong and refused to be downed.

King Dranus looked on in wonder, taking note of every feature and tucking it away in his memory. Had they faced this Shieran force on even terms with this flagship at their head, they would have been annihilated! It turned out that the Shierans' biggest weakness was their cowardice. But still, a beast was most dangerous when it had nowhere to run. They had all underestimated this marvel.

Slowly, methodically, the South Star Fleet bombarded the flagship from a distance and as fires grew and the lower ranks took on water, the onslaught of enemy fire subsided.

Taking this moment, the two flagships ran upside of the *Fire's Folly* along with some of the other Varz ships and secured a line to one of the middle decks. Once they had secured planks and ropes the Varz and South Star marines flooded the enemy vessel with orders to take no quarter. King Dranus himself joined in the advance, drawing the Sword of Righted Guard and making his way through the bowels of the beast, seeking its hidden heart.

The king burst into the melee on the highest deck, his sword deflecting a blow that he followed with a boot. Admiral O'cule killed the man as if he were simply resting the tip of his sword on the deck and the man had just been in the way. The two men grinned wildly at one another. Dranus scanned the layout of the upper decks and found a set of stairways that were heavily guarded, holding off many more Varz marines. Among the frenzied warriors trying to break through, one cried to his fellow folk...

"For the Wife of the King! For Commander Kaelel!" Not a soul among the Varz warriors held their breath; all repeated the cry. Even Dranus, who felt his body weaken and shiver by the cry, screamed his fury. And it was fury that grasped him then, in response to this cry; such vile, insensate fury. While he may have blamed the Book for his wife's death, it was the warriors of the Four Realms that were the direct cause of her death. The people of Varz were ever a vengeful ilk and Dranus's lust for vengeance came rushing to the surface.

Dranus glared at the stairways, hating them. His rage perverted the timbers and they buckled under his sorcerous gaze. The enemies protecting them fell and screamed as they died. He grinned and waved for ladders to be brought forward.

Dranus himself was the first up the ladder and was met by the final contingent of the flagship's warriors. He found a certain morbid glee from taking these men's lives, theirs was not the blood of those who had killed his wife, but then those would die at his hand too. He knew this to be the battle haze that his ancestors had felt, enraptured by the death and gore, and relishing the superiority of their skill and sorcery. But with every empty stare that met him at the tip of his blade came a vision of his deceased wife.

And with that, a guttural madness.

Finally, the men stopped resisting and dropped their swords, the enemy admiral came forward and appeared at the head of his force.

Dranus did not stop the slaughter, cutting down weaponless soldiers as they fled.

"Stop your assault people of Varz! We surrender! Take the ship, it is your prize, and make us your prisoners, we will resist no more." The admiral was dignified in spite of his panic. By normal standards King Dranus would be compelled to accept his surrender. The admiral had led well and he no doubt held valuable intelligence.

But this had long since ceased to be a battle in a war following an honorable code. This was a vengeance-driven massacre.

The king stomped towards the defeated leader, his dark eyes set and seeping with rage. The man put his hands forward to be taken away. The king only raised his sword.

"You must accept my surrender!" Terror riddled the enemy admiral's features.

"I am King of Varz! I MUST do nothing!" With purpose he stabbed the sharp edge of the Sword of Righted Guard down into the man's throat and into his center, skewering the honorable man like a pig on a spit.

"Kill them all, burn the ship." It was a simple order and the Varz sailors filled it with glee. Dranus tugged his sword from the admiral's corpse and returned to the flagship to meet with his admirals, his blood-lust slated for the moment.

"The flagship sacrificed herself to let the rest of their forces retreat. We managed to sink many through our charge, but we estimate that a little more than half of their ships have made it away." Admiral Burgiss, who technically held rank over the younger Admiral O'cule, handed the king a hastily written report giving the predicted numbers.

Dranus was in no mood to receive such a thing and in stride took it, handed it to O'cule, and passed the pair en route to his personal chambers.

"No matter, we will have their lives in time."

Overall, a large portion of the deployed Shieran forces had been destroyed. The number of sailors and soldiers lost was even greater than the loss of their ships. But the Varz navy had suffered at the hands of the Shieran flagship more than he had anticipated.

Finally he reached his personal chambers aboard *The Dawn's Fury* and slammed the door behind him, huffing still in his armor, sweat covering his body. He set the Staff of the South Star in a corner with the reverence it deserved; it had won him an unwinnable battle.

But the madness still didn't leave him. They had not paid enough yet. Not nearly enough. But they were all dead here, there was no one left for him to kill.

And she was *still dead.*

Dranus pressed his forehead against the outer wall of his room hard and screamed all the viciousness that still boiled over inside of him. But as the sound of that scream died out, so did his wrath and his fury and the strength they had given him. He stumbled to his knees, head still pressed against the wall, and wept silently to himself.

She was *still dead.*

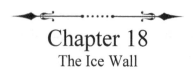

# Chapter 18
## The Ice Wall

T he pursuit of the Shieran navy continued night and day, but with due patience. At times, unfavorable winds allowed only the South Star Fleet to gain on the fleeing enemy, but they always managed to stay just out of range until the South Star set for the evening and the chase would have to be aborted. Still, the enemy was never far out of sight from the Varz navy and soon they would get their first glimpse of the Shieran Isles. There they were likely to meet resistance along the way. The outlying islands created a sort of gauntlet of land-based projectiles with expert artillerymen who had trained at their post long enough to know the distances and the winds near perfectly.

The king spent his days at sea in deep thought about his wife. Since the bloodletting and the rallying cry for vengeance in his deceased wife's name he had been inconsolably depressed.

He pored over the boundless information that the Book maintained. Its secret access to even unattainable texts, including those Forbidden to all but the King of Varz, was a constant source of both convenience and perturbation. But such perturbations were negligible in the face of his gloom. In near darkness he searched through all of the old knowledge for some piece of information he had forgotten or misinterpreted. Kaelel was dead, but her body had been recovered and what was left of it buried. Perhaps he could....

At times he had to stop himself; he felt like he had become obsessed with the idea of a woman that had briefly been his wife and who had brought out some terribly bright feelings within him. Then again, that ignored their long history as friends and as lovers. Kaelel was not the meaningless connection he wanted her to be given his current state, and he mourned her because she had changed him. He tried to convince himself every night that this change had been for the best, but he found it hard to gather evidence in favor of this thesis.

Still, he locked himself away below decks for hours and contemplated the nature of how Queen Luna and King Vulcan had been resurrected in a sense from their dead sleep. He recalled the distinct scent of pine both in the underwater castle and the sealed vault of King Vulcan which was not present once Queen Tempest had apparently awoken then passed once more. But what could such an insignificant smell mean?

In each case, they had been powerful sorcerers who had each ended one of the Great Wars, even Queen Tempest the Undying. Did this make them special? Perhaps it was no coincidence they had the power to end generations-old wars? There were stories of the red eyes of Varz, interesting only because even its use as a visual literary device would be strange given their already unnatural sclera color. Some of the oldest texts referenced a greater power than what they had; it was described as something not just at the extremes of their abilities, but as something categorically different but so rare as to be mythical. They were referred to in ancient terms in the same way that one might speak of a monster hiding under a young one's bed: as the eyes of a Devil.

He considered further the nature of the Shield of Second Life. Though he did not have the thing, nor could he use it now to resurrect his wife, it was proof of magic that could defy Death. What was the source of such blasphemous sorcery? He had read the account of Queen Tempest's casting; neither the queen herself nor any number of sacrifices had perished in the casting from violating such an existential constant. King Faust the Reaper, who was known for mimicking what he believed was the physical manifestation of Death, had claimed to have the answers to these questions and these answers supposedly drove Tempest to attempt the casting originally. Ultimately, Dranus had to admit that this was the difference in power and skill between the masterful monarchs of the distant past and himself; even reading the many secret works of Faust bore only confusion.

No matter how much he searched and conversed with the knowledge the Book held, he could find no way to reject Death without perishing himself. And that even if he failed! Felled vermin aboard the ships and too curious gulls served as test subjects for the king's experiments with terrible magic. He consumed drugs which he originally brought for strength in battle which increased his mental capacity like the brews of the Varz Dens, but much more potent. With the limited resources available to him he slaved over potions to expand his understanding. He attempted all manner of chant and rhyme and twisted what logic he could over and over so that at times he felt slip his grasp on which was truth and which was lie. But only for short moments, he was sure.

Over these few days he came to the frustrating conclusion that if once the ability to overcome Death had existed, it had since ceased to exist. However, the nature of Varz sorcery was the rejection of reality. By the very act of admitting that this was the reality of the situation, he inadvertently solidified that such a thing remained possible to a sorcerer of enough skill and willpower.

This conclusion, being the only one he could reach while retaining his relative sanity, gave the king some strange sense of closure. He could at least rest knowing that he had committed his greatest effort to bring her back in spite of his deteriorating mental state.

After weeks at sea, they spotted the outermost of the Shieran Isles, with a number of pleasant surprises. Most importantly, the wind was greatly in their favor from the north, so the outer islands were skirted at a safe distance without losing too much time. Secondly, they seemed to meet little resistance from installations en route. A few well-trained marine teams that were sent ahead had managed to sabotage most of the catapult embankments along their path and the handful that remained were apparently too understaffed to mount an offensive worthy of his attention. The admiral took this as a sign that the enemy was massing their forces around the capital for a final effort to endure a siege until reinforcements could arrive. The final surprise was brought from a messenger hawk directly from Varz; a message which told of the Arendrum forces retreat from their land and a sighting of one of the Warriors of Pyrán near the Urhyllian border in a brief engagement. All of these things signified that Dranus's plan was moving forward accordingly, and the united front of the Four Realms had scattered to protect their own holdings.

In discussions with his admirals, King Dranus decided that it was likely they would face a member of the Warriors of Pyrán in defense of the Shieran capital. However, their naval forces had to be diminished and Shiera hardly had a standing land force to speak of. Dranus expected a surmountable force to try and hold but knew that with his superior forces and position he could take the city before relief arrived. The single Warrior would be trouble, but they could be outnumbered and overpowered by superior sorcery.

Admiral O'cule suggested a feint with a small force to try and draw out the enemy, but the king dismissed this without a thought. The enemy had no reason to leave the protection of their port harbor and had to be getting wary of the tricky stratagems employed by the Varz forces. As much as he would have loved to insult their intelligence with another gambit, he at least respected their skill enough to believe they would not be so foolish.

By the time the sun reached its zenith on the next day, they were closing in on the island which held the capital. Passing through a narrow gap in the islands, a call came down from a nest that scouts were seen on shore riding back to the capital with news of their approach. King Dranus made no attempt to stop them. Knowledge of their position would do them no good. There was only one place the Varz army could be headed. In the end, they would take Shiera by pure force and the Lessers would be powerless to stop them. Even if there was a Warrior of Pyrán there, a sole fighter could not hold off an entire fleet of sorcerers.

A few hours into the afternoon and the bay which held the city of Shiera came into sight. It was a sight, however, that set the many Varz sailors to scratching at their thick raven hair in confusion. Spanning the harbor where the enemy ships should be was an ice wall nearly two hundred feet tall! Rapid reports came in to confirm that the wall stretched too deep to go under and from one shore to another.

"Curse those Warriors of Pyrán!" Dranus shouted as he tore away the scope from his eye.

His shouts were met with the splintering cracks of the ice shifting under its own massive weight. It would start as a rumble, an almost visceral aching as the unnatural ice struggled to hold its shape amidst the currents of the harbor.

Dranus took a few moments to inspect the wall. Would they have to move to a land-based siege? No, that would put them at too great a disadvantage and take too much time. Time is what the enemy needed, and he would not give it to them so easily.

He turned to order ships into position to bombard the wall, but Admiral O'cule was a step ahead of him.

There was little for him to do at that moment other than

summoning the South Star Fleet. With a bombardment in mind, he willed the Fleet's organization and tapped the Staff against the deck to release the cerulean light of the South Star Fleet in a line of ships at the head of their formation. Those in the Staff had responded to his will and had already readied their catapults and seemingly intangible projectiles.

"We will have the greatest chance of success if we attack together," Dranus commented to O'cule who looked on at the wall in consternation. He would be hatching some backup plan already most likely. "Everyone prepare and fire on my command."

It didn't take long for the trained sailors to uncover and prepare their long-range siege machines, but they were low on projectiles that would have enough mass to harm the massive wall. They could hurl fireballs at it, but it would never melt with any speed.

The sound of a few nearby splashes in the water, testing for range no doubt, signaled that the Shierans knew of their presence and were preparing a bombardment themselves. If the mass of their fleet was behind this wall, they would soon be at the mercy of a literal rain of fire.

"O'cule!" Dranus barked, "signal the Magemaster to prepare defense against projectiles!" The king's gaze darted back and forth across the ice wall, looking for a weak point to exploit, looking for signs of scouts, looking for any avenue to a simpler victory. How could they be gauging their firing distance from behind the wall?

"My king..." O'cule's voice stammered, uncertain. The man was rarely uncertain.

Following his admiral's gaze, he saw Magemaster Zed (ZED) on a neighboring vessel, waving his arms frantically with a number of assistant mages trailing behind him with heaps of scrolls.

He saw the man's lips moving quickly, trying to relay a message, and so enhanced his hearing to cover the range but was instantly deafened by the creaking ice and the low rumble of the wall scraping against the ocean floor. Reeling almost to the ground Dranus cursed quietly to himself at his own haste.

"Looks like he has some sort of plan, my king," O'cule said softly. "His ship is approaching ours. What shall we do?"

Dranus had recovered and returned his hearing to normal. As he had trained to do, he stopped and took stock of everything around him in a flash of seconds.

The ice wall. His fleet. Incoming bombardment. Warrior of Pyrán. Strong impacts in unison. Heaps of scrolls. O'cule's demeanor. The Magemaster's odd expressiveness. Decision.

"Hold fire but stay ready." Dranus rapped the Staff on the deck and Admiral Burgiss appeared before him already in a low bow. "Admirals, can I leave defense of projectiles to you and the South Star Fleet? Do not expend lives on defense unless you must."

The two men nodded in assent and Burgiss disappeared to return to his own forces. O'cule frowned but headed to the upper deck to prepare a concerted spell with others of the Magemaster's corps.

Meanwhile, Magemaster Zed's own ship was coming about to pass close with his own. His plan better be a good one.

But these thoughts afforded no extra time as the world moved forward. The first salvo of almost liquid flame flew over the top of the ice wall in massive sheets. It was light and so the wind altered it easily, but the sheer width of the bombardment was enough to ensure the hungry flames would spread among his forces unless....

Flame met shimmering green vibrating furiously in the air and dripped down the side of the airborne shield before falling short into the sea where it burned still for too long. Could the Warrior of Fire be here as well?

Suddenly Dranus was back at the Rift. The dirt in his lungs. The sweat drenching him through. A ferocious heat burst into the air and fell at their western flank. He recalled the wild panic fill his body as the Archer's Brigade was consumed by flames that licked too high and burned too hot. Unnatural flame. Flame that threatened the only thing in this world he had come to care for in truth.

A crack like lightning from the ice wall brought Dranus back.

No, this was not the flame of the Warrior of Fire. But if it were.... He was still frozen in place staring at the fire dancing on the tips of the waves. He wanted to think to himself that if the Warrior responsible for his wife's death were here, he would bring to him or her the most exquisite death imaginable...but he couldn't. He was as ice cold as the wall towering before him. He was...afraid?

"My king! My king!" Magemaster Zed stumbled over the plank connecting their ships in a hurry, seemingly out of breath. "Thank you for hearing me out!"

Dranus shook the feeling of dread from his bones and turned back to the issue at hand. Zed was already pointing and directing his assistants to arrange scrolls and maps on a table hastily brought above decks.

"Be quick with it, Zed," Dranus said, flicking his gaze upward at the straining O'cule who seemed to have taken the first bombardment almost singlehandedly.

"Apologies, my king, but a forward bombardment will do nothing against a wall of ice this size." The Magemaster pointed to a map where he had drawn a thick line over the harbor of Shiera and scribbled a few notes.

"The Shieran bay slopes rather steeply downward because, as you certainly are aware, the current Shieran Isles are merely mountain tops of the sunken nation. Thus, a forward impact will diffuse greatly into the mountain and generate compression in the wall, potentially strengthening it and certainly not harming its structural strength. The depth of the bay would keep the wall from toppling with the forces of the water pressure on the lower half." The Magemaster had a piece of charcoal and was sketching a diagram of the ice wall and all the relevant features as he described them, likely ruining the map he used as parchment.

"I'm not hearing a solution in this!" The king motioned furiously for him to get to the point.

"We need to perform a *backward* bombardment! This will pull the wall down the slope, creating tensile stress on the surface between the friction of the sea-floor and the weight at the top of the wall! Ice is naturally resistant to being compressed but not to being pulled apart!" He drew with careful measurements made by eye, scratching in numbers here and there as he performed calculations in his mind's eye while another wave of fire and stones clashed against a stronger green shield and the rumbling of the ice waxed and waned.

"Are you suggesting we *pass the wall first* and then bombard it from behind? Have you lost your senses?" Dranus was near to fuming at this waste of time.

"No, my king, no!" He traced along a vertical representation of the ice wall, scratching out numbers at specific points and then placing one finger at the top of the wall and drawing an arc with another finger pointed outward. "Here." He pointed to the point where his arc and the wall met. "If we can embed several anchors along this line of the wall and then use the force generated by the catapults linked to...."

"Linked to the anchors in the opposite direction to pull them towards us...." Dranus finished as he caught on. "What do we need to prepare?"

The Magemaster grinned widely in victory. "With your forgiveness, my king, I have already begun making preparations as I knew that you would see the wisdom in my plan."

Rather than reprimand the man for disobeying orders, Dranus was actually impressed by his foresight and determination. He would never punish those who made achieving his goals easier.

"Continue, then. What do you need from me?" Dranus offered his services since the South Star Fleet would be acting mostly autonomously at this point.

"Each casting will be handled by one of my mages, but the coordination of such efforts so that the force is distributed evenly and all at once requires a great will. One such as only the King of Varz can supply." Zed bowed deeply, humbling himself in an effort to remain in the king's good graces.

"I will prepare, then. Time is against us, let us do this quickly but precisely," Dranus said without looking back and moving to the ship's forecastle. Far behind him on the rear deck was O'cule, standing with a spread-leg pose and his arms folded across his chest. There was a look of great focus in his eyes as he performed a similar service as Dranus prepared and which someone like Ven was used to filling, though Ven did it with chilling efficiency that even the king lacked.

Sitting cross-legged on the forecastle, Dranus closed his eyes and opened his mind. He dulled his hearing against the creaking planks, the sound of waves, the cracks and groans of the ice wall, and the shouting of sailors so that he could focus on his inner voice. Almost immediately a vision of the ice wall with all of the markings Zed had drawn on the scroll flooded his mind, and it was as though he watched the battle from far in the air over his own forces. He could see the sweeping arc that Zed had drawn and a few points where anchors needed to go. For ease, he transformed these locations into names. Not of those he knew but of those who did not exist but now would. These beings were not humans with thoughts, values, and histories, but mathematical locations with bearings, height, influence of the wind between them, and as many other countless features as a person would have. The mages preparing their own individual spells

197

would use these figures as they would learn about a friend of a friend, to craft precision into their own workings of magic.

Steadily he saw imaginary lights spark up on the decks of a select number of ships as mages from across the fleet connected to him like they had with Ven at the Rift. Dranus had entered that complex web of consciousnesses momentarily during the battle and could hardly fathom the weaving links between individuals that Ven had crafted. By comparison, the webbing he formed now was like a child's toy wooden hammer next to the most deftly crafted steel mace. It was simple but it would do, after all, this was not his calling as it was Ven's.

One by one, strong anchors were shot into the ice wall at the specified points. They sank deep into the ice, not relying on any sort of physical tether to tie them to their point of origin. It took time for them all to be in position, but time was such an intangible thing, even more than normal, here in his sorcerer's forge. He could tell that defenses were straining against the constant bombardment of the enemy, but the strong wills of the South Star Fleet helped bolster their strength. When distributed across so many mages, the shield could hold for hours before taking a lethal toll from its casters. Perhaps the ghostly sailors of the Staff even had some greater resistance to this effect.

That single tangential thought had consumed more time than he would have guessed and already the anchors were in position. Catapults and mounted trebuchets were also prepared with heavy burdens and launching loads for maximum distance and thus, force, but without payloads.

"Everything is prepared, my king," Magemaster Zed's voice trickled into his mind and for a moment Dranus saw the entire layout, all of the angles, and indices of force, friction, stress and strain, the weight of ships, the movement of currents below the surface of the water. And without effort, he *understood*.

"Hold," Dranus whispered in response to the hundreds of others in his web. He watched the numbers and angles and every factor bob around like a wayward dingy on rough seas, waiting for the right moment. He struggled against mental burden and exhaustion to keep up with the shifting numbers and the sharp pull with which his attention clawed at him for more resources to one thing and then another.

When the moment came, it was more of a feeling than a discreet thought that signaled the appropriate conditions.

"Now!" Dranus shouted through his web, but this was not the signal. His control over those in his web coordinated their magic through his own, tying the position in space of the siege weapons' beams to the back end of the anchors.

He felt, all at once, the catapults and trebuchets releasing their tension in unison and their force transfer was like being drawn and quartered but not by horses, but by the natural forces; implacable and mighty as they were.

Across the fleet, the frames and beams of the weapons strained, and ships even lifted slightly out of the sea, pitting their weight and the force of the weapons against the mass of the ice wall! Countless magical experts distributed force as evenly as they could but still several weapons splintered and cracked under the massive strain.

Dranus clenched his jaw and tightened his resolve against the pressures, stabilizing the complex spell so that, with cracks that splintered ears like divine-shod lightning, the ice wall began to reveal crevices along the line of anchors that warped the ice wall towards them. It stretched and resisted the pull but the weight and force of countless weapons of war pulled at just the right points and at just the right angles at just the right time forced the wall to them, causing it to buckle under the tension with a raucous sound that was at once the earth-shattering sounds of every war, every battle that had ever taken place! It was the sweetest sound King Dranus had heard in weeks! He saw it first in the minds and eyes of hundreds of linked sorcerers and then raised his eyelids to take in the sight with his own black eyes.

The ice wall had fallen!

# Chapter 19
### The Sack of Shiera

The mass of Varz ships falling back into the water and the huge chunks of ice falling caused the bay to erupt in waves that crashed together, sending spray up tens of feet in the air and threatening to capsize dozens of ships! Dranus's own ship rocked so much he lost his concentration and nearly his grip on the Staff of the South Star, causing the ethereal navy to vanish. As he held himself firmly against a nearby railing, he barely caught a glimpse of a ship teetering so precariously that one of its booms dipped into the water before bobbing back out.

After the initial surprise, the Varz sailors went back to their training, using a combination of nautical and magical means to stabilize the ships across their fleet.

Curiously, the water on the other side of the now fallen ice wall was incredibly calm, as if the waves crashed against some invisible barrier.

That could not be a good sign.

Worse, still, their enemies had already begun mobilizing while the Varz ships still struggled to regain their composure and reconstruct their formation, not to mention put away the heavy (and in many cases, recently destroyed) siege weapons.

No doubt they had considered a new strategy since confronting the Varz Titan Ships on the open sea. They were charging directly for them. Dranus surmised they must be trying to close in and fight hand to hand rather than exchange volleys with the impenetrable Titan Ships. And yet...something was off. Their ships were too few and moved far too quickly for a natural ship!

Shrill, high-pitched whistles started to sound from within the Varz ranks and one by one the Titan Ships, with their stout profiles protecting them from the rough waters, began a counter-charge. Gradually, ships further back in the formation where the fallout from the ice wall was less severe resumed their earlier barrage, trying to pick off incoming vessels or at least deter them.

Dranus exerted significant pressure on his own vessel, steadying it through the certainty with which he understood its 'unique' buoyancy, or at least as unique as his sorcerer's mind could make it. He gathered himself, securing his footing on the now drenched deck that stunk like brine and rotting wood. With a heave of his lungs the water fled from Dranus's clothes, light armor, hair, and skin. He tried to ignore the shouts of men and women struggling to report to Admiral O'cule who had borne out the little storm on the upper deck. The man gave Dranus a significant look, a grave look, and then turned back to the numerous scouts, sailors, and messengers that flocked around him.

O'cule was right. Without saying a word he had expressed his discomfort for these circumstances. They had already lost one senior officer at the hands of a Warrior of Pyrán, and he surely did not want to be the second.

Suddenly a streak of projectiles flew overhead in a coordinated arc, aiming for the spot where the ice wall had been which was now filled with oncoming Shieran ships. They had recovered quickly!

But this volley would not find its mark. Instead, several geysers of water blossomed from the otherwise calm sea around the Shieran vessels and swept the stones and balls of flame out of the air like Dranus might swat so many flies from around his face!

Titan Ships surged forward and in many cases found marks on the outer reaches of the enemy formation, but at the center.... At the center they were launched from the water and flipped, landing upside down like turtles on their backs in the water.

Dranus's mouth hung agape. The Warrior of Water had *this much* power? Even before The Ultimate sealed away elemental magic, tales of it were hugely limited in scope. There had never been story or even hyperbole of magic like this!

Dranus waved attention from the Admiral above and behind him, pointing to the center of the enemy formation. O'cule nodded in agreement and signaled for the Titan Ships to move to the outer ranks and slowly surround the center.

But just as this order rang through a sequence of high-pitched whistles, a small explosion burst above the port of Shiera. Not an attack; it was a signal, but a signal for what?

The first ships breached their ranks moments later, pulling

alongside Varz vessels that rained arrows upon them but met mostly walls of shields held by the soon-to-be boarders from Shiera. Two raced towards the Varz flagship but were intercepted by others, including the vessel of Magemaster Zed who had taken on a similar guise as that of Commander Ven at the Battle of the Rift. He was coordinating a web of naval sorcerers and directing their efforts to slow the advance of the enemy into their formation. Here and there Shieran wooden masts burst into splinters, skewering the unwitting sailors; sails tore, falling over them like a blanket used to smother a rogue flame; rowing oars grew heavy, almost leaden, and slipped from the grasps of oarsmen into the sea. The Magemaster and his fellows had drawn an invisible line at the center of the formation past which no ship could hope to pass unscathed.

It was in this way that both sides diverted their attention to outflanking the other, but there was an imbalance in this competition. One side had their backs to safe harbor and the other....

A blaring trumpet from the west stole Dranus's focus. After a few moments, and by shifting his gaze like telescoping lenses, he saw the missing Shieran ships he'd been wondering after. That explained the signal over the city from earlier. Fortunately, this was not as troubling as it first seemed. The rapid flushing together of the two forces had made it impossible for Dranus to deploy the South Star Fleet effectively, but this…they could handle this.

Dranus ran aftward, practically floating up the stairs to the upper deck where O'cule still commanded the bulk of their forces. He nodded to his friend as they exchanged an unspoken understanding of what would happen next.

His pulse raced, beating against his chest and the sorcerous tome hidden behind his armor. With controlled urgency he righted his state of mind, thrust the Staff of the South Star into the deck, and was nearly brought to his knees by the immediate weight of the casting. It came with the multi-tonic dirge of the Staff roaring through his ears just before the cerulean navy of the Staff emerged in an appropriately defensive position. For the time being, a small corner of the ghost navy focused on further bombardments into the enemy's main force.

With the new threat delayed, Dranus looked back to the movements of ships at his front.

There was still something unnatural about the way the Shieran ships moved, almost like the Staff's navy, but different. This was no doubt the Warrior of Water's doing! To think that she could be calming the sea and moving the currents all while deflecting incoming projectiles and warding off Titan Ships...it was incomprehensible, even to a king of Varz! This was something beyond Varz sorcery, at least in its normal form. There was that old myth laid secret in the Forbidden Texts. A higher form of sorcery. The eyes of a Devil. But that was absurd...the enlightened folk of Varz did not believe in such things as Gods and Devils. No, there was some trick to this. Perhaps all of the Warriors together could channel their power into one...perhaps even over distances. The thought was terrifying, but not unconquerable.

Dranus was shaken from his deep thought by the shrill sound of the Titan Ships changing formation.

In a rapid sequence of glances he could see that the combination of becalming the enemy ships and keeping their own superior forces away from the Warrior of Water had worked. The Shieran outer ranks were decimated by the Titan Ships and now the stout vessels moved to surround and overwhelm the center of the formation.

With this change, Dranus could tell that something shifted. The water in the Shieran harbor was less calm and stranded vessels were abandoned. With nowhere to go, the remaining Shieran ships huddled close around a single ship that seemed to be glowing with a blue light like early night. As the projectiles flooding in grew in number and frequency, this light grew as well.

Once more Dranus willed his view beyond what was normally possible...and there he saw *her.*

It was like a dream, Dranus thought, like some ethereal vision of a living spirit of the sea or an avatar of the ocean. Despite the Shierans' hopeless conditions, the girl simply danced on the bow of the unnaturally steadied ship. She wielded a great trident that glinted in the reflection of the sun as it spun effortlessly around her. She moved with such ease...such beauty. The king was entranced by the sight; he could not tear his eyes from this view. It was tragic in so many ways that she danced like a school of fish in effortless synchrony, a sight he never expected to see again. And yet she must be snuffed out by his own hand, nonetheless.

Most tragic of all, however, was her appearance...oh how she resembled his dead wife Kaelel! The sounds of the battle seemed to fade from his ears and his vision narrowed to that deck, his grip grew limp, and he felt as though he were only half present.

The Warrior raised her hands, the trident pointed down. To her left she leapt with stunning agility and a wave followed suit, swatting a lead ball from the air and into a nearby Titan ship. With fluid ease the Warrior turned her momentum into a spin, her weapon held close to her body. Following her dance, the sea spun up into towering waterspouts that deflected arrows in a number of places before falling back into the bay as the Warrior came out of the spin into a wide stance.

Then the fluid form turned harsh. From the flowing movements sprang quick stabs of the trident in several directions. Like a pole she stabbed the blade into the deck and spun around it furiously. If it were still a dance, the song had changed and it was no longer a dance of serenity, but one of violence.

"My king...my king! King Dranus, what should we do?!" Admiral O'cule was shaking the king violently trying to wake him from his trance. Pulling himself back at once, Dranus regained his form.

"What?! What?!" His eyes swept the battle quickly, trying to gauge all that he had missed. And what he had missed was that the balls of fire now fell harmlessly into the water and instead of victorious Titan Ships moving towards shore he saw more than a score pierced from beneath their hulls all the way through the iron roofing by massive shards of ice.

"Valkhir's Rage! Have all of the remaining Titan Ships and bombardments converge on the last ship! Shoot it down, sink the thing like your life depends on it!" Quickly he turned to survey their western flank and was relieved to find that the South Star Fleet had held off the surprise flank and already that force had clearly given up on Shiera and fled back to the south.

The seas shuddered and shook, and boats were tossed this way and that by the whims of the waves. But from every ship now came lead shells, balls of flame, arrows and lances, every manner of attack was being brought against the Warrior of Pyrán and soon the ship was torn to splinters.

The Warrior still stood, steady atop the waves amid nothing but wreckage and foes. It was masterful, the way she handled her powers and kept herself from destruction with such grace. Still she resisted and toppled a whole Titan Ship with her waves; she was majestic and gallant and unthinkably picturesque. It was a growing shame that she must die.

But as Dranus's pulse began to calm and he felt his victory assured, something changed in the air again.

Something changed in the sea.

The Warrior had vanished from sight but beneath them was the refracted light the Warrior of Water gave off, spreading and piercing through the murky depths as if it took the form of something wicked and unknowable beneath the serene surface of the waves.

Then came the pull.

Without wind or manpower the remaining ships of Varz in their entirety were being pulled in towards the Shieran harbor. They were not pulled under as if by grasping claws but seemed almost lulled by a sweet voice to meander closer and closer to the shore. Did she mean to beach them all and engage in land-based combat? It would devastate the Shieran coastline, but it was their only means of combat now that what remained of their navy was sinking to the bottom of the bay.

That was what he had thought. But even a monarch of Varz could be wrong once in a while.

The gathering water pulling at the ships began to rise as it reached more shallow areas. It rose in ways the onlooking sailors could not fathom. The water rose so high as to obscure the city from their vision and it did not stop there. The water belittled them with both its size and its strength. At the peak of the wave, now monstrous in size and width, was a chaotic royal blue light. And behind that light Dranus felt a gaze, but this was no human gaze he had ever experienced. He felt the full weight of the world's oceans bearing down on him and in that moment he saw flashes of the Battle of the Rift: slabs of rock as tall as the cliffs toppled like toys, gusts of wind like an invisible strike through the air, and all-engulfing flame devouring a full branch of his military in a single moment.

The fear gripped his throat and held him as it must have done to every living soul in the Varz navy.

Then, without mercy or hesitation, the tsunami descended upon the powerless Varz navy.

Dranus whirled to O'cule, wild defiance in his eyes and shouted, "O'cule! Take pitch! I'll take roll!"

O'cule, mouth hanging slack and brows shaped to despair,

gathered himself too and nodded in response.

The admiral's hand joined the king's on the Staff of the South Star, Dranus's free hand on the guard rail and O'cule's on the wheel. Dranus had to remove the fear and dread of the oncoming wave from his mind and focus on the axis of his ship that ran down the center from fore to aft. He centered his resolve on that dimension of space, picturing his ship steady on calm seas even as he felt the vessel rise beneath him, exerting immense pressure on his legs to stay standing.

He drowned out the yells and shouts of weaker men and women struggling to keep their sanity. Focus on the axis, Dranus. Steady the roll, do not let the ship know that it should be heaving hard to port and rolling like a loosed barrel down a steep hill.

He became aware of the air thinning slightly and the spray of sea water weakening and then the lurch of movement as his ship rode the crest of the massive wave with sorcerous steadiness.

Dranus stole just a moment to look about him and nearly vomited from the sense of vertigo before his eyes slammed shut. Some other ships had known how to prepare for this, but they were few. Too few.

The King of Varz did not know how much longer they rode the surge but eventually he grew conscious of stillness. He no longer felt the press of roll on his understanding of the ship's axis.

Carefully, he opened one eye and found O'cule standing up straight, his hand limp at his side and tears cascading from his eyes in long streaks.

Steeling himself, Dranus turned to look upon the utter devastation.

Only a small handful of ships remained. None of the Titan Ships survived. They had been taken so far from shore that the central Shieran isle could hardly be seen in the distance. And in the wake of that path were the scattered remains of the splintered, battered, and drowned.

An entire Varz fleet...destroyed in a moment...by a *single sorcerer*.

He swept about with his eyes, stinging from the sea water that had tossed about in the upheaval, until he finally found what he wanted. But not what he expected.

Bobbing gently on the waves in the near distance was a solid sphere of ice dyed the dark color of the Warrior's glow. Dranus searched through overlapping fields of vision and detected the faint heat of the Warrior inside, but she did not stir and he could sense no thought from her, no variance to her rate of breathing, though breathe she still did.

She must have over-exerted and was now unconscious in what she thought would keep her safe.

Dranus felt every nerve in his body light up with fire and anger at the sight, but he had to think strategically.

"O'cule!" Dranus barked.

"Yes, my king?"

"Capture her alive. She will not be granted the luxury of death for what she has done this day."

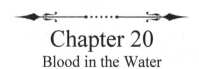

# Chapter 20
## Blood in the Water

It took a great deal of struggle and significant sorcery to dredge the massive shard of ice from the sea and to break through the protective shell to find the sapphire gem hidden inside, but by nightfall, it was done. The girl was taken to the brig and kept unconscious by the Magemaster and his guard around the clock. If she woke without them having complete control over the situation, they would be doomed. Already the King of Varz risked too much letting her live...but he could not deny the questions that called from the deep echoing pit of his mind.

Dranus had receded to his quarters to have long meetings with his remaining naval officers and with Admiral Burgiss of the Staff. By the time he made it in to rest, the sky had been covered in a thick blanket of rolling clouds. He sat on his bed for nearly an hour staring into space with no particular focus, deep in thought and reflection of all that had happened.

As proud as he had felt in his winning gambit at sea, he felt doubly ashamed for underestimating once again the Warriors of Pyrán. In a manner, he did not wish to punish the girl he had captured, for she had simply defended her home from an invading threat. It was he who had allowed her to cause such devastation to his forces. How had he become so overconfident?

The pit in his stomach deepened, then widened. He felt doubt weigh on him like a sodden cloak.

Before he had been confronted by Deleron Kaxus and obtained the Book he was desolate, practically wasting away from the emptiness he felt about his life. Where would he have been at this time had that boy not sacrificed himself for his childish beliefs? In the Book he had written "I will kill King Dranus" and in a sense he had. The Dranus that had lived until that point was, in a sense, dead. Would that version of himself have been so full of hubris and bloodlust as to charge into a well defended port where waited one who wielded ancient forbidden magic?

Since the night of the Book and the rising of the South Star he had found appropriate meaning and purpose to his life and was feeling more alive than ever before. Although he had married the late Commander of the Archer's Brigade as a political move, he had come to love her, hadn't he? Were those pleasant times and emotions worth the ones that had brought upon this military disaster?

Dranus winced at a sudden surge of pain in his chest. He saw Kaelel's smile, witty and clever at all times, but special for him. He smiled to himself as he recalled lazy evenings in debate and in love-making that had made time seem a thing of no consequence.

Without his bidding, recent memories of the Warrior of Water dancing on the deck and striking fiercely with her trident intruded on his daydreaming...but it was not an *entirely* sickening feeling.

Was it that the feelings he had developed for Kaelel were simply being mimicked in the presence of his wife's doppelganger? His enemy? Or was it possible that he did harbor some affection for the girl? No, he had to remember that their physical similarities did not make them the same person. A Lesser girl could never be a fraction of the woman Kaelel had been.

With that thought he pushed the topic from his mind and tried not to think about it anymore.

There were plans to be made. He had underestimated the Warriors of Pyrán for the last time. He could no longer go about this war in the traditional manner.

But then what should he do? In the immediate aftermath of the attempted sack of Shiera they had taken stock of their remaining naval strength which, while a small portion of their original number, was significantly more than the completely decimated Shieran fleet. Shiera did not have much land on which to battle so their navy was effectively their only martial force outside of the local Superior's personal guard. O'cule could take the capital and rapid calls for reinforcements could be made, but was that even the right choice? Would the other territories willingly weaken their own defenses upon hearing that the Shieran fleet had been completely obliterated? The only other significant navy was that of Myrendel, but they would be months away with their primary port resting deep within the Gulf of the Seven.

No, with the Warrior of Water out of the equation, O'cule could hold Shiera for long enough with what remained. Magemaster Zed was a powerful asset to have here; he had to have faith in those that served him.

Then there was the king, himself.

Already he knew what must be done next. The Book had been evasive, but on multiple occasions let slip, or perhaps purposefully planted, the fact that there was a fourth Relic of Power that he knew nothing about. However, that relic lie in the ruins of Pyrán and to go there as a citizen, let alone a king of Varz, was pure blasphemy. If he were to ascend the slope, would he physically be allowed to enter, or would the place reject him like a sickness? Not to mention that it was in the mountains between Arendrum and Myrendel; it was deep within the enemy's territory. Regardless, without the final relic he had no other means by which to secure victory over the Warriors of Pyrán.

That was, unless he could learn something from the Warrior they had captured.

Heaving a great sigh and steadying his resolve, he summoned his guard and instructed them to bring her to him tightly bound and blindfolded so that she could neither escape nor learn the layout of the ship.

The moments in waiting for this order to be filled dragged like bloody corpses towed in a ship's wake. Dranus could feel some subtle hesitation... some nervousness which made his heart beat out of rhythm. Did he suspect her to try and attack him? Though he had the Sword of Righted Guard and the Staff of the South Star, he could not hope to understand how her mastery over water worked. Still, if Zed could keep her under, then in the worst case he could subdue her in close quarters and simply kill her.

Even with that thought his anxiety did not lift. It wasn't the threat she posed that caused his heart to beat quickly and his palms to sweat like a boy at his first battle.

The door cracked open, and the limp body of the Warrior of Water was brought in. Clearly the Magemaster had done well in suppressing her consciousness. Once she was set down in a chair bolted to the deck and her arms and legs were secured, Dranus removed the blindfold and dismissed his guards.

He looked her over briefly. There were some similarities between her and Kaelel, such as the long black hair, but they were, as he knew, quite different. His longing to see his beloved again must have blinded his eyes to seeing her anywhere he could. This steadied him substantially.

He leaned over to stare into her expressionless eyes and there he searched for her consciousness.

Suddenly, Dranus saw from the eyes of a young girl playing on docks, fishing with a crew of men, and laying on the beach with her feet lapped by the waves. Countless memories passed and in each he was smiling wide and laughing. He felt the warmth from the sun like he never had and marveled at the grainy sensation of sand between his toes. He felt contentment in the simplicity of the world around him without the stress of rule and the burden of his duties as king.

But these were the Warrior's feelings, not his.

Then he was approached by a man cloaked in shadow and shrouded by mystery. The word "Guide" was clear upon wrinkled lips. He brought with him unfamiliar faces and a feeling of dread; he recognized one of the faces as the Warrior of the Sun whom he faced at the Battle of the Rift.

Dipping into only a fraction of her memories it seemed as though hours, maybe days passed.

He saw the bright lights of the Shieran capital fading in the distance from the rear deck of a ship, felt a comforting hand on his shoulder, and a tear slowly making its way down his cheek. Then he found her mind, wrapped in a ball of ice like he had found her body earlier. Unlike that time, in this world of minds and thoughts he could break that barrier simply by thinking it.

With a shake, the Warrior regained her consciousness and struggled in her bonds before locking her brown-ringed eyes on his sorcerous ones.

Dranus returned the stare, showing neither weakness nor hesitation.

"What is your name, hero?" he spoke slowly, with conviction.

"Why am I still alive?" She seemed both bewildered and furious at her capture.

Dranus remained calm, "What is your name? I'll not converse with one whose name I do not know." To overcome her will, he must use his wit and stay in control of himself while she became wild and unrestrained.

"I have no desire to 'converse' with you! You might as well kill

211

me and get it over with!" She was rude and harsh, thrashing about in her bonds and cursing, but her passion burned so bright.

"You appear to have quite the desire to die, young lady. But I'm afraid you've not earned that death quite yet."

She seemed perplexed, somewhat, by this comment and finally acquiesced. "My name is Raven...."

"Raven." He smiled and looked her over briefly. "It suits you well. My name is Dranus, and I am King of Varz." When he mentioned that he was the king the girl's eyes lit up and began scanning the room rapidly. It appeared that upon receiving this news she had gained a renewed desire to survive.

"You should calm yourself, you can neither harm me nor hope to escape; I can have your life at my whim. Cooperate and you may find yourself alive and well at the end of this war." He gazed uninterestedly at his hand, brandishing unwarranted bravado. He glanced at the craftsmanship of his sword hilt, anything other than her so that she would yearn for his attention like a duelist yearned for her opponent's respect.

"I'll never cooperate with the likes of you! You and your folk are evil! You bring nothing but death and destruction! It is my duty to bring down your reign of terror before it can ruin this world!" Again that passion sprang to life within her.

"And why is this your duty? Why do you fight against me and my people, Raven?" He remembered quite intimately the feelings she had experienced upon leaving her home to fulfill this duty.

"It is my destiny; it is my Fate," she replied with a matter-of-fact tone.

"I see, and what makes it your 'destiny'?" He could see in her eyes that she had perhaps never truly asked herself that question.

"It was foretold in prophecy, that we Warriors would rise against you. I was given the powers of my ancestors from the bosom of Pyrán, the Holy itself, so I must fight!" She had regained her conviction though it was subtly shaken from when she had commanded him to kill her.

Already she had given him new information. Though he had expected the Warriors were birthed from the ancient enemy of Varz, he only now had confirmation of this. Still, he could not let the shock show on his features. He must divert her.

"You must? Tell me Raven, will you die if you do not fight? Will an ancient God smite you from the heavens? Will the ground split and swallow you? You Lesser Folk seem so constrained by what 'must' be done, it is why you have not flourished like my kind. Your Shieran Admiral told me I 'must' accept his surrender. I did not. And yet, here I am! None the worse!" He made unnecessary gestures with his hands and body, but this was the way the Lessers expressed themselves. As much as she seemed relatively sharp, he had to stick with basic logic, not the complex understandings that those of Varz had mastered.

"Your disregard for what is right and wrong is the cause of all the suffering that I fight against. I must fight you because it is the right thing to do, and no other reason than that!" There again...she spoke of suffering but did not show the pain in speaking the word. What suffering had she endured, really, if she regarded it so casually?

"Oh, great hero? Is it that you fight me which makes you good? Is it because I fight back that makes me bad? Your realms have waged war before, surely that does not make them *bad*. And was it not the Arendrum forces which invaded my land first?" He spoke innocently, shrugging and imploring her to consider the wisdom she had taken advantage of.

"We invaded your land because you threatened our security! If we had not attacked first you would have built strength and then sent your armies to take our lands and enslave our people! You are in the wrong because you fight with wicked plots and deceit! You fight to own and control the will of others." She glared at him with eyes set.

"Ah! So that strategists are now demons?!" Dranus stood straight and chuckled at her naivety, shaking his head in frustration.

"How much do you know of this continent's history?" Dranus asked, looking down on her with a leading glance.

"I know that throughout the history of the Five Realms, Varz has always sought to control all through some misguided sense of superiority and done whatever was necessary to have things their way."

"Indeed," he conceded, "we are a race of warriors if nothing else, but proud warriors." This he let sit in the air for a moment. "But, do you know who ruled the realm of Shiera under King Valkhir the Rageborn after the First Great War?"

The girl shifted uneasily in her seat.

"No."

"Aha! It was Altus! *Superior* Altus! One of your own ruled even when you were under Varz control! And how many slaves have Varz Kings and Queens taken from your realm?"

She opened her mouth to speak "Countl...."

"None! Not a *single* slave has been taken in our history under order of a Varz monarch. We are fighters and strategists, but we are not barbarians. It is against our code, passed down for a thousand years!" And yet, his words were twisted like his magic. The fact they took no slaves was not born from nobility, but paranoia. Every slave was an extra enemy in waiting, brewing in their hate and desire for vengeance.

The Warrior of Pyrán had no response to this, it seemed that her resolve had waned and she averted her eyes. Where she had struggled against her bonds before, she now acquiesced. Dranus knew what the other nations thought of them and what she would have been taught through rumors and myth.

"Did not the Five Realms thrive under Varz rule once united?" The tone of his voice mounted, and he stared at her hard, insisting. "Answer me!" He grasped her chin so that she could not avoid the question.

But still she looked away.

It was a mistake, he realized, to have touched her. To feel her soft skin in his harsh grasp and feel the confusion in her distant gaze. For a lingering moment he saw Kaelel in her face, in her hair, even in the straightness of her back held proud against it all. How his mind fluttered and became clouded by the sensation. He withdrew his hand and turned his back to her, but the image of her was burned onto his thoughts.

"I apologize." How could he convince her of how little she knew?

"Tell me, Raven, you spoke of the suffering that my people have brought about. Pardon my insistence but I don't believe you truly know of such suffering. Your life was simple enough: fishing and spending time at the docks, enjoying the feel of sand between your toes on the Shieran beaches." Her head snapped to attention, and she stared at Dranus's back in disbelief.

"How do you know about that?!" She tried to shout, but a shout like that of a mouse.

"I saw it in your mind when I woke you. You lived a rather peaceful life until the Warriors and this 'Guide' came to call for you.

It seems to me that the only suffering you have experienced was being drawn from your home by the call of this 'destiny' you speak of." He sighed and turned again to face her, his look was soft and humble. "I felt your tears as you sailed away that night. How many nights after did you weep in longing for the life you had before?"

Again she was speechless. It was to be expected as she was still a child and was not suited for such talk. She had no deep understanding of war or politics or even the intricate history of the Five Realms. She had merely been taken from a relatively normal life without suffering to fulfill some destiny that she had been told was hers. Her power was real, so the fact that she had been chosen for something was undeniable, but the *necessity* of fulfilling that call was what he had to chip away at.

"Not like you've suffered..." It was almost a whisper, followed by downcast eyes and a soft glow of her cheeks.

Dranus's brows flared, his body tensed.

"I saw, too...what you've lost in this war."

Had she seen into his memories while he experienced hers? That was...not impossible.... But one who hadn't even manifested the Eyes of a sorcerer? In a battle of wills against the King of Varz? Had she resisted him out of instinct?

"In a war, both sides sustain losses. It cannot be avoided." There for a moment he gritted his teeth as he weighed the option of killing her then and there. He wanted to end her; to draw his sword and plunge it through her heart. It was these cursed Warriors that had taken his light, his answer! Now he thought he glimpsed Kaelel in this girl's face? Entertained notions of affection for her?! What sorry excuse for a king had he become?!

He controlled himself. In part, he had to listen to his own argument. Kaelel's death had not been the design of this young girl.

That look of innocence on her face, how she blushed and shrunk back at his overt aggression. On the battlefield she was a warrior goddess in human form, but the stark reality was that she was still a young woman who had only recently been drawn from a sedentary life that was far from luxurious, but which had its own familiarity and appeal.

He had brought her here for a certain purpose and he was on the cusp of fulfilling that purpose. So he again donned the mask of the calm, the controlled; indeed, it was a mask he had known many

215

times before.

"And yet I have never called your folk 'evil.'" He concluded.

"I do not believe my folk are inherently evil either. We do not spread like a plague among your societies. We are simply a different way: a choice between a comfortable life on the beach and a life fraught with death in answer to the call of Fate. You may see us as darkness because of this, but I see our folk as a radiant glow of civility and advancements spreading like the dawn's light." Dranus gestured broadly. She had tasted the power of sorcery and seen what it could accomplish, surely she could appreciate that at least.

"You do not appear to be so sure of your 'destiny' young Raven. I, not as king but as myself, believe it is your natural right as a living creature to question anything anyone tells you is required of you." Finally her eyes came to meet his though what he saw there confused him. He could not identify what it was that she was feeling or thinking, only that there was a certain calmness to her.

"If your kind had any sense," he continued quickly, "you would realize that you've already discovered the easiest way to defeat all the sorcery and power that Varz can bring against you! But you cannot see the obvious; your *eyes* are so limited." This was true: the only time Varz had been defeated and withdrawn back into their own territory was after they had conquered all the lands. They conquered by force, brought their customs and technologies to their new cities, and then grew complacent with no one to fight.

"Why are you this way, King of Varz?" It held some confidence, the question that came from the Warrior of Water.

"Why?" He pretended to think it over, rubbing his chin pensively. "I am myself. I have been trained to be a monarch of Varz all my life, but that is not my destiny. It is merely my title and my means to forge my own destiny. You have been chosen to be a Warrior of Pyrán and that is your title and a path presented to you, but it is not the only path, and it is not your destiny." Dranus was firm but was letting up a bit...already he had her questioning what was right and wrong. Given more time she may be convinced to divulge the secrets to her powers, but that was not something he could get from her so easily, not so quickly.

"In Varz we understand that nothing is absolute. We understand that reality is meant to be altered to our benefit. To live chained to an indisputable destiny is worse than death. If your kind could understand this, perhaps we would not find ourselves at such distant ends."

"So then you fight to bring unity and understanding to the Five Realms?" She was still hesitant, but a boldness remained in her eyes.

"No." He looked at the Sword at his belt. "I fight because it is in my blood. I do not know what my Fate is yet, but I fight to find it." When he looked back up she was staring at him with somewhat of a smile on her beautiful, young face.

"Then I will fight to find mine as well!" At this Dranus was a bit off-put...had she withstood his words? Had he underestimated her resolve? He guessed that his words had taken some kind of hold, but she was a different person, unlike his kind. To sway her thoughts would take time.

"You'll be sure to let me know when you find it, Raven." Truly he did feel some kind of connection with her. In ways she reminded him of himself when he was younger and less wise, believing that his kingship was both his title and his identity.

"Until then, I saw you during the battle. You cannot control the water while bound." He stated this as fact, not as a question, and she meekly nodded in ascent.

He opened his door and ordered the guards to take her back to her holding cell.

"Then if you do not try to escape or to bring harm to my folk, you will be taken good care of. If you make any attempt to escape or take the life of any of mine, I will keep you alive, but just barely." The king had taken liberty with her and shown her some level of humanity. Even if she had declared she would continue to fight, he felt that he could expect some level of cooperation from the girl.

"Feed her well. Only give her water in small amounts, never enough that she can use to some effect." He whispered this softly to the guard and then watched as she was unbound and taken from the room.

She left the room in quiet dignity. Her eyes were buried in heavy thoughts and philosophies of a treacherous sort, but her cheeks were rose-red, and her lips were curled ever so slightly. One last time Dranus saw the picturesque features of his dead wife and heard her lyrical voice ring through his head... but he could not hear the words.

*       *       *

Later that night Dranus examined maps of the area with Admiral O'cule in private, planning their next movements. O'cule would secure the city, slowly and carefully. A ground force would be deployed to secure the Superior and a light crew would be left on the ships in case the few remaining Shieran vessels tried to stage a sneak attack of some sort. Magemaster Zed would stay with them as insurance.

A small number of Titan Ships would reinforce them from where they still held the border. At this point there was no need to worry too greatly of a threat at sea finding space in their rear flanks. Armodus would continue autonomous control of the army and O'cule would organize the navy in his absence.

Of course, the man didn't know that part quite yet.

"My king, have you learned anything from the prisoner?" O'cule was hesitant to ask, thinking he may be out of line.

"Nothing of any great import, but I have learned that she is young, and her mind is yet to be fully molded. There is a chance, I think, that she may join our cause given the proper motivation and some time." Dranus was still absorbed in the maps, picking the quickest routes around the islands and the most strategically significant points to hold.

"With all due respect, Highness, I'm not sure the people of Varz would welcome a Lesser, especially not one of those damned Warriors, into our ranks." Again he shied away from being too brash or bold as to directly oppose the king since the normally dark ruler seemed particularly out of sorts this evening.

"I have no intention of assimilating her into our ranks, Admiral, she will merely be a tool at our disposal that we may utilize if the situation calls for it."

This seemed to pacify the admiral. Of course he had to consider the import of bringing the one who had caused the death of so many of his people to their side. It was, however, a vexation suited for another time. There was plenty with which to occupy his attention as it was.

"My king, will you lead the advance yourself? You have made no mention of the South Star Fleet in our plans." Dranus shifted the maps on the table until he looked at one of the mainland of Shiera,

218

that thin strip of land that was the shore of the inlet which housed the Shieran Isles. He took a deep breath and let out a long sigh.

"I will not."

"You'll return to Varz then?" O'cule inquired with genuine curiosity.

Dranus stopped looking at the maps and stared hard at his admiral. Could he trust O'cule with the information he held? Would he accept such a seemingly heretical decision?

"Admiral, no, O'cule...can I trust that if I tell you this, you will never speak of it again under penalty of exile?"

Rather than being intimidated by this, O'cule actually smiled.

"My king, I love you like I loved your father. There is no more faithful a soul in all of Varz. My loyalty to you is the salt in the sea." The man dropped his shoulders and beamed a smile of genuine pride and of compassion.

Dranus was calmed by the admiral's words.

"As it should be." King Dranus smiled, reassured that he had the best man in Varz as his admiral.

"The Book tells of some Relic which can defeat the Warriors of Pyrán, and I must seek it. However...it lies in the remains of Pyrán itself. Amidst the high mountains between Arendrum and Myrendel, it is there I will find the thing." His voice was hardly more than a whisper, making O'cule's response all the more jarring.

"To Pyrán?! Sire, no man of Varz has set foot in that place since before the age of the Five Realms! It is a blaspheme to all that we of Varz stand for! My lord, surely there can be nothing of use to us in that forsaken place!" O'cule was clearly agitated, the implications of the king's actions were numerous and grave.

"Settle yourself, Admiral!" Dranus's tone was tight and strict. "If the Book says it lies there, then there it lies. You've seen what just one Warrior can do alone! If we do not take drastic measures, this will be a war of attrition that we stand no chance in."

The King of Varz stared hard at the older man, daring him to refute this fact.

O'cule kept the stare for only a moment before looking away and cursing. "You are right as always, my king, I apologize for my outburst." He shuffled in place and pulled his uniform tight. "I will see that everything runs smoothly in your absence, but please be careful. You will be deep in enemy territory with no way to contact us. If something were to happen...."

"Fret not O'cule, remember that I will have an entire army at my disposal." He tilted his head to one side to reveal the multi-sided gemstone in the crown of the Staff of the South Star.

O'cule smiled, feeling foolish once more. Mayton's beard, he'd been rattled!

"I will chart my path through sparsely populated areas nowhere near Varz borders. Placing an army or a Warrior that far from the front would be tactical folly!" He reassured both his admiral and himself. An army could be bested with the Staff, but facing a Warrior one-on-one was unlikely to end in his favor.

"Then with the blessing of The Ultimate, make haste, my king." Of all the blessings that could be bestowed upon the king at the start of a journey to Pyrán, this was perhaps the most appropriate. It was certainly the most ironic.

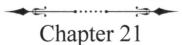

# Chapter 21
## The Souls of the Staff

King Dranus waited for a few days while the fast boat he had used to skirt the Shieran blockade was fetched from the border along with the new Titan Ships. It was important that everyone, including his own troops, believed that he remained aboard *The Dawn's Fury,* or at least in the general vicinity, and commanded them through Admiral O'cule. To maintain the ruse, his servants had been ordered to continue serving him, but with the added cover that he was to enter a deep sorcerous trance in an effort to discover a way to defeat the Warriors of Pyrán. This worked doubly in his favor, as it would appear he had simply created the last Relic himself after weeks of desperate work.

In the meantime, when he wasn't overseeing repairs or strategic meetings, he was ashore on one of the many abandoned islands or on his flagship fully testing the various properties of the Staff of the South Star. With all he had managed in recent naval battles, he had begun to wonder what other kinds of tricks he could pull off with the Staff.

In his time on the ship, he learned that he could summon any of the other three units onto his flagship or even over open water, though they dropped immediately into the sea (and quickly voiced their discontent). He confirmed that any number of the sailors of the South Star Fleet could be summoned or left off of their ships, but that each sailor or marine was bound to their respective ship and could not be summoned on another ship, though they could then cross to other ships after being summoned. Interestingly, he could not summon the ships underwater unless the Staff itself was also underwater, for whatever purpose that might serve.

On land he discovered far more peculiar things. Of the greatest delight to the king was that, like Admiral Burgiss, individual commanders and leaders of the various divisions could be summoned alone and held their personalities and character vastly intact. He found that he could not summon the soldiers into the air, and likewise could not summon them to a position that was more highly elevated than the one which he held. This, he assumed, was due to the position of the South Star and the refraction of its supernatural light.

Though he had been nervous about attempting such a thing, he made a humorous discovery about the South Star Fleet: that they could not be summoned off of their boats onto land...but that their boats could be summoned over the land. It was unfortunate, though, that they soon toppled, much to the dismay of their crew and the delight of the Varz onlookers.

King Dranus was in moderately good spirits while he waited, though he spent his nights deep in thought. What was he to do with the girl that was his prisoner? He tried to speak with her briefly each evening, if only to check on her care and health. He considered letting others speak with her freely so that she could see that his folk were similarly human, if culturally and intellectually more advanced. But that was too enormous a risk to take without someone moderating what they said or did.

Thoughts of the blasphemous ground of Pyrán swarmed his thoughts around the clock. Would he be safe in getting to Pyrán? And what would he find there? What was the ancient artifact that not even he had knowledge of? And why was it in Pyrán in the first place? Surely he would find no Varz castle or monarch from the past as with the other three. No monarch of Varz would dare to call that place home as it was against the very foundation of their nation.

And what of the Shield of Second Life? Its whereabouts were still a mystery, and he was no closer to finding out who was in possession of it. For all he knew, some thief had discovered it by accident and let it sit as a trophy, collecting dust, not knowing of its true potential.

All of these things strained his mind to its limits so that when finally it was time to begin his journey, he did so with enthusiasm and with hopes that he might finally begin to find some answers.

*     *     *

Only Admiral O'cule and Magemaster Zed saw him off in the early morning darkness. Because O'cule would not be able to keep constant watch over the captive, he found it necessary to give specific instructions to the Magemaster to watch over her. The proud sorcerer was told only that the king was leaving. The man was no fool and he had his suspicions, but he was as loyal as any other soldier of Varz and would sooner have his tongue removed before divulging any secrets that may be vital to the strength of his nation.

He did, however, have something to give the king on his departure. Before leaving the small merchant ship he turned and regarded his monarch. He approached quietly and placed a small silver ball in Dranus's bare hand.

"This is likely the last of its kind, kept in the Magemaster's care for generations, but you should take it. If there is a time for it to be of use to Varz, it must be now." The man treated the small orb like a small child, something fragile and precious which must be cared for with the utmost attention.

Dranus nodded, realizing what he held and marveled at the sight, for he had thought them all gone. "You have done a great thing Zed; I will remember this." He placed the marble-sized orb of silver in a cotton cloth and then shifted the cloth to be both firm and loosely giving to keep it from shattering.

With this, the Magemaster bowed low and took his leave back to *The Dawn's Fury* to care for the Warrior of Water.

The sailing was easy and his crew, the one that had taken him across the border in the first place, was well accustomed to the secretive nature in which their king moved. Moreover, they were all honored that they could serve him so closely.

In the short time it took for him to reach the mainland, Dranus summoned Admiral Burgiss to his ship and began to discuss the matters that plagued him. They would speak in his personal cabin, rocking gently in the afternoon with two glasses stuck to the table with sorcerously increased friction. The admiral could not partake, but it would be rude not to offer, he thought.

"By what means were these Relics of Power crafted, do you think?" Dranus sipped at the hot wine to warm him against the cold, cloudy evening. On the deck, the voices of his crew could be heard railing at one another while telling stories over the same wine he drank.

"I have only ever known the Staff, sire, but I know that it took a great deal of sorcery and a number of the realm's most powerful sorcerers to imbue it with such properties. The stone, however, was found. It fell from the heavens around the time we first saw the South Star." The long dead admiral of the South Star Fleet had lost none of his memories in his long sleep and Dranus found this information to be very telling.

"From the sky?! I presumed the gem was designed, like the Staff itself! Why was this not kept in the records?"

"Indeed, I remember the night vividly. I watched it fall as a young man, thinking it a star itself as it blazed through the sky." He looked into the sloshing liquid in his cup with a half smile, as if remembering the night and the light scar the falling star had made. He snapped his attention back quickly, however, recovering his tough, stoic expression.

"Queen Luna was actually completely uninterested in the stone at first. It was the Husband of the Queen, Jahnas, who was intrigued by its properties. It was under his direction that we came to learn, somewhat, of the gem's magical potential. They were very happily married, Queen Luna and Jahnas, even among the tribulations of the Great War. But when the queen became obsessed with the gem and what secrets it held, they began to drift apart." Dranus was swept up in the whole tale, almost in disbelief that he could hear his own nation's history straight from the mouth of someone who lived it.

"Jahnas was a close friend of mine. He regretted ever finding the gem which eventually took his life." Burgiss was noticeably solemn now, as though he had just considered for the first time that his good friend had been dead now for centuries and yet he still haunted this world somehow. A mixture of the private company and the thought of the wine loosened his long-frozen emotions.

"Was the Husband of the Queen enslaved to the Staff as well?! Can that be?" Dranus could not conceal his curiosity.

"No. But the Staff took away his wife, the majority of the Varz war effort, and virtually everything he loved. In that way it took his life." It may have been Burgiss's sudden change of mood or maybe not, but the king was suddenly overcome with sadness. He could relate to Jahnas's feelings, he thought. But instead of losing his life, he had forever felt that he not truly had one to begin with.

"Did he not accompany her to the Castle Beneath the Waves?" Dranus asked.

Burgiss looked puzzled at first by the king's question, but quickly accounted for the strange name he had used to call the castle.

"Unfortunately, Jahnas died from sickness shortly after the Staff was forged. I spoke with Queen Luna as she descended into her madness beneath the sea." Burgiss grew smaller then; his posture shrank, and his brow furrowed harshly. "She felt that it was her negligence which killed him and she never forgave herself for that. Alone in that damned castle with none but the souls she had imprisoned, she could only dwell on her regrets and the things she had lost."

Dranus looked across the room to where the Staff stood, strapped securely to a support by an open porthole that let the light of the South Star in. Suddenly the queen's posthumous title made more sense. What unbearable sorrow she must have endured to regret so much and to see in her people's eyes their diminishing respect for her as she lost hold of her sanity.

Fearing for his own mind he apologized to the admiral for bringing up such memories and delicately changed the topic to something more positive.

"Tell me about the First Great War...."

Several days later, the king continued on horseback, packed down with supplies that should last him for at least long enough for him to find a small town to trade with. In its scabbard was the Sword of Righted Guard, and strapped to the horse's side was the Staff of the South Star. In a pouch hanging from his side was the Book which guided him to the sacred mountain of Pyrán.

The pace that the king kept was strenuous at first, riding all throughout the day, stopping only when he suspected he might be discovered or to rest himself and his mount. The lands of Arendrum were mapped with exceptional detail so that Dranus could keep to dense forests, hills, and frigid mesas, avoiding any major settlements or military supply lines.

In the evenings, before the South Star had set, he had taken to communicating with a certain Commander Vintus (VIN-tuhs), head of the South Star Archers Brigade. Vintus was about Dranus's age but seemed to have had lifetimes worth of adventures more than he had. Commander Vintus had not known much about Queen Luna or the Staff of the South Star, but he was one of the primary socialites of his time and his tales grasped the king's imagination like none he had ever read in books.

"I tell you Dranus, it was a night I'll never forget! Before I was Commander, of course, but while I was working my way up through the ranks!" Vintus had been overly friendly with Dranus at first but had astutely pointed out that Dranus could do nothing to punish him and argued that they were from different times but of the same age. Besides, Dranus found it comforting to have a same-age friend who could address him casually and was neither a lover nor a book.

"You made Commander fairly young did you not?" Dranus was smiling, glowing from the light of the fire, but not like his companion glowed with sorcerous amber light.

"By your standards, I suppose, but it was relatively normal for the young to take charge in those days. Our passion and vitality made up for our lack of experience!" The young man had short feathery hair that was all black and a lean, fit figure though he could not remove his glowing armor.

"What different times we live in now...the people of Varz hardly know the meaning of passion! Now we put such a high price on experience and knowledge, being careful and sedentary. What do you suppose led us to this way of things?" It was something the king had postulated on for many nights since he had roused himself from this trance-like lethargy himself.

"Well, from what you've told me about what's happened, I'd say it's that we lost our ability to fight." Vintus considered, rubbing his chin thoughtfully.

"That is what I thought! Battle runs through our veins like fire! When we have nothing left to burn we can do nothing but fizzle out!" Dranus agreed, nearly jumping from his seat.

"Aye, but the embers will remain, friend. And embers need but a light wind to burst into roaring flames once again!" He made some dramatic gestures around the fire, joking and kidding with this king from another era.

"Yes, and I have tried to stoke the fire as much as I can. I believe our people go through a time of great change now as we reascend to greatness." Dranus stood and looked to the south where the dull red star was beginning to fade once more.

"I'll say! You're trying to do in a single lifetime what it took our people centuries to do! But you're a good king, Dranus, I believe you will revive the old spirit of our people. I look forward to seeing

226

that day." To have the faith of a man such as Vintus, who had lived in the prime of the Varz empire a mere handful of generations after the time of The Ultimate, was a boon to his confidence unlike any other. And given that the young man had been particularly critical of his deployment strategy at the Battle of the Rift, he believed the sentiment was genuine.

Dranus grinned at the man and then glanced at the last light of the South Star.

Vintus chuckled, standing up with arms spread, "You gonna kiss me goodnight, or what?"

And then he vanished in a whisp.

Dranus could not help but feel a bit sad that the man who was now likely his closest friend had, in fact, died several centuries ago. And though it was a simple reality that the people of Varz wielded magic so easily, even the king had to especially appreciate this magic which could unite two separate ages. He slept well that night, calmed by the confidence of Commander Vintus and the soothing sounds of the night.

His route lay mostly in the northern portion of Arendrum as he made his way to towering Pyrán. This area was not well inhabited because of the cold climates during the Night Season and though this made it so that it was unlikely for him to get caught, it also meant that his progress was drastically slowed when he entered the snowy hills to the north of the mountain range.

At this point he had no choice but to pull back his pace as his horse trudged through deep snow, furs and simple shifts of the mind keeping him warm. Eventually he was forced to head southward towards the capital city of Arendrum or else his horse would freeze to death, and he would have no game to hunt, no rivers to fish. There were no towns here, only small settlements where strangers would be met with open suspicion and hostility in all likelihood. He couldn't even disguise himself for trade and his supplies were beginning to run low.

The positive side, Dranus considered, was that he had further time to speak with those of the Staff. Because members of the Army and Archer's Brigade did not have horses, he summoned the Commander of the South Star Knights with her treasured mount. The woman was more the age of Commander Ven than his own, but the grays in her hair were not as prominent and her characteristic black hair was shorter, framing her battle-worn face. He noted a distinct scar on her face that went down between her eyes to her left cheek.

"Just a careless fault in judgment, nothing more." The Commander said, noticing the king's gaze. "I was overconfident in my youth and took this in a duel." She gestured to the scar. "Caused more problems after I got it, to be honest. Some people thought it was too similar to the crest the queen wore and my own little sister almost had me executed for it!"

Dranus had been all too intrigued to learn that this Commander Lena (LEE-nuh) was the queen's older sister. It was incredibly rare in Varz history for the eldest son or daughter to not become the next king or queen but there were instances like this when it happened. Lena had explained that Luna was simply better fit for ruling while she was better fit for fighting; the logic was straightforward enough to have convinced their father.

"Although sometimes I think it was just because Little Luna was jealous of me...." Commander Lena cackled. "I haven't been able to call her that ever since she became queen." She grinned to Dranus.

"Jealous? But she was Queen of Varz, should it not have been you who was jealous?" Dranus could not hide his suspicious brow, moving at a steady canter upon his horse. To her credit, the Commander reigned in her horse since it had no trouble moving through the snow at all; an odd feature that was shared with the ships of the South Star Fleet. It was as if the members of the Staff existed on a separate plane that overlapped his own.

"No, it wasn't that. Luna had always wanted to be Queen of Varz but our father, King Dranus the Steeled, always favored me because I was the better warrior and the first-born daughter. Even after our father died she felt the need to try and best me as though that would somehow change his final impression of her." Dranus was startled by the fact that her father was also named Dranus, presumably the first of the name!

"It was not until our younger sister disappeared that we ceased to quarrel over such trivialities." Commander Lena was an impressive woman; she had hardly shown a sign of weakness or hesitance since Dranus had first called upon her. But speaking of a younger sister, whom Dranus had never even heard of, cast her eyes downward and caused her cheeks to sag with open remorse.

"A third sister? I was to believe that Luna had only a single sister." The king, though he did not want to cause unnecessary distress to the woman, was becoming more and more curious with every talk he had with the spirits of the Staff. There were so many inconsistencies between the Forbidden Texts and the accounts of those who lived during those times. Then again, he supposed all stories told enough times transformed into mere facsimiles of their origin.

"She was very young when she disappeared. She was neither a strong warrior nor a good leader. She was incredibly insightful but spoke very infrequently and kept to herself. I'm afraid even as her sister there is not much I can say about her. She was unimaginably brilliant...she could have been a masterful sorceress if she had the chance." Her fist tightened on the reigns and her glow dulled momentarily. A small fluttering of noise came from the Staff but drifted off as quickly as it had come.

"Even when I spoke with Luna afterward, she always blamed herself for Lana's disappearance."

Dranus remembered his talk with Admiral Burgiss and the burden she had felt about her husband's death. Gradually all that he had ever known about Queen Luna the Mad was shifting. Even after meeting the woman, herself, he had only glimpsed the strong facade she had to maintain in an exchange from one monarch to another.

"Ahh, did this contribute to her madness?" Dranus asked innocently.

Lena's strong brow furrowed at these words, clearly taking offense.

"My sister was not mad! She was disgraced by that namesake! All of us offered her our lives for use in the Staff of our own will. Not a single one of us has regretted our decision." She looked away, ashamed of her momentary dissolution of composure.

"I know, I apologize commander." Dranus saw her then as the protective older sister that she was. Even though she must have spoken with Luna multiple times after her retreat to the ocean depths, she could only see her innocent little sister as she had always wanted to remember her: a little brat who needed looking out for but who's heart was pure and who's entire life had been intertwined with her own.

Lena turned as though something she had not quite thought of finally registered.

"You met my sister, didn't you? To get the Staff you must have

229

spoken with her." Dranus hesitated, not knowing what to tell the woman...should he tell her that her sister truly was insane or let her continue to believe in the innocence of a sister wronged by cruel history?

"I did. She was a wise Queen of Varz, and perhaps one of the most powerful in our storied histories." He could not hide his hesitation well and not even the steady flurry of snow could distract the luminous green warrior's gaze.

"Please tell me, my king, what did you gauge of my little sister?" Her hardened eyes stared at the king and Dranus felt it difficult to say the truth: that she had lost her sanity somewhere along the way, that even she admitted to her madness in the end. Before it would have been as easy as saying the words as they came to his mind, but now he found he did not want to ruin this woman's perception of her sister. "I beg of you, King Dranus."

"It is of no importance whether Queen Luna was mad or not, Commander Lena. She was a magnificent Queen of Varz and did great things for our people and our realm. She was wise and intelligent as can be seen from her deeds. You were a duelist; would you ever judge the entirety of a duel by any single sword-stroke? That she is remembered solely as the Mad Queen is an injustice without uncertainty." Dranus neither lied nor completely divulged the truth, but this was allowable in his mind, and it brought a small smile to the commander's lips. The tension of the subject quickly faded from the air, and this was clearly for the best.

"Luna was a terribly brilliant sorceress. Once her husband told her about that gem's properties, she had discovered how it could be used in a matter of weeks. That she was able to create such a thing as this staff, with a little help from the Black Mages, is nearly unbelievable in itself." Dranus nearly jumped out of his saddle when he heard her speak of the Black Mages.

"The Black Mages?! What do you know of them?!" Dranus had only seen some vague reference to them while he was searching for information about Luna in the Book.

"Almost nothing, I'm afraid. They answered and interacted solely with Queen Luna, though I had heard some of them matched or even exceeded her sorcery. I know neither their identity nor their purpose, only that they assisted in creating the Staff of the South Star and all apparently perished in doing so." Lena looked somewhat resentful, wishing she could answer her king more thoroughly but unable to do so.

"Exceeded the powers of the queen? That is nonsense! No one has greater power than a monarch of Varz, that is how our society is structured, it is the law!" Dranus could not believe that this could be true...the only way for someone to be stronger than the Queen of Varz was to create spells that not even she could know!

"That may be true, my king, but remember that logic is somewhat of a malleable substance for our people and has always been."

Immediately thoughts of the Shield of Second Life returned. Had some man or woman of Varz surpassed him and divined the Shield's location? Was some traitor plotting a coup in his absence at that very moment? Waiting, perhaps, for him to do all of the work and expend his resources so that he could come in at the final moment and take over?

Now he continued in obsessive paranoia over who might be planning against him...was it the Magemaster? He was an ambitious man and everyone knew that. He had shown his competency countless times and had even surprised the king with the presentation of the small silver marble that Dranus now carried. But those of Varz were fiercely loyal and he could not waste time thinking one of his own plotted against him. Outcasts and bandits, the lowest scum of Varz, these were the ones he might be wary of. For now he could not possibly know more of it and so he made an effort not to think.

"Certainly not the greatest sorcerer of my time, but a man named Geoffra had a particular skill with bizarre forms of magic," Lena added, noting the king's distress and hoping to change the topic. "He was an interesting old man with a thousand and one stories and a fantastic imagination. He claimed familiarity with night and sun magic, with summoning pacts, and ancient rituals. The story of how he became known as 'firetreader' was my favorite."

Dranus listened attentively as Lena retold some of the stories she still remembered from the kind old story-teller. They passed the time thus until the South Star set once more.

Then, after almost a month and a half of travel, he lay eyes on the nameless mountains that divided the realms of Arendrum and Myrendel and knew he must soon face the perils that led to the top of the world.

# Chapter 22
## A Letter to Superior Frau

King Dranus made camp among the low hills surrounding the great mountain range that split the realms of Arendrum and Myrendel. He had ventured dangerously south, just a short distance from the Arendrum capital city, to reach his final destination. He could have entered the mountain range further north, but that range was particularly dangerous and likely impassable in places this time of year. Unfortunately, he had no other choice. Still, he took care to make sure his tracks were covered and his impact on the surrounding area was as minimal as possible. To make matters worse, he was working on the last of his rations. He sustained himself mostly with potions he could brew with what little vegetation that the unforgiving Night Season permitted but he would need to hunt somewhere in the mountains where his work was less likely to be discovered. Over the last few weeks he had noticed a precipitous drop in his body weight as he fought to sustain himself as inconspicuously as possible.

Fortunately, he had finally reached the point where he was close enough to the mountain base. One could not miss Pyrán from this distance. It was a singular monolith among even the tall peaks of this range. It could have been his preconceptions playing tricks on him, but looking up at the point where he headed it almost seemed as though the peak were shrouded in mysterious shadow: a shroud of sacrilege and danger in equal parts.

Other than the dark cloud of breaking the greatest taboo in his culture, the morning was pleasantly warm, and the king was feeling refreshed, confident that the key to his overall victory was within his grasp. Despite his rough conditions, his recent communications with the spirits of the Staff of the South Star had greatly increased his overall outlook and his confidence as King of Varz. Incidentally, he had learned enough about the Staff and those that resided within that he felt as though he had truly mastered his mad ancestor's Relic.

Dranus sat on a downed tree chewing on stale bread and mostly frozen jerky, his last piece. He quietly considered the embers of the fire he had recently doused. With all his sorcery and knowledge, he still had to put out a small fire by hand. But the Warriors of Pyrán...they could create and destroy the elements on a whim and at a scale that had only been seen when a tremendous number of powerful sorcerers came together: like when his people sank the nation of Shiera.

Part of him dreaded that the Warriors would be waiting for him at the peak and that this was all part of some ploy by the Book. Was this another part of the prophecy the Book had spoken of? The text had not revealed much in the way of specific events, but it was just as cryptic in nature as his own magical tome.

The daunting task of climbing the great mountain furthered weighed on him. On a great climb, one needed the promise of reward, or of long-sought destination to drive you. But here he was heading to the one place no citizen of Varz had ventured to in more than a thousand years. Who was he to enter such a place? Who was he to go where those of Varz dared not go? Surely he was King of Varz but so had been his father, and his father's father, and a series of monarchs that preceded him for generations. And yet they had not dared even a plan to visit that place. But then why should they? Not even the Lessers who praised the holiness of that sacred mountain ventured to the peak. In every culture across the Five Realms it was a strong taboo to tread on that ground. It was not a place for mortals. Some folk religions thought it was the location of the afterlife itself! Now he was to assume the task single-handedly and face whatever mysteries stayed there?

It had seemed insane every time he thought about it. Every day since he left Shiera behind. Every night staring at the fire. What would his hubris bring about? What would he find there? What could be there other than ruins and the vestiges of their ancient enemy?

He did not know, could not speculate, and would not guess lest he shake his resolve.

Thinking hard about what he should do to prepare himself, Dranus took out the Book which he had scarcely said a word to since leaving Shiera. The two had made amends of sorts, but Dranus was not as trusting or reliant on the Book as he had originally been. Regardless, his confidants of the Staff had no knowledge of what to expect in the ravaged remains of Pyrán, so he turned to that near infinite well of knowledge with some reluctance.

"Oh, master! I've recently read something I know you'll love!" the Book instantly sprang to life with a chipper yet seemingly chapped tone. "How can you tell a Shieran ship from one of Varz?" The lost art of humor had recently begun to flourish once more in Varz culture, and it felt like every time Dranus opened the Book it had some new quip to annoy him with.

"Our craftsmanship and technology are far more advanced. Their ships tend to be somewhat larger than ours. Obviously we fly different flags." He was in no mood for such obvious questions.

"No, no, no! Varz ships aren't moored at the bottom of the Middle Sea!" The Book's papered laughter and the way that this particular 'joke' indirectly praised his own efforts in the war softened the king's mood a little and a smile broke onto his dry lips.

"Very clever." Part of him longed for the jovial adventures he had shared with the Book in familiar comfort when they had sought the first Relics of Power. But his trust in the thing had waned and he could not afford to be so forgiving.

"Book, have you any idea what lies atop the mountain of Pyrán?" He stared at the worn, almost skin-like cover as though he were speaking with the Book face to face.

"The ruins of Pyrán lie there, of course, master. Surely you know this already." Dranus was not amused at this.

"Do not be coy with me, tome. What lie within the ruins? Can you describe them to me?" The Book took longer than normal to consider before committing to an answer.

"The item that you seek lies there, master, the item that will allow you to overcome the namesake Heroes. There are no written records of the place's physical properties, only that it is now in ruins."

Dranus allowed himself a brief smile at this reassurance.

"So then how will we find the weapon? How could such a powerful thing of Varz have made its way to such a place?" Each of the previous Relics were masterful creations of some of the greatest monarchs of Varz and had been kept by their creators in their castles. But there were no castles of Varz in this place and the ground was unbroken by Varz blood since the time of The Ultimate. He supposed, on the other hand, if a monarch wanted to keep a particular weapon secret...perhaps they believed it to be too powerful?...there was no better hiding spot.

"The *item* will likely not be in any particular location, though it never leaves the summit." This talking in riddles would have angered the king had he not already become accustomed to these types of conversations.

"The *weapon* can move, then? Will there be another reanimated corpse waiting for me that has awoken prematurely?" The emphasis the Book had put on the word 'item' made him curious, he still had no idea what the Relic was or how it was supposed to help him against the Warriors of Pyrán.

"What do you believe it is that you will find there, lord? The item you seek is not a weapon for fighting or for killing, it is something much more subtle." Although the Book could not express emotions, Dranus was overwhelmed with the sensation of a snickering grin in the Book's tone.

"Not a weapon? And you are sure it was created by Varz?" Dranus stood now, openly unsettled by all of these mysteries, pacing as he normally did, touching the V-shaped scar on his cheek and staring through the snow-covered trees around him. All of the other sorcerous items ever crafted by notable Varz sorcerers were tools meant for killing, how could this one be so different? There was, for example, King Faust's cloak, but even that was part of his martial guise and was designed with combat in mind.

Suddenly, the Book practically hopped out of his hands. Its cover flew open and it flipped through pages furiously, back and forth until it stopped on a page where words were being written in ornate calligraphy.

"My lord! There is no time! You must leave now; you are in danger!" The Book shouted.

Dranus was not sure he had ever heard the Book speak with such nervous agitation.

"Why? What is it? Or are you trying to lure me away from my questions?!" He was ever suspicious of the magical book, but he took the time to take the Staff of the South Star from where it stood against a tree, just in case.

"No, master! It is a letter from the Arendrum Superior! Quickly, you must read it immediately!" The king was beginning to sense that the Book spoke the truth and anxiously spread the pages, watching as the words were carefully crafted with every stroke of a fine-tipped brush.

His eyes widened, his pulse jumped up, and sweat began to form on his brow. The letter read:

> We have just received word that Shiera has fallen, the Varz forces have moved more quickly than we expected. They must be strong to have so quickly overcome the entire Shieran navy. Communication is scarce with them.
>
> Furthermore, I have sent the Warrior of Earth after an invader. He has reported that there can be no more than three, yet their numbers seem to change from place to place. He has been tracking him for some time now but has been unable to discern a final destination. My last correspondence with the young man told that he would attempt an ambush just north of the city. We have fair reason to believe the intruder is of Varz, perhaps some small scouting team charged with mapping our lands so they may more easily be taken, but we cannot be sure. The ambush should take place today. Until we know more, take care of your borders Superior Frau (fr-OW), with the fall of Shiera we are all in danger.

The letter was signed by the Superior of Arendrum in long, flowing waves at that very moment. That meant...the ambush could happen at any....

Some ancient instinct forced the king to sidestep abruptly, just barely dodging an arrow that could have pierced his midriff.

"No! How?! I've been so careful!" The ambush had already begun! He had been so meticulously careful to leave no trace of his movements and somehow they had found him, had been tracking him! Even worse, the ambush would be led by the Warrior of Earth, that monstrous force that had almost wiped out the entire South Star archer units in a single massive upheaval of earth.

With no care for his things, save the Book and his Relics, he tried to saddle his horse. He had already unsheathed the Sword of Righted Guard and when arrows flew at him from varying directions the sword took each one to the side without so much as a thought from the king so that his defense from ranged attacks was nearly perfect. This did, however, significantly slow him and he could sense the tightening of a noose of light-footed archers and heavily armored soldiers.

This was not Dranus's first brush with near-certain death, however. Facing these kinds of conditions was normal, and critical, in the training of a Varz monarch or any other ranking officer. He was frantic in spirit, but his mind was steady. With flourishing thoughts the straps and buckles of the saddle wove in and out into their proper place. Meanwhile, his eyes surveyed the surrounding area, flipping through various types of sight to gather as much information as he could.

On the northern hills appeared legions of archers with bent bows. The flatlands to the south now sprouted soldiers like weeds. To his west was only Arendrum and certain doom. And to the east, between the king and his precipitously close goal, was the shimmering silver of the Warrior of Earth. It was a thorough ambush. In the distance he could see towering masses of rock being erected in any dips between hills, blocking foot paths and any venues he might take by horseback.

For every inconceivable situation, there was a conceivable way out. This was the law of Varz sorcery. The restrictions of things like reality were tenuous, like ropes tied loosely around his wrists: he need but shake them off to move forward.

A plan formed.

In a small lull of the near constant deluge of arrows Dranus split away from an image of his body as it mounted the horse. His true outline vanished into the cold air. He slapped his horse hard on its hindquarters and the loyal steed charged to the south, towards Varz. With his relative invisibility, for as briefly as it would last, he should be able to get through the perimeter and escape. He moved deliberately, planning every step so that he would not make any disturbance of the landscape around him. Although his footprints were hard to mask in the falling snow, he had tricked the snow into spreading his weight across a broad area so that they did not penetrate as deeply.

The line of men to the east came into sight and he froze, hardly allowing even a breath from his cracked lips, and struggling to keep his racing heart from betraying him. The enemy was advancing steadily, led by the Warrior in his silver armor and carrying his huge shield of gray stone. Dranus scowled at the sight of the Warrior of

Pyrán but was taken aback when the young man seemed to smirk in return, staring right back at him!

"You have many tricks, I see. Or rather...I don't see." The short youth laughed heartily and motioned to his men.

"As long as you exist and stand upon this ground...*my* ground, you cannot hide from me!" He laughed again and then pointed quickly, the motion was followed by a line of arrows. The arrows were not completely accurate, and all passed the king without harm. But his luck would not hold for long, and the archers would gain his depth in time.

Dranus had never fathomed that this Warrior had such mastery of the earth that he could see him presumably by the pressure his body exerted on it; that must have been how he had tracked him so efficiently.

Though he had desperately hoped to keep secret the fact that he carried the source of the South Star Army, he no longer had other any other options. With a dull thud in the snow, a bloody crimson light cracked as though through the fabric of space itself. The light flooded the scene and surrounded the surprised enemy warriors. Following the light came a legion of the South Star Army in full charge, knowing the situation implicitly through the king's magic.

To Dranus's mounting horror, the Warrior of Earth was like a mountain himself, knocking aside every soldier that came against him with alarming ease. His men crowded around him and fell upon the downed spirits quickly and efficiently. The boy strode closer to the king's position at a leisurely pace.

Dranus winced and took a few hesitant steps back, fear welling within him and threatening to break the concentration he needed to remain invisible. This was perhaps the worst of the Warriors he could face one-on-one. If this kept up, he could be killed, or worse...captured.

When the Staff slammed into the snow again, the Warrior's eyes darted directly to the spot and then up at Dranus's eyes. Amber light burned in the air surrounding the King of Varz and was soon followed by a flurry of arrows.

Unperturbed, the boy simply slammed the heavy shield against the ground and a wall of earth rolled from the land, consumed the arrows, and then faded like a rolling wave back into the earth.

Dranus could not hold! He took a step back and Teego, the

238

Warrior of Earth, took note of the moving of snow.

Again the Staff turned and now a low dirge of distant voices emanated from the thing along with a shining emerald light. He had decided no more risks could be taken and now a whole army of a thousand or more horsemen filled the valley! Dranus revealed himself, no longer able to hold his invisibility.

"You will not have my life this day, cursed Warrior! Now die!" Dranus's shout lacked the confidence necessary to shake his enemy. But even if he was a hero of some prophecy, he could not possibly stand against so many mounted men!

But giving away his exact location was just what the Warrior of Pyrán had been waiting for and his reaction was swift, making a series of rapid, heavy steps on the ground like some bizarre dance. Then, the viridian light that once filled the valley had vanished and near its center stood a large tent of triangular earthen shards converging some thirty feet over the king's head. Inside the prison of earth was none but the King of Varz and the Warrior of Earth.

"Well, I had my hesitations, but it looks like it worked." The young man's confidence showed on his face. Such nonchalant joy. Such disgusting power.

"What worked?" Dranus was nearly sick to his stomach...the power of the South Star could not be used without its light. Now he was contained in a structure that could be completely controlled by the Warrior that stood before him. It was more than a shelter; it was a tomb.

Though his eyes automatically adjusted to the darkness out of habit, he still held a major disadvantage. Any major spell that might free him would take time and at this distance he might not have that time.

"I was surprised when I heard we had records on that staff of yours." The Warrior took small, careful steps forward. "But it seems our ancestors dealt with it during the First Great War for a brief period. They surmised it was linked with that red sun you summoned." He smirked again, staring directly at the king. "I guess they were right."

He had to do something! Keep the boy talking, distract him, and then escape.

"And how do you know it doesn't have other properties?" He tried to lead the boy, but the expression of humor had left the Warrior and was replaced with a frown.

The boy made a quick, stern movement and the king's feet were rapidly covered by a blanket of heavy dirt; nearly knocking Dranus to his knees.

"Your tricks won't work on me, King of Varz. And I know you are the king, only the queen could carry the staff in the old days, and you have that mark on your cheek, so don't try and play dumb with me!" King Dranus had met quite a foe in this Warrior. Despite his apparent youth and inexperience he was an efficient fighter, an intelligent boy, and controlled a power that was, by all historical accounts, unimaginable. And unlike Raven, the Warrior of Water, he seemed quite resolute in his hatred for Varz.

"So then what will you do with me? Capture me? Kill me?" There was still some time. He ignored the boy's words for the most part. What he talked about was irrelevant so long as he talked long enough that Dranus could concoct some plot or recall some spell which might aid him.

"Well that depends on whether or not you resist any further. We had been wondering when you would make your next move but had not expected something like this!" To his credit, the boy held his shield in front of him as he slowly approached. He was being rightfully careful, but his hesitance also benefited the king.

Dranus took note of these words in particular. The news of Shiera's fall must not have reached him while he was tracking in the field. For this he was thankful. He expected the Warrior would be much less diplomatic with a lust for revenge gripping his heart.

"Well, that depends on...." He stopped abruptly, remembering the silver ball the Magemaster had given him weeks before. He ventured in his mind to find where the pouch containing the orb was and almost sighed in relief when he discovered he had smartly kept it on his person. With a small gesture as if to clear his throat and some subtle sorcery, the pouch was dislodged from its buckled position in his armor and fell into a deft hand, mid-motion to cover his mouth. The motion was corrected by his sorcery for any stray movements. His enemies would know to expect large spells and illusions, but the illusion that an arm in motion had not stopped for a moment when it actually had? The boy gave no indication of direct suspicion, though he pulled his shield closer in reaction to the cough.

"Depends on what? You may not be used to this but you're not

240

exactly in a position to be bargaining!" The boy still had his youthful arrogance. Good, it would prove to be Dranus's greatest advantage.

"Am I not?" A vicious grin curled onto Dranus's lips. "You are an expert in my ways now? Oh, woe is me. Outsmarted by a *child*." Dranus playfully feigned his weakness, though he could not keep the obvious sarcasm from his voice or the sinister smile from his lips.

The Warrior became cautious. He took a step back, raising his shield against some expected resistance.

"Know this, Warrior of Pyrán." Now the King of Varz emanated heavy arrogance and pomp which pressed its weight against the Warrior's retreating shield. "You may have great power, but you were given this power, it was handed to you for nothing! I have worked from the very moment of my birth to master the sorcerous arts! You cannot prevail against me because you have never known a true foe!" He paused, "today, you will learn!" The powerful voice of the king boomed in the closed chamber.

Before the boy could retort, Dranus threw the silver orb into the dirt and a bright flash like lightning illuminated the earthen shelter.

Next, spreading quickly over the snowy earth came an oozing, viscous liquid the same color of the orb which covered the area between the two combatants. The Warrior of Earth had regained himself after reeling from the blast of light and now seemed to be preparing for some great manipulation of the earth around them.

But before whatever he had in mind could be completed, a terrible screech sounded from somewhere beneath the dirt's surface. The boy came to a jarring halt with eyes wide. He stood still, breathless for a moment and then screamed, tearing at his chest as if trying to remove disease, threat, or Death itself. Sometimes he made a motion like he was trying to plug something...like a hole had appeared within him inexplicably and his body railed in response.

Dranus relished the boys suffering and bathed in the warm breath of air that quickly filled the dome. Another screech sounded, shattering the shimmering green light that was beginning to expand from the Warriors body. In its place was the King of Varz, illuminated in golden light, looking like some dark God greedily consuming all the world's light.

From the brilliantly shining portal burst a giant black hawk with a maliciously curved beak of yellow and a proud plumage of jet, blade-like feathers; its eyes were like a sorcerer's in that the colors were inverted, but instead of black, the knowing eyes shimmered rich yellow. The magnificent creature hovered in the air for a moment, looking about, and its glaring eyes caught those of the bewildered Warrior of Earth who could do nothing but look on in terror. Then the bird caught sight of its summoner. The Warrior visibly shrank back at the splitting scream of this animal from another age.

It took but a moment for Dranus to grasp the massive bird's talon with his free hand, having sheathed the Sword of Righted Guard. Then the mass of winged fury rushed at the ceiling and crashed through it, ripping the king from his earthen clasps, climbing higher and higher into the sky and letting out a triumphant cry. Below, all of the soldiers stood wide-eyed, rubbing at their eyes and questioning their sanity. Only the Warrior of Earth had regained himself and glowered at the fleeing King of Varz.

When they had reached a secure distance, Dranus climbed up the huge bird and sat in the ancient saddle, taking the specialized reigns and smiling wildly at his daring escape. For a moment he simply laughed, covering his face with his hand in disbelief himself. It was incredible that the summoning gem still worked in the first place, but that the great hawks his ancestors had bred still obeyed his command was nothing short of unbelievable. The hawks had been bred for war and knew nothing but war. When Varz decayed into times of peace they had been set free and had not been spotted for several hundred years! The saddle, he presumed, was part of the summoning spell as it was likely as old as the gem which summoned both it and the majestic bird.

Finally, sanctuary was his.

With immeasurable odds stacked against him he had managed to escape. Not only that, he now had the means to climb the treacherous mountain trails in a matter of moments! He and his saddled companion climbed rapidly through low blanketing clouds to the peak of Pyrán: the top of the world. In his ascension he mused at the stark similarities between his people and the creatures they had bred. It was curious that their sorcerous eyes were a different hue, but he supposed this was natural in a different species.

What would have been a nearly impassable climb had become a blissfully scenic flight. And in his ascent, he realized that his rescue was in large part due to the efforts of the Book in his armor. To control a force such as Fate...was this the power that the Book offered? Was that the true mechanism of such an improbable escape? Dranus realized that it was a mistake to consider such profound topics at that time, but perhaps that was the nature of this place.

Soon he found himself hovering over the ancient ruins, his elated mood quickly dampened.

Below lay shattered buildings of a place long forgotten by all in the world. Here was no great city, no impenetrable fortress or castle, hardly any true buildings had ever stood there.

No, below were the remains of temples, of towers of prayer, monuments to forgotten Gods, and gardens not tended through a millennium of neglect. Below was that most ancient of enemies to the folk of Varz.

Below was Pyrán, the Holy.

# Chapter 23
## Pyrán the Holy

Pyrán the Holy was calm in its perch at the top of the world. When the great mountain came to its summit the land leveled off unnaturally into a flat plateau. At an almost visible line just below the plateau there was the abrupt end of all things natural from the mountain. Moss stopped abruptly on rocks shorn flat. Trees grew sideways as if to avoid this line and their branches grew into nubs where they mistakenly approached the holy place. Below this invisible barrier was rough and scattered dirt; above it was neat, perfectly smoothed path.

A lone figure crossed the unnatural plane that separated nature from...whatever was in Pyrán. He had studied the barrier closely and, with trepidation, stepped up the last few feet and crested the plateau.

Nothing happened.

At least, nothing that he could tell at first glance.

The man continued with careful steps, feeling more and more torn at the very locus of his soul for coming to this place and treading so carelessly. Was it really possible that the legends and stigma his culture assigned to this place could unsettle him this deeply?

Or was there something else at work here?

He approached a garden with tall, earthen walls and stone columns crumbled by time…but potentially not as crumbled as they should have been....

Entering the garden he saw the remains of rose vines, long since unattended but not yet decomposed. It was said that this place had been unattended for a thousand years, so how was it that things looked so well preserved? Was this place death, itself?

King Dranus of Varz contemplated this thought and its implications extensively, feeling almost as though he could not leave the garden before he reached a conclusion. But a surprising calm befell him, and he carried on.

The glaring quiet of the place pressed on his temples and

tightened his jaw. Here was like a dream where things were not quite as they should be, and yet, *felt* like they belonged.

His footfalls, which he made no effort to hush, barely broke the silence as if muffled by the thick air between his ears and the ground. There was no sound of the wind blowing through the peaks nor the stirring of trees or fallen leaves. Although there were plenty of trees and leaves all about, there was no wind to push them, despite the strong winds he felt when saddled in the giant hawk which would not even approach the peak. With irregular frequency he caught glimpses of movement like some small animal that may have made its way up to this point only to find the way back down was too treacherous, but it always turned out to be his eyes playing tricks on him. In the forlorn stillness he began to see movement where there was none, hear sounds in silence, and feel queer sensations prickling at his skin. He had simply never gone so long without natural stimulation. Not even the gentle sounds of nature could be found. It was like a mock diorama of reality: perfectly still and posed for all time.

King Dranus stopped at a pair of tall statues which formed an archway over his path. The two figures facing each other were vaguely familiar to him: Gods of the old world according to the Book. He stared up at the giant statue to his left. It was of a man clad in armor all adorned with circles, his long hair radiating in all directions from his face like an image of the sun's rays. The God's arms were of a different stone than the rest of his body. They were huge and black as though they were chiseled from slabs of dark onyx. The right arm rose into the air to form the left half of the archway.

To his right was another of the Gods whose features were notably similar to the one he faced, though his armor was decorated with an array of sharp crescents. His hair hanging down his back, he raised a peculiar white sword seemingly coated in pearl. The blade was curved like the young moon in its cycle, its lower end serving as half the guard, and it rose to meet the black arm to form the right half of the archway. Dranus did not know why he took such time to consider these statues, but as he did, he remembered a Lesser tale about the Gods of the Sun and the Moon; brothers who constantly quarreled over who would own the skies.

Was it the spirits of these lost Gods that haunted his nerves? With the rise of Varz and The Ultimate in the Five Realms, the remaining followers were said to have fled to the west for sanctuary. But those were dimmer times, could there still be those who believed the world was once held in the palms of Gods? The Book, an almost limitless hoard of knowledge seemed to think so, but its thoughts were based solely on human writings. Humans from a thousand years prior believing in Gods did not make them real. It was only by considering these things, which he knew to be simple and logical, that he could contain himself in this most sacred place.

Further and further into the ruins he traveled, leaving the garden behind him. The less he could see the physical boundaries of this promontory, the more he felt he had entered some alternate realm once inhabited by the dead but since abandoned even by them. No matter his effort, he could not identify the feeling that made him feel so alert, and yet so eerily at ease.

From the corners of his eyes he thought he saw shadows of things that had no form, or shadows that split into illogical directions; sometimes he guessed a shadow showed what a structure had looked like before it was destroyed by wear and tear and gravity. But whenever he looked to inspect it more closely, it appeared as simple, uncloaked normalcy.

Possibly the most disturbing aspect of this place was its unshakable familiarity. Everywhere he looked he had some innate sense that he had seen the thing before. Statues, buildings, even subtle patterns in the stone pathway; it was all as a memory from a dream. It felt like...like the buildings and statues were projecting their memories into him. They forced him to remember someone else's memories, to feel someone else's feelings, but who's? And then, at the barest conscious scrutiny, the feeling was gone.

Was such a thing possible?

Here, at the origin and apex of all sorcerous might, he believed that anything was possible. Even the King of Varz could scarcely be prepared for such realities.

It was the remarkable sense of familiarity that set the king to thinking about how much he really knew about Pyrán, the Holy. What he really knew was far less than he wished he knew and even this was mostly speculation and myth. He knew only that this place had always been the seat of magic and power merely by the nature of its existence and no other reason. Still, there were stories and the like

246

that ordained this place as the home of the old Gods; that the power here was merely that which was left behind by the Gods when they chose to leave this plane to its own devices.

What had actually occurred here? What had been the true purpose of this place before it was destroyed? He needn't ask who wrought such destruction on this holy place, for it had been none other than Dranus's distant ancestors. But he could not shake the feeling that something was amiss, that by no means or logic should he be in that place, and that his very existence in such a sanctimonious location upset the balance of all things.

All he knew for certain at that point was that he could not stop. He had made it all this way and he could not leave without the item that would help him defeat the Warriors of Pyrán, whatever it may be, and wherever it could be hidden.

For the first time, considering he had not yet heard solid answers from the Book, he took the text out of his armor and addressed it as he had always done.

"Book, I am here in Pyrán, now you must tell me where the relic is." It took some effort for him to remain calm as he spoke, the sound of his voice was stifled and choked by the atmosphere around him.

The Book was silent.

"Book, I am your master, you cannot resist my questions!" His nervousness was now obvious, and he struggled to keep himself from shaking both from the cold and the unnamable sense of doom he felt.

Still the Book was silent.

A thought occurred to the king as he prepared to punish the traitorous tome and he tried to shift his vision, to see into other dimensions of space or to see heat, to see anything which only his eyes might grant him.

He could not.

None of his trained twists of logic had any effect on the place or anything in it whatsoever. This was immensely puzzling, though it revealed the source of the Book's silence. He could not fathom a reason why his sorcery would not work here, of all places. Was it his antithetical heritage which the mountain simply would not allow to manipulate reality?

With every step, it seemed, a new question arose.

Among the ruins Dranus came to a set of seven large stones laid in a circle enshrined by an outer ring of strong columns. Set into the stones were indentations. In one was a place for a monstrous sword, in another was a place for a pair of daggers, and there were such stones for a shield, a bow, a trident, and a long chain with small blades at each end. As his eyes followed the ring of stones, they fell at last upon one that was nothing but a pile of rubble. The king poked gingerly at the stones with the toe of his boot, moving them aside slowly. Inscribed on one of the gray stones was the symbol of the crescent moon, its upper tip missing from a fracture in the rock.

Dranus recalled the towering form of the man with the long crescent blade. He knew there must be some connection but could hardly guess at what it was. One thing began to make sense, however. The prophecy had mentioned 'The Seven' but only six had shown at the Battle of the Rift. Originally, he mistook this for an error in the text, or perhaps it was that only six of the seven had been summoned by then. Now, he hoped, one had already met their end.

The remaining stones were in near-perfect, unmarked condition. While he did not dare to touch the site of such holy relics with his bare skin, he examined each of the stones in turn. The trident's form and the size of the shield were familiar to the king, and he recognized them as the weapons the Warriors carried. This was among the least puzzling discoveries he had made in this place as his captive had already hinted that their powers came from this place. Still, he had never quite considered that their powers might be the providence of holy relics.

Could it be that their powers to control the elements emanated from their weapons? If he took their weapons from them would they be unable to retaliate? Would they, in turn, allow *him* to control the elements? Was it possible that this was the secret he was supposed to find atop the mountain? If so, why hadn't the Book simply told him this? He wished he could just ask the thing, but he could not, so, deciding to err on the side of caution, he assumed this was not the purpose of this visit and continued onward.

Soon he neared the center of the ruins, a fact he could not so much prove as feel.

When he stopped abruptly, it could have been for many reasons. It could have been that the ground raised before him to form a small hillock, or that on the other side of the hillock was what appeared to be a perfect mirror of what he had just passed through. It could have been that now he finally felt a little wind on his skin, heard the soft rustle of his clothes, and realized he had not smelt a single thing until that moment.

It was none of these, exactly.

It was that there was, now, a very familiar scent that shook him to his core: the scent of pine. Indeed, the hillock was surrounded by a randomly placed assembly of conifers bristling with strong-smelling green needles. Dranus immediately recognized the scent as identical to what he had inexplicably smelled in the Castle Beneath the Waves and the Castle Surrounded by Stone and which was curiously absent from the presence of the thrice dead Queen Tempest. Only this time the source was clear, and that clarity blossomed into further understanding. Inexplicably, innately, he knew that those previous smells had somehow been generated by these same pine trees.

His whole body tensed and his jaw clenched. There would be an undead monarch here as well, then. But who? Who would dare to have set foot here and how had such a fact been expunged from their records?!

Atop the hillock there was a short tower of only three floors. Its windows were tidy, its roofing strong, and its wooden construction looked as though it had been freshly coated and painted. It was clear that whatever specter awaited him, and whatever Relic they possessed, waited for him in this humble tower.

As much as his beating heart begged him to turn back, he had to press forward and climb the hill.

His ascent up the slope was labored and suddenly more silent than his advance through the ruins. As soon as he reached the door his sorcerer's soul sensed an overwhelming presence almost as though the structure itself radiated pure magical essence. Truly, this was the center of all magic in the world.

Slowly, he pulled the wooden door open.

His first step was like a rodent gingerly testing a branch to see if it could bare his weight. Upon discovering that his form did not instantly disintegrate upon crossing the plane, he entered in a quick movement. The moment his whole body had entered the place, the cold of the Night Season vanished. He felt warm and comfortable as if sitting by a perfectly controlled flame. He no longer felt that nagging sense of doom about him either. Rather, there was a calming aura to this tower and something about the layout of the first floor reminded him of his own bedchamber, though he could not say how specifically.

This building had withstood much of the ravages of the past miraculously and there were still some simple effects lying about. An empty table and chair sat in the corner of the room, and it seemed that once there had been a fireplace, though it was now destroyed. He wondered, then, how he felt so warm while outside the fury of the Night Season still swept about him.

It was simple enough for him to assume that in this place of sorcery and given the nature of the particular sorcery that he and his people used; the ordinary laws of reality did not have significant hold.

To the right of the entrance was a simple spiral staircase leading up to the second floor. As if drawn by some unnamable force, he ignored the rest of the room and carefully took to the stairs, testing each step with just a little weight to make sure that it would still hold him and not collapse from rot. But the steps were pristine.

The atmosphere grew warmer as he ascended and the area he came into was empty and small, partitioned from the rest of the floor. To his right and left were open doorways and he chose the right one, stepping into what appeared to be...a kitchen. And not the wreckage or remains of a kitchen...an active one. Over a fire there was water boiling and on a tiny table in the center of the room there were various vegetables steaming with fresh heat.

Had the zombified monarch of generations past been idly living in this place? Could anyone live in this forsaken place?! All the times before the corpse had been unanimated until he attempted to take the Relic. Had he seen the Relic already? Was it the tower, itself?!

He heard some movement from the room next to him and quickly drew the Sword of Righted Guard, but this only frightened him further as the sword felt heavier than it had ever felt. It moved like a normal sword, with no volition of its own and none of the serpent-like movements it was renowned for.

His heart now threatened to leap from his chest and flee that wicked place. His skin was electrified, he broke into a sweat, and the sword in his hand shook despite the feeling of calm that was like a pressing hand against his mind.

By nothing more than pure will power and his pride as King of

Varz he edged close to the open doorway to the next room. The wafting smell of fresh brew and food pulled at his starved senses. With a deep breath the King of Varz rounded the corner and his black sorcerous eyes could not comprehend what they saw.

"You are late, King Dranus." The words came from a tall, youthful figure with short black hair. He was not decayed, not a corpse at all. His facial features were distinct and handsome, and the symbols on his robes were easily recognized.

Before King Dranus VIII stood the ancient, the origin.

Before him stood King Baklar the Ultimate.

# Chapter 24
## The Shadow of Fate

D ranus awoke in a cloud of psychological haze. His thoughts moved sluggishly through waist-deep contradiction and thick, cloying disbelief. He had been prone on the floor, sword in hand, but he quickly stumbled to his feet. The mix of his heart racing and his mind moving like molasses was disorienting but in a quick moment his body was calm and his mind clear.

Too calm.

Too clear.

His eyes first converged on the young man sitting across the room, lazily flipping through the Book which now seemed almost fully black with everything densely written on the pages. He had never seen the thing present information this way before!

"You...you are..." His mind balked at the information his eyes fed him. The man standing before him had died over a thousand years ago! This man was a legend, a myth, almost a deity in Varz! How was it that he now stood, looking hardly a day older than himself?!

"I am King Baklar (bah-klar) of Varz." He spoke calmly, without so much as glancing up from the pages of the Book.

"That's not possible! You are dead! You have been dead for a thousand years or more!" This would not be *entirely* problematic if the man before him shambled like a corpse. At least then there would be precedent set by Luna and Vulcan and, presumably, Tempest. But this was a man of flesh and blood, fully alive by every definition he could conjure.

"You should be calm, sweet son of my sons." This time the man looked up and met Dranus's gaze. His voice was like a warm breeze that blew through the room; it was gentle but powerful and in an instant Dranus became calm and collected again.

"You are, then, The Ultimate?" Dranus was still nervous, as much as his physical senses seemed to ignore this. The implications of what he witnessed at that moment were innumerable.

"I am. In every way that you know of me and more. I am the true King Baklar that you refer to as 'The Ultimate.'" He closed the Book and set it on a small table next to his chair, standing. Once The Ultimate stood, Dranus instinctively knelt and lowered his head, though he had never performed this action in his life, not even to his own father.

"My Ultimate...how? How can you be alive? And *here* of all places?! I have read of your death! Your legacy...the lineage of monarchs...." There were too many questions to ask now, he hardly knew where to begin.

"Ahh, you have heard of my *attempted* murder." He smiled an ironic smile. "Well, I suppose the murder was successful, but...impermanent." The Ultimate picked his words carefully as he rested a gentle hand on Dranus's shoulder then bade him rise.

The current King of Varz obeyed.

"But then how have you lived so long? Even Queen Tempest could only live three lives through her spells. And why here? Of all places in the world, this is the site of our ancient enemies, this place represents everything we stand against. The irony of your being here is...." His mind fumbled over too many words that tried to escape at once, his thoughts were all roiling chaos and madness.

"It is because I am here that I have lived this long and am in such good health. The fact that this place is such sacred ground has been the only defense I have had for the last millennium against someone finding out that I am still alive."

Dranus shut his eyes in consternation trying to place events, people, places, in a logical order.

"Let me explain, child." He sat Dranus down in a hard, sturdy chair that had not been behind him before. "Pyrán is the center of all magic and sorcery in this world. Here the laws of reality are most malleable and unstable. Nearly anything is possible here, it is even possible for there to be no possibilities, as you experienced in the gardens." Dranus was unmoved by such paradoxes, as they were typical for a sorcerer of his skill. "You have no doubt heard the story of my inner circle's betrayal and my resulting death. But when those closest to me turned their blades inward and stole my very heart from my chest, there was one who gave everything she had to bring me here. By sacrificing the very stuff of her life-force, my wife King Dranus, *eroded* bringing me to this place so that I could live. Here, it was not necessary that I have a heart to live." Though stolid since

253

their meeting started, the corner of The Ultimate's lip dipped momentarily and his fingers tensed.

"Perhaps it is better not to have such a thing," he continued, the mask all Varz Kings wore falling back into place.

"Once I was recovered, there was nothing left of my wife. Nothing for me to bring back. Nothing." It very clearly pained The Ultimate to recall such a thing...even after a millennium to forget. "As I said, here anything is possible, but that does not mean there are no prices to pay."

Dranus felt an aura pass through the air and in a single instant he became overwhelmed with thoughts of Kaelel and the misery he had suffered since her passing, but a thousand times over.

When The Ultimate's emotional miasma lifted, Dranus saw, just for a fleeting moment, the image of Raven, tranquil like the sea.

"Over the centuries I have learned everything there is to know of this place and all of Pyrán is now mine. The reality of this place is completely under my control so long as I stay here. And so long as I stay here, I will never die. I can remain whatever age I choose." The Ultimate moved to the table and stroked the worn leather of the Book fondly. "It is why your sorcery has no effect here and why this book no longer responds to your will."

Dranus stared in open amazement. That someone could so thoroughly control the power of this world's magic to the point that reality itself became something that one created by their mere existence was...unthinkable, it was a paradox that even Dranus could hardly grasp. If ever anyone had questioned why Baklar was given the title The Ultimate, they need only meet the man to be assured. He was greater even than his fiction!

Slowly but steadily, as Dranus's mind put historical events in place with new information and his understanding of sorcery shifted slightly, things were beginning to make sense. The histories of Varz were not so well detailed at the birth of their nation. Of course Dranus had read how Baklar's Circle of Ten had been enraged by their king's decisions in the wake of Pyrán's destruction and how they had turned on him, as powerful sorcerers they each were. In the end they had taken out the man's heart and left him for dead to move the nation further. This was, however, of the greatest kept secrets in Varz and was knowable only by the current monarch. It was a lesson passed down from Baklar's own son after learning of the treachery later in life. It had been from this example that Kings and Queens of Varz had come to demand such unquestioning loyalty.

A memory returned, unbidden.

"My Ultimate, before, you said that I was late...did you know I was coming?" Now that he thought about it, why was there food set out if he needed no sustenance to live? Had it been in preparation to receive him as a guest?

The Ultimate laughed at this and pointed to the Book. "The Book told me, though I expected you a few days prior."

Had he misheard? Did he say that the Book had told him he would be arriving on a specific day, what must have been hundreds of years in advance? The Ultimate read the obvious dumbfounded expression on Dranus's face and sat himself across from Dranus. It was not until that moment that Dranus had truly taken in his surroundings. The room, combined with doorways ostensibly leading to other rooms, was entirely too large to fit into the size of the tower he had seen from the outside. It was beautifully furnished in classical Varz style. The wood floors were polished and sturdy unlike the stairs. Tapestries of violet, mauve, and dark purple lined the walls with delicately embroidered depictions of unfamiliar scenes. Looking back to The Ultimate, his modest chair and table had become a small but grandiose throne of carved marble and gold, the Book resting on one of the arms.

"You know very little about this book, outside of its abilities to gather information, that is. Its power is much more subtle than what you can guess from looking at it or speaking with it." The Ultimate sat cross-legged and seemed to be enjoying himself, and why not? Had he not been in solitude for more than a normal man could bear?

"I...I don't understand my Ultimate...how did you have the Book? How could it know that I would come here so far in the future?" Though his body was still calm, likely because of The Ultimate's control over him in this space, his head throbbed and he tried to stick all of the pieces of this puzzle together, but every time he snapped one piece to the next, the picture grew exponentially in size.

"You know very little about my past as well, I think. Relax and recuperate here, young one, and I will tell you a story not told in a thousand years."

Suddenly Dranus, too, was in his own familiar throne from Varz. He had on one arm a jug of his favorite wine, and this he could tell by the unique smell, and on the other a plate of his favorite delicacies. Again, Dranus felt unnaturally relaxed but this time he embraced it and cleared his frantic thoughts so as to not miss a word of the story he was about to hear. He must pay attention to every word, every inflection and tone, even the most minute of details in this story if he had any hopes of understanding everything that was happening to him at that moment.

To understand all that had happened before.

"In the time of my father, the power of sorcery was universal. All of the three continents enjoyed its use, and a kind of military stalemate was widespread. That is, until I was named monarch of what was then a small collection of autonomous towns in the south of our realm. I established the nation of Varz on the principles of power, discipline, and pride and raised a force of sorcerers the likes of which have never been matched. Together we waged war with a single ultimate goal: supremacy. In that time we sank the nation of Shiera, which was the strongest established force on our continent. With help from foreign allies we held, but resistance was heavy as other parts of the world hoped to maintain the global armistice. Many in our own ranks wondered why we went to fight when we had managed such peace."

Dranus felt a certain level of understanding of this situation as he, himself, had been subject to such questioning at the start of his journey.

"All of this you know quite well from the Forbidden Texts, I'm sure. What you don't know is what really happened next and why it happened." The dark black eyes of the current king focused hard on those of The Ultimate, knowing absolute truth awaited him in the next few words.

"The reason the world could use magic was Pyrán. This place is the source and it maintained itself, spreading throughout the world. At that time it was protected by the single Guardian of Pyrán." The Ultimate's stare hardened, and Dranus could almost see harrowing battles play out in the man's eyes.

"She was a sorceress of even greater strength than those I had assembled. Her power was awesome, Dranus, control that you could not even fathom over the elements and all manner of things. She could raise armies like endless fields of grain. She could steal a weaker man's soul with nothing but a motion of her hand. She was the Watcher of the Mount. She was the One. She was what the Gods left in their wake. Perhaps she was a God herself." The Ultimate's fist shook. Whether it was in anger or fear of this memory was unknown to Dranus.

"We waged war on that. For me to establish Varz as dominant I had to take away that power from the rest of the world; I had to subjugate Pyrán." The Ultimate stood abruptly and went to the next room without a word.

Dranus considered many things. He considered the history of his people and understood why Pyrán was the place of blasphemy such as it was. He considered the Guardian of Pyrán, and all that The Ultimate had said of her unknowable power. He continued to refuse, however, the notion of Gods which The Ultimate used so simply. The facts and memories of Varz that he had once believed to be clear became muddled and then straightened in a single pass. In the moments of silence he considered his present situation; clearly the Warriors were somehow related to this Guardian, though their powers were split and paled in comparison. Perhaps there was some secret he could learn from The Ultimate to defeat them as his originator had done so long before.

The dark and imposing figure of King Baklar reentered the room with a red velvet pouch in hand.

"The Guardian of Pyrán was too much even for me, at first. Then I found this book, I can hardly remember where or how now, but it just seemed to find me. Much like you, I spoke with the thing, and it told me of a manner in which the Guardian could be defeated. It led me to create this." He pulled from the innards of the velvet pouch an oval-shaped stone that was dull but comprised of several intermixing streaks of color.

An item to defeat the Warriors of Pyrán which could move as if carried by a person. Surely, this was what Dranus had come all this way for.

"This is the Stone of Pyrán's Plight, as I have named it, we have always been dramatic in this sense, have we not?" The Ultimate let out a chuckle before sitting again on his throne. "This mere stone, clod of dirt and dust, is the end of the Guardian's power. I crafted the stone somewhat crudely, with the instructions of the Book, so that it could only be used by one with my blood. But its power is limited; you must get the stone close to the Warriors for it to drain their elemental powers. Even then they will have their skills, weapons, and whatever sorcery they have unlocked elsewise to defend themselves." He held the stone upright and showed it to Dranus.

He dared not reach to touch it quite yet.

"You have come for this, son of mine, and with it you can end the Warriors of Pyrán as I ended the Guardian a thousand years ago. It is Fated like the turning of a wheel." The Ultimate hesitated for a moment and looked away.

Before Dranus could contemplate the significance of this expression, the mention of the Warriors dislodged another memory. "The Warriors of Pyrán! They were here, in your realm! You could have ended them then and there, why did you let them escape?!" With the power The Ultimate commanded in this place he could have simply blinked them out of existence as easily as he might blink his eyes!

"It is no longer my place to interfere in this world, young one, I must only observe it. I had my chance to forge the destiny I wanted and despite my best efforts, I failed. I...have come to accept this." He tensed visibly again, and his eyes flicked momentarily to the floor above them. "Were our meeting not beyond my own power it would not have occurred."

These words were carefully crafted. The edges of them as they left The Ultimate's lips betrayed a certain incompleteness to the truth he presented. Then again, how could he question the wisdom of his thousand-year-old ancestor?

"There is more to the story, however...." Already Dranus was hearing so many things for the first time. Why was there no record of the Stone or the Guardian? Why were the histories so twisted? Was it that The Ultimate's betrayers rewrote history to their favor?

King Baklar let out a heavy sigh. "In my youth, I was ferociously vengeful, but in the way of our people. You see, when I conquered Pyrán and stole the Guardian's power, I did not kill her." He locked eyes with Dranus. "I defiled her. I took from her the light which bestowed hope upon our enemies. I made her impure such that a force like hers may never rise again to stand against me and our folk."

Dranus was surprised to see such remorse in this man's face at an action that seemed both logical and warranted in his eyes. Then the dangling vines of cause and effect reached down through the ages to find King Dranus.

"So the Warriors of Pyrán...they are also your descendants? That is why they can use sorcery as we can. And because they are also descendants of the Guardian they can manipulate the elements to a somewhat lesser degree than their ancestor." Dranus's features sagged as the magnitude of what he faced settled before him.

"To kill any one of them would be to kill one of my children, like killing you, Dranus. I could not bring myself to do it even if I had a say in this world. It is as the Book said back then." The Ultimate stared at the Book on the arm of his throne.

The Book! Dranus had been so enraptured with the story that he had forgotten the simple fact that King Baklar had used the Book as he did! Now he was calmer and had somewhat more of an understanding of things that occurred in the world around him.

"My Ultimate, what is the Book? What is its true purpose and potential? I think you know much you are not telling." The Ultimate stared at the Book for several more moments as if searching for a lost memory.

"It is called the Book of Fate's Desire." He started slowly.

"But the Book claimed to have no title." Dranus countered.

"True, the Book has no title, but it has a name. As I'm sure you've noticed, you must be overly specific with the thing to glimpse something of the truth. It almost got me killed twice before because of the damned way it gives its answers!" Dranus was surprised, but not nearly as much as he had been upon finding the Book. He had always known there were secrets he could not access, something about the Book that just was beyond anything else in the world. And he related to his Ultimate's experience as he blamed a great deal on this Book of Fate's Desire.

"To answer your previous question, the Book did not so much tell me with certainty that you specifically would arrive at any specific time, but it seemed to intuit that it was very likely that one of my descendants would make their way here around this time. It was not, in this way, specific to you or your current circumstances. Had things played out differently in the intervening years, you may not have even been born, but someone of my blood would have made their way here for one reason or another."

The Ultimate explained so matter-of-factly that Dranus actually understood with relative ease. This explanation was far more likely than a specific prediction, as the future could be guessed at but never known.

"I have watched the Book from here since I cast it away, and I believe I have some understanding of its purpose, though it is difficult to be certain." The Ultimate pulled back his dark raven hair and regarded a wall face which, with almost unnoticeable distinction, became the view of Varz, his home city. He watched people walking around the palace, saw soldiers collecting volunteers for the draft, and he saw Commander Ven busy keeping things in order. Everything he saw he knew intuitively was happening at that very moment back in Varz. More of the puzzled fractions came together.

"It appears that the Book is an item of Fate, as indicated by its name. But I have been unable to determine its...direction. Sometimes it appears to use individuals to serve Fate's desire and other times it appears to allow the individual's desires to carve Fate to their own will. I believe I was its tool more so than the other way around, but for what ends I am unsure. Unfortunately, I am less sure about your Fate, Dranus. It is heavily clouded by uncertainties and events that have yet to unfold." Baklar seemed to empathize, expressing a sincere look of knowing condolence.

To use or to be used. It was a question Dranus had contemplated since discovering the enigmatic book and being subjected to its whims.

He thought back to the traitorous Deleron Kaxus who had incidentally brought him the Book. Was it that the vengeful youth had been used to bring the Book itself to Dranus's hands? For him to have begun a war, to have found himself here in Pyrán to meet The Ultimate as predicted, he must have the Book. Was all of this a series of preordained steps to a Fated end? Did he dangle like a puppet from the strings of some higher power?

"So then I am its instrument with which it crafts Fate." Dranus began to feel that old nagging, that heavy feeling of emptiness on his mind and heart again.

The knowing eyes of King Baklar gleaned his descendant's sequence of thoughts. "I cannot be sure; you have done things which neither I nor the Book would have predicted. Indeed, you arrived later than the Book's predicted margin. You doubtless maintain at least *some* control."

The Ultimate's words did nothing to reassure him.

"Regardless, you should not fear the Book of Fate's Desire. Though it may be the shadow of Fate, it has always led to greatness

260

and you would be a fool not to utilize its power to the fullest. Make no hesitation and give it your trust...though a wary trust it should remain." Dranus took these words to heart as wisdom from a being without match.

An image flashed across the wall and Dranus saw Commander Ven reading a letter that had been wrapped around the hilt of a dagger.

"There! The results of whose blood was on Queen Tempest's dagger! What does it say?!" His mind returned to familiar routes of thought. Now that he had learned so much, the greatest question that remained was of the whereabouts of the Shield of Second Life.

"Yes, I see, you still worry about the Shield." The Ultimate squinted at the scene. "It appears that the blood was certainly of Varz but was...diluted somehow, it was not pure."

In an instant another piece had fallen into place!

"Then it all makes sense! I had thought perhaps one of the Warriors had heard of it from their histories and certainly with their powers they would have no problems reaching Tempest's castle and finding it. From what you have told me they have diluted blood of Varz, could it be the seventh Warrior?"

At this, The Ultimate raised a curious brow.

"You saw the stone. Though I have searched endlessly, I have not been able to locate the seventh Warrior of the Moon."

The scene on the wall fizzed into a haze and then reformed in an instant. Dranus saw the Warrior of the Sun, that young girl that had almost taken his life at the Rift, surrounded by sand.

"The Warrior of the Sun has no apparent knowledge of the seventh, though if anyone would, it would be her. If history were to continue, they should have been sisters." The Ultimate swept his hand from side to side, moving through different scenes of desert with huge stone pillars reaching towards the sky. "She should have been born a Urhyllian at the least." Again they looked at the quiet, freckled features of the young Warrior.

"My Ultimate, if they have access to some sorcery and some of our blood, why do they not have the Sorcerer's Eyes?"

"They simply have not awakened them yet. The eyes mark our people as the only folk who have inherited the magical source in our blood. They have that same blood, but they have not awakened their true potentials yet. They are like one of our children before they have mastered the basic understanding." Like those at the festival in Viél, children of Varz learned the basic fundamentals of their sorcery at different rates. Unlike Varz children, they had no one to instruct them or teach them the methods of thought.

"Could the seventh Warrior have the Shield?" Dranus still watched the young girl.

The Ultimate did not respond as quickly as normal. He looked away, calculating, picking his words carefully. "No. I am certain that the seventh Warrior of Pyrán was never born, and I have only the slightest inclination as to why." The Ultimate looked at the ceiling again for a moment, looked through it, and continued. "But it is possible that one of the others managed to retrieve it, however unlikely."

"Then at worst I may have to kill one or two of them a few times." Dranus replied with a sour grin. "I think I will enjoy that."

The Ultimate felt a bit of forgotten pride well within him as he placed the Stone of Pyrán's Plight into his young one's hand.

Dranus stood and then knelt once more out of respect and accepted the item graciously.

The current king cradled the stone like a fragile child, marveling at the beauty of it. While it was smooth and oblong like a large river stone, it was painted almost naturally with dull tones of red, green, white, and many others. Among the more subtle colors, strips of vibrant, shimmering purple stood out like the night sky tinted by the moon's soft light.

"My Ultimate, you have given me so much..." He accepted the stone with grace and honor. "I am keeper now of more knowledge then any in my line and I will not take this duty lightly." He stopped for a moment trying to gather his thoughts; to fit everything together into a cohesive understanding of all he had learned.

At the base of the mountain he was a simple King of Varz with a somewhat impressive collection of relics. At the peak of the same mountain he had gained something that Varz monarchs valued far greater than any weapon ever made: knowledge. He had gained such knowledge that no other in the world, save The Ultimate himself, could know.

"I have only one final question, Ultimate." His countenance grew grim and Dranus shifted uneasily once more in his throne. "You conquered Pyrán and shifted the very laws of the world with the

Ultima spell, and no greater spell has ever been conceived since...will you teach it to me?" The Ultima spell was one of such power that it could not be described, though Varz poets, scribes, and nobles had attempted to do so for centuries. It was so simple that it could hardly be comprehended. It was a paradox of such great magnitude that it could be the origin of the concept. In their history alone the Ultima spell sank the country of Shiera, defeated the Guardian who King Baklar described as nothing short of Godlike, and split the continent near in half when forming the Discidia Rift. This was a spell by which the world was shaped.

The Ultimate's gaze flicked to meet Dranus's eyes, then aimed down to his lap where he crossed his arms. Back to Dranus.

"I am sorry, good son of kings, but you cannot perform the Ultima spell...you do not have the correct eyes."

The correct eyes? Before Dranus could consider what this meant, he felt unnaturally heavy. It was not that his clothes or even his body had become heavier, but his *existence* pressed upon him like a thousand leagues of ocean overhead. He struggled to stay upright in his chair as his mind fended off a constant barrage of rapidly changing thoughts, ideas, feelings, and sensations.

When he looked back to The Ultimate for an explanation, he stared dumbfounded into eyes that burned crimson red like boiling blood.

"The Devil's Eyes. The pinnacle of our people's sorcery. One must ascend to the Devil's Eyes to perform such a spell." His wrist flicked and the whole of the tower shuttered as if every plank of wood and nail moved a hair to the right and then back in an instant. "In the history of our folk only the Guardian, myself, and my most favorite of daughters from the time of the First Great War have achieved it. You are strong and you are a talented sorcerer Dranus, but you will not unlock the Eyes in this life, I think."

The Ultimate's orbs hazed back to black, and the weight was instantly lifted from his spirit though he could not help but feel disheartened that he was somehow of inferior stock than his legendary ancestor.

The Ultimate sensed the dismay in his favored son's countenance. He looked at no place in particular on the wall which had shifted back to normal and racked his mind for information that had once been his. An idea arose.

"Dranus, you have the Staff of the South Star, how much would you suppose you know of its properties?" The Ultimate rubbed the thin black beard at his chin.

"I have spoken with its spirits extensively and have practiced every manner of its use, I know all there is to know." Dranus was puzzled by such an abrupt and unrelated question.

"Then tell me, if you will, how many souls were imprisoned in the Staff upon its forging." The Ultimate wore a secret smile that the king could not help but question.

"Twenty thousand. There were twenty thousand split among the various forces. I'm told the cut of the gems in the staff-head dictated such an auspicious number." He was skeptical; though he knew his answer had to be true.

"Incorrect." Now the living legend smiled openly with a bit of ironic joy in his eye. "There were twenty thousand and *eleven* souls taken into the Staff, but only twenty thousand of them were soldiers. Flip the Staff and inspect the base carefully."

Dranus became suddenly panicked that he was sitting comfortably in a throne. No scabbard. No Staff strapped to his back. He nearly jumped from his seat until his eyes were led to a near corner of the room where Vulcan's sword and the Staff of the South Star stood. Before he could stand to retrieve it, it appeared in his hands lying across his lap. He breathed a sigh and calmed himself.

However, Dranus was becoming increasingly more confused at the words of his ancestor. Everything he had ever heard, even from the very spirits that took residence within the Staff, was that there had been twenty thousand who had sacrificed themselves willingly for the Staff. Not knowing what to expect, he rotated the Staff and squinted at the base, reflexively trying to use his sorcery to aid him to no avail.

His mouth hung agape when he saw, set deep and centered in the spike which he used to summon the ghostly spirits, a tiny glimmering black gem almost as insignificant as a speck of dirt.

"Another gem? What is its purpose? Why is there no mention of this anywhere?" He let out a frustrated groan. "Oh, are any of our records accurate?!" What could it mean? Why were there so many secrets even among those of the same lineage? As he asked himself that question he immediately knew the answer: Varz was a nation ruled by power and keeping power meant keeping secrets.

"I cannot explain to you its purpose, but I believe I know how it may be used. Flip the Staff upside down and use it as you normally would if you find yourself in the most dire of situations. It should have some effect. You must only use it thus if there is no other way and in no other circumstances." King Baklar's brow furrowed intensely from his previous jovial state. "I cannot warn you enough, Dranus. I cannot know nor be responsible for the consequences of using the Staff in this way. But I know that whatever happens will be unchangeable." The Ultimate's words held great gravity that burdened the king's thoughts.

Dranus felt the words of The Ultimate pass through his mind as though it were a straightened arrow of truth. Although he could not quite place it, he felt in his sorcerer's heart that there was a notch in this arrow. Baklar had watched everything that transpired from atop the world. There was something he knew, something he was hiding.

"Still, if you do this, I think you may find that the Ultima spell is not completely outside your grasp."

This shook Dranus from his stupor of questioning and curiosity. He practically drooled at the chance to make an impact on the world such as the one The Ultimate had, but part of him hoped he would never have to use this for he feared the implications greatly.

He rested then, letting his body fall limp, trying to bring all of these new facts, new truths of secrets never told and lies too well accepted.

The Ultimate was holding the Sword of Righted Guard though Dranus had not seen him collect it.

"There is so much I can learn from you, King Baklar...." So much, in fact, that he wondered whether or not he could even absorb such vast information.

"Fear not, favored son, we will have plenty of time to talk in the coming days. I cannot stop the Warriors, but neither can I let one of my own meet them unprepared. You will be my guest for a while, and I will train you here."

Dranus's heart leapt into his throat and his body filled with energy. He could hardly accept that this was happening!

"In particular, there is one spell you must master before I can allow you to continue on your journey...."

# Third Movement

"If I were to characterize those of the newly formed Varz, I would say that they are misunderstood. It is not that we misunderstand them, but they who misunderstand themselves. They are driven by something primal, though their intelligence is great. They adore paradox because it is their nature, I think. Their king, Baklar, is...he cannot be described in a word. He is a visionary the likes of which this world will never see again. I believe that given the time he could one day rule this entire world, perhaps indefinitely. He is that kind of man. I will not allow him that time, but I fear I will lose myself in the fight, nonetheless. He comes."

-From the journal of the Guardian

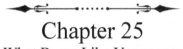

# Chapter 25
## What Burns Like Vengeance

"I'm leaving."

"Voradore, you can't leave!" Leon, the Warrior of Wind, chased after the youth clad in the same shining silver armor as he.

"Why not, Leon?!" The Warrior of Lightning turned. "In just that short time Varz defeated the entire Shieran navy! They defeated..." Voradore clenched his fist and electricity arched from point to point across his armor.

"...they killed Raven, Leon."

"We don't know that!" Leon tried hard to hold onto his naive hope that their comrade had simply been taken prisoner and still lived.

"Get your head out of the clouds, sky-boy! Our enemy is Varz! The darkest, blackest, most soulless creatures this world has ever seen! There's no way they would have spared her." Voradore had seen far more tragedy and far more violence in his lifetime than the sheltered Warrior of Wind. His face twisted in pain as his imagination went to work picturing all of the myriad ways the Black King might have tortured and killed his friend.

"So what...so you're just going to march into the middle of their fleet and kill them all single-handedly? What about the Varz army ahead of us?" Leon stabbed the edge of his massive sword into the dirt of the Varz plains.

"We've come so far into their land since the four of us returned. We have a chance to push through and capture their capital." Even with Teego staying behind for a tracking mission in Arendrum, they had made their presence felt on the battlefield.

"Forget the capital! What worth is a single city when whole realms are falling? Their king is clearly with them, what could we possibly gain from holding their capital city other than an indefensible position surrounded on all sides by the enemy?" Voradore was growing impatient. He had long since discredited the strategic advice of his opposite in the Warrior of Wind. Unlike the pure armor of his comrades, Voradore's armor was accented by streaks of black chain that trailed up and down the length of his plate mail, held there by the constant pull of magnetism he could emit. It was to this length of long chain his hands moved as his temper flared.

Leon felt the electricity in the air and his grip on the legendary sword of the wind tightened reflexively.

"You think I don't want to leave and go protect my family?" Leon was trying hard to keep this from escalating. They were all full of passion from the recent news and yet exhausted from constant fighting.

Voradore scowled at these words. "Your family. That's right, you think you've got so much to protect just because you're the only one of us who still has a family. Don't forget that most of us had adopted families just like yours and that they were taken from us by those demons!" The chain came loose from his armor and rattled to the ground where the two bladed ends grounded themselves in the dirt. "That's your problem, sky-boy. You don't burn like the rest of us with hatred. You haven't lost your family...yet."

The air grew thick with pressure as a breeze blew past the pair. The wind swelled around the towering form of Leon and circled like a zephyr around the sword at his side. "Your heart is so filled with hatred, Voradore. How can you be a Warrior of Light when you surround yourself in such darkness?"

"How can you be a warrior at all when your heart is so soft?!" The piercing dagger-like edges of Voradore's chains sprung from the ground and stabbed forward like darting serpents. Leon flexed and a surge of wind burst from his sword, pushing away the chain.

In a single fluid movement Voradore twirled his body and moved in quick, precise movements to change the direction of the chains in their flight. Wrapping around his back a single bladed edge spun like an uppercut, dragging along the ground then shooting up into the vortex of wind. With the crackle of electricity the edge cut through the barrier, making room for the second edge to dart into the empty space.

"Ok, Voradore." A kick of his armored boot shot Leon's giant sword into the air and then a stiff gust blew it back down, pinning the chains to the ground, their current absorbed by the thick leather padding of the sword hilt. Leon was like a feather when he controlled the wind, his agility surpassed only by that of the teleporting Warrior of the Sun. With his power he leapt forward with the momentum of his sword, bounding high into the air and descended boots first.

The Warrior of Lightning repelled the chains from around his body and ducked out of the way, leaving a waiting noose of chain for Leon. Voradore grinned at his expected victory, but his face soon soured as the Warrior of the Wind seemed to float aloft a breeze like a fresh-fallen leaf.

Voradore grit his teeth, letting his frustration get the better of his judgment. Overhead, dark clouds gathered in a hurry and thunder rumbled low across the ground. The boy's silvery armor grew shrouded in a cloak of black light as his powers were more and more unleashed.

Leon, who was smiling as he drifted lazily on the wind, taunting his ally, finally saw the growing aura and tensed. In a flash of energy his own armor emitted a bright white light as if lit from above by a growing hole in the black clouds.

Atmospheric pressure grew and grew at this focal point in the sky as the two Warriors battled for control over it, warring as Warriors of opposing elements often did.

Suddenly, Leon's sword rushed back to his hand and the boy's power increased several times over. The maelstrom of clouds overhead dispersed like a puff of smoke swatted away by the hand of a giant. An immense wind descended upon them and pressed Voradore into the dirt; Leon followed, pinning his arms and legs with his weight and that of his plate armor.

"That makes thirteen for me, twelve for you," Leon said between labored breaths. His heart racing, he tried to crack a smile and ease the tension as both of their lights waned.

Voradore struggled beneath him but could not topple the great weight from his body. He had been foolish to let his legendary weapon leave him and not pull it back as Leon had. It was uncommon for one of their bouts to be decided by an error in judgment, usually Teego stopped them, and a winner was declared after the fact by whoever was there to watch.

"Get off! This doesn't change anything! Just because you managed to pin me doesn't mean I'm not still leaving to protect

Myrendel!" Though the fight had ended, electricity still arched all across the pinned boy's body and small whirlwinds sprouted in crowds as far as 20 feet away.

Leon dropped his massive sword but did not get up. "I may not have lost as much as you have Voradore, but Raven was my friend as much as yours. Still, we have a responsibility to these people to be where they need us. We were given these powers to fight for them against evil when it sprouted again in our lands."

Voradore's chest was tight, and not because of the weight of his victorious foe, but because of the sadness he had to harbor every day of his life. He turned his head, trying to hide the tears that had begun to pool in his eyes. "It's not fair. We are right, aren't we? We're fighting for good! Raven fought for good. She shouldn't have died."

Leon lurched to the side and stood, extending a hand to help his friend from the ground. The loss of a friend was a serious blow to the young soldier, but Voradore had experienced nothing but loss since he was born. Leon could hold his emotions back, but compared to Voradore, the cold and calculating Warrior of Lightning, well...he could not hope to fathom what that young man felt. Nor did he wish to.

The tall soldier of the wind held back his tongue but thought to himself, 'the prophecy never said that we would all survive this ordeal. We mustn't forget our place in history, no matter the cost.'

Voradore got to his feet and gathered his chains while Leon took up his sword. They were silent as they thought about all that they had been forced to face since the prophecy had come true. None had protested following this calling like Raven had. She had never been wronged by Varz like most of the Warriors and had consistently spoke of how unfair it was that they, not even adults yet, had to bear the Fate of the Five Realms on their shoulders. Voradore considered the overwhelming irony of the fact that she had been the one to give her life for a cause which she never fully believed in.

"Think how Keine must feel. He never even got a chance to tell her how he felt about her." Leon thought about how much the little bundle of sunlight in his life, Olette, meant to him. He feared for her every moment of every battle they had endured. If he had heard that she was the one to die...no, he refused to think about that.

"I haven't seen him since we were told." Regretfully, Voradore acquiesced and would, at least for the time being, remain with the other Warriors. They started heading back to their camp.

"I'll find him. I'll talk with him and the general and see what they think we should do. I'll tell them you want to leave, but you have to think, we are considerably stronger when we're together. We should try to stay together." Leon tried to comfort his friend. For as much as they fought almost constantly, they were still comrades and friends.

In a flash of golden light, the frantic form of Olette, the Warrior of the Sun, blinked into existence from the bright rays of the sun overhead.

"Leon! Keine is..." Her freckled face was bent in a frown, her eyes searching, panicked, for reassurance.

"Keine is gone!"

*       *       *

Fire.

Fire cleanses everything. It burns out impurity from the tainted like steel in a forge. Fire is the solution to all of the evils in this world. And all things will eventually end in fire.

Fire.

Fire burned the blood and oil and fat on the Warrior's knuckles, but it did not burn the Warrior. Over and over he smashed his flame-licked knuckles into the slaughtered mess that was once the face of a Varz soldier. Every time he removed his fist he saw the laughing face of the King of Varz. Over and over he sought to destroy that face of pure malice with cleansing fire.

For several minutes this had been the scene. If at one point in time the charred husk beneath the seething, raging body of the Warrior of Fire had been a man, it was that no longer. It was a faceless object. It was only an object the Warrior used to perpetuate his fury.

Eyes that might have once been filled with hate and sorrow held only that bizarre crimson light that had shown at the Battle of the Rift. Insensate anger was all that came from those eyes, like a raging fire with no will, only an insatiable desire to burn more and more. Even the tears which yearned to stream down his face turned to vapor instantly.

His fists finally stopped as they reached the bottom of the crater and rested at the Warrior's side. The fire that ran the length of his body flared and leapt high into the air. He raised his head and yelled his insanity at the wind. His cry was the voices of all those who had died in this war; of all Varz had made victim in their long, twisted history. It was a cry of despair; it was a statement of vengeance.

It echoed off the walls of a smoldering crater twenty feet deep and a hundred feet wide. Littering the crater were human-shaped ashes in all sorts of grotesque positions. Here and there stubborn armor still flamed and slowly melted into pools so that from above the crater shone in the reflected light of midday.

At the center of the crater was the Warrior of Fire.

Outside the crater was the conflagration that had previously been the Varz advance camp.

When the Warrior of Fire had fallen from the sky like a meteor, most of the soldiers had stood their ground and prepared to fight. But he had not come for a fight, he had come for a cleansing.

Outside the crater some two-hundred sets of black sorcerous eyes stared blankly at the sky, or at the dirt from fleshless faces and hollowed skulls. Not one had escaped, the Warrior made sure of that.

"Embers and ash." Keine spoke through chapped, parched lips as painful images of the Warrior of Water flashed through his mind, replacing the shadow of another from his thoughts. "For what they've done...nothing will remain of them but embers and ash. This I swear."

Further outside the camp, every brush, tree, blade of grass, even bits of sand burned and melted into glass. A mile-wide radius of flame had fully cleansed this place. It had not been Keine's will to destroy so indiscriminately, but he was pleased with the outcome, nonetheless.

The inferno continued to burn even after the weary Warrior of Fire trudged back to his own ranks. It burned all night, becoming visible from both sides of the camp.

The soldiers of Varz and those of the Four Realms recounted the haunting evil of the mighty yell that had been unleashed from the no-man's land. To each, the cry of something purely cruel had preceded the glare on the horizon that never waned. It sank the hearts of men and women on both sides; the shadows of what they could not see forming into the darkest nightmares this war had spawned in their own minds.

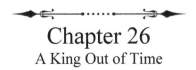

# Chapter 26
## A King Out of Time

Before taking flight, the giant hawk of Varz threw up its wings, tossing up a rain of black feathers that nearly blocked out the twilight moon. The beast let out a terrible scream and one by one new feathers grew into place like a thousand daggers sliding gracefully into invisible sheaths. The new feathers seemed almost oily in the moonlight.

King Dranus of Varz waited patiently as the hawk preened here and there about its new feathers. He had no knowledge of this ritual, if ritual it was, but the hawk refused to be mounted until it was finished.

Finally, the massive bird exchanged a glance with the king, golden-yellow sclera meeting black.

Almost before he could put his weight fully into the saddle, Dranus collapsed, grasping desperately at the saddle's horn.

It had been one week since he first came to Pyrán. One week since he had met King Baklar, since he met The Ultimate. And it had been one week since he slept last. Although sleep had not been relevant in the realm that King Baklar controlled, once he stepped foot off the mountain's plateau he felt the strain of uninterrupted physical and mental training catch up to him. A week of wear on his muscles and a week of constantly pushing the boundaries of his sanity hit him in waves until he could barely stay conscious.

Once the shock of it all wore off, Dranus became aware of the whistling of wind through the fresh feathers of his hawk partner. They were descending like a spear down the cliff-face, nearly invisible in the shadow of the towering mountain.

Somehow he had stayed mounted through it all. Had he formed a spell reflexively? Did the saddle itself have magical properties beyond the few he knew of?

Trivial thoughts were washed away like dead trees in a landslide.

Dranus's head throbbed with secrets too numerous to count, too incredible to believe, and all too important to risk sharing with another soul, living or dead. He felt his grasp on reality grow more and more tenuous as riddles of logic and mazes of comprehension that he had drilled into the very fabric of his thinking threatened to dislodge all that he had gained in his week at the top of the world.

The hawk banked sharply and suddenly Dranus's senses turned back to the outside world.

He was in control again.

The Ultimate had taught him a great deal about sorcery and the nature of their people's connection with it. Slowly but surely these lessons returned to their sorted positions in his understanding of the world. Baklar had been right, organization had been critical in maintaining his relationship with reality 'without the right eyes.'

Of the other important lessons he had learned from The Ultimate, he now recalled three: that he should embrace the Book of Fate's Desire, that he should deal with the Warriors of Pyrán sooner rather than later, and that no source was stronger in this world then the bond of love between two sorcerers. Romantic love, familial love, platonic love; each of these could fuel a miracle if exploited properly. In fact, King Baklar had spent much of their resting moments recalling his wife and the time they had shared while she lived. It never ceased to amaze Dranus how human The Ultimate was...when all throughout their history he had been revered as somewhat of a more divine sort soaring over the chaff of the world. And while that myth was not entirely accurate, neither was it completely inaccurate. But in the end, the man was still a man.

That is to say, he was now a man. Laced between the loving moments of peace with his wife were tales told of gruesome horror. King Dranus had never considered his ways or his people inherently evil, but The Ultimate in his youth was, by any definition he or the old king could muster, evil. His people had ever been of a ruthless and murderous nature, but they lived for the fight and the struggle; The Ultimate relished in suffering, despair, and cruelty magnified by a mind which could conceive of atrocities beyond normal understanding. It was a thing of wonder, how much a millennium of solitude could change a man, if it had, indeed, changed him.

He would have a great deal to discuss with the Book once he was rested and prepared for such a battle of wits, but for the moment he wanted only to rest his mind and return to his fleet in Shiera. As his consciousness faded once more he saw images of his lost wife Kaelel against his eyelids and flashbacks of the Warrior of Water, dancing on the waves.

*     *     *

Dranus awoke dangling upside down in his saddle, his arms limp beneath him.

Flustered and confused, he tried to gather himself and move the whipping hair out of his eyes. His hawk partner screeched in approval and then turned back up while careening dangerously to the right.

The bird's body was tense, and Dranus could feel the shifting of great muscles beneath his legs. He had to get a sense of what was happening! Were they under attack? Was the bird simply trying to torture him?

Suddenly the hawk folded its wings and dove, sending the king's body reeling and straining his back. This point of vantage while they descended had one upside: it made clear that he was under attack and by whom.

A massive shard of earth like an arrowhead flew straight up just a few meters in front of them. Had they continued, it would have skewered the great bird and him in a moment.

As his mind cleared, Dranus took full stock of his situation and exerted his will. The wind steadied around him, his vision cleared, the reigns came to his hands, and a calm fell like a slab of rock over his anxiety.

With some effort, he forced control over the bird, urging it to dive further beneath the clouds instead of rising back to safer heights.

Finally they broke through a layer of gray clouds and the outline of a large valley took shape with the sparkling silver armor and massive stone shield of the Warrior of Earth at its center. The king grinned as another arrowhead of pure rock formed on the surface of the plain and was launched at him with an earth-shaking leap from the glowing Warrior.

Feeling pleasantly refreshed from his nap and the adrenaline of his waking, he pulled the reigns to dodge and summoned the Stone of Pyrán's Plight to a gloved hand.

Now a steady stream of arrows arched up to meet him, but they

275

were far too slow and inaccurate to pose any real threat. The Staff of the South Star alone would be enough to wipe out the tag-alongs; he need only focus on the Warrior of Earth.

For the time, he worked to synchronize his will with that of his mount. The bird was far more intelligent than he had expected and even seemed to have some rudimentary understanding of sorcery! Working in tandem, they rolled to the side then spread wings to catch a draft and rise rapidly. With every movement he could feel the hawk's muscles tense beneath him, and his own muscles tensed in response. It felt as though they shared thoughts, with neither vying for control. They shared a pure symbiosis of tactical precision encased in a cloud of the free joy of flight and grace.

Ultimately, the cooperation became natural enough for the king to focus his attention on his next moves offensively. With a gleeful grin he looked down like a child sneering at a field of little toys all preparing to move about and battle and eventually be smitten by the God of his own little playroom. He had gained so many new weapons in his sorcerous arsenal; he had to at least try a few out.

So Dranus flew down dangerously low, taunting the Warrior of Earth. The boy took the bait and flung a smaller, more slender spear of rock up after him. In the slowly passing moments that the spear chased them, Dranus plunged into his thoughts. He saw the spear and he knew of his palm. He skirted the knowledge that he could not will the rock to move as the boy did. But he was a man of strength, he could press over a stone with his hand if he really tried.

And so he tried. He thrust his palm to his side with all his strength and felt the firm resolve of the stone shard. At the moment of impact he brushed aside natural perception and understanding of force and settled on the mechanical force of a well implemented tool.

In a burst of pressure, the earthen shard shot off to the left while Dranus and his mount veered dangerously to the right.

Hah! He'd done it! The king pressed his hair back with his hand, releasing the reigns and laughing fully into the wind. It had come so easy to him then, though it seemed metaphysically impossible only a week prior!

More! He needed more!

He began to steer his black mount in a large ring in the sky.

The illogical routes of distorted reason from before were still so fresh in his mind that he almost heard The Ultimate's voice on the wind. He recalled the bright light of the midday sun above the clouds as well as the millions and millions of water crystals floating in the layer below it. It was, in his estimation, the proper place, time of day, and moment of need to alter the space more and more.

Once satisfied, his eyes bulged with ferocious joy and his chest felt near to bursting with power. He once more used his free hand to point at the center of the circle he had flown and then descended upon the enemy ranks.

Before soldiers could raise swords and bows, a beam of hot yellow light pierced the clouds from above, drawing a line of destruction in the path that Dranus chose. It rent the ground beneath their feet and melted steel, baking bodies and boiling blood. He moved the ray lazily through the ranks, unconsciously projecting the loud boom of his laughter to those below him.

Unprepared for such a slaughter, the Warrior's ranks broke almost immediately and fled, leaving only the boy glaring mountains from behind his shield.

To Dranus's great pleasure, his sunspot could not penetrate the wall of earth that flew up and over the Warrior like a soft blanket. His sorcery was strong, but the Warrior's defenses seemed impenetrable so long as he had the earth beneath him.

Acknowledging this, the wildly grinning king brought the hawk in to land, leaping from its back and brandishing the Sword of Righted Guard in one hand, the Stone in a pouch at his side. Filled with the lust for battle inherited from his ancestors he dispatched a few of the soldiers that had grouped around the Warrior with as many expertly placed strokes of his sword; the gaps in their armor seemed to invite the tip of his blade. He relished in the warm blood of his enemies running down his face and took in the sight of the Warrior of Earth in as large of gulps as he could.

"I'll make you pay!" The youth shouted and charged with shield raised.

Dranus shifted his sight in response.

He could see it all: every move the boy would make before he made it, every inch of earth that moved suspiciously, every avenue of attack he could feasibly explore given his speed and direction. The powers the boy used were unrefined and tied strongly to his emotions, this made his intentions easy to read. He showed the obvious hallmarks of someone who had only ever fought those that were like unarmed children compared to him. He had no mind for battling an equal.

Dranus stepped to the right, deflecting a rocketed stone with his sword supported by a gauntleted hand. Ever forward he continued at a steady walk while his opponent rushed to close the gap, launching projectiles all the way.

Each one was more easily dodged then the previous and he found himself stabbing through the rocks, shattering them into shards that rained on his armor. A few small cuts opened up on his face, but these were worth it. At this point, he wanted to do more than kill the Warrior of Earth. He would *break* him.

Every step brought them closer until finally a two-handed blow from King Dranus crashed against the sturdy shield which the Warrior held. Though the large stone held, the Warrior's feet were pressed hard into the ground. The boy pressed his shield forward with sudden force, trying to knock the king off balance but the shift in density of the ground gave away the move and Dranus leapt backwards. However, his landing was disrupted by hard ground made suddenly slick like mud and Dranus fell to his knees.

Dranus suddenly became aware of a shadow on the ground beneath him and he rolled instinctively to the side, narrowly dodging the descent of a floating boulder.

That was too close. He was getting too sure of himself. He must not forget The Ultimate's warning.

He was back on his feet, holding the Sword of Righted Guard in a protective stance. He made sure to secure his footing with every move. He could not magically affect the earth, but he could affect the bottom of his boots.

They circled one another slowly and the boy's eyes moved between the king's own and the ground before furrowing in confusion.

Dranus responded by reaching to the sky again, channeling the sunlight through the clouds. But before he could gather enough, the Warrior moved in a set of movements he distinctly recognized.

Once again they were encased in a fortress of rock and dirt, blocking the sun away and sealing the Fate of one of those inside. King Dranus let out a wild laugh, his harsh black eyes glaring through the darkness at the panting Warrior of Pyrán.

"I heard what you did to Shiera! I won't let you get away with killing all of those people! I won't let you get away with killing RAVEN!" With his shield raised, covering most of his body, the Warrior inched closer step by step. His body shook with anger and the prospect of getting revenge. Even in his own domain his wild eyes darted around, expecting some sorcerous manifestation that would rob him of his retribution. With every step the walls of the dome constricted tighter and tighter around the furious Warrior and the confident, grinning king of Varz.

"Unfortunately, boy, there is nothing you can do to avenge them. Would you like me to tell you how she died, at least, before you join her?" Dranus snickered and sneered at the boy, lying and hoping to get some greater outburst.

The boy's features boiled and his face bristled with insensate rage.

"It was not quick. An arrow first took her in the leg...."

Only a few meters separated the two.

"...and then another in the stomach, terrible wound that was...."

The Warrior never stopped. Just continued marching on.

"...a lead ball crushed her arm and pinned her to a deck; oh, you should have seen the delicious despair in her eyes!"

The space was tightening more and more around them, but Dranus could feel the boy's emotions climbing while he was calm and in control. He could be pierced from a thousand angles by one of the boy's earthen spears, but Dranus could see the lust in the young man's eyes, thirsting to deal the blow with his own hands.

"Oh, you should have seen the way she struggled! It was so painful!" A nonchalant wave of the king's hand dismissed any presumptions. "Not for me, of course, I rather enjoyed it, but I assume it was for her."

The Warrior of Earth grimaced, a blink of sadness, anger, and despair flashing across his features.

"And I, myself, threw the spear which pierced her heart. It was a beautiful death." He let loose a roar of laughter, just a few feet from the approaching threat. His senses lay sharply in wait of any sudden attack.

Fury could bear no more insult.

"I'LL KILL YOU!!!" The Warrior's life reached its passionate climax as he sought to bring the shield down atop him and skewer him like a pincushion from every angle. The dome stabbed at him even as it collapsed.

Dranus saw it all play out as if in slow motion. He devoured every pained look in the boy's eyes as the Stone of Pyrán's Plight came to his hand before gently touching against the raised shield. Suddenly, solid stone walls became dirt again and fell harmlessly all around him.

The Warrior's expression rapidly flicked between rage, confusion, and finally, terror. The shield grew heavy and tumbled to the side, its wielder dragged to the ground with it by the strap attached to his arm.

Dranus sauntered over and rested a heavy boot on the boy's arm, ensuring he stayed trapped by the thing he had relied upon so much to give him strength.

"As I said before, boy...you can do nothing. And do you know why?" He put his weight on the arm, amplifying it with his sorcery. "Your power was handed to you, presented like a wooden sword to a small child. When you chased rodents and stepped on insects, you felt as though this power was rightfully yours, but it is not. While I have trained every day of my life to create power, you have done nothing. None of you have." Dranus raised the Sword of Righted Guard and aimed it at the boy's exposed throat. His other boot moved swiftly to pin the second arm that tried to catch him off guard.

"You pitiful Warriors will all fall, your efforts will be for naught, and history will forget you and your sacrifice. The day you chose to stand against Varz...was the day you chose death over life."

The wild and terrified eyes of the Warrior of Pyrán, still trying to understand what had happened, looked up into the face of the King of Varz. He saw the mad eyes and wicked smile of this horrible fiend and knew the world was doomed. Dranus thrust the Sword of Righted Guard with piercing accuracy, making sure to sever the spine. It was a swift death. He had broken the boy, he knew. Now, as a warrior, he could show respect in the only way he knew how.

The saviors of Pyrán, the Holy, numbered four.

After taking a moment to catch his breath, he eyed his mount feasting on the bodies of the dead. This was the beginning of his new reign. With the power he now commanded, no one could stand against him, not even the Warriors of Pyrán might hope to defeat him.

He stared up at the clearing sky as if he saw it for the first time, having finally burst forth from the cocoon of his past, emerging as a true King of Varz. He was a figure of the past, stepping out of time.

The Ultimate had been right, the weapons these children wielded were nothing more than tools to be utilized in prophecy. Without the power inherited from the Guardian the weapons were simple things.

Dranus's heart raced still but he quickly calmed himself, waiting for his mount to eat its full. His mind was cleared now, he knew only of what steps must be taken next. With all that he had learned and gained from The Ultimate, it was time again to bring the rule of Varz to the Five Realms.

*  *  *

With his new feathered friend he made excellent time back to Shieran waters and was pleased to see Varz progress among the Shieran islands. The Lessers were putting up a fight, but O'cule had deployed their reinforcements intelligently. In the handful of days that it took him to fly back, Dranus had lots of time both to consolidate all of the information he had gathered and to speak again with the spirits of the Staff.

His objectives therein were twofold: to find out more about the black gem in the Staff and to find out what using it might entail. The spirits of the Staff were unable to do anything but speculate and even then their speculations were based on nothing more than supposition and gut feelings. None of their suggestions seemed to have much merit in Dranus's eyes and he supposed the only other source he might question was the Book of Fate's Desire. Even so, he guessed the Book's reaction would be similar to that of The Ultimate, who had never seen it used thus but guessed the outcome. It could be that the only difference between the two would be that The Ultimate would not even suggest what he thought might happen, giving the current king only a heavy warning.

Dranus had set up camp on one of the smaller, uninhabited islands among those of Shiera, still wanting to keep up the appearance of having been there all along. However, it was likely that word had spread to the other realms that he had been spotted and identified near Arendrum and this news might easily make it back to his own forces. He would need to find a boat so that he could release his mount back into the wild. The great beast was a wonder to behold, but there was no need for him to keep it, and the pact that once its kind had with his forefathers was long since forgotten. Remembering the warm blast of air when the portal opened, he wondered at where the bird had come from and if there were more of them there.

These topics and more vied for priority in his thoughts like a court of gossipers yelling ever louder for his attention. The rote process of wandering around, gathering pieces of dried driftwood, kindling, and something to buffer him against the wind gave plenty of space for the courtiers of his conscience. It was only when he had finally struck a fire at his makeshift camp that he was able to settle.

It had been two months since he had left *The Dawn's Fury* and only the Shieran ports most inland remained free of Varz flags, and those were abandoned. O'cule had done his work with startling efficiency given his resources; he was ever a capable man simply waiting for his opportunity to prove himself.

The king sat on a large stone and stared at the leaping flames, rising and falling in waves like those which lapped gently against the shore. Everything was calm. There was only the smell of the sea, the crackling of the fire, and the wind through underbrush. Now and then a bird flew from a tree nearby or something surfaced among the waves before retreating. It was, if he dare think it, peaceful. He thought to summon his friend Vintus from the staff but then stopped.

They would return to the fleet soon, perhaps it was time for him to confront the Book for the first time since his leaving Pyrán. He fetched the thing from his tent and held it with both hands in front of him. It was silent. From it he feared both the implications of its existence and the answers which it might provide him regarding the Staff. He focused briefly, re-imbuing the tome with the power of speech.

"You are the Book of Fate's Desire." The king's tone was stiff; deliberate.

A few pages stirred.

"Oh, you mean me? I began to think you had forgotten about me. Yes, I have been called by that name." The Book seemed both recalcitrant and secretly excited to speak with the king once again.

"But you said you had no name when we first met!" Dranus challenged.

"No, master, you asked me what my title was, and I am most certain that I have no title."

Dranus smiled, remembering the words of The Ultimate. "Then who was it that gave you that name?"

"Who was it that gave you your name, master?" The Book retorted quickly.

"It was my father." The answer was simple, and the king waited to see where the logic went.

"And who gave him his name?"

"His father, of course. But what does that have to do with you? You are a piece of writing; you have no father like I." He was beginning to grow irritated again, but in the same way he had when they were on better terms.

"Indeed, master..." The Book hesitated, "...well I suppose my wit has dulled a bit in my weeks of banishment. The point is that my name was given to me, but I know not by whom, it may have been by myself, but I cannot be sure." The Book seemed legitimately confused about its own origins and Dranus thought this a bit tragic, to have nearly unlimited knowledge of the world and none about yourself.

"I see, well do you suppose The Ultimate gave it to you?" The Book seemed to leap in his grasp, pages rustling in a flurry of surprise.

"King Baklar! You met with him?! Aha, I knew you would!" There was even a hint of pride in the words of that magical tome, but he should have expected it; it was the Book of Fate's Desire, after all, who told The Ultimate to expect him.

"I did, upon the peak of Pyrán. Though he mentioned that either your prediction was a bit early or that I was a bit late." The memory of his first meeting with the great king of the past came to mind briefly, nearly prompting a blush of embarrassment.

"Then it was that you arrived late!" A quick challenge was issued followed by the familiar ruffling of paper that he always assumed was akin to a laugh. A part of him warmed to the idea of having this relationship back in his life although his suspicion and caution felt close like wet clothing. The fact remained that even this comment from the Book implied that it was an unavoidable certainty that he would have been there at that time. Those thoughts of being controlled and used as a plaything of Fate itched at his thoughts.

Still, he could not help but smile at his friend.

"He told me many things, about his history with you, about the history of Varz, about things that might still be. He told me I should trust you and embrace your power...and I have decided to do so. You have my trust Book of Fate's Desire. For now." His countenance turned serious, as though the Book might somehow see that he did not take this lightly.

Instead of expected hesitation, the Book was quick to reply.

"Then you have my strength and my knowledge, King Dranus. I'm sure you learned a great deal from Baklar. I may have the ability to read anything that has ever been written or drawn, but Baklar sees and has seen all." The Book clearly had a great deal of respect for the first King of Varz. That great king had the strength and will to cast the Book away, to cut himself off from such strength and never look back. If the relationship between them had been anything like his with the Book then he might see why the Book recalled those times fondly.

"I must ask you one question before we continue this way Book." King Dranus thought long and hard about this question, he had been doing so since leaving the mountain sanctuary of Pyrán. Was he the Book's tool? Was he some pawn of Fate's desires or was it Fate itself that bent to his ambitions? Did he even want to know the answer to such a question? One thing was sure, if he were to ask the question, he must do so with perfect words lest he be cornered by the Book's wit.

The Book was patient in waiting for the question, but Dranus could not force himself to ask it. It was not yet time.

"You know of many things that are unknown. Do you know what the black gem in the Staff of the South Star is and what secrets it holds?"

"There is a black gem in the Staff of the South Star?!" The Book of Fate's Desire nearly bounced from his grasp in genuine shock.

A bit caught off guard by this exclamation, Dranus smiled wryly and placed his hand against his forehead with a heavy sigh.

"As helpful as ever, my friend."

# Chapter 27
## Storm Cloud Squall

By use of the South Star Fleet and intricately drawn maps of the Shieran waterways, King Dranus VIII of Varz arrived in the capital city of Shiera the next day with the setting of the South Star. The great hawk had already been seen off, flying west over the Middle Sea. Although he was loathe to see such an important part of his nation's history lost, he wished the creature genuine good fortune and hoped he would see his like again one day.

Upon reaching the city he acted as though he had never left, coming in to the now conquered High Hall as though he were conducting a routine inspection. Admiral O'cule, who had just returned from an expedition in the north himself, locked eyes with the king but kept his nerves. He acknowledged the king's presence but nothing more; he knew they would have time to speak later that night once they were in relative privacy.

That time seemed to pass as if by passing through a threshold from the High Hall onto the hidden rear balcony of the Varz flagship; the brief interlude something of a dream in his later recollections. King Dranus had so much to tell, such plans to lay, and so little time in which to lay them. The night brought silence among the floating ships and the ever-watching sliver of the waxing moon like a cat's eye in the night. Admiral O'cule and Magemaster Zed arrived moments later, careful not to break their king's pensive mood.

Turning to greet them, Dranus moved towards the Magemaster first, placing a firm hand on the man's shoulder next to his bowed head. "That which you gave me at the onset of my journey was that which made it possible, Zed. Your deed saved my life and for that, all of Varz is in your debt. I will require future service from you, and you should be cautious to guard your life." The man raised his head, hope dazzled in his eyes. "For if you still possess it when Commander Ven becomes unfit for her position, it shall be yours."

The tall, broad figure almost seemed to jolt with excitement but held his emotions in as best as he could, showing the control of self that was characteristic of a master sorcerer. "It was only my pleasure to be of service, my king. I am honored to accept your graciousness and swear that I will not betray your generosity. We will make the Lessers sleepless with fear of our magical might, my king." His reservation while speaking such passionate words was admirable and Dranus had no question that this man was the rightful successor to the position of Commander of the Mage Corps.

Taking note of the growing silence between them, the Magemaster gave a stiff bow and exited the balcony to return above decks. The two that remained, Dranus and his friend O'cule, leaned against the metal railing in a stiff tension until one of them smiled and the other responded in kind.

"My king, I am relieved to see you back. We intercepted most attempts to send word outside of Shiera, but it seemed as though the news of Shiera's fall reached the enemy regardless. I worried that they may have discovered you or that you might have run into one of those Warriors of Pyrán." O'cule's concern was genuine; as one of the king's father's confidants, it had fallen on O'cule's shoulders to worry for Dranus's in place of the deceased former King of Varz.

Dranus grinned a wicked, terrible grin and the image of the bloodied Warrior of Earth flashed back through his thoughts; his muscles tightened.

"I did happen to come across the Warrior of Earth, as a matter of fact." He spoke with no apparent importance, simply referring to the incident as though it were a passing moment of no great significance. His eyes wandered and his smile lingered.

"And you managed to escape?!" O'cule was alight with concern, marveling that his king still lived and walked free!

"I did more than that, O'cule. I crushed the fool like the pebble he really was." The old battle-lust of his ancestors spiked in his blood as he recalled the event. "There remain only four Warriors to impede our path and they will fall as easily as the Warrior of Earth did." His arrogance showed like it had at times before.

O'cule was not entirely unfamiliar with this guise, but there was a subtlety to his voice that had not been there before. There was a hunger and a delight in all that he had accomplished beyond the lethargy with which he had once boasted petty victories. Something beyond the confidence imbued by single-handedly defeating a Warrior of Pyrán had changed in Dranus, something truly momentous.

"My king! To have defeated a Warrior of Pyrán by yourself! But how? The Army of the South Star? But that Warrior...he could nearly wipe out our entire army like so many ants beneath his boot!" O'cule made no effort to disguise his shock and pride in spite of the reserve of a Varz officer.

Again the king made no splendor of his achievement, though he relished the praise of his subordinates like he had not before. "The Staff of the South Star was unused, old friend. Those Warriors have a much greater threat to fear now." Dranus removed the Stone of Pyrán's Plight from the pouch which held it and presented it to the Admiral. A few noticeable veins of green had been added to the quiet purple. The two colors stood out in a vibrant glow against the other swirling, intermingled strips of color stained onto the stone.

As disbelieving as the admiral had been when he heard that the Warrior of Earth had been defeated without the use of the Staff, he could not trust his eyes when he saw the thing in his king's hands.

"...My king? ...a rock...?" He was unsure how to act. Though he knew he should not disrespect his king by questioning the item's usefulness, how was he, an Admiral of Varz, supposed to believe that the final and most powerful Relic in Varz history was a rock? A smooth and colorful rock, but a rock nonetheless!

Dranus, though he felt no anger at the Admiral's amazement, had to be cautious about what information he gave the man. He could not admit that he had met and trained with The Ultimate; he could tell no one of this. But he could tell him of the Stone's properties since only the King of Varz could utilize it.

"It is not just a rock, O'cule. It is a magical item crafted for the sole purpose of defeating the Warriors of Pyrán. It draws their elemental powers from them and leaves them weak. And it has done so once already." Dranus traced the line of green across the round surface of the stone.

O'cule marveled at the thing, daring neither to touch it nor ask how it was made as it was not his place to do so. But he was still skeptical, as Dranus had originally been, of the nature of its crafting. The other Relics were weapons, a sword and a staff, how could one of their ancestors have made a simple stone when destruction ran through their very souls?

"If it is your word lord, then I will not question it. Though I look forward to seeing the stone in action. Will you use it on the Warrior of Water?"

Dranus paced the room, rolling the Stone in his palm repeatedly while he considered this question as he had often done. "That will depend a great deal on her attitude. She has great power and a weak resolve. If we can bring that power to our side then it will be greater to harness than to eliminate. How has she behaved in my absence?" His interest showed in the way he stopped suddenly, his eyes focusing with a gentle expression.

"The Magemaster reports that she has been absolutely no trouble at all. She has cooperated in order to remain alive though she complains of boredom without cessation." Dranus smiled at this and took a seat, signaling to his admiral that they could drop some of the formality.

"Has she made any comment on her opinion about our people and the stuff of her destiny?" Now Dranus pretended to lose interest, almost as though he were speaking with the girl at that moment and not the admiral himself. While it was not uncommon for an officer as highly ranked as O'cule to have rights over a prisoner aboard his own vessel, Dranus had given explicit orders on how she was to be treated and with whom she might converse. O'cule's gilded tongue had been a valuable asset to King Roboris the Thick-Hearted in settling an agreement with the kingdoms of the West and he hoped to utilize it as his father had.

"I did speak with her one night. She wanted to know what it was like being a regular Varz citizen, it was an odd conversation at best, my king."

"And how did you describe it? Did she seem perplexed? Swayed? Doubtful?"

"I told her the truth: that our people are prosperous and we enjoy a period of superiority, a simplicity of life accentuated with the thrill of war. I told her about life for the common folk, about the Dens and experience of walking down a street busy with sorcery and sweat now that we have been renewed. She noted that our festivals and the like were similar to those she was familiar with, if not a little odd." He paused, attempting to recollect her reaction and wishing he had taken specific notes.

It was the simplicity and matter-of-fact tone that O'cule, perhaps unknowingly, employed which was so convincing. As a brilliant sorcerer of Varz must do, he stated opinions and points of view as indubitable fact in such a way that the listener could not refute his words.

"And what of our history? Of our customs?"

"She seemed interested in our appearance above all else, especially our eyes. Of course I spoke of the natural use of sorcery in our everyday lives. I told her about the Mask of the Monarch festival and how the Eyes come to all of Varz blood." O'cule let out a chuckle as he stared into the distance seeking his own memories. "She had such bizarre questions, that one. She asked me if I knew my own destiny!"

"To which you replied?" But, of course, the king knew the answer.

"How could a man of Varz not know of something which he forges himself?!" The venerable admiral shook his head at the utter absurdity of the question.

"She didn't appear to react much, just nodded and seemed very pensive. She does not speak much, that one."

Dranus shook his head, knowing that it was her pensiveness that would eventually lead her to his way of thinking. "'He who speaks least,' O'cule. She is bright and beautiful beyond her years."

O'cule nodded in agreement, though it seemed that Dranus had been far more enamored by her appearance than any of the others. She was, after all, a Lesser by blood. He was not so bold as to bring this up directly with the king, despite his worry. The girl bore some passing resemblance to the late Wife of the King and the last thing they needed was for the king to sink back into depression and lock himself in his room for a week doing all sorts of forbidden experiments.

Dranus, sensing the stutter in the conversation, decided to move forward.

"I will visit her tonight and test her resolve. Regardless, I will be leaving shortly for Varz to rally our ground forces. We are at the peak of our power and our enemies are disorganized and will try to send relief to Shiera. If we act quickly we may take advantage of their weakness and wipe them out in a single pass. I will bring the girl with me and see if she cannot be put to use." Dranus rose from his seat, resuming the pose and posture that must be upheld when a king takes his leave from an officer. "I leave the command of our forces here to you, O'cule, and trust that we will hold what we have taken."

O'cule snapped to attention like a spring trap and bowed to the King of Varz. "My king! I understand, I will have a small force readied to escort you whenever you have made your preparations to depart. And I swear by my line of noble ancestors that I will not relinquish a single Shieran Isle." Admiral O'cule was always one to be counted on, that was comforting. Dranus had no doubts that this was a task well within the reach of the old admiral. His forces would also be the first vanguard against any foreign threat from the North if any should make an attempt to ally themselves with the Lessers, though he doubted this greatly.

"Rest well admiral, there is much to be done." The king rested a hand on the older man's shoulder, looking him in the eyes; black orbs frozen for the passing glance.

"My king," he acknowledged and then excused himself to oversee the night's work.

Dranus stayed a few moments on the private deck listening to the waves lap against his ships and breathing in the briny air. It was not the most pleasant smell, but it carried a certain martial comfort. Here, like his home in Varz, was a place of tranquility in a chaotic world.

The waxing moon spied him once more.

To the southeast were the restless folk and the dancing pyres of light running up and down the twilight streets of Shiera, still brimming with life under Varz rule. General Armodus had always taught that a taken city left in luxury and apparent peace would stifle any thoughts of rebellion in the masses like a smothering blanket.

There in the ever-vigilant cold of the Night Season he felt at peace with nature. Still, he sensed that something loomed in the distance, some unseen danger. A cold gust blew and the rustling of furled sails overhead disturbed the melancholic hum of the night.

The king raised his gaze and watched the horizon for some unlikely sign of unrest. For several minutes he watched diligently, somehow expecting something to appear besides knowing that nothing would get so close to them without ample warning. Unless....

There was nothing.

Nothing more than a few clouds in the distance.

He tried to shake that nagging feeling, fighting to retain his peaceful demeanor from just moments before, but it continued to flutter in his bowels; it began to quicken his heart. If the sorcerous Book had been on his person he might have sought its guidance, but it rested in his own cabin.

Instead, it was to his prisoner that his thoughts turned, complicating and multiplying his unease like pouring oil on a fire instead of water.

Before he knew it, he had arrived at the small chambers of the Warrior of Water. His stomach was still in knots, but he quieted himself with a combination of self-control and self-sorcery.

The Warrior of Water had been moved to an actual room and was given a bed though she was still heavily guarded at all hours. These guards now bowed low to their king and permitted him entrance, knowing that they should keep their distance and be sure not to eavesdrop.

The girl was laying on her bed, staring at the ceiling, when he entered. Her hands and legs remained firmly bound. She did not notice him at first and appeared to be deep in thought. For the few moments that she was entranced with her ruminations he watched her carefully, musing, like he had so often done, at her similarity to his late wife. He could not deny that he had thought of her often while away, even if those thoughts enraged and perplexed him. Perhaps he had missed her, or missed the passing of time during which he would be twisting her mind and forming it for his own purpose. Yes, that had to be it.

Finally her attention was broken, and she seemed startled by the presence of a man she had not seen for more than a month. She sat up and stared hard through the King of Varz though she seemed noticeably more calm and accepting of her predicament than when he had first met with her.

Raven was obviously confused. Had she thought that he would visit her often? Perhaps torture her? She seemed surprised that she had been treated with dignity and relative kindness so long as she did not cause trouble.

She had pleasant talks with the admiral of Varz, himself. He had been an icon of a man, not like the king was, but in the way that a local merchant might be known for his honesty and good nature. By the day she became less and less certain about all she had heard of the demonic peoples of Varz. At some point, she had begun to hope for an audience with the king, for clarity, if nothing else.

"I see they've given you a room, you must have taken my advice." The king's expression was gentle and he held a slight curve to his lips.

"So you have been away...." Her eyes narrowed as if trying to see through his gentle exterior and find his true intentions.

"I am a king! I have no time to attend personally to a single prisoner when there is a war at hand." He was calm and spoke as if this were common knowledge, walking slowly into the room. "Tell me, Raven, what have you learned of your destiny in your time among us? Do you yet struggle?"

The girl looked down at her bound hands and away from the figure who strolled evenly around the outer wall of the room.

"I have thought a lot about what you said back then...."

"Please, you may call me by my name, Dranus." He interjected, sensing her hesitance at how to address him.

She flushed a strawberry red over her pale features and continued to stare at her lap.

"Dranus." She cleared her throat and calmed, "I do not struggle, but I feel that my destiny will not escape me much longer. It is less now that I battle with shadows and more that I am waiting to see a friend I have known I would meet for the entirety of my life."

Though she looked away, Dranus could see a quiet confidence in her eyes, an iron will. She was being stubborn and she would continue believing that the path set for her was right, he assumed.

"And what makes you think that? You are my prisoner, your nation has fallen to my strength, and even now my people gather resources and further diminish your people's chances of success." Her response got under his skin. How could she still hold to such a silly ideal in the face of impossibility?

The Warrior smiled and looked toward him, an almost longing gaze in her eyes.

"Just a feeling, nothing more."

Such a beautiful smile. The longing he saw in her features was for something else, somewhere else. Something far from her current reality. Was it to be that their paths were destined only to cross as enemies? He wondered if he should seal her powers away now and avoid any undue risk. She spoke now not knowing he had this power...perhaps he could use that.

"And was it a feeling that set you on this path in the first place? Did you join the other Warriors based on such a feeling? I fear that your feelings, the whimsical impulses of someone as young as yourself, guide your destiny, not your mind." He took a seat in a chair across from the bed and assumed a pensive pose, ready to engage her.

"Is that so bad, king? To follow one's heart?" She turned to face him but pulled her legs tight to her chest.

Was it a phrase that held many meanings to the girl? Why was it that she said a thing like this with such obvious hesitation?

"Is it not what you and your people do as well? You told me that you fight because it is in your blood; is it not your heart that moves that blood through your veins?"

For a moment he was shocked, she had wit to match any Den Maiden! He now saw why Admiral O'cule had found it so entertaining and yet confusing to speak with her; she was more like they then her own kind...although this was of little surprise to the keeper of Varz's recently amassed secrets.

"Do not play semantics here." He poked in a soft but sturdy tone. "Were it that I lacked a heart I would be a far greater king." Now Dranus found himself quoting that herald of Varz's dominance, King Baklar the Ultimate. "To be king is to know what is best and to lock that knowledge where the heart cannot see, lest it know its true self."

Dranus kept his composure and showed no weakness to the girl. These were merely statements of fact.

"I think you could stand to rely on that heart a little more; you might find it wiser and more resilient then you believe it to be." Now she diverted her eyes again and Dranus almost thought he saw her blush. And what madness when his own pale cheeks flushed with color!

No! He was King of Varz, and no young warrior of legend would make him question centuries of tradition and expectancies. He bit into his lip and regained control of his body.

"I admire you your youth. You are in the Dawntime of Life and your passion burns like the early morning rays of the sun. But do not think that simply by rising to your zenith that you will look down

293

and see that your destiny lies before you like a fresh new world. Your naivety will only get you so far." She seemed enamored by his words and for the first time he saw her smile; his heart fluttered as if to remind him that it was still there.

Then all at once she was sullen as if remembering something that brought her great trouble of mind. "You don't need to concern yourself with my destiny, King Dranus. However much I wish to craft my own Fate, I am burdened by my responsibilities as a Warrior of Pyrán. So long as you threaten all that I have known and I bare this strength, I will resist you and your ways...whatever ways they may be."

The king took note of everything he experienced from her and logged them like still paintings in his mind. She was resolute in her words, but her emotions betrayed her remorse. She was questioning even that power which she had been given and certainly her view of Varz had changed. Unlike the previous time, there were no outlandish accusations, no looks of disgust, and a calm resolve that replaced her frantic uncertainty. Now was the time to let her feelings stir and to let her continue thinking. Now he could visit her whenever he pleased and would find what needed to be done to convince her that his truth was superior. Such was the nature of his people, the nature of Varz, and even the nature of sorcery itself.

"You are in no position to make threats, Water." Dranus smiled a devilish grin and then stood from his chair. "Fight who you must to find your destiny, Raven. Even if the one you must fight is yourself. Consider what I have to offer. Consider your own wants and needs." And he said nothing more, for to be vague was to build bridges to new places of thought she never knew to explore. Raven was an intelligent young woman, he would need to lead her there, not drag her kicking in the dirt.

He left her as she had been when he entered, staring in thought at the roof of her cabin. And as she had not changed, neither had the king. His heart was still aflutter with alien sensations and a hesitation towards the future. He could not refuse that he pined for the embrace of that girl like the warmth of sleep among his own things and the safety of his fleet. In a state of furious reverie he had to accept that each smile she gave, each thoughtful aversion of her soft eyes and delicate skin, filled him with forbidden hope that she battled with the truths of her existence for his sake, if not for hers.

He found himself upon the forecastle of his flagship alone, his back to the sea. He stabbed his nails angrily into the guard rail and grimaced, wishing his uncertainties away like a coward. He contemplated the merits of being direct with her. If she felt the same would it make her choice easier? But if she did not? What a fool, what a moronic scab he would show himself to be! How could a proud king of Varz even consider such things?!

Clouds filled his mind. He felt every bit of give of the brine-sodden wood as he dug deeper and deeper, threatening to crush the rail or himself in equal likelihood.

He turned to show his agony to the stars. The sky, too, was filled with clouds; rushing storm clouds that seemed to race at him like a wall of charging horses and chariots. He saw furious flashes of lightning in the night and felt the wind pick up around him as the squall came. He contemplated all that the Warrior of Water had said as his dark musings turned ever darker. With each passing moment the storm grew larger, angrier. Its full force would be upon them before midnight.

Dranus feared the approaching storm much more than he feared the Warrior of Water or any of the Warriors of Pyrán. It was not the unrest it would bring or the troubles of the sea. It was simply the presence of the thing which set his brow to furrow and his heart to sink. It was the ominous portent that it brought that made him feel as though all that had happened so far had merely been the brisk winds of fortune. Now the true storm came.

It brought glory in one hand and ruin in the other. Each hand rested before him, reaching out to him and calling for him to grasp. But he felt the clouds misled him: that he would reach for glory only for the fingers to open and reveal doom at the last second.

But this was just a feeling, nothing more.

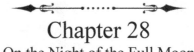

# Chapter 28
## On the Night of the Full Moon

"**A** week of storms! *Weeks* of rain! And here we are on guard for the fourth night in a row!" A Varz marine clad in dark blue sailors garb tried to warm himself from the cold and the rain that fell relentlessly around him. His gloves radiated a soft glow of warmth, but it wasn't a boundary he was good at pushing.

"That's our duty! We should be honored the king's entrusted us with guardin' his prisoner for four nights in a row." Another guard tried to reason with his friend but he, too, was feeling the wet and the cold chill turn his loyalty to ice.

A week after returning to Shiera, Dranus had set off again with a small group of ships for Viél and ultimately, Varz. The Warrior of Water remained on his ship in her bindings, though she enjoyed a rather lavish room and very few leaks. Many of the soldiers were discontent with this situation, but they knew better than to question the ornate and unknowable workings of their monarch. In the end, Varz was a place that rewarded greatness; they had no one to blame for their relatively lower ranks other than themselves.

"That's all right and well, I agree, but by Vale's engorged gut I wish this damned rain would stop!" He spat on the deck and flexed his legs, trying to get the blood moving through them after standing sentry for so long.

The pair stood on the main deck of a ship much smaller than *The Dawn's Fury*, outside a door which led directly to the Warrior of Water. At every other entrance to the innards of the ship were two guards as well, each pair doused in the pale light of the full moon.

"Full moon tonight. Whaddaya suppose our chances of seein' a God-storm are?" The second guard shifted uneasily as he tried to peer through the blackness of the driving rain into the rolling seas.

"A God-storm? You actually believe in that old myth? We've been sailors now for nearly twenty years. Have you ever heard even a whisper that could be taken seriously?" A joke in bad taste it was to speak of a God-storm. Sailors that invoked the name during a full moon could be seen as bold or stupid, because regardless of how unbelievable the tale was, a sailor knew better than to tempt the seas lest they rend him to the dark depths.

"I'd say," he continued "that with some of the best sailors and sorcerers aboard the king's own personal vessel, not to mention King Dranus, sorcerer-God that he is, that this ship is nigh unsinkable."

A similar conversation was had by the pair across the deck from them and they saluted one another, not wanting to raise their voices and risk waking everyone. So they continued to complain and whisper crude jokes with their partners. They distracted themselves from the cold and practiced petty spell-work and ignored the baleful moon hanging among the stars.

This was the way of the night since Dranus and his crew had left Shiera weeks prior. The storm had chased them all the way down the coast and there hadn't been more than a passing cessation of the rain the whole time. The seas were rough for a typical vessel, but the masters of nautical sorcery that manned this ship made the act of sailing out a storm a relatively safe venture. They would arrive in Viél in a matter of days, though their approach had been slowed. Still, the soldiers all thought they had braved the worst parts of the storm and celebrated their merit for doing so unscathed. In their confidence they chose to discount the old tales of the legendary God-storm, said to have been summoned by a God of the Moon to destroy the Varz navy during the Second Great War. Those that survived had spoke of impossible things at sea and it became a way to scare new recruits quickly after that. Modern sailors liked their superstition but feared nothing of Gods or such impossible conjurings of nature.

The king, however, remained suitably wary of what terrors could be wrought when the heavens and the seas were aligned in their wrath.

\*     \*     \*

The soldiers on deck barely noticed the change in the rolling of the waves, in the frequency of distant thunder, or the excitation of the winds. They were cold, wet, and tired from a long night on watch. The South Star would rise in another hour or so and that would be their cue to switch shifts. This was all that they could focus on, the relief of their duty and the few measly hours of sleep that they could attempt before resuming their responsibilities.

They were taking turns dozing against the doors they were to protect when the sea fell.

Like being dropped from a cliff they plummeted into a trough in the waves only to be tossed back up by a large wave, waking all of the guards and putting more than a few of them on edge. They had dealt with such seas for many days now, but their earlier talk of fitful winds cursed by Gods to sink every soul of Varz to the deepest depths lingered in their thoughts.

The king awoke in the sudden upheaval and had his wits about him in an instant. Like the guards, he had also spent many sleepless nights amongst the churning of the stormwinds and the loud cracks of thunder that bade him awaken. He avoided a drugged slumber in case something were to happen to the ship that required his efforts. He'd not settle for a Fate so lowly as drowning in a sleeping stupor just short of his dreams being realized.

Like he had done every night he stared at the ceiling, thoughts abounding like their ship on rough seas, kept tightly to the bed through sorcery alone. It could be like every other night they had experienced, nothing was that different and they had known to expect a surge in the early morning.

Still, something was off. Dranus could feel it.

He knew that night was the night of the full moon and he knew as well as any other the stories of the God-storm. What he knew that others did not was that the story was based in truth. There was a massive storm during the Second Great War that had greatly damaged the Varz fleet, though the attribution of divine intervention was added in later years.

Sprawled on his bed, Dranus tried to pass time by contemplating the source of such a storm, but this merely served to fill him with greater unease. The discord in the flow of all things he had felt in Shiera had followed him to the high seas, but it was closer now. Closer than ever before.

Nonsense. This was natural weather. A storm as any storm he had braved in all his years.

He tried to shut his eyes and fall back asleep, but some annoyance kept him yet awake. It was not just the uncomfortable feeling he had, nor the pitch and roll of the ship, but some light that agitated his eyes. When he raised his heavy lids again he searched the room for the source and found it curious to see paper thin strips of blue light shining through the cracks in the planks that separated his room from the room next to his.

The Warrior of Water's room...!

Memories of bright colored lights shining across the Rift rushed into his mind all at once. Before he could react, he was thrown from his bed, ripping through his magic, and crashed against the wall. Dranus panicked, he knew what this meant and he had feared that it would happen when he was unprepared, as he was then.

With haste he pulled on his belt and his pants and unsheathed the Sword of Righted Guard. All the while he stared at the glowing blue light and fought to hold his balance.

Then, the light moved, trickling through the wood, and it was gone. Without so much as a simple shirt he burst through his door, his chest taking the full force of the cold, wet wind of the storm. The shock of the blow set his mind spinning and he gripped the door frame trying to reorient himself.

Through darkness his eyes darted, seeking signs of the girl and those placed to guard her. The main deck was deserted. A dozen well trained and seaworthy marines and not a soul remained! Washed into the sea, presumably!

A violent lash of lightning whipped from the clouds and the light brought his gaze upwards. Flickering between the deluge of rain was that brilliant blue light of holy power. Had the tidal forces of the full moon amplified her powers somehow? Was this the night she had been waiting for?

He saw her, then, seemingly floating above the foredeck wrapped in scintillating sapphire. He screamed into the wind's howl, calling the girl's name, but his words were lost. Grasping anything that might give him a hold onto the ship he crawled along the wall of the aft cabins towards the center. He tried to will his control over the ship, but he could not hold it.

He glared again at the awesome image of the girl on the foredeck, seemingly unaffected by the weather around them. Though the decks spun and moved wildly she had no trouble maintaining her balance or her strides towards the front of the ship. The wind, though it tossed her hair about like it did the briny waters of the Middle Sea, did not appear to impede her advance. He was taken back to the vision of her elegantly dancing on the waves in the defense of Shiera. Her grace was astounding! She was not moved by the water because she *was* the water!

But what was her plan? Would she jump into the near frozen waters of the ocean and attempt to swim to shore?! Even with her power could she survive such an endeavor?

He eyed the central mast and made a desperate dash for it, throwing his hands at flailing rig lines blown loose and finally clutching the mast to his chest, knocking the breath from his cold lungs. He would have hurt had the frozen rain not already thoroughly numbed his skin. He could barely feel the splinters of the mast digging into him. He was fading...no! Concentrate!

He dashed again for the staircase that would ascend to the foredeck but was taken by a sudden jerk of the waves. He rolled onto his side and tumbled towards the seas. His heart leapt when his back hit the railing and he wondered for that split second if the swollen wood would support him.

Staggering to his feet Dranus wiped matted hair from his eyes and like a beacon he continued to endure the awesome vision of the Warrior of Water. Reaching the staircase had worn his body and his mind; his skin frozen and his grip on the Sword of Righted Guard tested with every passing second. His thoughts raced. His mind was a flurry of emotions and outcomes which he feared. He found himself frightened by the thought of her leaving, even by the thought of her being in danger. This was not the way things were supposed to go!

"What are you doing Raven?!" He screamed as loud as he could though he knew she still would not hear him. As if in answer to his question, a bright strike of lightning illuminated the night and terror consumed the King of Varz who looked up at a gargantuan wave like an angry Titan of the sea baring down on his small ship with wicked intent.

He grabbed onto the rail next to him for his life and awaited the terrible doom that would come crashing down on them at any moment. But to his surprise, no water spilled on him other than the normal downpour of the rain. Instead he felt a hard lurch that surely would have knocked him overboard had he not secured himself. He felt the ship rise into the sky and a new wind pressed against his left side.

The ship was being carried by the wave, just like in Shiera! And for all he could guess, it would carry them to unfriendly shores where the Warrior of Water no doubt planned to escape. It was anger which consumed him then.

How could he have been so foolish?! To allow this girl, among the greatest threats to Varz, to live among him and his people. Was this all the machinations of the Warrior? Had she used him in some devious ploy, some ruse? Blinded by his affections towards her he had set his own Fate and that of his entire nation at risk! Could anyone know such torturous remorse as he?

"No! I will stop this!" With his anger a certain clarity and rage-fueled warmth filled the king, and his body began to adjust to the movements of the boat as he forced his will on the reality around him. He was Sorcerer King! No child with nascent elemental powers would best him, not this night!

He took measured steps up the stairs to the foredeck and saw her again, standing at the edge of the foredeck looking out into the storm as if in a trance. She was like a magnificent figurehead with her legs hanging limply in her tattered dress, her arms outstretched to either side. Her glowing sapphire gaze looked as though they judged the waves, or else commanded them with absolute authority. She was in complete control, a specter of Godly power.

One by one his footfalls led him closer to the figure from which the blue light emanated. His heart was racing. The constant thump of it against his chest followed the rhythm of the Stone of Pyrán's Plight which seemed to pulse in anticipation at his belt.

"Raven!" He was amazed he still had the energy or breath to scream against the wind like that.

She turned and he could see the holy light radiating from her eyes, from sad eyes. For a moment Dranus thought she wept, but no, it was surely the rain. Somehow she had heard him, or else felt that he approached her.

Her face was the image of mastered calm but still he sensed some sadness in her...some feeling of dread which he likely mirrored. And though the words that formed on her lips spelled "stop" he continued to move towards her.

A chilling wave struck his side, but he held his ground, his feet planted securely to the deck with his sorcery. Another step towards

301

her brought an even greater wave of that icy water and a twitch of pain shot through the young girl's face as Dranus cried out.

But again he held firm. The bright blue light around the girl dimmed just a bit.

Finally he had reached a distance in which he could hope that his words might reach her.

"You must let me go King Dranus! Nothing can change from our meeting, nothing!" Her voice was so smooth and clear, as though it resonated through the rain to reach him. "My Fate was chosen for me, and I must fulfill it... Please, just stop!" She pleaded with him; with genuine concern she begged him.

The anger within the king fled as he witnessed the truth laid bare across her features. If anyone had succumbed to the Warrior's ruse, it was Raven herself.

"Is that it, then?! You've lost your battle with yourself?" he shouted in genuine disgust and outrage; he had hoped for so much more from her.

But the girl shook her head and attempted a smile amongst the chaos of the storm.

"How can I lose a battle against myself?"

"The only way to lose a battle against yourself, is to give up, Raven!" He heard both of their voices so clearly then, as if the storm had hushed itself so that they may speak one last time as King of Varz and Warrior of Water.

"I'm sorry...but I must do this. You have the power to end all of this King Dranus, but if you will not, then I must!" He knew then, at that moment, that she wept.

A massive wave crashed down atop the king, consuming him like a river, running over him like a stampede. And from this downpour came a powerful force, and a prideful voice. "You're right," he muttered, "I do have the power to end this."

Suddenly he held the Stone of Pyrán's Plight aloft. It resonated with the powers the Warrior of Water commanded as though it thirsted for them. The power of the stone nullified some of the effects of her control where he held it and parted the sorcerous waves where they threatened to strike the king.

"You said to me..." he locked desperate eyes with desperate eyes, "that you were burdened by your responsibilities as a Warrior of Pyrán." The blue light pulsed quickly, desperate panic consuming her features. Still, her beautiful blue irises showed through the mist, he could see them clearly. Dranus took several labored steps to close the remaining distance between them; there was nowhere she could run to. The waves now affected him no more than they did her; his resolve could not be shaken.

"I will take that burden from your heart." She did not fight what came next, but closed her eyes as the Stone touched her forehead and hungrily feasted on the blue light emanating from her body. It swirled and gathered around them both but moved like a whirlpool down into the Stone. Then it was over, and a snaking line of blue settled in among the others.

With this, the storm lost its fury and the wave which had carried them returned gently to the seas. And like the wave itself, Raven fell into the arms of King Dranus. He tried to support her tired, soaked body but his weakness was great and the two fell to their knees upon the deck.

What a sensation it was, to touch her! His sword hanging from a thong around his wrist he felt her skin on his fingertips for the first time. For all the driving rain, the freezing winds, and the salty seas, her body was warm to the touch and it filled him with its warmth. Deep in his chest, in his once forgotten heart, he felt connected to her as he had never felt before. And this all from the weight of her body in his arms!

The seas began to subside, and it appeared that the massive wave had at least served to get them away from the main body of the storm. The deckhands, feeling it was somewhat safe to see what had happened then, began appearing on the main deck.

On the foredeck King Dranus considered his next move, his mind still trapped in the hectic wrath of the storm that continued to swell within him. On the one hand, the girl had proven herself a threat, though she had just lost what made her a threat. How many of his guards and his soldiers had she killed that night? Still he could not deny the feelings that spread through every inch of his form, that had developed ever since the first moment he laid his demonic eyes on her. And he knew; he could see, hear, and feel, that she shared those feelings. He had opened her mind to a new level of understanding and set her free from her curse of destiny as a Warrior of Pyrán. For all that she had been a mortal enemy, he had the gnawing impression that this young woman was an integral part of the Fate that he

303

crafted.

His body acted, ignoring the indecision of his mind. With a sudden move he lifted her, eyes opening a bit, and he pressed her body against his, embracing her.

He could hardly describe that which he felt from that moment. All that he had longed for, all that he had regretted losing in his wife, all that he had hoped he might once find again came rushing back into him. He felt life and a whole new genre of emotions which his time with Kaelel had only hinted at. It was as though everything he had ever desired manifested itself in that single bursting moment.

And Raven, no longer the holy Warrior of Water, wept. She wept for the powers and sense of purpose she had lost. She wept for the shattering of her conceptions about the world and the loss of innocence. But she also wept for the freedom she had gained. And she wept for the forbidden feelings she could now embrace, as she embraced the man she had once thought a monster in disguise, a terrible barbarian of a man bent on destroying the world. Such a war she had fought in her heart of hearts! A decision she had forsaken, made possible once again; made reality all the more!

Through the tears and the steady rain they held each other, neither thinking to say a word. Through the thunder and wind they lifted their buried heads and pressed their cold lips together, and they kissed for the first time under the light of the full moon.

# Chapter 29
## Rise and Fall

A single word buzzed on the lips of every man and woman as the dawn brought light and peace aboard the king's ship: God-storm.

It was already circulating among the ship hands that the violent weather they had experienced early that morning was due to none other than the mythical storm of ruin. Sailors recounted how they were tossed as if in a losing fist fight with the motion of the waves, the mere walls and floors of the ship delivering knockout blow after knockout blow. Many recalled seeing the ship carried upon an unnatural wave of gargantuan proportions through the portholes. What most could not fathom was how they had survived a legendary storm which had once sunk an entire Varz fleet! The select few that had come on deck before the king vanished with Raven (by some effort of the exhausted king, himself) knew that it was their almighty Sorcerer King who had vanquished the God-storm!

Haunting yarns of Dranus's battle with the enchanted forces of nature moved from mouth to ear across the deck, in the mess, and at every passing brush of shoulders until it was common knowledge that the glowing figure atop the forecastle had been the King of Varz exerting his authority over a thing which may have been a God in disguise! Songs of that feat would be sung by Varz naval men for generations to come.

To the king himself, who had known the truth of what happened, mention of it even in passing brought a haunted look to his eyes throughout the day. It was, however, a blessing for Dranus to find that an explanation for such outrageous events had manifested itself, whispered through the planks! This would be added to his ever-exaggerated legend which was both a blessing and a curse. His people would have no fear, no disloyalty or cowardice even in the face of God-like beings, but all of their hopes now rested solely on his shoulders.

Heavy is the mantle of legend.

Still, there were more pressing matters that demanded his attention.

Where were they, for example.

Dranus had been in a frenzy of chaotic cognition the night before and had lost all perception of time passing. For all he knew they could be back in Shieran waters, half way to the West, or deep into the nothing of the Southern Seas. They had escaped the clutches of the storm that had followed them since Shiera, but how much had their path been delayed? Would he be able to return to Varz in a timely manner? There was still the chance that they had been set into some trap before Dranus could stop the girl. He had to consider every possibility.

Dodging deftly between deckhands scrubbing the decks clean, his heart thumped in his chest with the remembered vision of Raven hovering above the ship in her azure light. The storm was pure pandemonium, but the space around the girl was hushed and peaceful like the reflection of the moon in a still pond.

He awoke from his daydream as he slipped into a hallway where the navigator was awaiting with a controlled smile. Good news at last!

It appeared that Raven had only known to direct them shore-ward, potentially expecting they still bordered Arendrum, and had not passed the point where the Rift met the ocean. Thus, in the worst-case scenario they would have to sail back out to the main current and lose a day or so, but in the best case, they could arrive a full day or so early by navigating the inland currents!

This good news came and went through Dranus's mind the same way a wave washed up from one side of the deck and off the other. In a war, a difference of up to two days could change the entire momentum of their strategy. But compared to the war between his head and his heart, it was nothing.

What must he do with Raven? What did he desire to do with Raven? What did she desire? Could she be trusted now that her powers had been sealed away? The moment of their embrace had afforded them no time for discussion before Dranus led the girl back into her chambers and back into what remained of her bonds. He said only that she must stay that way until it was safe.

What of his folk? They had but recently celebrated his marriage to

Kaelel, who's burial mound was still brined by the sweat of those that dug it! It was not customary he take another love so soon, but then again, they were in a war and he was the king. Varz monarchs had hardly shied away from breaking the more arbitrary traditions in their past and the populace simply had to accept their will. It was not impossible.

Her appearance was another problem. Though she was half Varz, descended from The Ultimate himself, she appeared as a Lesser! His people would never accept the presence of a Lesser at their king's side. That was to spit on the foundations of their society lain by Baklar's own hands.

He touched his fingers against the V-shaped scar on his cheek in deep thought. He considered the intense irony of the circumstances under which this war had begun: a half-blood son of Varz seeking vengeance for his father who had committed the very sin he now contemplated. Dranus loved the twisted combination of cruelty and irony as much as any man or woman of Varz, but this was something he could not take credit for.

"Your hate for me was well-deserved, Deleron." Dranus cracked a smile at the thought as he reached his chambers.

They would reach Viél in a matter of days most likely. He had to speak with Raven, he had to decide how to handle this, but he did not have to do so alone.

He reached across his desk for the Book of Fate's Desire, hoping he might glimpse some valuable insight from the tome.

"I need your council, Book."

"My knowledge is at your disposal, master. You seem distressed."

Dranus sighed, was it that obvious? If the tone of his voice gave away so much to a book, how could he hope to convince his crew that nothing was amiss? They would expect the proud boastings of a sorcerer who had just recently bested a thing of lore brought to life!

"Something happened during the storm last night." He was cautious how he should phrase what he said, not entirely sure what the Book knew of the information that had been shared with him by The Ultimate.

"You mean *besides* the storm?! I've not been tossed around like that since..." The Book immediately thought better of bringing up the fury of his current master after the Battle of the Rift. "...well since the second time I almost got King Baklar killed! Of course it was his wife who did the throwing then and I was more instrument then cause, but still!"

Curiosity grew within King Dranus, but he had to stay focused, there would be plenty of time for stories later.

"Yes, the Warrior of Water attempted an escape, the source of the storm, and I was forced to take away her power with the Stone." He paused, picking up the Book and moving to sit slouched on the edge of his bed. "But after that...well, I could not hide that I harbored some affection for her, and she returned in kind." The king felt the resurgence of fire in his cheeks. He looked away as if ashamed to tell this animated book all of his worldly problems.

"Aha! Yes! I had hoped something like this would happen!" The Book was jubilant, excited like it had been when its prediction of his meeting with The Ultimate was affirmed. Dranus grew suspicious again, feeling as though he might have been manipulated into this affection. These feelings were new to him; what a simple pawn he would make to something as powerful as the Book!

"What?! Did you know something of this and not tell it to me?" He was not yet angry but had to know the truth.

"I had no knowledge, master, I assure you; but I had my hopes that something would come of her capture." The pages of that mysterious Book rustled like leaves blown by a strong wind. "It is a strong coupling, my lord, what holds you back?"

"What holds me back?!" He stood and paced about the room, his head in his hand while the Book remained on the bed. "Isn't it obvious?! I am King of Varz! She was until recently my arch enemy, my prisoner, and moreover she is a Lesser! If I even suggested her as a member of our people, let alone a part of the royal family, I would have outrage and rebellion sooner than the words might leave my lips! Even contemplating the idea I risk a multitude of blasphemes on a millennium of tradition!"

Brief sounds of rubbing pages came from the Book like an old man's cryptic chuckle of hidden knowledge. "She is a Lesser as far as she appears, is she not, master?" Dranus's head turned quickly at these words, and he stared hard at the worn leather cover.

"It is as you say, she is a member of Varz in some part...she has inherited nearly all of the appropriate appearance...it is only her eyes..." He stopped, touching the scar on his face again.

Like a budding flower he began to form an idea; it was small at

308

first then burst into its full beauty.

"Her eyes!" Dranus took the Book in his hands and flipped the pages hurriedly, searching for a set of pages he had studied when he was a young child.

"The Ultimate mentioned that the Warriors of Pyrán had simply not unlocked the power of their eyes and that the Stone only took away their elemental powers inherited from the Guardian! If I can tap into her sorcerous power and activate the Sorcerer's Eyes in her, then she may yet be accepted." A grin crept to the king's lips and that subtle crescent veiled his brilliant plans.

"There is one further thing you must consider, however." The Book spoke up, still in the king's hands.

"And what is that?"

"The girl, master. Could it be that she was roused in the moment last night? After a night considering herself she may again turn to escape when we reach land. If you plan to make her a part of Varz then you must first be sure that this is what she desires or she will only bring you destruction."

Dranus was unmoved by this warning. Recently he had been inundated with warnings from many sources, it was time for him to make his own decisions, reckless or not. Besides, the Book had not been there for all that he had experienced with the girl. They had only known each other a short time, but they had spent countless hours deep in conversation. Moreover, the psychological bridging they had experienced initially had bound them in knowing of the other's true past and motives. He was sure that she had been considering his cause ever since that fateful meeting. She had even expressed that she was reluctant to become a Warrior of Pyrán. Whether it be her wiles convincing him of some illusion of affection so that she could take advantage of his kindness, or it was true affection and change...he did not care.

The Ultimate had livened him somehow, along with everything he had experienced so far. He felt nothing like the person he had been, sitting alone on his throne considering the worth of his life from dreadful moment to moment. Now he thought of such things with passion and weighed his worth like his ancestors had, by their accomplishments both on the battlefield and off.

"If she has not seen the light of our ways yet, then I will cast it upon her. I will make her a fitting woman of Varz, you will see." He was confident and without hesitation claimed his cloak from the wall and attached his belt around his waist.

"You will see." He smiled and flaunted these words at the still Book that lay, somewhat amused, on the soft silks and furs. Dranus then hurried to Raven's room with a stern face, dismissing the marveling gazes of the guards that thought him divine. He entered, locking the door behind him.

What caught his breath first was the state of the room. In the hush and hurry of the previous night he had not seen what damage the girl had done. Anything not secured lay broken or splintered on the floor. The bed, which was secured to the deck, was intact but it was as if the room had been flooded to the brim.

On that bed, curled in a ball against the wall, was the young woman that made his chest tighten and his mind zig-zag. At first, he was frozen, merely staring at her miserable state in tattered clothing, sodden and shivering. In a flash of horror, all his gaudy confidence fled him. In the space of time that she kept her head buried, refusing to check who had come in, he played through a thousand potential scenarios.

Finally, the long silence was curious enough to raise the girl's head and she peeked a single eye over her arms then lifted, noticing who it was. Dranus smiled at her, but she did not smile back. Instead she gripped herself more tightly and locked eyes with the King of Varz, glaring like a caged animal given just a tantalizing taste of freedom before returning to the keepings of a wild beast.

"Raven."

She winced at the word as suddenly as it came from the king's lips. In response, he became devastatingly unsure of himself.

He did not dare get closer to her now, though he had intended to do so originally. He was stunned. He hadn't expected such a cold reception and found himself with no idea what to do next.

A sudden shiver from Raven snapped his wits back to him, if for nothing other than an immediate problem-solving mindset.

"King of my Father, Raven, I didn't realize..." he cursed at himself; he should have been in to see her sooner. "Hold still, please."

Then his thoughts dove into the thickness of the room, sloughing through a reservoir of residual magic while shyly avoiding her physical form as much as he could. He separated the water from her clothes first, then from the sheets and the bed, so that it would fall to the deck. Material stretched unnaturally, forgetting the limits of the extent fabric, so that it more modestly covered her body. Finally, a difficult bit, especially in his volatile mental state, but he focused with the precision of a monarch of Varz and shared his body heat with her. He could feel that more was lost to the room than he would've liked, but he was desperate to improve her situation.

Raven reacted first with shock, then suspicion. Her freezing muscles clearly unclenched a little from the warmth, but her posture was still defensive and alert. Her eyes still cut him.

Next, Dranus noticed the cuffs around her wrists and ankles that still remained where her bindings had once held her. "Let me remove those cuffs." His first step towards her made her shy away slightly.

What was happening? Had it truly been as the Book said? Just a moment of passion? He had no experience in this area, no books of knowledge to help him. He was lost in an unmapped sea!

He stopped, still several feet from the bed, their eyes still locked on one another. With a few simple movements of his wrist and a flick of his ankles, the cuffs split and fell from her body. Still she did not move; only looked where the cuffs had once been then set her eyes to Dranus once again and spoke hesitantly.

"Are you sure?" It was almost a whisper, the words she spoke from behind crossed arms.

"Of course, your bonds have been useless since last night, there is no reason for you to continue wearing them." It was a simple enough question, but just as he thought he was regaining a grasp on the situation, he lost it again.

"Not that!" she practically shouted. "Me," came the next whisper. Her voice was stronger now and her eyes were harsh, an icy blue stare of something that reminded him of accusation.

"I don't understand what you mean, Raven." And he truly did not; he took another step towards her.

"You and I are enemies, Dranus! How can you have feelings like this for me?! How could I possibly trust that?" She buried her head again and he caught just bits of what she said under her breath, "How could I...?"

Dranus's countenance hardened with frustration. "Enemies?! For what purpose are we enemies? Because some power was thrust upon you and then directed towards me by another? That chain has been loosed from your Fate already! There is nothing to keep us as enemies now!" He took another step closer.

"It's not just that!" Her head snapped up again and one arm shot out to hold her forward some. "You're the King of Varz and I'm from Shiera, I am one of those your kind call 'Lessers!' You can't possibly believe that just because I've lost my magic that we can just be together and everything will be fine!" Tears welled up in her eyes as she yelled her anger at him, screaming frustration at that which she felt she could never have.

Dranus faltered watching her, wishing only that she wouldn't be sad anymore and knowing what to say but not knowing if he should say it.

"Raven...there is something you don't know about yourself...a well-kept secret that you may not want to know." He looked away, could he afford to give up such important information so early? All of that which he had learned from The Ultimate he had planned to never tell anyone else, but was that necessarily the right thing to do?

"Raven you...."

"I'm what?!" She glared, a lancet of accusation that begged him not to give her too small a hope that it might leak everything from inside her.

"You are also a member of Varz. By your blood, we are the same."

She was dumbfounded, shocked silent by such news that was hardly something she could ever believe to be true.

"No, that's not..." she stuttered and look down at her lap, confused.

"To be a monarch of Varz, one *must* be a descendant of King Baklar the Ultimate, first King of Varz. It is because my blood is tied to his that I am permitted to be king."

"What does that have to do with me?" Still she stared at her own body, questioning her very flesh as if it had hidden this secret from her all her life.

"The power you wielded as a Warrior of Pyrán was inherited by your shared ancestry with the original Guardian of Pyrán whom The Ultimate defeated long ago. But in the aftermath, a child was born. You and the other Warriors are descendants of that line. Your lineage is a shared one of the Guardian as well as The Ultimate. Though it may have been diluted over several generations, Varz blood still runs in your veins." He watched intently, unable to tear his sight from the image of that girl struggling to comprehend her true past and what that meant for her future.

Her eyes darted around wildly in her skull, searching for some missing fact that would make this all make sense, though it eluded her.

"But my eyes...all of your people have those black eyes and mine are blue." Finally she looked back at him, some stifled joy remained in her eyes.

"*Our people* have the Sorcerer's Eyes because we have inherited some command over reality. We use our eyes as gateways to impose our imaginations on the world around us and that is what *we* call sorcery. You have this ability like I do and once you have begun to master this skill your eyes will awaken as well." Finally he sat next to her on the bed, but she seemed too distracted to notice.

She looked at Dranus, so innocent and confused, it was clear that she still wondered if he was not tricking her with lies. She had always been taught that the people of Varz would speak only in lies, but what she had heard and what she had experienced so far had proven this to be a falsehood; and this was one of many falsehoods she had come to appreciate while captive.

"Could you teach me?" The long braid of her black hair swung as she turned her body, moving an inch closer to the king. Her body was rigid with uncertainty at how physically close she should get with him; everything was moving so quickly that it was difficult for her to make even the simplest of decisions.

"You could have no better teacher in all of Varz." He smirked to himself at his own boasting, despite the truth of his words. "I will teach you, Raven. You will learn our trade and I will teach you our ways, but only if this is what you truly desire..." He remembered the cautionary words of the Book of Fate's Desire and knew that he must first discover what she wanted and respect that. "...if you start on this path, you can never go back. I can make you a citizen of Varz by blood, by character, and by mind. I can make you mine, but you must want these things, I will not force them upon you."

She turned her eyes away, blushing wildly, and considered his words. What was it that she wanted? Growing up she had always felt she was meant for great things but never felt that leaving with the other Warriors of Pyrán was it. There was always something inside of her, something cold and calculating, detached from the others that lived near her. Was this the Varz blood that Dranus had spoken of? Had she always been a bit of a Varz citizen but never known it?

"The other Warriors talked a lot about their troubled pasts. We were all born orphans but most of them had been wronged in some way by people of Varz. They hated your kind fiercely." She considered, for a second, her use of 'your kind' in her wording. "It was why they were all eager to join, but nothing like that ever happened to me. I was happy with my life in Shiera and originally I turned them down. But eventually the Guide convinced me that it was my destiny."

The reference to this 'Guide' assaulted Dranus's senses and he battled himself to keep from interrupting her story.

"Of course, I was raised learning that the folk of Varz were bad and were our enemies. I can still hardly believe how much of that was lies."

She looked to be juggling a hundred different clashing thoughts. Even with her particular past she was timid in her acceptance of Varz. Dranus considered, what would have happened had he captured any of the other Warriors? Other than the obvious attraction between them, would he have been able to convince one of the others that his side was innocent. He doubted very seriously that any other set of circumstances than those the Warrior of Water had experienced would have led one of their order to him this way.

"Do you remember? When I first awoke? We...I don't know, we *saw* each other. Was that your doing?"

"It was not," and it wasn't. "I've never experienced something like that before. I cannot be certain if it is because of your powers, our distant blood bond, or something else. But I'm fairly certain that there could be no deception in what we saw of each other."

She smiled and nodded in agreement, then continued, clearly satisfied.

"I still don't know my destiny, but I know I want to find it. That is what I want." A crooked smile, curved to the left of her cheek, met the watchful eyes of King Dranus and her hand took his on the bed. "And I want to do that...with you."

Like a soothing wave he could feel all of the tension and anxiety bleed from his brain down his body and into the swollen timbers beneath him.

Dranus squeezed that small hand he held firmly and stood, lifting her from the bed and pulling her into his arms. She fell into him, clearly shy and awkward, but she did not resist him. In time, she would find comfort and security in him, and he would find the same in her kiss. Such a kiss it was to break through the doubt and the worry! What a sensation to release tension and press it into passion from his lips.

"I will return in the night. Until you are fit to be one of us we cannot be seen like this. I will have you moved to a safer room; you will not be bound again." He dreaded that he must soon let her go and return to his duties as king. He had not felt the pull of responsibility as nagging since his time with Kaelel, but he had not fully appreciated that until she was gone. He would not make that mistake a second time.

"Tonight I will begin to teach you the art of our people. It will be difficult, but you should find it somewhat similar to the use of the elemental powers you had as a Warrior of Pyrán." He brushed his hand down her coarse black hair and admired her youthful frame, his fingers trailing down her back.

The girl seemed to have lost all hesitation then, enraptured by the doting of the king, she held the appearance of pure acceptance. For all that she was a young woman in the prime of her beauty she had never been touched like this before, never been appreciated like this before; or rather, she had never allowed herself to be appreciated like this before. The affection and emotion, it swept her up like a cyclone and lifted her high. She could barely even consider what might come that night, but she smiled at her king and held him tightly.

"I will do my best." She too, was reluctant to let him go but they had to part until the veil of night could cover their secrets in shadow. Refusing to look back lest he be drawn back in, Dranus exited the room and took to making his rounds of the ship.

# Chapter 30
### To Craft a Citizen of Varz

The king was overwrought the rest of the day, able only to focus on the task at hand as far as he could keep other thoughts at bay. The South Star set first, and the sun followed it beneath the calm ocean. After his final rounds he dismissed the guards at Raven's door for the night, commending them for having stood guard since the morning. A simple lie and congratulations from their Sorcerer King was all that was needed.

When rare idle moments found him, Dranus reviewed basic texts that he had read as a child, recreated on the pages of the Book of Fate's Desire. He had never taught someone how to use magic, but he was a master if ever there was one, how difficult could it be? With a sack of some materials he left the Book in his own chambers and stalked through shadows to the girl's new room.

Raven was perplexed to see the lock move, the door open, and then close again with not so much as a sign of any presence. She stood as though ready to defend herself but relaxed when Dranus revealed himself from the magical shroud of shadows he had cast about himself.

The girl was openly amazed, rushing quickly up to him only to stop short and hesitantly poke out a single digit to test if he was really there or not. When she found him as solid as ever her eyes widened.

"Are you going to teach me how to do that?!" For all her indecision and hesitancy earlier she seemed excited and eager to begin learning with him.

"Not that one, I'm afraid. You will learn that there are a number of spells kept that only a monarch of Varz may know." He shook his head but smiled at that unabashed enthusiasm which she showed so spiritedly.

"Spells? None of the Warriors used spells. In fact, it was oddly natural the way we used our elements. I feel like we each had an inborn affinity to our element." Raven sat on the edge of a table bolted to the deck in thought.

"That is likely true, given your ancestry. In fact, I've hypothesized that in each generation there are a specific seven who would fulfill the prophecy, were it needed. With as much time that has passed, the Guardian's bloodline is presumably quite robust." Dranus laid the sack of items on the table beside the former Warrior as he spoke idly, revealing all of his secrets now with a small slice of comfort.

"Hmm, it's true that none of us remember meeting our parents ever. Vorad—the Lightning Warrior said it must be some curse attached to the prophecy."

Dranus considered this in a controlled manner. His mind had immediately gone to the idea that Raven could feasibly bear the next iteration and then mysteriously die suddenly. But that was only if the prophecy would continue on after having already been fulfilled once. It was not a concern for that moment either way.

"When we used our powers, we didn't really *control* the element, they were more an extension of ourselves that 'responded to our will.' We didn't really have spells." She made an impression like she was quoting someone then and Dranus tucked that little piece of information into his mental storage of things related to this "Guide" figure. Beyond that, what she spoke of was an ancient form of sorcery which even The Ultimate had used. Indeed, it was a basis for many simple magics used to this day, including the motion he had used earlier to remove her cuffs. It tied the state of the sorcerer's body to the state of other things.

"Not spells, really..." Dranus began slowly, trying to decide on the most appropriate wording to use, "As I said, we of Varz use our knowledge and expanded minds to bend and mold reality and logic in our minds. When we have reached the actuality of the change we wish to effect, we use our will and our eyes to project that reality into the world around us. However, many of the more complex 'spells' have specific routes of reasoning or certain philosophies that have been documented to be particularly effective. These are what I may refer to as spells, but they are many stages away from what you will learn tonight."

While he spoke Raven sat herself in a chair at the table, listening intently, absorbing every word he said while her energized hands went to toying with the pile of mysteries Dranus had brought her.

He motioned that she could take the items out of their satchel and examine them. Meanwhile, he examined the new room that had been fixed for her. This was the bosun's bunk and as such it was small but had a few extra amenities. A small table in the corner of the room with two chairs, a hammock stretched from the far wall to the wall where the entrance was, and a small but private keg of drinking water that rolled about with the lolling of the ship. It was an interior bunk which meant it was protected against the worst of drafts and didn't smell quite as much like brine. Indeed, the bosun had a metal cage of dried fruits, spices, and flowers secured beneath his hammock which wafted a subtle but pleasant scent throughout the room.

"So what are these for?" Her sweet inquisitive voice snapped Dranus back to attention.

"Learning," he replied.

"First, you must learn that reality is only that which you accept as reality, and that it can be altered at any moment." He paced the room, pointing to her and all about as if the room was 'reality.'

"I was raised with no parents, on my own, taken from my normal life and given elemental powers to fight a nation of power-hungry sorcerers because of some legend ONLY to find myself captured by those I tried to defeat and eventually convinced that it was with them that my future lie." She smiled a cheeky little grin. "I think I can handle that part."

"Perhaps, but you must accept it into your heart. You must know this to be true at all times, without even thinking it. Understanding that all is malleable has to be as natural as breathing." This point had to stick. This was fundamental to working their sorcery effectively.

Raven replied with a serious nod.

"Typically, children in training spend considerable time on mind-altering drugs, hallucinating, and accepting the variety of experiences they have. It can be rather enjoyable, but such drugs are not available to us at sea." He watched a wash of emotions go across the girl's face as he spoke: a bit of horror, skepticism, and then relief.

"We will just have to start simply," he said, picking an orange from out of her hand and sitting in the other chair.

"What color is this fruit?" He held the orange openly in the palms of his hands.

Raven fixated on the fruit; clearly it was orange but that must be some sort of trick.

"Orange. It is orange."

"Are you sure it's not blue?" His inquisitive tone was underlain by a sort of comical voice.

"Of course it's not..." she began, confident in her ability to see. But when she looked back at the fruit her mouth hung agape and she grasped the fruit, turning and twisting it in her hands over and over, amazed.

"It's blue...but...."

"Blue? Are you ill? It is quite certainly orange." He smiled wickedly to himself; he couldn't help but enjoy confusing her like that.

And again she was befuddled by the color-changing fruit. "It is orange."

"Wrong again!" He took the fruit back. This time it was a bright green color and while Dranus tossed it in his hand it changed colors with every time it touched his palm.

"You see, this fruit has no definite color when held by a sorcerer. Its color is only that which the sorcerer gives it. In order to be correct in guessing the color of it while I hold it, then you must control it beyond me and impose your reality upon it." He handed her back the fruit and it returned to its normal orange color.

"So if you think it's blue, but I think it's...green, what color will it be?" She stared at the thing, trying to tell it with her mind to become green.

"This is an insightful question! This is where the 'wills' you mentioned before come into play. When two sorcerers come into conflict, the victor depends on the strength of one's logic and the immovability of one's will." Dranus stared at the orange for a moment, thinking he was missing one...or several...elements.

"Of course, this is complicated by the original nature of the manipulated aspect of reality. For example, to change an orange to the color yellow is substantially simpler than turning it black because yellow is more similar to orange than black."

"Who decides what is more similar or less?" She asked, puzzled.

"Another excellent question. All things have a 'nature,' or in other words, a manner of reality that existed before there were sorcerers to manipulate them. Varz scholars reason that there was a primordial time before ours in which all things were given all of their features and properties. The last thing to be developed in this primordial time was the concept of sorcery, which dissolved this essence of certainty into our time. Of course, this is just the prevailing theory." Dranus felt a rush within him he had longed to experience again: the feeling of cognitive challenge. He was considering the very foundations of his people, of the world, and of reality itself, digging up years of research and tutelage surrounding the topic of sorcery.

Raven mulled these things over in her mind before picking up a quill pen and ragged parchment that clearly had been soaked and then dried out...probably by her. With these she drew out some of the concepts, including a sort of timeline of how things developed according to theory.

"So if I think that a thing is different from how I've always thought about it, and that new version is not too dissimilar from the original way...then it will become my way?" She puzzled through the concepts one at a time, pointing to each with the tip of the pen as she went on.

"No. Our sorcery is not so simple as mere 'thinking.' To alter the reality of the world around you, you must know without the most minuscule shade of doubt that the thing you envision is a reflection of your will. You must consider logic beyond that which you have taken for granted and apply it to the abstract. When you give the abstract a form you mold the stuff of truth like a sculptor. Once you have reached the knowledge which you desire, you must only force it from your mind. It is an *understanding* that supersedes your human senses, our sorcery." Dranus watched the girl repeat some of the words he had said to herself, one hand wiping hair from her face and the other furiously doodling new things in between the concepts she'd drawn before. While crude, he could see the way she made sense of what he said through these glyphs and depictions.

Finally, she looked up from her notes with curiosity shining through her bright blue eyes.

"Wouldn't it be most effective, then, to simply apply the logic that the 'primordial' version of things had always been the way you wanted them, but to anything that you could think of?"

"If only. The primordial time was before the advent of sorcery by definition and thus cannot be affected...that or the theory is flawed in other ways." She seemed to accept this answer and scribbled a thick

320

black line at one point on her timeline from one edge of the page to the opposite edge.

"Let us practice. Pick up the fruit and *tell* me what color it is." This time he watched her, inspecting every expression, every thought that might glance through her mind, looking for flaws in her logic or reasoning.

Raven was cautious as she picked up the orange; manipulating the elements was as easy as moving her body but that kind of thinking couldn't be applied to changing the color of a fruit.

Or maybe it could?

If she was to manipulate the laws of reality, could she not make it so that moving one's body was like altering another thing's physical properties? The way in which she began to believe that this was possible seemed to come naturally in light of her fantastical experiences with water and ice. Within a few moments it was as though she had considered this to be the way of the world since her birth.

Dranus watched closely as the girl raised her left foot and, as if commanded by such an odd gesture, the fruit grew larger. She tilted her head to the side and the fruit seemed gradually to turn to stone. She lowered the hand not holding the fruit towards the floor of the cabin and finally the fruit changed to a rich yellow.

The king looked on in amazement, both in the speed with which she had learned to manipulate the physical properties of the fruit and in the odd manner by which she accomplished such a feat. He cocked a brow and tightened his lips, trying to surmise what logic had brought her to such movements.

"Well...it's a good start, but we'll need to eliminate that odd thing you did with your body."

She regained her normal posture and the fruit turned back into its normal form.

Dranus smiled, puzzling over the possibilities which had brought this about. In the ever-turning cogs of his mind he concluded swiftly that her previous powers had imposed the will of her body over reality where their sorcery imposed the will of the mind. It was an interesting transmutation of the skill, or rather, perhaps it was that she hearkened back to the very origin of their sorcery. After all, what could someone know more flawlessly than their own body?

Raven pursed her lips and furrowed her brow as she stared harshly at the orange. "But it's not 'right,' right?"

Dranus laughed.

"Do not worry about 'right,' you will soon learn to remove that notion from your halls of knowledge. You should be proud! If ever you *or* I wondered if you were truly a child of Varz, there should be no more doubt as of now." He smiled genuinely and placed a comforting hand on her leg.

Raven smiled brightly in return, glad for such approval and for feeling like she was where she belonged for the first time in ages.

So the night continued for several hours as Dranus attempted to hone her skills and her focus. The deeper hours of the night brought them to a point they were quite familiar with. They spoke largely of philosophy and the truth of the world's current state, and they discussed how philosophies of varying natures could be applied differentially to sorcery. Dranus had not shared such riveting conversation since his late wife and the ancient souls of the Staff of the South Star. But this was different as there was a novelty and wonder about the subject to Raven. Her enthusiasm was like a rampant disease, he just couldn't help but revel in it as well.

By the time the South Star peaked a hesitant ray of crimson over the ocean, Raven could alter the color of the fruit on command, something that had taken the young king several days to master. In the early morning hours they found great pleasure in each other's company, holding hands, and sharing intimate stories of their lives.

Little by little Dranus's gaze softened, and Raven's eyes grew sharper.

*    *    *

After several sleepless nights of laughter, sorcery, and longing gazes, the King of Varz and his entourage reached the port city of Viél. With Dranus's kingly mastery over short-ranged illusions, he managed to get Raven off of the ship and into his suite of rooms while pretending that she was meant to be kept in absolute isolation in a cell that was, in actuality, empty.

The first day after they arrived, Dranus acquired a particular concoction of herbs and fungi that could be brewed and amplified for beneficial effects. He made one such potion for himself, to put his body into a deep and restorative sleep so that he could regain the strength he had lost at sea. For Raven, he brewed a similar sleeping potion but with an added drug that would awaken her consciousness while she slept. He instructed her to practice in the dream worlds where the stuff of reality was inherently decided by the dreamer; it would be a good way for her to acquire the natural sense about sorcery that one needed to unlock the Sorcerer's Eyes.

The next day found Dranus relieved and Raven exhausted. He had feared that sending her off to the dream worlds might have been hasty; those that were not sufficiently trained could lose focus on the border between that cerebral realm and this one. He helped her to rest and then went about his duties as king.

He sent orders to gather troops from around the realm and issued a declaration of intent to the governments of the Four Realms. More of a challenge then anything, he made it clear that he would next take Arendrum and that his forces would march on the city of Medi (MEH-dee) in two months. This was no ruse, though the enemy would likely think it so, but a way to show that Dranus was sure of his power and that there was absolutely nothing they could do to stop him.

If he could gather the entire allied forces in one place, and all of the Warriors of Pyrán in one place, he could wipe out every threat in a single pass. It was risky, but now that he knew so much about the Warriors and had diminished their numbers, they were much more of a knowable threat. In time, Raven would be convinced to reveal the extent of the others' powers and their demeanor. If he had learned anything from the boisterous Warrior of Earth, it was that many of their number were hot-blooded teenage boys, full of unearned confidence and bravado. Likely they would each attempt to take his life single-handedly, which was the perfect circumstances for him with the Stone.

Thus it was with humble hope that the King of Varz left the fort at Viél with not much more than a private letter to O'cule and a 'royal messenger' caravan breaking the outer edge of the city in the early morning. The path across the plains should be peaceful and easy for riding. As the two new romantics traveled together they shared more stories of their youth and of the journeys they had each been on. Dranus told Raven about his quest to gather the Staff and the Sword, and she recalled the tale of climbing the peaks of Pyrán with the others, though her story ended abruptly at the point when she claimed the trident strapped to the side of her horse. They trained in the sorcerous arts at night and Raven progressed with stunning rapidity. At other times he would introduce her to members of the Staff, including his friend Vintus, who he had not had a moment to speak with in some time.

He was, predictably, cheekily upset at this small slight but was pleased to be introduced to the first new person he'd met other than Dranus in a few hundred years.

Commander Lena was particularly fond of the girl and spent afternoons of slow and steady riding teaching her various tricks and shortcuts in sorcery that even Dranus had never heard.

He and Raven bonded quickly; he felt like he had with Kaelel for those precious few days and at times that terrified him. But it was now several weeks into their courting and there were no threats to their blossoming affection. Each day their love grew stronger, their bodies closer.

One early afternoon, an uncharacteristically warm and clear sky found the pair traveling over the arid stone desert near a small town southeast of where the Rift came inward into Varz territory. The cracked earth was spread with delicate sands and hardly held a single patch of choked vegetation for every mile. This terrain was home to only the most stalwart of vermin.

A cool breeze reminded the king that the Night Season yet lingered in the barren desert, but for the time they would take advantage of the high spirits the warmth brought.

In the distance King Dranus made out a small camp that flew a flag of solid black above its four rust-colored tents. Dranus sneered and curled his nose in contempt.

"Bandits...the lowest scum of Varz. There is a standing order to kill on sight for all military forces, but with the war I have heard they have been much more active." He stopped his horse and Raven followed suit, looking to Dranus for what they should do next.

"If they are so hated, why do they fly a banner announcing who they are?" She could only assume that this was the way that Dranus had so readily surmised that they were bandits.

"As I have said before, it is an important trait which all Varz men and women share: pride. A sorcerer's art is only as powerful as their will and without pride, the force of their will is diminished. It is not a blind pride, but one that must be fed from time to time by the daring and inadvisable." He turned back to the camp and motioned.

As a commotion started up around the perimeter of the camp, he decided that now was perhaps one such time for them as well. His horse started into a slow walk toward the camp and Raven's followed.

"My dear, all citizens of Varz, from cobblers to bakers to farmers, are fighters in one way or another. Did you know that it is required that all children learn some form of combat as part of their basic schooling? Those who are not physically able are trained extensively in tactics and strategy."

"Really? That seems...practical." She had not heard this before, but it didn't exactly surprise her.

"'There are no dull blades in the Varz armory'," he quoted in response.

"Of course you are no stranger to combat, but you have not faced Varz warriors without your power over water. It is time you learn an important lesson in combat." With practiced efficiency he began to twist and contort his thoughts, to understand more than was there to understand, to control that which could not be controlled. His hand began to glow, and a thought of irony passed through the king's mind until he conducted a bolt of energy to the bandit's flag, setting it ablaze in challenge.

"Dranus, what are you doing?!" Raven was instantly alarmed, tugging on Dranus's arm and glancing back to the camp to see what reaction might come. One came in the form of several armed riders charging directly at them, all of their armor glowing an unnatural white light that could be seen shining through the hazy desert mirages.

"This is your first test as a citizen of Varz. Take your weapon and execute these bandits, by order of your king. I will not help you, and they will show you no mercy. To survive you will need to use your wits and your skills, but most of all...you must show them no decency that they won't show you. These are warriors and sorcerers, and they wish only for your death at this moment. They will think of nothing else."

Raven was still, quiet and she began to shake as she moved to untie her trident. For all that she had fought in the Battle of the Rift and at the Sack of Shiera, she had help then both from her allies and from her powers. Now she was alone, only herself to rely on.

"What if I lose, Dranus?!" She pleaded with him one last time, but the king looked only at the advancing rabble.

"Don't lose." He said only those words then turned his horse to leave her. He had seen her fight...he had every confidence that she could overcome a handful of bandits.

Raven dismounted and unstrapped her large trident, feeling at once comforted by the familiarity of its weight and the firmness of the ground. She closed her eyes for a moment, clearing her mind, listening to the sound of hoof beats coming closer and closer. She took her stance; legs close and slightly bent, right arm bent behind her holding the trident with the head facing down at her heels, left arm crossing her chest, and head held high. From this position she extended her feelings beyond just her flesh, eyes, and ears.

The familiar twang of a loosed bow caught her ear and with lightning speed she ducked and lurched ahead, the force of her kick-off empowered reactively. She stayed low and sprinted forward, kicking up the sand around her like a dust devil. Approaching the first bandit, her pace slowed and she dodged to the right of the horse. As the heavy head of the bandit's axe bore down on her she crouched below it, bending her legs like a spring to leap behind the downward swipe. She rose with a rotating motion, the pole of her weapon pressed against her back, turning to face the bandit and take him on the side with the flat head of the trident. The bandit fell dazed from his saddle, trying to piece together exactly what had just happened to him.

The unnatural movements of her body put strain on Raven's muscles in ways she had never experienced before. Her perception of the movement of things was...different. It was as if she had seen this move play out in her mind, with all of its impractical redirection of force and stopping, and her body had simply responded with the knowledge it would hold.

She couldn't stop to think.

She had her feet under her quickly and turned in a tight loop to plunge the three barbs of her weapon through the glowing armor. The armor did not yield. The aura around it seemed to hold the attack at bay and before she could strike again she tumbled to the side, avoiding another mounted attack. The three other warriors watched in amusement, assuming it would take no more than one of them to deal with a Lesser girl.

The one who had fallen got to his feet with a grin and paced around her, a heavy axe in each heavily muscled grip. The man's look told her that he thought her movements before had been luck.

Raven resumed her stance; one she had learned from an ex-naval officer when training with a fishing spear on the Shieran Far Docks. She mirrored the circling motion of the bandit as the others watched on with folded arms and smiles.

Something was not right. If he was so confident, why didn't he attack...he was stalling! Again she bowed forward and sprinted forward with remarkable speed and agility. But the man's grin widened and he clenched his fist, causing the ground directly beneath Raven to become soft like mud. Losing her footing, she reacted instinctively, stabbing the sharp head of her trident into the shifting ground before she fell on her face. With this motion she propelled herself into the air; the shaft of her spear *would not* break, it *could not*. With this motion she leapt over the advancing brigand and landed too hard, sending a shock through her feet and legs, and causing her teeth to grit hard.

The bewildered man spun quickly but met the extended reach of Raven's trident at full pole, the sharp daggers on the tips of the weapon cutting through the man's exposed neck from right to left. The weapon continued in its spinning motion around the girl's body until it rested again behind her.

Now the other three stopped smiling and took up a formation. One of their bunch had been downed like a stalk of wheat to the farmer's scythe and they knew that this was no ordinary Lesser girl. Their movements formed a horizontal line so that all three came at her in a wave, the archer in the center loosing a few arrows which landed harmlessly behind her rapid movements. It was strange how the archer's accuracy was so poor...his shots *seemed* on target at first and then listlessly drifted to the side as if hit by a stray wind protecting her.

Raven's mind flew faster than her feet and she calculated her next move. For a moment she felt as though the acuity of the scene sharpened. It seemed that things may have slowed down a little, and everything she saw began to take on new meaning.

Even without her powers she moved like the rushing tides, the head of her trident like a tail behind her. She raced forward then swerved to the right, sliding on the harsh sands beneath the rightmost horse and now the movements of the world slowed. She saw every moment like a picture, moved her body so that she would not be struck by the horse's limbs, and saw the strap which held the saddle in place. She appeared on the other side of the horse with the buckle of the saddle in her hand and soon the rider had toppled and fallen to the ground, his steed as gleeful for the freedom as the rider was bewildered. Before he could even press his hands to raise himself he felt the piercing sting of a three-pronged blade strike through the back of his neck; a quick, accurate death.

The third rider, seeing how his two partners had faired while mounted, decided to come down on his own and wielded a short sword with a mismatched shield. That pesky archer shot another arrow and this one grazed her exposed arm. Now she was bleeding from her arm and from her leg where she slid across the ground. Her energy was beginning to wane, so she took her time cautiously approaching her recently thrown weapon and dislodging it without breaking eye contact with the mounted archer.

The man had been focused on her for a long time, he had given her the strangest of looks but they were not quite centered. She tried to follow his gaze until she finally realized he was following her weapon, not her! Before she could hide it she felt the thing grow immensely heavy and drag her tired arm towards the ground. She could not lift it.

Now the marauder on foot set on her, confident and bold, charging closer and closer. Clearly they had all noticed that she did not have the Sorcerer's Eyes and now they felt secure that victory, and revenge, was theirs. Raven began to panic; she could not fight without her weapon and the loss of its use was more a blow to her confidence than to her actual fighting skill. Her nerves went mad as they had been before the battle. She had to focus. She tried to calm herself and remember all that she had learned.

She steadied herself and concentrated on her knowledge of her weapon, that which had been a part of her since she wrested it from the rocks in sacred Pyrán. Her focus broke at an intimidating shout, an arrow she had to dodge. She danced around her anchored weapon and felt as though she closed an inner eye. She knew that the weapon was not light, but that she had commanded its mass with ease before. When the pole had been filled with water, she moved it about like it was practically weightless. It was, she had understood and now remembered, an inherent property of such a legendary weapon to be...weightless. Her inner eye opened as her vision faded to black behind closed lids.

She pictured the trident in her hands and her body relaxed. Then, all at once, she became rigid.

The raven-haired warrior lifted her trident from the ground and the advancing warrior stopped in his tracks. Black orbs wide with fear, he took a few steps back in disbelief, glancing back to his partner to see if he had stopped his sorcery for some reason.

When he looked back to the woman who had challenged them, his eyes met harsh black globes with white irises staring back. Those soulless eyes held deep understanding and they thirsted for blood. They were the eyes of a true warrior of Varz.

Racked with confusion the man slashed wildly, charging and hoping that the spell would at least slow her down. Raven watched the blade fall as if from afar and caught the worn blade between the prongs of her trident. A quick rotation of her wrists snapped the man's blade in half like the most brittle of rotted bones. Unable to recover, the bandit barcly had time to raise his shield against the coming attack. But the shield could do nothing but splinter against the sheer force of the attack and even the magic armor split with the intense power that knocked the man to the ground.

Everything about the girl was calm and serene, though she pulsed with an air of malice. Raven pulled her trident loose of the dead man with a self-satisfying crunch. Everything now was more clear than it had ever been in her entire life. She could see *everything,* and she could see *more.* The world around her seethed, bubbles of reality boiling up and then popping into other realities. The word logic hardly held meaning anymore.

Her black eyes flicked to the last rider fleeing, the shoddy plate armor he wore open in the back. Raven grinned a wicked grin and lifted her trident in her right hand and posed herself low, her left leg forward. She remembered something that Commander Vintus of the South Star Archers had said and launched her bladed fury after the coward. The trident glowed and straightened in its path, not once losing momentum until it struck the back of the final bandit. The limp body fell to the ground some ways away, the staff of the weapon erect like a flag of her own proclaiming her ascendancy from the dead man's back.

King Dranus stared with his lips parted, he could hardly believe his eyes. He had known her to be an excellent fighter but what he had just witnessed far surpassed even his own skill in combat. She had not only defeated the four men and their sorcery, she *humiliated* them. As he had hoped, in the heat of battle she had subconsciously tapped her sorcerous potential. At first she was enhancing her body and modifying the properties of things in small ways to make her outlandish style physically possible and effective. It was likely she hadn't even realized that those arrows missed her because they had been altered very slightly.

Then, she had unlocked the Sorcerer's Eyes and even Dranus from afar could feel the whole atmosphere settle. That last spell, Vintus had explained it to her once...*once!* It was a high-level combat skill that usually took years to sync with one's body and the properties of their weapon. It was why his forces at the Rift had all used special uniform spears.

Raven's blood, her training, and her prophetic station were all unique. With the right training in sorcery she could become the most fearsome warrior that Varz had ever known. Even without her elemental powers, her agility and precision, her timing, and her unheard-of skill of learning sorcery made her the perfect warrior. She was one in a generation, undoubtedly.

Except that she wasn't. She was one of six, now reduced to four.

Dranus shuddered to think that the remaining Warriors of Pyrán were anywhere as powerful as this...and they still had their elemental powers. Had the Warrior of Earth simply been a less skilled warrior? He had a shield and no real weapon to speak of, though his elemental powers were great. Perhaps he had underestimated the other Warriors based on that boy's greenness. When he had recalled Raven's fighting at the Sack of Shiera he typically recalled the beauty of her movements, but in reality, she had held off an entire besieging naval force almost single-handedly for a time. In the end, she had *won!*

Could he convince Raven to fight her old comrades in his stead? If it had come to it, could he have defeated her in a duel? Could he defeat any of the others in a duel without taking advantage of their weak mental states?

His mind swam with questions, complicated by the purely

breathtaking display he had just witnessed. But besides all of his secret fears he began to grin wildly, watching her calmly reclaim her trident and her horse and ride back towards him. Her still-dripping trident left a deliberate trail of blood in the sand, sticky and wet.

That she was his, and what a woman she was, delighted Dranus just as it set his spine to shiver. He knew that a display like this in front of his people and all in his realm would know that she was a true citizen of Varz. Now that she had the eyes, she was the only woman who could be Wife to the King.

He only hoped, in the deepest recess of his mind, that she would not one day challenge him for a throne that could rightfully be hers....

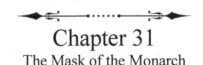

# Chapter 31
## The Mask of the Monarch

If the king had left the capital city of Varz in the most humble manner some months ago, he was now met with the other extreme upon his return. The people of Varz needed to see him as strong and to see his new love with at least the same level of exuberance as his previous marriage. Thus, he'd made sure to send messengers a few days ahead to prepare in advance.

And prepare they had!

People flooded crowded streets as the king's retinue escorted him and his companion through the magnificent northern gates of Varz. Impossibly tall were the gates great oaken supports. Impossibly beautiful were the hand-crafted decorations across the gate's lintel. Impossibly bright was the sunlight shining off the bronzed, swinging doors to the city.

The large meeting center near the main gate was like oil on water in its colors and flowing masses as ranks of onlookers surged forward only to be pressed back by royal guards. Banners were hung from every roof, balcony, or window sill in praise of Varz and in wishing for tokens of great fortune and praise upon their honored king. From the cultured dirt and from every manner of vase bloomed flowers of the most fantastic hues; blue striped stalks with white flowers, plants of shimmering shades of red that reflected light like metal, buds with patterns of black and purple in the symbol of Varz, flowered vines woven into complex tapestries of nature depicting the natural abstract. In some places it appeared that whole methods of gardening, perhaps even *colors* had been invented just for his arrival!

Music blared from instruments not played by ordinary means in centuries. Music had mostly fallen to the niches of Varz culture, with musicians pressing air through instruments magically. But now there were a whole stand of women carrying instruments of all shapes and sizes, forging chord and discord. The crowds swayed in time with the rising and falling of rhythms.

It was not very good, but the cacophony of sounds drove the masses to frenzy, cheering as though they had already won the war! They showed signs of uncommon patriotism, waving huge flags, their faces painted in black and purple, and all manner of effigies of the elite of Varz; of the king himself, of General Armodus, and even one of the deceased Commander of the Archer's Brigade stood watch from a tower in the South.

King Dranus, lauded monarch of such festivity, beamed with the excellence he felt from such a welcome. He marveled at the sights around him from atop his mount. Was this really his home city of Varz? Had these streets seen such frivolity in all of their history? He remembered the crowded Dens and the empty squares of years prior and tried with all his imagination to fuse the image with what he saw then, finding it near impossible. These were the borne fruits of his quest! This was the life he had brought to himself and to all of his people by invoking the old ways. He had wakened them from a dreary slumber of neglect and lassitude, as he had awoken himself. His pride swelled with every passing moment.

Raven, former Warrior of Water, was a mess of conflicting emotions. Upon hearing in Viél that she would be presented to the folk of Varz she was nervous, even though not a soul in the city would possibly recognize her for her former identity. But after her achieving mastery over the Eyes and several days and nights hearing of the Varz way, she had learned an important lesson about pride and confidence that she knew she must draw upon to impress herself on the Varz onlookers.

At the sight of such praise and such flourishing culture all around her it was easy to draw the guise of the prideful about her. This was what she had always dreamed she might experience as a Warrior of Pyrán. When they had presented themselves first in Myrendel and then in Arendrum and made their powers known there was a grave appreciation for their strength, but no fanfare celebrated their coming. In the battles that followed they were abused as mere weapons of war to be used however the strategists saw fit; moved around without concern for their wishes like pieces on a board.

This was different...different from anything she'd ever experienced in Shiera. That she had ever thought of the folk of Varz as associated with darkness, evil, or hatred now baffled her. There in that moment of celebration, the people of Varz had created something wholly unique in the world; something beautiful and terrible, music and all! And for what? Their king returned after less than a year abroad? What life they had!

What life *she* would have!

Here she could embrace the smiling faces and the twisted grins she had come to adore in Dranus. She watched the colorless stares of thousands fall on her and continue in their cheering and spectacle. Where she expected suspicion there was welcome; while she waited for jeers, she met only the roar of wonder like a waterfall!

This, she knew, was her home.

It was in this manner that the King of Varz and his beautiful new companion moved toward the center of Varz.

When they reached the central plaza, Dranus made an unexpected announcement. Much to the shock of all present, including Raven herself, Dranus revealed the true identity of the woman at his side. He spoke loquacious tales of his conquests in the north, how he had felled the Warrior of Earth and enticed the same of Water to their cause. He displayed the girl like a trophy, accentuating her rise to unlocking the nature of Varz, omitting, for obvious purpose, the way in which such a feat was possible. In verbose, lyrical rants that Raven would soon find were common of these types of speeches, the king glorified her as his greatest triumph, the value and loyalty of whom could not be disputed.

The crowd was nearly ravenous with the long-winded tales of victory at the hands of their storied king. How could they question such a king? As clear as the air that swept her long braid was her apparent affinity to the folk of Varz.

Still the king sought to put to rest any suspicion or hesitance in her acceptance and so called up several skilled warriors from the Varz Army, as had been planned in advance.

Clearing a circle among the throng, Raven went down into the ring where she was handed a wooden sparring spear, her nerves afire with the passion of the moment and the expectations placed upon her.

"Show them what you showed me, and they will love you as I do." Her king's words were all she needed to comfort her against the closing encirclement of Varz soldiers with dulled ceremonial swords. This was a mock battle, but the swords were heavy and she was unarmored. They would not kill her, but they could cause serious damage if she wasn't careful. Plus, given that he'd practically left her to fend for herself against blood-thirsty bandits, she didn't expect that this would be a staged fight or one where her well-being was not actually at stake. The guards would back away when they were presumed "killed" but she didn't presume that they would play fair. Her kills would need to be unquestionable, ruthless.

"People of Varz!" The king's voice tore her attention away, "I present to you the newest of our family! May her actions overshadow any doubts my words have not put to rest!" Dranus's final call, echoed by the close walls of the plaza, was the signal for the display to start.

Raven had resumed her previous pose, the spearhead pointed down behind her. A glint showed in her Sorcerous Eyes that made the hardened warriors of Varz hesitate in their advance. She was calm, her mind open and moving.

One guard darted forward from behind her and his sword met the stiff retort of Raven's spear, kicked backwards from her heel. She followed in the motion, seeming to unravel as she turned, never taking away from the momentum of her weapon. She motioned the spear further up then quickly down, ripping the sword from the soldier's hand and then thrust the wooden tip into the man's chest, knocking him off his feet.

One down.

The others took this as the true start of the melee and swarmed the girl. She pulled herself towards the spear, shifting its weight like water in a tilted glass. The soldier leading the charge stopped short as the spear stretched out towards him, reaching full pole where he knew it could not reach him. Then it stretched *further*, striking him between the eyes and knocking him off balance.

Two.

From the side came another guard, his chest-height swipe towering over the crouched girl's stance. She stuck the spear between the man's legs and swiped left, then right with a bit of added sorcerous weight. The man grimaced as the spear next went to his groin and slid up his chest.

Three.

With the tip in the air, she planted the base of the spear and used it as a pole to reposition, darting past strikes like she danced with her

335

weapon at some grand ball. The guards swung wildly as if at shadows, making them seem simple novices until, with their frustration at a new high, they entered a practiced formation and advanced cautiously.

By then Raven was smiling, moving about with a playful gait. She thought she might try a spell she had been working on.

All at once her features became rigid as she took one powerful step towards the soldiers. Then, as if in an instant, she was on the other side of their group and the men were all barreling over. Each believed that only they could possibly have been injured in that short time and each were mistaken.

That's all of'em.

Suddenly a splintering pain surged from her eye sockets into her brain and her hand started shaking at the stress.

The crowd sank deep into a fog-like hush. These men were seasoned practitioners of the sword, one of them had even survived the Battle of the Rift! And yet they were like children playing with sticks before the spear-wielding woman.

Dranus appeared at her side instantaneously with a knowing expression on his face.

"I told you that you weren't ready for that yet," he said with a smirk and only a little sympathy. "Take deep breaths, you need air. You did not compensate your heart rate."

Dranus had spoken at length about the dangers of going beyond one's skill in sorcery and now she was getting a small taste of that first-hand.

A few gulps of hot air later and she returned mostly to normal, the pain turning into a dull ache, while the euphoria of the battle burst through the suffering like a splintered buckler. Raven let out a yell of triumph and the scene exploded into a riot of cheers, yelling, and screaming. In a matter of moments she had won the hearts of every man, woman, and child of Varz. Even Armodus and Ven, present in the king's entourage, were near speechless at the display of skill she had shown. They who had witnessed the atrocities committed by the Warriors of Pyrán firsthand were most wary, but the girl they watched dancing around the battlegrounds with such fervor and elation, commanding the laws of reality so fluently; she could not be a Lesser by any conception. She could only be a citizen of Varz. And Ven saw the way that Dranus looked delicately at the girl, how he cherished every movement and sensation, and how he relished in her acceptance. She saw the love that had returned to his heart as she had hoped it would.

The ancient monarchs of Varz were unmatched, unstoppable. Now that one, perhaps even two, had risen from the tomes of their history, what hope might the Lesser Realms have against them?

*    *    *

Later that evening, Dranus held court for the first time since the war began. Watching all of the practiced movements and traditions play out as he had thousands of times brought back not so distant memories. He remembered sitting as he was, nearly dulled to death by the meaningless banter of nobles and the hushed whispers of servants in wait. He recalled those feelings of desolation he had once known as if they were merely memories of a dream forgotten. He saw in his mind the dashing confidence of the young half-blood Deleron Kaxus who had sought so foolishly to defeat the King of Varz by himself. He had grown to pity the boy since then; a young man led to his doom by the whimsical workings of the Book of Fate's Desire, a Fate Dranus had only narrowly avoided on a number of occasions.

As petition after petition arose for an increase of resources here or the rights to produce weapons from a specific family there, a thought struck him like a bolt from heaven.

"The Mask of the Monarch." He interrupted, derailing a fairly important report of incidents on the Varz front lines without the slightest hesitation.

All of the nobles present were silent, casting glances back and forth between one another at this proclamation. They knew of the yearly festival, of course, but that was not for another couple months.

"We hold The Mask of the Monarch festival now." He declared, testing his subjects as he often liked to do.

"B-but the festival is not...." a noble started, sheepishly.

Dranus glared at him, provoking him to go on with a 'so what?' look of contempt.

"It would not be fair to the Candidates who should still have time," another spoke up in defense of the man. This woman was well-respected in the court and known for her dedication to tradition.

"Ven?" Dranus looked to the official keeper of Varz traditions and rituals.

"The Mask of the Monarch serves Varz by preparing our young to meet the standards of our society," the old woman started, "but its purpose is, above all, to serve Varz."

"Then it will serve Varz by increasing morale and welcoming Varz's newest daughter," Dranus immediately picked up on the hint that Ven had given him.

"That would certainly be in service of the greater good." Commander Ven agreed. Her look of approval was met with an overall sound of content and with no further objections.

"When should it be held, then?" Ven asked after a relative silence returned to the court.

"Tomorrow night," Dranus stated.

Once more the chamber burst into uproar, but not in protest, in the flurry of preparations and things that must be done.

Like slamming into the walls of Varz, herself, the court proceedings came to a sudden and utter stop. Servants were sent in every direction and nobles hurried to their homes to prepare for the social politics of the festival.

Orders were disseminated throughout the night that the festival was set to occur the very next night. It was only by the presence of elaborate preparations such as those made for the king's return that made such speed plausible, but it was still very little time to prepare. With all of the extant arrangements complimented by those that would be tirelessly worked at overnight, the festival would be on a scale the people of Varz would never forget! All that was left to be done was for the youths to fashion their masks and their wares. Surely every son and daughter of Varz had a favorite!

His sweet Raven was nearly overflowing with unchecked excitement as she made her own preparations; she had nearly leapt into the ceiling when Dranus had explained to her what the festival was. In preparation as much as elation she refused sleep and instead spent the first part of the night reading, and the early morning hours conversing with the spirits of the Staff. In a single night she hoped to learn the vast but well-kept histories of Varz Kings and Queens.

Dranus, for all his effort in recent times, was content to relax for a single night and to sleep to his mind's desire.

The South Star had set. The sun followed on its heels. Waves of burning scarlet blanketed the city of Varz as the last rays of the sun's light trickled through crowds like chalk drawn across the sky in large swaths.

As brimming with people as the streets had been throughout the previous day, they were now equally deserted. Some houses hung lanterns and others did not. A calm quiet held the worn stones of the capital as a cool breeze swept the mass of decorations to and fro. By simple workings the banners had been changed to reflect the event. In a mad dash of entropy the arrangements of flowers had been randomized to the best effect the most abstract minds in the city could accomplish. But other than the fading light of the sun, the city sat in near perfect darkness.

On the southern wall the statue of Kaelel, arrow drawn facing the north, was silhouetted in that dying light. She would stand watch over this generations-old festival and bless it and all those who participated.

In the final moment of sunlight slipping behind the walls the city exploded into life! Fires erupted from massive pits of tinder so that all of the city seemed to be illuminated by fanciful spirits of flame. Shrill cries of the city's youth sounded as doors were kicked open, revealing the barely contained energy of young boys and girls sprinting through the streets.

All of these young of Varz, released from houses bearing special lanterns, wore ornate masks that mimicked the likeness of any one of the great monarchs that had sat upon the obsidian throne of Varz.

There was Queen Luna the Mad with a miniature Staff of the South Star racing ahead of King Vulcan the Rock with a stick in the familiar shape of the Sword of Righted Guard. Queen Tempest the Undying leapt over a small pit of flame, though her telltale shield was absent so long as that secret was well kept.

Dranus spotted Vikra in fine splendor from his winning the Candidate Festival in Viél. The shining gold reflected the firelight from deep within a black-as-shadow cloak. He had donned the guise of King Faust the Reaper, wielding his signature scythe with a gold-coated blade.

King Valkhir blustered with red cheeks as his stubby legs chased down Queen Mena the Ichor. Queen Mena was a favorite among the younger candidates because they could douse themselves in homemade goo, mimicking the acidic excretions that leaked from the famous queen during battle. Kings Maccus the Major and Miccus the Minor were the popular choice of young twin boys while many younger boys imitated the laughable King King the Jester, whose very name had been the most crude of jokes and who's life as king had been more so.

Dipping and dodging between the children with nearly untraceable speed was the tall and beautiful woman of Varz, Raven. At the unrelenting behest of the charmer Vintus, she had donned the mask of Queen Luna and paraded around the city in a fit of youthful joy. She carried with her a South Star replica that was about the length of her arm in diameter. She would toss it into crowds of smaller children and watch as they smacked around the soft stuffing or jumped onto it, only to roll off the other side. Raven herself, was bursting with her own light of life. He had never seen her so happy...had he ever seen *anyone* so happy?

What all of those children in masks with their replicas of relics held in common was that they had recently ascended to true citizenship in unlocking the Sorcerer's Eyes. This was their culture's annual celebration, and this was their night to be recognized as full-fledged members of the sorcerer's ilk. They would run free through the city nearly all night, collecting treats from the different bonfires, mocking battles between figures born centuries apart, and using any manner of sorcery they wished without threat of reprimand. This was a night for creativity and imagination to be rewarded in its highest form!

"The Mask of the Monarch, master? Why now?" The Book was held open in King Dranus's lap as he watched over the proceedings from a high balcony. By this point the adults and the rest of those who would cater and enjoy the festivities alike came from their homes to gather up their young and take part in the familiar traditions of the Mask of the Monarch, though they were exponentially more extravagent this year compared to any other year before.

"Is it not obvious to one so wise as you?" The king gave the Book a sardonic smile.

"Wise I am not, you would remember. Knowledgeable? Very. But wisdom is such a thing that escapes me." The tome itself was in quite a jovial mood; happy to have the sole attention of the king once more.

"But you give suppositions! You are more than known for your vagaries besides. Surely the merit of such suppositions and the like lend themselves to a certain wisdom." A liar the Book was not, but a more crafty practitioner at slight of words could hardly be found. Everything the Book said held some semblance of truth, though it was often buried deep in misdirection.

"Ahh, if nothing you are far more wise than one such as myself, King Dranus. Perhaps I do contain a certain notion towards some truths over others. You must remember that all of my conclusions are based in knowledge written by others which often conflict. My assumptions are, at best, an amalgamation of congruent evidence; whichever side wrote most of their argument is generally the side you hear of."

Dranus considered this as he watched over the marvelous dancing of those below him. What an interesting method of forming an opinion...it was perhaps the most logical in a sense given the assumption that those thoughts most written were those most supported. Then again, fanaticism could easily overthrow such sense. A single scholar with a thousand hours could influence truth as much as a thousand scholars with a single hour. For a moment he thought to reconsider past disasters caused by the musings of the Book, but his lightened mood banished such dull thoughts.

"With such a scrutinizing view it is shocking how frequently you are wrong!" Dranus showed a more appreciative smile than before, and the Book simply let out a laughing sound like the flap of pages in the wind.

"Wrongness itself is a more subjective thing, master! It is a matter of reference if you like." The king closed the Book in a playful gesture, admitting that he had once more been outwitted by the tome.

"Yes, yes. Of course. In this peculiar case you are right!"

"But am I?!" The Book challenged. "Reference, King Dranus! Reference!"

Life had returned to the King of Varz as it had done for his city, and he belly-laughed somewhat contemptuously with the enigmatic relic. Down below the children were gathering in their multitude of decorated masks, trailing in a line behind the swaying braid of Raven.

It was bizarre, in some part of the king's mind, how this young woman who was only recently a paragon of the Lesser Realms had so easily fit into the Varz lifestyle. The children adored her, even the parents felt no hesitance in letting her lead them through the city like a caravan. Were they all under a glamour? Was this some unavoidable end of Fate's design as the Book had hinted at? Or was it simply that she had unlocked blood hidden beneath generations of dilution as The Ultimate had suggested? Within the circumstances, the answer was irrelevant to the king, so long as the outcome was thus.

"We welcome our new daughter Raven to Varz!" A man standing on etched stilts of ornate workmanship boomed his voice over the crowd as the legion of masked children funneled onto and around a large stage.

"And we honor her with the Mark of the Monarch for her portrayal of Queen Luna the Mad!" A riot of cheers and whistling drowned out the constant drone of music flowing throughout the city. First the faux South Star bounced onto the stage, followed by Raven in her giddy splendor. She tempered that free spiritedness momentarily to bow stiffly, as if accepting some magnificent achievement.

The contest was predetermined, of course, by King Dranus. What Raven required was a feeling of oneness with his people and acceptance by those people. This was the primary reason he had revived the festival at this time. This was a time of impressions that would be frozen like an imprint in sand. This way, he could form every single citizen of the capital city in a single night, casting Raven in the greatest light possible while simultaneously giving Raven an experience of her new culture that would revolve, through careful manipulation, around her.

Raven smiled wildly as her mask was painted with the three-pronged crown upon the forehead. Perhaps the greatest irony of the evening was that though the event was staged, Raven's costume had come directly from the spirits of the Staff who had known the queen. She bore such resemblance as to bring back haunting memories of the zombified queen he had met with beneath the waves of the South

Sea. She was, for that reason, most deserving of the Mark of the Monarch though no one would truly know why.

The passing of the Mark was the signal to Commander Ven who appeared high above the streets with a troop of her Corps.

Dranus stood, adjusting his own crown of Varz with a smirk. This was his time to address his folk as he had done at the royal union near the outset of this war.

"Sweet sons and daughters of Varz! The Mask of the Monarch is a tradition started by our beloved Queen Tempest the Undying." He paused to allow a number of the masked children to cry out in vicarious triumph. "She who emulated King Faust the Reaper! She who conquered in the Second Great War! She who taught us to honor our great ancestors in this festival!"

Further cheers.

"Let us not forget to honor ourselves on this occasion, for we have achieved greatness all our own! And greater achievements await us in our shining future! Let us take that future to the Lesser Realms and spread like the wind over barren plains of ignorance and inelegance." The people swooned with the beauty of the king's words; enamored by all that he represented.

"With this festival I commend you all, but so too do I request a favor."

The crowd yelled in anticipation of their charge.

"Anything!"

"Name it!"

"Give us your words and we shall forge them into steel!"

Dranus raised his hands to calm the mass.

"Never forget." His words were soft, solemn. The crowd looked about in a fit of confusion as they echoed the words among themselves.

"Never forget your past." Soft-spoken words. "Never forget what has brought us here." His tone rose as did his gaze, staring at the long-gone horizon. "Never forget all that we have done to accomplish our goals." Higher and higher his voice rose.

"Never forget the sacrifice of our soldiers and that which their families have forfeited! Never forget the required death of the few to benefit the many! Never forget that their deaths are of the most noble because they are of our blood!" Like a song in flowing crescendo the forceful notes of his words flourished ever louder and bolder! The bass and the treble, the ululating choir of the people of Varz at his feet swept up in the melody. The fortissimo of the king's final command in their ascendancy!

"Never forget that WE ARE VARZ!" Hysteria burst from the grand finale, ringing from the bright city over the countryside. It all came from their love for the king and of their homeland. This was the fervor that had won countless wars over the last millennium. The Lessers loved their homes, but the folk of Varz *were* there homes. It was why their nation, their capital, and their people shared the same name. These things were interchangeable.

Commander Ven and hers reflected this love to the blanketed sky, weaving tales of light in the sudden darkness of the hushed fires. The people crazed by their king's speech watched pictures of Varz monarchs in battle, clad in the same ancient armor that Dranus wore when he took to the fields. All triumphant, all showing mastery of their various weapons in bouts against faceless warriors from around the Four Realms. A show of fire and light in the sky forever etched in the hearts and souls of that lustful folk.

It was a night that none present would ever forget, as their king had commanded. It was a night that heralded the onrushing glory of the Dark Realm.

It was the Mask of the Monarch in every way.

# Chapter 32
## The Battle at Medi

Although the peak of his hill was nowhere near as dizzying, King Dranus was reminded of holy Pyrán as he stared like a statue down at his assembled forces. There he had felt the ominous pressure of a thousand-year history and the God-like king of legend, The Ultimate. Here, he felt that same pressure welling up beneath him. This was his moment to be remembered or to be forgotten. This was his chance to ascend to such status as those taught to young children to instill Varz pride, the paragons of their long and victorious legacy.

It had been weeks since one such celebration, The Mask of the Monarch, had rallied his folk beneath the fervent banner of a victory that must be inevitable. His had been a bold claim, but thus far he had met the expectations of his former self. He had arrived just south of the Arendrum city of Medi in the night, precisely on the day he had proclaimed.

To the citizens of Varz and to his army it would seem a sure sign of success how simply such a force had been collected, but Dranus knew the truth. He had hardly slept more than a couple of hours a day since that night. Raven had been submerged in the vast ocean of Varz tradition and sorcery. Strong brews and novel concoctions with wine had fortified him through the exhaustion and the loneliness. In a few weeks, he had become an efficient automaton of a human being, running through preset programs with precision and speed. When it finally came time to rest his gears, he had hardly ever had the heart to wake his sleeping lover. There would be plenty of time for them to enjoy one another after the war was won.

General Armodus had led the incursion to Arendrum while Dranus rest in a sorcerous slumber. He was refreshed and the cool, crisp air brought him an incredible sense of clarity. He had set the placements of his forces personally and spent most of the morning in talks of strategy.

From this peak Dranus could just make out the outer wall of Medi, a city set half way between the capital city of Arendrum and the Varz border. Historically, it was the first line of defense against the Varz aggressors and was thus heavily fortified. It was for this reason that the Allied movements had quickly gone from peculiar to enigmatic.

Originally, the Allies had assembled in a large circle surrounding the walled city while the remainder of their forces no doubt waited behind the walls. The remaining Warriors of Pyrán, too, would be present in the city; moreover, he counted on it. This was the anti-siege formation that the King of Varz had expected from a fortified stronghold of a city in its own territory.

However, upon sight of the Varz forces, the enemy had abandoned their defensive position and marched into the field. Dranus had immediately called an emergency council. By mere protocol they had multiple strategies ready to be employed in such a scenario, but it was exactly that which unsettled him. These strategies were deduced by routine, not by any expectation that the Allies would meet them in open battle instead of through guerrilla tactics and anti-siege measures. Doing so with the Varz forces positioned so favorably was too close to strategic suicide for him to take lightly.

Had his declaration of intent given them so much time and knowledge that they felt emboldened by some imagined advantage? He could hardly imagine that anything less than the full force of the Allied armies came against him purely by the unceasing outpouring from the tall gates of Medi. Were the Lessers so base that they thought they could overpower him by sheer force of numbers? No, just as Varz had a long history of victory, the other nations had detailed histories of how *not* to defeat a Varz army. They would not be careless here. The only logical conclusion was that the presence of the remaining Warriors of prophecy assured them that Fate was on their side. Indeed, the last time the two forces had met en masse, the Warriors of Pyrán had single-handedly won the battle.

This time would be different.

A derisive chuckle escaped the young Commander Bourin from the convening circle of officers. He was all haughty pride, prancing about like one of his own steeds. In his mind, this battle was something of a formality before Varz assumed control over the Five

346

Realms once more. Dranus knew better.

Finally, Commander Ven with her patched eye notified him that the council was ready. She, along with General Armodus, Commander Bourin, and the newly appointed Commander of the Archers Brigade sat in a tall tent discussing which strategy would best fit their scenario. The myriad colors of their glowing armor lit the area in a festive ambiance as narrow shafts of light came through the gaps in the tent. While a spot had been readied for Raven, a skilled warrior in her own right, Dranus had thought it better to leave her in Varz to continue her training. While he and his kind often delighted in the twisted tragedy of such ironies, this particular king thought it better to spare his new love such a cruel irony as to bear witness to the death of her former comrades.

Surrounding the council's tent were the brilliant goldenrod members of the Archers Brigade set in formations for long range bombardments. On the ground at the base of the mountain were the bustling bodies of the Armed Forces, setting their formations just an inch further to the left. Lining the slopes of the narrow hill were the jagged rocks of amethyst, the swollen ranks of the Mage Corps. Since the Battle of the Rift, they had more than tripled in size and constituted a substantial part of the Varz ground forces. The only force missing was the forest green Mounted Forces, though they were not unoccupied.

Set and secured into the ground of a ledge overlooking the field was the Staff of the South Star, its multi-sided gem pouring out ruby light, the melancholy dirge of low chanting sluggishly drifting on the morning air. For this battle they would need numbers above all, and the South Star Army still numbered over 10,000; a major contribution to their ranks, they made up the vanguard of the Varz forces. Behind and to the right and left of the South Star Army were the Varz soldiers in ranks facing outward, their backs to the hill. Combined, they formed a horseshoe formation with the hill at the center. This way, if it appeared the battle was going poorly, they could retreat along the side of the hill while the South Star Army held with the ability to be recalled instantaneously.

This was, however, not the only reason for this formation.

"Ah, it seems the enemy has finally settled on their strategy." Dranus led his council from the tent and assayed the layout of the battlefield from his ledge. To the west was a dense sea of trees that

347

went north and surrounded the city of Medi. To the east, as well, were scattered thickets of dense foliage. Because of the positioning of the Varz forces and the constraints on the land of the forests, the enemy had chosen a simple formation: a stacked line of battle on the plains north of their position.

Now with his council close by, the king openly considered the audacity of the enemy forces. "We are of the high ground, we have established our formation, and they have a walled city to defend...why would they march to meet us here where our position is most advantageous? Do they truly believe their numbers so superior?" Thick wrinkles appeared on the king's brow as he considered this conundrum again, poking and prodding his logic for flaws he had previously missed. Did they have some special scheme in their third hand? Something that the most brilliant minds of Varz could not have predicted? The mountains and hills to the east were littered with Varz scouts and their rear was soundly secured; they could not be flanked without ample warning. Two months was a short period of time...they could be expecting reinforcements...but estimates of the myriad armies indicated that the vast majority of the enemy had already arrived. What could a late engagement of reinforcements accomplish if they could not gain advantageous position?

Dranus racked his brain over and over, playing the battle out in his mind a hundred times over and a hundred times more. His council argued behind him but their voices wisped past him like so many fluttering leaves gone unnoticed.

Row upon row of Arendrum soldiers formed an impassable line of men and steel that approached but did not quite reach either the western or eastern forests. Their plan was simple and obvious, they would charge and wrap their forces around the mountain, using their superior numbers to surround them. It was exactly as Bourin had suggested, but were they so predictable? Or was it the gravity of the battle that unearthed the king's nerves and set them aflame?

From his rear came several scout captains all giving their reports. Their rear was secured, there appeared to be no further reinforcements coming from Arendrum, and their artillery had not yet been discovered. The fortresses guarding the path through the mountains to the east reported no activity or signs from either Urhyll or Myrendel. It was as he had expected.

In his mind, Dranus could hear the reports in the lilting voice of the Book. The tome always spoke so simply and reassuringly but hid so much from his ears and eyes. The looming specter of Fate cast an invisible shadow on him but what else could he do?

"We will continue as planned for this outcome." The command was simple and a chorus of "My king" sounded the council's acknowledgment. Each Commander mounted their horses and moved to their positions. Bourin, a cocky grin still plastered on his features, made some small signal in the air. In the east and the west some agitation of the emerald forest signed a knowing movement of trees and men.

Everything appeared to be moving forward as planned and all of the king's forces were in position. Commander Ven gave her signal from below that they were prepared to start the casting whenever the battle began. Finally, he received a piece of paper from a field messenger and read it swiftly. The last piece was set, the artillery was in place and well hidden. It was time to begin this decisive battle that would prove once and for all who deserved to rule over the Five Realms.

There was a hush on the battlefield, a hanging silence between the two forces as they postured in their respective formations. Each side knew what was at stake. Every soldier from the most dispensable of front-linemen to the King of Varz knew that more than their lives were waged in this battle. Dranus marveled for a moment in the clawing anticipation for battle that he knew his ancestors had once lived for. He appreciated the array of colors massed before him, noticing that the allied forces appeared to have donned pure white armor as a symbol of their unity. Leave it to those who were least united to concoct a display of their unity for the lingering eyes of their enemies. They were bland and simple...everything that his forefathers had loathed about the folk they knew to be Lessers.

A series of horn blasts broke through the calm and the war machine of the Allied forces began to trudge forward. Then from the top of the hill came a mighty battle cry, a song of glory and pride that all Varz soldiers, new and old, knew. Soon the little valley rang with the symphony of tens of thousands of Varz warriors! The prideful chords of the Varz soldiers lain over the thumping beat of the advancing enemy; the melody of the crooning Staff of the South Star unimpeded by the strong silence of nature as it awaited the results of this battle.

King Dranus thrust his palm to the skies and a bright flash of crimson light shot into the air, taking the shape of the slanted V; symbol of Varz royalty. At this, the sky north and west of Medi erupted into arcing streams of flame.

A lightning bolt struck upward from the city, spidering outward and shattering a large swath of the great balls of destruction. Others had their flames compressed as if by giant hands until they went out. Still others were swept away by a powerful gust.

It was as they had planned. As with the Warrior of Water, if they could keep the remaining Warriors busy with defense of the city, they could defeat the ground forces without worry of their frightening power. For this reason all of the artillery weapons had been thinly spread and hidden by magical means from scouts. The enemy would have to locate and deal with each one and that would take time, or else endure the onslaught for the duration of the battle. Either way, it gave the Varz forces time to gain an edge in the battle without interference from at least some of the Warriors of Pyrán.

Dranus's cheek twitched at the sight of two small contingencies turning from the mass and heading back to the city. Still, the line of white soldiers like the advancing realm of the dawn advanced upon their formation. And still the armies of Varz sang in marvelous glory and lust for battle, their sorcerous eyes glowing with malicious intent.

Just before the two forces met, a rain of arrows came from the back ranks of the enemy forces, trying to catch the Varz formation off guard and set them to defend while the foot soldiers attacked...a classic strategy, however dated and predictable. Commander Ven was ready and before the arrows could even reach their full height, a huge translucent green wall appeared in the sky overhead and disintegrated every one of the arrows. Instead of a disorganized and chaotic mess of troops, the allied forces slammed against the stern and resolute ranks of the South Star Army.

Every one of those ghostly soldiers knew this was their time to prove their use, not to their king or their long dead queen, but to themselves. This was their time to affirm that the decision they had made so many centuries before had been worthwhile.

Those men were more artists than soldiers on that battlefield, wielding their curved swords and shields like the focused painter with his brush and his pallet. Every brush stroke painted the marvelous shades of red which emanated from their ghostly form. Their enemies supplied the canvas. Every one of those men fought like ten. These were the masters of sword and sorcery alike that had fought in the First Great War and their style entranced the king who had failed to see them fight from such a vantage before. They made laughable sport of the ill-trained men of the Allied forces.

With no concern for their furthered existence, no feelings of pain or exhaustion, they were nearly invincible. Still, their job was not to slay the enemy single-handedly and they slowly but surely moved backwards with the precision and efficiency expected of a Varz army.

As the front-line battle raged, the west and east flanks moved in and began to curl around the hill, trapping the Varz troops with only one way for escape. And as those forces met the respective flanks of the Varz formation, they too began to draw back towards the hill.

Elsewhere, the Varz Mounted Forces, their faces painted to the vibrant green of their surroundings, hunched low on their restless steeds. They caught only the slightest of glimpses through the dense forest of what happened on the field. They listened to the clash of iron and steel and the wild shouts of the men and women doing battle in the field.

Commander Bourin deigned to bow himself in his saddle. He held himself with pride among his warriors. His features were alight with nervousness as much as anticipation of the battle to come. With the other half of his forces in the eastern woods he knew that this stratagem was one of great risk, but which also held the promise for a great reward. They would be charging blind into the field, seeing the state of things only as they cleared the line of trees so that a signal would not betray their arrival. The eastern forces would have to move in tandem or the two-sided flanking maneuver would lose some of its effect.

In the end, it all came down to the foresight and cunning of the king. It was a reliable source on which to wage one's life, the Commander thought to himself.

Commander Ven's mind was in constant flux as it integrated the thoughts of her warriors; their observations, their predictions, and their reactions to all they saw. It was only a practiced mind such as hers that could retain its identity amidst so many competing thoughts and voices. With every minor shift in the tides of the battle the Commander coordinated the focus of their casting. Their structure was such that all of the spells used to enhance their forces originated from her. Their minds interlocked through age-old sorcery.

The western flank was being pressed too rapidly. With her eyes closed she saw through the eyes of a thousand mages or more who lined the slopes of the hill. She shifted herself to the western flank and the soldiers there felt their skin harden and bounce back blades like the well-crafted armor they wore. Filled with a wicked sense of invulnerability they pushed back against the pressing weight of the Allies.

In the back of her thousand minds Ven saw a ball of fire loose from the woods around Medi. Then she saw a flash of bright light, a silver warrior falling from the sky. Then she saw nothing.

She shuddered and cringed, the pain of unexpected death breaking into her stream of thought, coloring her thousand views crimson.

The pieces were set. From the King of Varz's view he saw every movement of the battle unhindered by the crowned helmet on his war table. Clad from neck to toe in the armor of his ancestor kings he was like a statue of baroque black. That armor which had generations of spells imbued in it and had seen more battles than could be counted seemed almost to pull towards the fighting. Like the king's blood it yearned for the thrill of battle, for the life-or-death struggle of swords and shields and complex sorcery. Yet the composed king held himself. He knew that his job was here; ever the king moving his pawns about the board.

His mind drifted back to endless days spent with The Ultimate atop that sacred mount and pulled forth a new addition to his arsenal. His thoughts swam through seas of infinite coherence, dashing quickly from sanity to insanity and back again, taking all that one might believe to be real and bending it to his will. He turned to face the archers behind him, each with an arrow which had no tip, but rather, a seed in its place. In a single volley an arc of arrows spread and landed near the center of each enemy formation in a precise line per his will.

Those warriors hit looked down at the ground, stupefied that they had lived with nothing more than an annoyance swatting at their armor.

Then came the quaking earth.

Like a nest of starved snakes their came vines that shot from the ground where the seeds took hold. They came up some thirty feet into the air and weaved together, caring little for the delicate bodies of the soldiers that impeded their progression. Within a few terrifying seconds a wall of thick vines and skewered corpses separated the Allied ranks.

Confusion and disarray reigned among the enemy formation as it hacked and chopped at the unyielding vines. It was almost time for the Mounted Forces to play their part. As much as he had suspected trickery or deception at the outset of the battle, the Lessers truly were playing into their hands marvelously. Was it, then, mere nerves that had set him to worry and to obsess over unseen threats?

It was not.

Before Dranus could give the signal for his forces to press outward from the hill, he saw the splitting of trees precariously near his own hidden forces. In the northeast a hidden cavalry bearing the flags of Myrendel emerged! Even with the enormous force that came against them in their unending ranks, there were yet more of the enemy? Dranus watched patiently, though his throat was tight as this new cavalry barreled towards his own unsuspecting cavalry. The new enemy was trying to move through the forests, meaning to use it as cover from the main fight and flank their rear from the east! What clever Lessers! They had finally acquired a taste for more finesse in their strategies, and what a time it was for such advancements!

Dranus clenched a fist and lifted the Book of Fate's Desire from his table, flipping through pages seeking details of this ploy. Had he missed this in his perusing beforehand? Had the Allies feared spies and not communicated their plans on paper? It could be any number of possibilities, not the least of which was the personal machinations of the Book itself. He closed the Book with a thud and set it back on the table, a wary glare cast to the worn leather before returning to the battle.

Even if he sent a signal to his forces in the east at that moment they would not have time to withdraw in an orderly fashion. They were positioned to charge, not to form ranks and retreat. They lacked the leadership of Commander Bourin but still held many skilled leaders among them. Dranus kept his head level and tried to devise a way to recover from this setback. The cascading consequences of this development ran through him like the blood in his veins.

The seconds he had been counting in the rear of his consciousness were nearing the zero point. Once more he raised his palm to the skies and a red light ribboned into the clouds towards the east. The enemy may see the ploy, but they may also see this as a warning of the new enemy.

From the western forest charged the Varz cavalry, led by the screaming Commander Bourin, trapping the split and disoriented left flank of the Allied forces between cavalry to the west, soldiers to the east, and an impassable wall of vines to the north.

By the time the western cavalry dove into the Allied ranks, the eastern cavalry had been engaged by the Myrendel force and quickly moved to flee back to the south, being careful not to be trapped by the unknowing allied forces on the Varz right flank. Just as the enemy forces were destined for a route in the west, his disorganized cavalry to the east was all but doomed. Indeed, rather than support the flailing contingent of mounted soldiers, Ven had focused her spell weaving on the eastern ground forces to try and press the inner wall of enemies.

With a simple bit of sorcery, Dranus transcribed a thought into words as a message and sent it with a messenger for the western flank. With victory in simple grasp on that front, they would need to hurry around the back of the hill to prevent the enemy from securing their only means of escape.

Everywhere around the king was the whistling of arrows at their own pace, sending a constant rain of death into the enemies back ranks who had since developed a fairly effective shield made of stacked men and wide, thick shields.

He had underestimated the potential of enemy reinforcements to disrupt his plans. He had intended to act quickly, but even with the disarray caused by the artillery, the enemy had acted preemptively.

Dranus stood up straight with a shiver down his spine as, moment by moment, he saw that the Lessers were not without their resourcefulness.

On the northern flank raged the most fierce of the fighting. There were warriors glowing crimson, doused in the blood of their enemies. They shifted almost as a single entity against the lolling tides of soldiers coming against them in waves. They worked as a cohesive unit, having trained with one another their entire lives they knew almost instinctively what the soldier nearest to them would do next. Their weapons length and size were ever changing and their armor flowed like a viscous liquid around their bodies, countering blows at improbable angles. Their brothers-in-arms came to finish the off-guard enemies so that the battle moved with a constant, exact rhythm.

One man dug a glowing cleaver into an enemy's neck and took the dead man's sword, molding it to a serrated edge that sawed with a single forceful pull through a helmet of white metal. Two enemies' blades sought his unguarded back, but the South Star soldier hardly noticed their deaths at the hands of two comrades freed up by the attention their brother drew. A shield stretched to a lance in a captain's hand and speared two men through the stomach. Heads and limbs fell like apples from a tree amidst a Dusk Season storm.

In this way the South Star army butchered and demoralized the front ranks of the Allies. These were the men who had trained their entire lives for battle, who had mastered every offensive art, and who lusted for battle like nothing else in the world. They could not be distracted for such things as tactics. To them there was only the narrow arena of battle. There was only the sword in their hand. There was only the enemy's mortal coil in need of loosening.

Dranus eyes rolled back into his head as he split communication with Commander Ven. Their entire eastern cavalry had been dispatched or fled. The forward ranks of the South Star were surging beyond their intended length and though this had not explicitly been the plan, it caused the eastern ground forces to slowly withdraw, fearing that the ghostly warriors would pierce directly through their lines.

He paced back and forth on the craggy overhang of rock on the hill. Beside him sang the Staff of the South Star. He had to decide quickly if he would withdraw the South Star Army in order to bolster the eastern flank and protect them from the advancing cavalry. The sorcerously enhanced flank was holding beyond its means but how long would it last? Then again, what would fill the massive gap at the center of the battle when the South Star Army retreated?

Suddenly his stomach lurched and he took to scanning the field again. There was something missing. He had been transfixed on the movements of his eastern flank so long he had neglected something...something important....

The artillery!

The artillery had stopped firing! Could it be that the Warriors of Pyrán had already dispatched his scattered artillery forces?! They were supposed to have more time! The western flank was being won even more favorably than the Allies won to the east, but if the Warriors of Pyrán came from behind them it would spell disaster!

"It is alright, battles never go as expected. Our force is still strong. We are strong on two of three fronts and have many reserves. Our route of escape is still clear." He listed advantages to himself nervously like a mother trying to comfort her young. He was hardly able to force himself to accept the truth of his words, no matter his skill at sorcery.

Then, like damnation from the sun a bright flare reflected from polished white in the southeast. From behind another hill marched yet another force of considerable size! These flew the flags of Urhyll and advanced rapidly towards their rear.

"Impossible!" His mouth hung agape. "We scoured every inch of those hills!" He was nearly foaming with outrage. "That Warrior...could she...an entire army?" Dranus briefly recalled the words The Ultimate had once spoken to him about the Guardian manifesting whole armies from nothing. It was not out of the realm of possibility, as few things were when it came to the complex sorcery of Varz.

Dranus's thoughts raced in panic as he accepted this truth. He suspected that had the ground been more level directly behind them, that the enemy would have spawned directly in their rear. At least this way he had some time to react.

"How can our estimates of their strength have been so wrong? Their timing...their luck! They will have us surrounded if we do not retreat now." Now he struggled to remain calm, casting a piercing glare at the Book in a spare moment. His knowledge of strategy was unmatched, but tactics took experience. He began feeling the panic of the Battle of the Rift set upon him. Memories of waiting helplessly, incapable of deciding on the correct recourse flooded his skin like a river of needles. Had he led his forces to slaughter again?!

This was unnatural! They could not possibly know of the Books power to intercept their written word! There was not the slightest indication that their hidden forces had been discovered before the battle!

As if in response to his cries of growing desperation, there was a crack of lightning that caused his head to swivel to the west. An unnatural wind gathered strength in the west and a row of towering flame consumed the walls of vine, disintegrating them almost instantly. Then, a flash of light blinded him from above and he saw the face of the Warrior of the Sun in splendid silver for a moment before she was gone again. Something fell at his feet and suddenly Dranus was still, his face set in a frown. Rolling in the dirt before him was the still-smirking head of Commander Bourin.

The Warriors of Pyrán had arrived at the battle.

# Chapter 33
## The Ultimate's Price

Dranus kicked the head of his former commander to the side and stepped hastily to the ledge hanging over the battle. The sounds of yelling and clashing steel still droned beneath the singing Staff of the South Star. The king looked closely at each area of the field, analyzing each section intently so that he could make his next move.

The western flank was holding and pushing the enemy back. The pincer movement from the hidden cavalry had devastated the Allied forces and what remained of that part of their formation was in retreat. He turned his head to stare at glowing crimson warriors at play. The vanguard was outnumbered and yet they pressed the Allies back here as well. All of these things worked to Varz's favor.

Below and on the eastern hillside Dranus spotted Ven doing all that she could to relieve pressure from their besieged flank. The second hidden cavalry had already been routed and retreated from the Myrendel cavalry who even now moved slowly but implacably into position just south of the eastern Varz flank to remove the possibility of retreat. Placing one hand over his left eye, his vision blurred and then cleared to that of a scout on the opposite side of his lookout. The Urhyllian forces moved uninhibited into place at their rear with whole legions jumping ahead amidst repeated flashes of sunlight. In a few moments they would enclose the southern retreat path so that only the western forests might offer them reprieve but the Warriors of Pyrán undoubtedly moved inward from that location.

The warriors were powerful, but they could be overwhelmed if a decisive charge down the hill could be mounted. Perhaps the South Star Cavalry could spearhead...but then his center would be completely exposed. At best he would be sacrificing the majority of his eastern flank for a small chance of retreat to the west. At worst, he risked complete and total collapse of his formation. As he lifted his hand from his eye and clasped a hand firmly onto the Staff of the

South Star he knew that the time for an orderly retreat had passed.

The King of Varz stood his ground on the top of the hill where his camp was set. Already nervous whispers came from the Archer's Brigade at his back. He breathed the chilled air of the Night Season and felt the tingling burn of the cold on his face as a strong slicing wind blew over the battlefield. His brow furrowed, his eyes narrowly scanned the scene and steam fumed from his nostrils. Everywhere around him his brothers and sisters fought for the pride of Varz.

And everywhere around him they died.

His dark eyes closed in brief reflection. He recalled everything that had brought him here. He recalled all that he had. He thought of The Ultimate and he thought of his home city. He thought of Raven.

Was this his time to die? Had his Fate been met so soon?

"No."

He had come too far, done too much to give up at that point. They were surrounded but not well and their losses were still relatively low. The main Allied force had been tied with the ferocious South Star Army and these casualties were incidental at worst. His lids rose like shades embracing the light. Quickly, he mapped the entire layout of the battle in his mind's eye, trying to see things as a whole, rather than small parts. He stared with the most translucent hope at the west. There was only time left for something bold and daring.

A strong wind of warm and comforting air brought some life back into his body and with it came a soothing green ambiance, emanating from the hill sides of the Varz forces. Where once the Aura of Valor had given his men strength, now the Aura of Respite soothed their pain-riddled bodies and filled them with supernatural energy to continue fighting. His folk would pay this energy back in double over the coming week, but it gained them a great advantage: the enemy would be tiring on the front lines and the battle had become too erratic to easily transfer in fresh troops from the Allies reserves, whereas the Varz soldiers were sustained by magical means. This would be the deciding moment.

The thin line between victory and defeat.

"Issue all remaining forces to retreat up the hill, pull in as tightly as possible. Archers! Provide cover for our retreating allies and try to make some room between them!" As his orders were shouted, they were shadowed by messengers and officers until the bitter-sounding horn of retreat was sounded in all directions from the hill.

To the west and the southwest the enemy ranks were thin, though the Warriors of Pyrán fought there. The fresh South Star cavalry would have to be their final gambit to break the encirclement and escape towards the west. If they could make it to the sea, his forces from Shiera could provide them with reinforcements and a place to rest...but then Varz would be vulnerable. It would be better for the army to move to the coast and for Dranus, with the South Star forces, to return to Varz over the secret passages through the Rift.

He paced over to where the Staff of the South Star was stuck into the ground, and he stared for a few moments at the glowing red gem face. He admired the craftsmanship of the head and how it had kept so well for so long.

Eventually his eyes rested on the base of the staff. There was one final option available to him, but would he be forced to unleash powers he could not understand? The Ultimate's warning rang through his mind again as he touched the Staff, pulling it up from the ground.

He tapped the base against the ground and the ruby light, the somber chanting, disappeared. Seeing the enemy in retreat, the Allied forces took this time to reform their ranks before pursuit. Dranus had underestimated the combined strength of their armies and had been outmaneuvered since early in the battle. Now in the early afternoon, when the sun rose high and the South Star began its descent, the allies underestimated the resolve of Varz and left their western flank thin. No doubt they expected that blocking in the Varz forces with their back against the chasm of the Rift would be enough to finish them off. The western route seemed almost too tempting. But it was their only chance.

Dranus's forces retreated up the hill and regained some form, allowing a gap to open between the outer circle of the enemy and the inner circle of the Varz forces in all directions, and this gap was quickly filled by the South Star Army. They were redeployed as Dranus willed them and they knew that their job was to hold their thin line while the Varz forces regrouped.

The king gave instructions for all forces to mass on the western border and for the glowing ruby soldiers to push that flank out as much as possible, whatever the cost. Their casualties were impossible to count.

The western Varz flank would spearhead behind the South Star riders and next would ride the Mounted Forces who had remained in the west, centered by the Mage Corps and Archer's Brigade, with another line of soldiers and the occasional still-mounted cavalrymen to cover their rear.

The ancient warriors of Varz, kept alive only by the lost sorcery of the Staff of the South Star, fought with unmatched bravery. They massed to the west and everywhere else they fell in droves. No matter how difficult they were to kill, they were not immortal, but neither did they die without taking several enemies with them.

Finally, his forces had massed but the enemy was quickly breaking through the eastern ranks and heading around the hill, they had to attempt their breakthrough now or it would be too late!

Dranus slammed the base of the Staff into the dirt again and rotated the shaft in his hand so that the emerald face looked out at the sea of foliage and men. With another strike the emerald clad horsemen formed into a wedge formation. Still at full strength and their numbers many, they would be unstoppable by the small line of reserve soldiers. Behind them the Varz forces rallied and believed fully that their king would grant them another miracle as he had in the face of the God-storm. Dranus himself had moved down the hill and rode at the front of the Mounted Forces, taking Bourin's place as commander.

"Now we break free my loyal warriors! So that we may be avenged, let us strike through and..."

King Dranus's speech was interrupted by a loud harmony of horns, but instead of the glorious chord they had first struck at the Battle of the Rift there was a dark, sinister tone to it. He turned his attention to the west where the Allies struggled to fatten their ranks, the Varz strategy readily apparent well before that moment.

A beam of radiant white light, thick like clouds, burst into the sky unseeably high. A dark ray of menacing black crossed it. Beneath the point where the lines of light crossed slowly crept a massive pillar of red that dwarfed the others. These lights were echoed by a sonorous call that no horn could have made. Each mimicked but refracted the sound of the previous so that it was like a chorus of one split like a rainbow into minor pentatonic cacophony.

What came next horrified Dranus. It drained him of the last of his will and shook him to the depth of his glaringly mortal soul.

While he had been rallying his men he had not noticed the

gathering clouds amassing above the spot where the Warriors focused their energy. He could not have seen the blackening funnel gaining force in the sky. Now King Dranus, for all that his eyes could see things no other living soul might see, lay eyes upon a swirling vortex of vengeful wind and lightning descending like divine wrath from the heavens. The cyclone touched ground with a terrible blast of noise. It passed through the pillar of light and erupted into a raging inferno, pulling flames into its form and mixing its essence.

Spitting flames in every direction as it spun, it was the product of ancient and terrifying sorcery, and it was the Warriors herald of inevitable doom. Staring at that firestorm as it approached from the west, cutting off their only hope for escape, was to stare at the ember eyes of Death himself. Belligerent and full of fury the vortex would consume the Varz forces and leave nothing but ash.

Armodus appeared at his side and shouted something lost to the combined sounds of crackling lightning, roaring flame, and deafening wind.

Dranus was frozen, his eyes were set on his doom as it loomed ever closer.

"My king, we must move now or we will all be lost!" Commander Ven's voice rang in his mind with uncharacteristic panic. This was an ancient and powerful sorcery forbidden of his people...nothing they could amass would stop it.

The king contemplated his coming death and without noticing, found that the Book of Fate's Desire had appeared in his hands.

Dranus looked down at the Book and it spoke softly to him, piercing through the noise. "It is time, my lord, to decide your Fate and that of the Five Realms."

He turned in his saddle to face the Staff of the South Star as it seemed to emit emerald light like a guttering brand; the light it poured and the screams like banshees crying their death-song seemed to fight the presence of the firestorm. He glanced again at the winds, moving slowly but steadily with the tall regal posture of a deity bringing justice.

Before he even realized it, Dranus had spun the Staff of the South Star in his grasp so that the head pointed at the ground, and he locked eyes with the tiny black gem at the base. He felt eyes looking back at him from within.

"Everyone get back! Spread and get as far away from me as possible!" No one understood the words of their king, but they knew that they could only trust in him for their salvation. Those in the center pushed outward and away, but the cyclone pressed back. It cut at their skin and the intense heat of the thing bore down on them.

The king dismounted and smacked his horse away, his heart raced and his mind was scattered. Here he could lose everything. Here he might forfeit all he had worked so hard to accomplish. His life, the life of his people, the glory of Varz, and the Fate of the Five Realms; everything came down to this single moment in his existence.

Now that the main gem faced down, the emerald warriors had vanished, but the chanting only increased in its frenzied pace as if it sensed the urgency of the moment. With a lump in his throat, Dranus slammed the crowned head of the Staff into the ground!

Silence.

The incessant chanting of the Staff had stopped. There was not the raucous whirl of the winds. There were no shouts and screams or the clamor of metal. An unnatural silence had beset the scene.

Everywhere around him were the frightful stares of his men and horses trapped in their fear. Not a soul moved, not even the firestorm which was frozen in place like a waiting fire giant.

Then, slowly seeping from the tiny black gem came airy black wisps of smoke. Like shadowy wraiths they swam through the still air gradually gaining form. Eleven in number, they became ever more material. They settled in a circle around King Dranus, ten men and women in black robes, and a final one covered in silver trim. Their faces were concealed by black hoods.

The one in the ornate robe stepped forward and spoke in an obviously young but stern, feminine voice, "My king." And all of those remaining echoed in a blur of voices. Instantly, Dranus recognized the voices as those that made up the chanting which had come from the Staff when it was at full power!

"Who...are you?" Dranus hesitated to ask, though he began to think he knew the answer.

The one who stepped forward was short and her frame was tiny, but Dranus felt an incredibly imposing presence from her. It was like a gargantuan shadow stood behind her, looking down on him from above. It was a presence he had felt from only one other in his lifetime. She removed her hood to reveal a youthful face that was at once familiar to the king.

And eyes as red as blood.

"I am Lana, younger sister of Queen Luna and leader of the Black Mages. We are the descendants of the ten great sorcerers who came together with The Ultimate to forge the nation of Varz from the chaos of the times. We were once loyal servants to the queen, until her wicked sorcery trapped us in that gem to fuel the Staff's powers." It was as though she knew the questions he would ask and was too impatient to wait for him to ask them. "But you are not her and we remain loyal to the throne." Her voice was calm, and her form held subtle grace while Dranus's was shaken and his posture unsettled.

Finally all of the pieces came together! Finally Dranus felt his mind clear with certainty as his logic fit the last piece of the puzzle into place. He recalled the remorseful eyes of Queen Luna the Mad for the briefest of moments.

Now he stood before the favorite daughter of The Ultimate; the only one else to have unlocked the Devil's Eyes, the only one who could be stronger than the reigning Queen of Varz as Commander Lena had spoken of, the source of the incomprehensible sorcery of the Staff of the South Star...and Dranus's last chance at the Ultima spell.

"What do you require of us, my king?" The others were quiet though they moved with notable unrest. Only the monotonous voice of one of history's greatest sorcerers and her overpowering essence broke through the void of frozen time she had no doubt created.

"Can you cast the Ultima spell?" Still Dranus was hesitant because even he did not know what the spell truly consisted of.

Lana raised an interested brow and surveyed the scene around her for the first time. "I can, but only if you are prepared to accept the consequences. If you make use of our strength, you will set forth devastation that cannot be revoked. The havoc that you bring will not be just, and it will not be clean; it will be stained with the darkest of magic." It was evident that she took this very seriously, as The Ultimate had.

"Furthermore, we will destroy the black gem that holds us prisoners and with us go the powers of the Staff." Though this consequence was much more tactically significant she gave it no more than a passing mention compared to her previous warning.

As a decisive king of Varz, descendant from every previous king or queen, Dranus took no time to make the decision that was his only choice. He nodded his consent with grim countenance.

"Then, what is your desire?" As she asked this she made a broad motion to her side and looked away...perhaps to the other ten members although they barely reacted.

"My desire?" Dranus was confused, why had she averted her gaze from him?

"The Ultima is absolute in strength, though finite in scope. Whatever it is you desire, I will create it." She seemed somewhat impatient with the king, as though she expected him to be well versed in this subject. Perhaps he should have been.

"To destroy the enemies that threaten us and to see no more Varz soldiers die at this battle, that is my desire." Stalwart in some newfound conviction, Dranus only hesitated for a moment before declaring what he knew must be clear.

At this, the young sorceress fixed her gaze back on him.

"Then by your will, my king." Lana returned to her place in the circle and replaced her hood as they all began to chant, but a different chant than the one he was used to. Where the other was flat and monotone, this was rich with sounds that ranged from near-strangled cries to despairing moans and groans. There was a distinct sadness and some agitated anger to the chant. Indeed it felt as though the Black Mages regretted their deed even before having done it.

The world's refrain ended abruptly.

The roar of the winds and the despairing cries of his men flooded his ears. He felt the burning heat and the weight of his armor. In a circle around him he could see the shadows of the Mages where they had been, but it was apparent that no one else perceived them as he did. Instead, every one of those around the king stopped one by one and stared with mouths hanging open at Dranus.

The great King of Varz radiated some engulfing black glow that most felt more frightening than the cyclone baring down on them. It clawed about like the tendrils of a crazed sea-beast and not a soul dared approach. It was not that they feared some threat to their mortal form, but that the darkness reached out to grasp the very fabric of their being.

What was this energy, Dranus wondered? Why had nothing

changed but his form? Was he to be the vessel through which his people might be saved? His panicked gaze suddenly stiffened and drifted upward.

The skies of blue and white and darkened gray were replaced almost at once by a suffocating sheet of utter blackness. Like sudden twilight, the air around them grew dark and heavy. In the distance, over the city of Medi, grew a bulb of the thick, pulsating darkness. Nearby, the catastrophe created by the Warriors of Pyrán was sucked into this black abyss.

Then, tragedy.

Death fell like oblong tears from the skies.

Black shafts, shards, spheres, blocks; every chaotic shape randomly formed crashed down upon the Allies. As the enemies of Varz were touched by the amorphous things, they died quickly and without sound. The combined forces of the Four Realms brought up shields and they hid behind trees, but still they died. They ran and they stirred their horses to their limits, but no matter how fast they fled, they died. By the hundreds, by the thousands, they died. The warriors of Arendrum and the remnants of Shiera died. The proud riders of Myrendel died. Even the crafty assassins of the Urhyllian desert, who had hardly participated in the battle, died.

None were spared.

The Varz forces stared about, stricken by horror.

This was no clean death they offered their enemies. There was no fight to be made against sorcery such as this, neither pride nor satisfaction could be found in these deaths. This was nothing but unchecked devastation and grim, dirty death. At once there was loud, vibrant life and then with the gentlest touch of the horrid forms to skin, there was emptiness.

Among the shrieking Varz soldiers, anyone who was touched felt nothing but a sense of oppressive calm. Those who had been approaching Death's door seemed to recover miraculously, though they could only surmise that they had, in fact, died and reached the most abysmal circle of the afterlife.

Even Dranus, king and paragon of everything Varz stood for, stared about him at the unholy carnage he had wrought. He knew without question that he had brought some evil upon the world that it did not deserve. Some atrocious act like his ancestors had done. But had they felt this kind of remorse? Was it the likes of such sorcery which drove Queen Luna mad?

After what seemed an eternity the sky cleared and like the beginning of the battle, there was a hush all about them. The Aura of Respite dissipated, and the glowing members of the South Star were nowhere to be seen. Some black dust fell from the base of the Staff and mingled with the dirt. No shouts of victory ensued, not a single warrior dared move a muscle as if in fear that they would be taken up into the receding darkness. All around them was unclean death.

Every soldier that had come against them was now dead. Tens of thousands of lives fighting for their beliefs. He had wanted their defeat, of course, but not like this.

The bodies lay peacefully on the ground or slumped against their horses which still stood patiently, waiting for commands that would no longer come. Blood painted the scene red where there had been fighting but in the untouched ranks of the rear there was only death. There was no sign of insult or injury. There was, however, the unmistakable expressions and contortions of fear blanketing the dead. They cringed and wept and huddled in masses. Some reached out for unobtainable salvation amidst their final steps. Well-trained warriors did not fear death and the Allies had shown that they were indeed well-trained. But this was something far worse than death and not a single face accepted their hellish Fate in their final moments.

Dranus returned slowly to the hilltop to better examine the result of his deed.

He had not yet realized the true extent of the devastation he had brought about.

In the distance, where once had stood the vast city of Medi with its innumerable thousands of citizens...women and children, young and old, those who posed no threat to Varz....

Dranus's gut clenched and he threatened to heave without a force of control he had been trained to muster.

Where once had stood the grand city of Medi and its people, there was now a deep, black crater; a scar on the planet that would forever bare his name.

Was this the Ultimate's price? Surely he had known that if Dranus summoned the Black Mages he would use the Ultima spell. He had warned him against it. But Dranus could not have fathomed consequences such as these. Even when Lana, the young girl who shared his royal blood, had warned him of the calamity he would unleash on the world he could not have imagined *this*. Had The Ultimate, the legend of Varz, seen this type of carnage a thousand years prior? Did he watch now and weep from atop holy Pyrán?

Dranus did not weep for the loss of so many, though he wanted to. His reserve...no, perhaps something in his blood kept him strong and resolute. Those that remained of the Varz forces relied fully on that strength.

*     *     *

In the morning, Dranus had set his formation to stand against the Allies at Medi. The Four Realms had sent nearly every man and woman they could muster to end the villainy of Varz as foretold in their legends. By the evening of that same day, each of those mustered had died.

Every last one of them.

Countless Varz warriors huddled close in their tents, shaken by the horrors they had witnessed. Some complained of nightmarish visions of unnamable black things hunting for their souls. Though many rushed to a nearby river to wash themselves of the blood and dirt of battle, too many remained there, shivering in the icy waters. They complained that they could not become clean no matter how long they bathed. They scrubbed at their skin for hours, some even resorting to peeling away bits of their flesh to rid the filth from their bodies. Many had to be dragged from the river to avoid hypothermia or self-inflicted death.

King Dranus showed no pity for those who suffered and rewarded those who matched his feigned strength. It was a mask he did not want to wear though he found it fit his face quite well.

In the morning they searched the battle for the Warriors' corpses but found only two. The Warriors of Wind and Lightning were dead, their white and black lights added in a storm of yin and yang to the king's Stone. Two remained: the Sun Warrior must have escaped the influence of the spell, but the Warrior of Fire, too, was nowhere to be found.

The king considered what should be done with the piles and piles of grotesque dead. In his unearthed heart he knew that the least he could do would be to return the bodies. But his awakened blood told him that he had come too far already, he could not pretend to be honorable in the wake of such foul sorcery. He had the bodies stacked in a massive pile that would, along with the crater that was once Medi, remind his enemies that only death awaited them.

Ahead of the army went a small contingent of Varz warriors led by General Armodus. They took the severed heads of the Allied leaders to the walls of Arendrum. They presented them plainly so that in a week after what would soon be known as the Medi Massacre, Dranus stood in the Arendrum High Hall and their Superior knelt at his feet. They had no more armies with which to resist the still strong Varz forces.

They had only whispers that two of the Warriors of Pyrán still lived, somewhere. They had wavering faith and desperate hope that these Warriors might still bring salvation.

It was this hope which Dranus knew he must crush next.

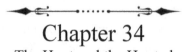

# Chapter 34
## The Hunt and the Hunted

A month or more passed after the battle of Medi, and yet the scars of that battle were still being formed as word spread. Tales of the battle moved from lip to lip quickly from messengers of Varz and were taken abroad by those fleeing the conquered cities of Arendrum. Ironically, those who crafted the stories and myths of that day, rather than exaggerating the truth, rarely approached it. Fearing that they might suffer a similar fate, almost all of the Arendrum cities offered their surrender on simple terms: no more fighting and no more death. The innocent must be spared; the rest is forfeit.

Although the monarchs of Varz were hardly the kind to show compassion for the bested, historically, the atrocity at Medi had more than satiated the newly kindled lust for battle and death in the heavy-eyed king. Where he could salvage life, he did. For some time the king allowed the Arendrum Superior to serve on the council that would run the city though the man quickly lost his constitution for such workings in the face of brutal Varz politics.

King Dranus took this time to consolidate all he had gained and all he had lost.

With the Staff of the South Star now more of a decorative piece than anything, their military strength had been more than halved. Fortunately, none of the Lessers could know this and he had his best sorcerers searching for a way to reactivate it, going as far as calling the Magemaster from *The Dawn's Fury* in Shiera.

Even if they did find this out, the military strength of the enemy realms was now all but non-existent save for Myrendel. While they had lost their cavalry forces, they were sure to have a formidable land force as well as a meager navy. Fortunately, the years of peace had crippled none like the haughty folk of the Crystal Towers. Far from the latent Varz threat and thinking themselves protected by the holy mountains at their border and their sacred lake, their cavalry was their largest force by several lengths. At the moment they posed very little threat.

Most pressing for their martial security was finding a replacement for Commander Bourin. The young man had set a high standard for tactics and discipline in his short tenure and left no line of succession. Instead, competitions of all nature were held in the camps to determine who might be a suitable replacement. The man or woman to replace Bourin must not only be an accomplished rider and warrior, but a strategist and a leader. All of the other members of the War Council were often in the back ranks directing forces at large or casting spells, but the Commander of the Mounted Forces was the front-line leader and thus the replacement had to show these characteristics as well.

So far there were many sent to the medic tents but no new commander.

Without the possibility of any major land battles needing the full strength of the Mage Corps, Commander Ven took charge of Arendrum and King Dranus returned to Varz and the relieving embrace of his love. While he was away, she had trained under the very same tutors that trained members of the royal family. If she was going to one day become Wife to the King, she would need the knowledge and skills to fill that role, as Kaelel had. She was trained in all things that the king had been trained in, all but her skills in combat, for those were already unmatched. Most importantly, she was taught the ways of the Varz people: how to act, think, and reason like they did.

Dranus came home to a woman who was enraptured by everything she was learning, and he had never felt so happy as the times he spent with her. When with her he could forget his duties as king and remember what it was like to be in love; he could experience one of the things that had made The Ultimate as great as he was. But he could only experience this in his waking hours, for when he slept he was visited by nightmarish demons and wastelands of doom.

*Black, amorphous shapes raining from the sky and chasing him, hounding for his soul. He would almost wish, in those dreams, that they held more menace, showing gnashing teeth or baleful stares. But the death that came for him was unfeeling and uncaring. In his flight he saw Lana of the Black Mages and he saw King Baklar the Ultimate, but they would offer him no help. They stared at him blankly with those blood red eyes, Devils both they were. They accused him as the onrushing souls of those he had slaughtered accused him. He saw the bulbous darkness swelling over Varz instead of Medi, consuming it. It would consume him.*

Dranus woke.

He sat up in his bed quickly. His mind cleared rapidly as he recalled the same images he had seen nearly every night since Medi. He looked first to his left and admired the soft skin of his lover's naked back, thankful for her safety. He smiled, as he did every time he saw her. Though his conscience was dirtied by what he had done, his feelings for this girl far overshadowed all of his doubts. But how long could that last?

He looked to his right and saw a letter with the Admiral's seal on it, resting on his stand.

A letter delivered in the night? It was a simple sorcery to send letters without disturbing the recipient but what message could be so urgent it could not wait until the day? With a bit of hesitation he reached for the paper and opened it, anxious that he might find some news that would tear him away from his love.

> My king! I bare wondrous news! Word of your great endeavors in Arendrum have reached our shores and in cowardice, those that have held out against us thus far have come to surrender peacefully. Shiera is united once again under Varz rule, and we have already made great strides in improving their ways. We have met with emissaries from the Western Kingdoms and bartered a treaty of peace that should arrive for your approval in a short time. I must congratulate you, my lord, for you have accomplished in less than a year what our ancestors could only do in generations of fighting! History will not forget you my king and it has been an honor serving under you. Your father would be proud.
>
> -Admiral O'cule

The news was good, indeed, even if it left a sour taste in his mouth.

It meant that already three of the Five Realms were under his complete control but the remaining two still had their champions in the remaining Warriors of Pyrán. Furthermore, Urhyll had its natural protection from the great desert known as the Screaming Sands and Myrendel might still have a force to do battle with. He could not have the Sun Warrior assassinating any more of his commanders and he could not underestimate the devastation the Warrior of Fire could produce as he had done at the Battle of the Rift.

Moving carefully so as to not wake the sleeping girl, he got up from his comfortable bed and stretched, breathing in the morning air. He had never before appreciated such things as the taste of dawn but now he found them to be among the most satisfying experiences of his day.

Taking a robe, he walked to his study and sat at a desk where lay the Book of Fate's Desire. He read over the letter from O'cule once more and sighed, shaking his head. To compare him to what his ancestors had accomplished was akin to claiming he'd slain one of the giant hawks of his people when in truth he had merely slain a caged bird no bigger than his fist.

He had fought with a laughable force against a mere 50,000 or so enemies combined from all of the remaining realms. In the time of the First Great War, Varz's military forces had numbered almost 80,000 and the combined might of the Four Realms approached 200,000. Warriors of the past from both sides had trained from childhood for the soul purpose of battle. He had seen how the South Star soldiers fought; it was no surprise they had brought about such miraculous victories. In the centuries of peace both sides had diminished in strength to mere shadows of their former military glory. That he had managed to gather the majority of his enemies onto a single battlefield and completely annihilate them was his only true merit in this war. And even that was made possible exclusively through the sorcery of centuries prior.

"Good morning master, I see you have read the letter from Admiral O'cule." The Book had also become rather cheeky and almost joyful since returning to favor with the king, especially with his newfound happiness.

"Yes." Dranus paused. "It is a great relief that our borders will not be invaded by those from the West. We have never had to fear those of the North before, I doubt we should consider them a threat now."

Dranus opened the Book of Fate's Desire and skimmed through the pages as he had done every morning since returning to Varz. Every day he searched for some clue as to the whereabouts of the remaining Warriors of Pyrán. Until he had an idea of where to find them, he would not risk an invasion in one realm that might be undone by a counter-invasion from another.

"Ohhh, those barbarians in the north. I hear that the strongest wines are made there, though! Perhaps when you have conquered the Five Realms we should take a trip there! It's been ages since the last time I visited!"

The king took note of this suggestion but did not bother to ask about the Book's history; he had learned over time that no real answers would come of it. Instead he continued sifting through page after page of reports on casualties and efforts to mount a defensive force in Myrendel. Likewise, he read letters to and from Superior Frau of Urhyll on the benefits and consequences of surrender.

"Oh dear! My lord, please flip another three pages!" The Book seemed frantic. Was there something even it had not expected to appear? What could it be? Dranus flipped three further pages and watched as words formed on the page, one by one, addressed to him.

"Favored son, I mourn for the tragedy you have brought about, but I blame myself. I believe I should have been more upfront with you about the consequences of using the full power of the Staff, though I knew it was something you must experience on your own. Despite my vow to not interfere in your world, I feel that you have proven my judgment somewhat unwise. As recompense, I will tell you all I know of the Warrior of the Sun's location, forthwith. Bring glory to Varz and fulfill your Fate, Dranus."

The message was signed by King Baklar the Ultimate.

Dranus stared at the dazzling signature of the ancient monarch in disbelief. He should have expected that one like The Ultimate who had such knowledge of the Book could utilize it thusly. He only wished that he could communicate back to express his gratitude, but he supposed he could do so by following the old king's command.

On the next page he found an intricate map of the Screaming Sands with its tall, rocky crags. Near the center of the Sands was a wide area circled in red ink. At the bottom of the map more words appeared on the page: "I have spotted her in this area, go there. Worry not about finding the girl. She will find you."

*     *     *

So it was that Dranus rode at the head of a force nearly three thousand strong which already tired from the difficulties of the desert. After leaving Varz it had taken them little time to reach the desert, but their progress through the harsh sands was much slower. The Screaming Sands were an enigma of the Five Realms even among the sunken Shieran towns and the Discidia Rift. There was a Lesser myth that told of a ferocious battle fought between the Gods ages before man arrived which was said to have occurred in this place. The Lessers believed that the God of the Sun had scorched this place in his anger and so it burned hot through all seasons, ignoring the normal laws of the weather. There was once a Varz king who claimed ownership of the deed, but Dranus knew, as all other monarchs had, that this was untrue. That it was a terrible feat of sorcery was unquestionable, but that it had been wrought by a God was unthinkable, unacceptable for a King of Varz.

The desert was the greatest line of defense that Urhyll had. Their ocean borders were jagged cliffs and could not be assailed from the sea. It had taken the cunning brilliance of King Vulcan the Rock to finally overcome the difficulties of the Sands.

Dranus rode far in the lead of his men with the Book in his hands, contemplating the nature of the desert. His horse struggled over dense sand dunes that rolled for as far as even his sorcerous eyes could see. Sometimes he approached tall, craggy pillars of worn stone that were randomly strewn about, such that the Lessers thought these the handles of the fallen swords of the Gods buried deep in the earth. Strong gusts of wind sent clouds of the fine sand into the king's skin like thousands of tiny needles. It was this combination that gave the desert the name the "Screaming Sands." The strong winds passed over dunes and dove into valleys to make deep, hollow moans. They whipped around the etched rock and let out loud, high-pitched shrieks that could be heard as far as one could see!

It was in no small part to this that the Sands had been such an effective defensive feature. The haunting sounds were too familiar to not feel meaningful but too bizarre to be of any sort of natural occurrence. All along their difficult journey his men exchanged superstitions about the voices of the Sands. Many believed that it was the remnants of ancient sorcery cast before The Ultimate had claimed all sorcery for their kind. Many of those present who had participated at Medi thought them the cries of the defiled dead chasing them still from distant Medi.

Like Dranus, they spoke of nightmares and being chased by unnamable blackness.

Were the voices unique to each person who heard them? Was that the reason so many forces had gone mad and lost themselves among this hellish place? Did the Warrior of the Sun battle such demons here, or was she welcomed by them?

In his light armor and thick padding, the king tired quickly from idle musings. With the Warrior of the Sun about, he could never be unready for battle, despite the sweltering heat and the thousand daggers of the hostile desert that stung his face.

Urhyll had always been the weakest of the Five Realms by numbers and military strength and yet now Dranus could see why they were the last nation to be overcome by his ancestors. The sooner they found the Warrior of the Sun, or rather she found them, the sooner they could advance to the capital and demand surrender.

Dranus knew that his target would likely reside among the rents in the towering rocks and so studied their patterns at every chance. While he traced a gloved hand around the sides of one such tower, his retinue was finally able to catch up to him.

Closing in near the head of the ragged formation was Raven, newest member of the Varz elite and former Warrior of Pyrán. Dranus had explained to her in great detail what they planned to do, how they set out to kill her former comrade. She was upset briefly to hear of the downfall of the Warriors of the Wind and of Lightning, but it seemed that she had come to terms with her situation and considered them necessary casualties with the cunning calculation of a Varz woman. Still, while she insisted she would have no part in the fighting, she did not want to stay cooped up in the castle without him for another several months so soon after they had come together. So she traveled at his side and continued her studies en route.

Even as they neared the center of the location The Ultimate had circled, two older women rode next to Raven, staring intently at every inch of her body and the way she held herself. Periodically one would poke her in the back or the side to correct her posture while another would shout instructions or yell at her for not riding "like a royal lady of Varz." The young girl was nothing if not frustrated by this, but she was glad to be with Dranus when she could and enjoyed her newfound perks as the king's lover.

Dranus tore his attention from the rocks and watched her, his eyes softening even under the harsh light of the sun overhead. He rode next to her and dismissed the protesting women to ride at a distance.

"My sweet savior!" She exclaimed, a cheeky smile on her lips. How marvelous that the heat had failed to tarnish her beauty!

"How are your studies coming?" Dranus smiled and held out a hand to take hers, his other stayed on the reins.

"Well! Very well! I had never known your society to be so structured and traditional..." She shied and furrowed her brow, reprimanding herself. "Sorry, our society...."

Dranus rubbed her hand with his thumb. "Do not worry, my love, it will come to you with time." He looked ahead at another hill to climb. "We have our ways, and they are set. They have brought us dominance for countless generations and so we leave them as they are. Soon you will hardly notice the structure as it will be second nature."

A third voice emerged between shouts of the Sands. It was rich and young; a voice that Raven had come to learn of, though she knew little of that which housed the voice.

"And the king should know!" The Book spoke from its open pouch at Dranus's side. "When he was young, he was quite the rebel against such structure!"

"Oh?" Raven's interest was piqued, though Dranus's smile turned to a frown.

"Yes, yes! I have countless letters from his instructors pleading with King Roboris to instill some discipline in the child. He used to move the castle stones and reroute the hallways to escape his teachers!" Raven laughed, trying to picture a miniature King of Varz running about in robes far too big for his body with a big grin on his face. But it was not a grin that had adorned the king's features.

"Moving the walls?! What a devilish little trickster!" Raven and the Book had a good laugh and Dranus tried to soften so as to not ruin their mood.

"When I was very young, my father took me to the Castle Surrounded by Stone where King Vulcan the Rock had ruled. I learned all about the moving passages they used to disorient their enemies and I thought it fantastic." A memory came back to him from his childhood. "I remember once I trapped Ven in a loop of hallways. She didn't realize it for several minutes! Even then she almost led herself to outside of the walls in her efforts to escape."

Raven loved to see her lover smile though she could not see the hurt behind those eyes. What the Book could not recreate and what Raven did not know was that it was not disdain for responsibility that had driven him to juvenile pranks unbefitting of a Varz prince. It was the empty, dazed look of disinterest that his mother had given him whenever she was with him. It was the unfeeling, cold hand of near contempt with which she had handled him in his youth. She had eyes only for the king and hardly even spoke with the son that was so desperate for attention he turned to wicked chaos and rebellion, only to draw scorn from his father. His father was enraptured, somehow, by that desolate creature he called wife and showered her with every affection he could muster. Were it not for the surrogate love of Commander Ven, Dranus might not have turned out to be the gentle soul he was.

"I bet you were a cute little troublemaker." Raven teased him, still grinning. She sensed the turmoil surfacing in her lover and tried her hardest to drive it away. In this she showed her age and naivety, but the king was glad for the genuine affection she offered.

He leaned across the space between their horses and kissed her. "I have been many things. Fighter, strategist, King of Varz, and even troublemaker, but I have never been 'cute.'" He challenged playfully.

"Oh, no?" This time it was she who closed the distance to place a sweet kiss upon his lips. "Then...handsome!" She squeezed his hand and laughed.

"Debonair!" The Book chimed in, its pages rustling in laughter.

"No, no, no!" The king feigned modesty. His grin stretched as he enjoyed the moment. "Disarmingly reverent..." They all laughed together, suddenly unaffected by the oppressive weather of the Sands. Dranus had only recently found that laughter had this peculiar effect on the mind.

"And quite a connoisseur of diction! A loquacious lute! A silver tongue of sumptuous style! A riveting writer of raptured...."

"Yes, yes, you've made your point, tome!" The king took the Book in his hands with a bit of frustration.

Raven watched on at the bantering between the pair she had come to expect and adore.

"How rude, master! I had at least two more to finish!" The Book opened to show a list of long-winded phrases and foreign words.

"Well of course you do! You've literally every word ever written! That doesn't mean you have to sputter off every one that comes to mind!" He closed the heavy cover of the Book and replaced it in its pouch. He frowned only to mask the obvious humor in the curve of his lips.

This continued for a few more moments as the bemused Raven watched on. She hoped that this war would be over soon so that they could be like this forever, living in peace and comfort. They made an unlikely family: the King of Varz, a Warrior of prophecy, and an ancient book that represented some force of Fate. But to have a family, to have love, was more than Raven had ever expected from her life.

"My king!" A panicked shout from their rear caused Dranus to cut his bickering with the Book short and spin in his saddle, his hand released from his love's. A member of the Mage Corps, clad in the signature purple of his ranks, tumbled forward to catch them.

"What news?" Dranus's face was set, his eyes stared hard at the man; though he was softer with his lover he was still the King of Varz. He was still feared by all in the Five Realms, and he managed this guise with calculated efficiency.

"Great king, we have detected traces of movement among the stone columns nearby! But we cannot maintain its location! It seems to disappear from time to time, only to reappear on another column!" The messenger panted from his exertion and the exhausting heat while Dranus turned his horse and squinted, looking from stone column to column for some sign of movement. Mingled in with the swirling screams of the Sands he thought he heard another voice. Did it call to him? Was it another manifestation of the Sands? Or was it the Warrior where The Ultimate had said she would be?

"Form defensive ranks and tell the men to be on guard for anything." The hand which had held his lover's moved to the pouch at his belt holding King Baklar's sorcerous stone.

"We have been found at last."

# Chapter 35
## Eclipse

After a brief relay of orders, shouted over the sporadic roar of the desert, the Varz army tightened around their center with those on the outer edges holding large shields and those in the center with their weapons pointed upwards. This way there would be no room for the little teleporter to jump in, kill someone, and jump out. She would have to attack from above and would meet only a ceiling of blades. This way his army would be safe while he dealt with her personally.

He hoped.

Though he respected her power, she was an assassin who wielded daggers; she had to get in close to fight and the closer she got to Dranus the easier it would be for him to seize her powers.

He surveyed the tops of the columns with his sorcerous sight, looking for signs of the slightest movement. It was because he focused on such intricate detail that he almost missed the pronounced figure standing proud some distance away, capping the most monolithic of the stone columns.

From that distance Dranus could not see the girl very clearly but somehow he felt the heat of her stare like the glaring rays of the sun. This was all the sign he needed. Turning to make sure his force was prepared and that Raven was also on her guard, he removed the pouch which held the Stone of Pyrán's Plight from his belt.

He hesitated at the moment when the incessant screams of the desert were pierced by a ravenous shout of intense grief and anger. The noise was hushed and irritatingly distant at first, as though he only listened to the fading echo of her cries.

Then like a sonic boom the yell exploded from the shimmering Warrior of the Sun bursting into existence next to him like a supernova, hanging in the air long enough to kick the pouch from his hand. She fell for a moment, evidently expecting to immediately teleport away. As Dranus looked around and recovered from the unexpected blast of noise he cursed himself that he had been caught off guard so easily. There was no sign of the young girl.

Frustrated by this setback he drew the Sword of Righted Guard. Had she been more aggressive she might have killed him before the fight even began! Now that his sword was drawn, she had no chance of landing a blow. Dranus looked about, sweeping the area for her location and preparing himself for the next attack. He felt the Sword tug at his grip as if it actively sought the next attack.

The strike came quickly from his right, and the Sword reacted with speed to match. It blocked the strike and easily knocked back the small weight of the enemy's blade. Her greatest strength as an assassin was her greatest weakness in a one-on-one duel; she was small and often struck from the air. The Sword of Righted Guard's strength was more than enough to knock her from any stance so that she could not use her speed to attack sequentially with her twin blades.

Another pause of silence drew tension around Dranus like a cloak. His eyes darted all around hoping that he might catch a glimpse of her and not just let his sword do all the work. The second his eyes strayed to the pouch that lay in the sand another attack was upon him, coming head on in front of him, but before she reached him she disappeared again! Only to reappear at the same trajectory but behind him!

The Sword of Righted Guard reacted faster than Dranus could think, and he felt tearing strain on his arm as the sword flung over his head to parry the blow to his back. He turned his horse trying to get a bearing on her, but the sand made it too difficult to maneuver, his reactions would be needed if he hoped to keep the Sword from breaking his arm.

"Mage Corps, the Aresona transformation!" As soon as the command was heard the focused few of the Mage Corps set to the complex task of turning the shifting tides of sand in the area into hard, stable footing. But he could barely get the words out before another flurry of attacks came at him in rapid succession from different angles. She was learning, using the force of her being thrown backwards to increase a forward strike on his opposite side. A few bouts of this sequence were all that a skilled warrior such as Dranus needed to adapt to the style.

Ignoring what his eyes saw he held his sword forward to deflect attacks and in a steady cadence turned with his shield to block the second attack.

Eventually she realized she was getting nowhere and stopped for a few moments. Dranus took this time to dismount and send his horse away. He stood on ground held firm by the Mage Corps' spell and took a defensive stance. He heard a call from Raven behind him but paid it no heed, his attention must ever be on this life-or-death dance of blades.

It could have been the tension and the adrenaline from repeatedly stepping in and out of the shadow of Death, but when he heard that next cry of despair it washed over him like a powerful wave. It was tinged with sorrow and disdain, a sense of impotence and frustration. It was a call that heralded a shining golden light from atop the nearest stone column. Her silver armor turned red hot and was quickly dispelled from the lithe body of the Sun Warrior. The exposed mess of weathered rags and tanned skin glowed even more brightly than the polished silver of her armor!

He spun to see what would happen, expecting some attack on his men. Instead came a whirlwind of rapid attacks that seemed to come from every direction at once! His sword moved more than two steps ahead of the king, pulling him this way and that. What little he could see before was worsened by the light from the Warrior. He had only the faint impression of light zipping around him as he grew weary and dizzy from the jerking motions. His sword arm had already been jerked painfully out of its socket, but ironically this actually allowed the Sword to move more deftly.

For a moment he dreamed that he saw the torn face of the young girl screaming, her features rippling with rage, her eyes radiating a holy golden light. He could not continue this way and survive!

As if sensing his desperation, her movements increased in speed until he felt a nick on his arm, then another on his other arm, a scratch on his face, at once he felt three shallow wounds! Even to his eyes, which saw things no other might see there appeared to be three of the Warrior flashing about! Could she be moving so fast as to appear in three places at once?! Or, could it be that she actually *was* in three places at once? The sun completely covered this vast expanse of desert...could she too be everywhere at once? Was such a thing possible?

He had no time to muse about this conundrum as he focused on defending himself. Even against the once-thought impenetrable defense of the Sword of Righted Guard she scored minor hits through padding and on the rare bit of exposed flesh in his light desert armor! Such speed, such power! Even after several encounters, the powers that these Warriors wielded was beyond Dranus's most absurd expectations!

The cuts he took grew deeper and surer though his sword and shield protected his vital points. His legs were weakening from the constant flailing about and the many cuts too difficult to block even for the sorcerous sword. The girl must have discovered by then that she could cut him without a counterattack, but clearly, and thankfully, that form took its toll.

The barrage ceased just as Dranus thought his body would give out from all of the strain. Then she appeared standing in front of him several yards away, breathing heavily. He couldn't stand to look straight at her from all of the golden light shimmering across the sands. But that holy light was tainted somewhat by the seething hatred that poured from bared teeth and teary eyes.

"Why won't you just die?!" When she yelled the light pulsed; not even his closed eyelids could keep the light out! "You're supposed to die! The legend said if we stood against you, you would fall! He said we couldn't lose!" Her leg twitched slightly, and the light waned for just a moment. Her fists were clenched around two ornate daggers that reflected the brilliant light of the Warrior.

"You're so evil! And...and wasn't it our destiny to stop you?!" She shouted at Dranus, the source of all her sorrow. "You killed all of those people at Medi! All of the soldiers! You killed my friends!" Tears streamed down her face. "You killed Teego, Voradore, Raven," her voice turned to a guttural growl, "you killed my Leon! How can you not die?! You deserve to die!"

Dranus was stunned, speechless. Never had someone put such emotion into their words...she was elegant in her tragedy, he thought. Truly this must be the most beautiful moment of her life. Unfortunately for her, he knew it was not his Fate to die here.

Still, he could only stare back with a blank expression, his sword arm hanging limp by his side. But again, the light that came from her faded as her leg began to give out.

To neither of their fortunes, another figure ran up from behind Dranus, a massive three-pronged weapon in her hands. She had seen the trouble Dranus was having and rushed to assist. The Warrior Olette appeared to have just noticed that one of her enemies, clad in traditional Varz armor, was none other than her former ally.

"Raven...you're alive!" No hope or clarity of soul emerged with these words. The young girl seemed to surmise the situation very quickly. The armor, the position, the eyes...she wasn't killed...she betrayed them!

"If I can't kill him..." and this was almost a whisper "...then I'll kill you! Traitor!" Desperate passion was the only thing that could fuel such a charge. Dranus watched closely, the wince of her face with each step not wasted on his trained gaze. She did not teleport. Was there some time limit to that form she had taken? Or was it simply that her body could no longer bear such strain? He realized, watching her charge towards his love, that the leg giving way was the foot she pivoted with.

"Incredible power wasted on the unskilled." He muttered under his breath.

Raven, having sharpened her skill even further but unwilling to kill her former friend, held the girl at bay. She struck high with the head of the trident, but Olette ducked low, springing upward at Raven's throat. A quick sidestep and downward swipe of her trident from the side pushed the Warrior of the Sun off balance. Holding the trident at full length she tried to keep distance between them.

This was to no avail, however, as the sandy haired girl's glowing light pulsed with anger. But while she flashed around the area with great agility, her attacks were sluggish and forced. Raven, who was as keen a fighter as any and not tired from battle, reacted to the attacks with the most subtle of movements, the length of defense that her long trident afforded her was far more effective in warding off attacks from different directions. A tranquil calm surrounded her, and the ripples of the Sun Warrior lost all force when finding her, like an arrow into water. She dodged and replied with strikes of her own, but only with the pole end or flat of her weapon.

Dranus had almost been too mesmerized by Raven's skill and the way she unintentionally embarrassed her opponent to remember the Stone of Pyrán's Plight. He ran to find it among the dirt and took the stone from its pouch. It pulsed with streaks of violet, blue, green, white, and black, having taken more from the lifeless bodies of the Warriors of Wind and Lightning. Like a task he had done every day since he was a child, he conceived falsehoods as facts and manipulated reality in his mind until his outline became hazy, and he faded into the hot sands. Only the movement of dust kicked up by his footsteps on the hardened ground betrayed his presence.

Olette clearly couldn't keep up the fight anymore, she had been fueled only by her rage thus far and even that faded with the devastating blow that was her dear friend's betrayal. She threw one of her daggers at the woman she had once trusted like a sister. Now she was just a soul as foul and blackened as the dark King of Varz, himself.

Raven didn't even bother to move as the blade fell short. Her black eyes were full of pity and fear, her normally steady hand trembled with uncertainty. She wanted to plead with her former comrade to join them, but she knew her words would fall on ears made deaf with insensate rage.

Dranus had taken the necessary movements to put himself in a favorable position. He stared at the young girl whose chest heaved with each labored breath. Her impassioned words rang in his mind.

He saw it in her eyes; he saw the final assault build within the Warrior. With nothing left, cheated by Fate, her anger was ready to flood out into the world in a last chance to exact some twisted form of revenge.

There! The girl burst with a final flash of sunlight, blazing forward at full speed. She raised her last dagger high over her head and pointed it down like a scorpion's tail at Raven. The Varz woman held her trident straight ahead of her in both hands. She waited to swing it left or right to deflect an attack from anywhere but in front of her, knowing that brilliant light signaled an incoming teleportation.

Dranus simply held forward the Stone of Pyrán's Plight before him as the girl rushed past him. A look of confusion blossomed on her features at the invisible thing her raised arm had hit.

That same look of disbelief and shock was reflected on the former Warrior of Water's features as the triple prongs of her trident pierced rags and skin like placid water. The little desert assassin shook violently from the shock, her final choked coughs muddled with blood. Skewered like a piece of meat she struggled to speak one last time.

"Are...you...happy...?" She wore a scowl to the end.

Then, among the roaring desert, the Warrior of the Sun slumped over on the pole, dead.

It was some dark force from within Raven's heart that prompted a shuttering "Yes" from the budding woman of Varz. But it was too much too soon.

Something within her broke at the realization of what she had done...what she had been forced to do. Her instinct at sorcery responded quickly, encasing those feelings in a cage of ice that numbed the onrush of emotional anguish.

She stood trembling for several moments, having dropped the trident almost immediately. The Warrior of the Sun fell to her knees, though she was held up by the weapon that pierced her chest. Raven's hollow stare and quivering lips struck her dumb for several moments as the last few seconds played back in her mind in super slow motion. What had happened? Why didn't she teleport? Why didn't she dodge? What had she done?

*What had she done?!*

Dranus emerged from the nothingness he hid in, carrying the Stone which now showed a brilliant golden light that shined brighter than all the rest. His brow was furrowed, and he stared down at the stone. The winds of the Screaming Sands whipped ever onward, and it sounded as though a new voice had been added to the furious choir. Was it the echo of the Warrior's cries? He looked up at the glaring sun overhead.

"Were it that her passion had reached me...." He spoke quietly, swimming in a mix of emotions. He reflected on all the Warrior had said as he mentally cowered from the look of disbelief and grief on his lover's face. Had she been right? Did he deserve to die for his crimes? To have committed such foul atrocities and still relentlessly march against those enemies that remained...would Fate eventually punish him for these transgressions?

A wayward wisp of a cloud drifted along and eclipsed the sun momentarily, casting a slender shadow across the trio.

It was a fitting end.

*     *     *

The days that followed were plagued by memories. Raven was inconsolable after what she had done. She was like a fierce mother bear backed into a corner protecting her young; she would not let anyone so much as approach the corpse of her former friend. She had slumped down herself to look into the dead eyes and whisper some sorrowful words.

After that, Raven became distant. She refused to speak with anyone, especially Dranus. She had her own tent erected and refused her lessons.

Dranus, too, was haunted by the screams of the girl whose tragic death he had brought about. Every shout from the whirling sands sounded more and more like the cries of contempt she had leveled at him. He felt his mind ebb back to the depression he had once known so well in the absence of his lover. His body, too, was healing from the wounds he received in the fight and contributed to his lethargic mood. Now that he was so close to his goal, could he fall apart so easily at the maddened dribble of a Warrior who had lost even her pride?

Eventually, the Varz army approached the gates of Urhyll under the flag of armistice. King Dranus and his men paraded the body of the fallen Warrior of the Sun through the city to the High Hall. Though he knew it was what his ancestors would have done and what he should do, he couldn't help but feel soured by the experience.

Regardless, when he met with Superior Frau he was the strong and resolute King of Varz and nothing less. He placed his heavy boot upon the kneeled head of the broken man and demanded their surrender. There was nothing left for the Urhyllians without their Warrior. Though Dranus expected some rebellion from the city that was known for its assassins and mercenaries, he knew that in time they would be flushed out and silenced.

Fortunately, Urhyll was dominated by the Screaming Sands and so held few actual cities. These were focused at the edge of the peninsula near the coast. It would be a simple matter to have them watched from the capital.

A proper burial was allowed for Olette at Raven's behest, but Raven did not attend.

The sun, source of all light in the world and standard for every bright possibility in the Five Realms, had been slain. Surely darkness would devour the continent, leading to eternal night.

But a single shining light remained for the Lessers; a final glimmer of hope among a people consumed by despair. It was that final possibility that stood in the Crystal Tower of Myrendel, looking out over all those he knew he must protect.

There was just one left: the First Warrior of Pyrán.

# Chapter 36
## The Crimson Eyes of a Devil

Two moons passed since the addition of Urhyll to the Varz empire.

In the home realm, the people were in a vivacious frenzy, having rediscovered what it is to truly live as a citizen of Varz. Young men and women were pledging to join the armed forces daily, hoping to contribute to the success of their nation's rise.

The cities were afire with uncontrollable inspiration. In a matter of days, a new tower would be erected, a new statue built, each more beautiful and elegant than the last! Production of goods had never been higher and the prosperity of Varz overflowed into its new territories. The realm's greatest builders and architects poured into Shiera and Arendrum, renovating High Halls and important locales to suit the tastes of a Varz ruler.

And though the Lessers feared those of Varz like a plague, they found that their lives had become surprisingly peaceful once again. All of the rapacious behaviors they had come to expect from the rascals of Varz were nowhere to be seen and the implementation of Varz culture was more adaptive to their own rather than replacing what had been there. The leaders of Varz were nothing if not practical; they wanted the world to know that these realms belonged to the one and only King of Varz, but they had no need to tear down whole cities only to build new ones. Their ancestors wished for supremacy by eliminating all competition. The modern folk of Varz knew they had no competition when it came to superiority, so control was sufficient.

Still, the problems were not in re-imagining the Lesser cities, but in the integration of the multiple societies. While Varz influence brought some enhancements to the Lesser Realms, the people of these realms were resistant to the kind of change Varz brought. Likewise, the majority of Varz citizens did not dare sully themselves by intermingling with the Lesser Folk. There were a few of the Varz citizenry eager to mingle with the new peoples of their empire. Those in kind with the late Deleron Kaxus, who had once spouted hopes of a Varz nation living in tandem with the Lessers, were the first to move to the captured capitals and offer friendship to the conquered folk. It was a begrudging step forward at best, but it was a step forward, nonetheless.

Meanwhile, Dranus and Raven had elected to stay in Urhyll for the time being while Armodus oversaw military placements from Varz. Their relationship had taken several blows from their battle with the Warrior of the Sun, but they mended quickly. With the busy days and lazy nights, the pair pressed the memories from their hearts and filled the space with each other's love.

After a few weeks of rigorous work setting up the new provincial government, the city became a welcomed retreat for the budding couple. Dranus had never enjoyed someone's company as much as he enjoyed his young love's. Their lust for each other was unmatched, but their lust was not so shallow as to be contained by simple carnal needs. They spent hours in the courtyard discussing politics and philosophy, enraptured by each other's mind. As she had shown herself a true woman of Varz in battle and sorcery, Raven also proved to be of sound mind and reasoning, a trait that had originally attracted him to her. They discussed how best Dranus might integrate Varz culture into those of the Four Realms with the least resistance and her council was as true as it was wise. There were occasions when he got the idea that she might make a better queen than he made king...but that was mere insecurity and a Varz monarch had no need for such things.

Contentment was nearly his, and yet something lingered in the recesses of his mind. It barred his way to fully enjoying the life he had made with Raven. So long as Myrendel stood against him, and the Warrior of Fire still lived, he could not rest easy. The truth was that a powerful enemy remained that threatened all he had built, and Dranus himself did not know just how true this was.

Inevitably, another mysterious letter came to the king's desk. It was Raven who handed him the letter, wringing her hands with downcast eyes.

The envelope bore a seal in the shape of a solitary flame in red wax.

Somehow Raven took significance from this seal that Dranus

could not understand, though he guessed it easily enough.

> King Dranus of Varz, it is time for us to end all of this. I
> challenge you to a duel to the death to decide the fate of my
> realm. If you accept, then you may march your army to
> Myrendel where I will await you. You may bring whatever
> trickery you desire so long as you face me alone. If I fall, then
> Myrendel is yours.

The letter was signed again with a calligraphic fire emblem and
Dranus needed no more clues to surmise who had written the letter.
The Warrior of Fire had challenged him to a duel of honor and his
Varz pride would not allow him to refuse.

He stood abruptly from his chair, his palm down over the letter.
The Warrior had made no specifications as to what happened if he
lost, but perhaps there was no need for such a thing. Without their
king and no rightful heir, the times would be ripe for rebellion led by
the Warrior of Fire, and the boy had already shown he could destroy
an entire army in an instant.

The stakes were high: complete control or total collapse.

"Raven, return to Varz in the morning. I will not have you watch
another of your former comrades die by my hand." His head was
bowed, staring at the letter and all it signified.

"No! Dranus please don't go! Don't fight him!" She grabbed his
arm with both hands and pleaded with watering eyes. He was firm,
resisting his reflex to throw her off.

"It does not matter what you say Raven, I am sorry but the
Warrior of Fire must fall for my empire to be completed." She
muffled a small sob in his sleeve then looked up again, trying to
contain her emotions.

"No, it's not him I'm worried about...it's you. You are powerful
but...but Keine is more powerful still!"

What?! What nonsense was this? Did she truly believe that he
would fall to a single remaining Warrior when he held the Stone of
Pyran's Plight and the Sword of Righted Guard?

"More powerful than I?! How can you believe such a thing?!"
Now he did wrest his arm free from her grasp, disgusted at her lack
of faith in him.

"Keine is not a better fighter than I. He is not as quick as Olette, he does not control his element as well as Teego, he does not lead as well as Leon, and he is not nearly as brilliant as Voradore." These names were unfamiliar to the king, but he guessed they were the names of the deceased Warriors of Pyrán with Keine being the last remaining.

"And yet I have defeated all of those in turn, more than once in one-on-one combat! What could I possibly have to fear from this weakling?!" He turned his back, anger filled him and flared from his nostrils. His body was rigid and tense, his Varz pride urging him to action.

"Keine is the First Warrior of Pyrán and the rightful leader, have you never wondered what makes him worthy of this title?" The thought had never, in fact, occurred to him though he was mostly unfamiliar with the ways of the Warriors.

"He is an archer, is he not? Is it his skill with the bow?"

At this Raven let out a contrived chuckle. "When we first met, he could barely string a bow, and he has not grown so much since then."

"Then what?! What is it that I must fear?!" He threw his arms into the air flailing about in frustration.

"I don't know how to describe it. You've seen when we tap into our powers and glow light from our bodies. When this happens to Keine he...he changes. At the Battle of the Rift, it took the remaining five of us to calm him down after the fighting stopped! He is practically unstoppable in that state!" All at once memories he had tried to forget came flooding back to his mind's eye; scenes of the holocaust at the Battle of the Rift, images of towering terrors of whirling flames baring down on him at Medi. He recalled a rumor that one of his camps had been savagely slaughtered and set to flame by a single enemy! Was it true, then, that this Warrior posed more of a threat than he had planned?

"Unstoppable, you say?" He paced about the room, considering all that he had at his disposal. Raven's experience was credible intel, but none of these instances seemed evidence enough to stop him.

Dranus halted abruptly in front of her, his finger shaking as he pointed at her. "We will see which of us is unstoppable! He must have already used the Shield of Second Life to escape the Ultima spell!" He stomped away, speaking under his breath. "And I have my final trump to play still." He hustled from the room with Raven close at his heels.

Raven knew nothing of the shield he referred to, but there was much he kept from her. She chased him, though dared not touch him again.

"If you go to fight him then you go to your death!" Her stare was hard through the tears, there was no doubt she believed what she said deep within her heart.

Dranus played out multiple scenarios in his mind, ignoring her words and picturing how the fight might go. It was true that he had a single trump card remaining, something he had only been able to perfect in secret in the last two months of peace. It was his greatest weapon against the Warrior of Pyrán and he knew that it would lead him to victory.

This choice was simple. He knew that he must face this challenge or lose all faith from his people. It was fitting that the leader of the last hope of the Lesser Realms might face off against the 'Wicked King' in a final decisive duel. But still, there was some part of him which held doubt...Raven was a genius of a warrior, a natural at sorcery, and yet the thought of him facing this Warrior of Fire had brought her to tears at the prospect of what she assumed was his imminent death.

In Varz, however, there was no room for doubt. Dranus shook it from his mind, willing it away as he might close a door to the inner sanctum of his mind.

"Then to my death I must go."

*     *     *

As the Dawn Season neared its end and the Day Season returned to prominence, the Varz army crossed the border between Urhyll and Myrendel. Across the Trias river they marched until they reached Lake Hyacinthus, tribute to the founder of Myrendel. It was said that if one looked into the calm waters of this lake that they could see their true self, an image of what lie beneath the skin.

When King Dranus, sorcerous tyrant of Varz stared into the clear cool waters he thought that he saw a grinning Devil staring back with eyes as black as night. It was a good omen and a fitting effigy, he thought with a matching grin.

Behind the king camped some eight thousand Varz soldiers, more than twice than even the most generous estimates of the enemy's strength. But the only Varz warrior that would fight that day was Dranus and he wanted as many of his forces as possible to witness this final triumph.

So it was that King Dranus advanced on to the pressed dirt roadway that led up to the walls of Myrendel, a huge bronze gate looming in the distance. At the foot of this gate was a single warrior clad in dazzling silver armor, his helmet removed and a sturdy bow in his grasp.

Raven had warned him of the boy's glowing eyes, the likes of which signaled a pronunciation in their elemental powers. From that distance it appeared no light came yet. If he could defeat him quickly, before he activated his full power, he could make this the easiest of his battles. He smiled in confidence to himself.

Dranus was dressed in the armor of kings: the complicated black plating that his ancestors had worn for generations, preserved by magical means over centuries. Built into the helm was a spiked crown showing his position as King of Varz. The metal shoulders of his armor were trimmed with sharp barbs and there were thin blades in rings around the side of his arms. For the monarchs of Varz this armor had been as much a weapon as it was a shield. In his left hand he held a circular shield of black plating, the symbol of Varz emblazoned on the front in subtle violet. In his right hand was the sword of King Vulcan, the Sword of Righted Guard which held perfect guard from attackers. At his waist was the Stone of Pyrán's Plight, his gift from The Ultimate himself and the final key to his victory against the Warrior of Fire.

The Stone glowed a pearlescent rainbow, missing only one final color.

Of the various magical properties of the equipment he wore, the most important was the odd feature of his armor which made it seem as though he wore no armor at all. This armor had been passed down through hundreds of years, with monarchs adding persistent enchantments to it with delicate expertise. The number of unique properties it carried were almost uncountable. It would absorb blows gradually and dissipate force. It would cast mirages of sword swings to throw off an enemy. It could even resist the armor melting sword-spell that he'd used in previous battles.

Dranus could move with all the strength of an unencumbered

fighter and with all the knowledge that the Forbidden Texts provided him. The Texts were meant to solidify the king in his power as a fighter so that none might challenge him. There was no better test for him than a duel. His eyes would be sharper, his swings stronger, his legs faster, his body resistant to pain or injury. He could shear through armor like silk and paralyze flesh with a single touch. It was the first time he had ever invoked so many of the forbidden spells at once and yet his strength was high with anticipation for a bloody battle.

Recounting all of his advantages like this reminded him that Raven could not have known of many of these factors. It was rare for him to use any of such spells as the sorcerous load was heavy, he would spend many weeks recovering before he could tend to his newly conquered realm.

King Dranus stopped a good distance from the Warrior and focused his eyes on the boy. He was not muscular or fit and he was not tall or stout; he was average in every way.

However, his voice carried the full distance and filled the king with renewed doubt. While he had expected some brave and defiant voice from the boy, what came from his lips was soft and light. It was deceptively tender, and yet there was a decided ferocity that backed the words.

It was the voice of a woman. It spoke an ancient tongue long since forgotten by all but the kings and queens of Varz.

"King Dranus, you have raised the fallen banner of your ancestors against the Four Realms when we had finally reached balance. For this you must be punished." The woman's voice rang unnaturally from the boy.

Dranus could barely keep up with the complex speech patterns he had learned as a matter of course for a Varz monarch. "You share many things with Baklar, but you must realize that you cannot hope to match the strength which forged his legacy."

Clarity came to the king over many moments of disbelief, discovery, and horror. He could never have heard the voice before and yet it held a certain familiarity he could not place, as the ruins of Pyrán had. With clarity came despair, for Dranus understood, then, that he spoke with the original Guardian of Pyrán, the one King Baklar had defeated over one thousand years prior. Or at least some incarnation of the woman.

Finally, all of Raven's warnings became too real, too fresh in his mind.

"Prepare yourself for death." The words were not a threat, they were an execution order. They held such immense power, such gravity that he felt weakened by their very sound!

But how?! The eyes did not glow! He appeared normal! Maintaining his control, trying to believe that this was a simple ruse and nothing more, he focused his mind to see a clearer image of the boy's face.

He locked his black orbs with those that stared back at him…and gazed into white irises steady in a pool of deep crimson.

His heart sank, his courage fled, his very existence felt strained as if his mind fought constantly to maintain itself as a reality of the world in which it existed.

"The Devil's Eyes…." Just saying the words threatened to drive away his sanity.

The Guardian moved like an enigma, drifting from one style to the next with seamless efficiency. Around her rose flames as if drawn from the earth, the winds obeyed her bidding, the earth churned beneath her, puddles of moisture formed in the air above her head, and her whole body sparked with electric arcs across her luminescent armor. She shouldered her bow and pressed a gloved hand to the ground, pulling out of the earth a large sword with a gray moon-like crescent as its blade. It was worse than Raven could have known.

Was it the Eyes that allowed the Warrior of Fire to control all of the elements with such apparent ease? Or was it the Eyes that channeled the Guardian's spirit? The power of the Devil's Eyes was unmatched; all was possible.

She vanished, leaving hardly a wisp of smoke behind and Dranus braced himself for death. Four arrows came all at once from above and his reactions were just quick enough to block them with his shield which immediately burst into hungry flames, melting the black iron as it burned. He cast off the shield with a shout and stepped away from it.

The earth shifted beneath his feet, and he was only able to hop away as the ground split, threatening to swallow him whole. A flying shard of ice came from his rear and the sword of his ancestors managed to knock it aside while putting immense strain on his arm. Were it not for his armor, the arm would have broken there, and the battle would be over.

A strong wind blew Dranus off of his feet, even in his heavy armor; the hair that fell out of his helmet stung his face as it whipped about.

He quickly regained his footing as the ground opened again. Now he was running, moving by instinct and sorcerer's intuition. Lightning struck in thin bolts all about him. He moved in predicted patterns, guessing where the bolts would strike and avoiding them enough to escape death, but not without losing feeling in his limbs on more than one occasion.

After surviving this initial onslaught, he regained some knowledge of himself. He was still King of Varz and he still held one card yet to be played.

The Guardian appeared in front of him. "You are not without skill, Dranus, but be assured that you will die here." The movements of the Guardian only hinted at those he had seen from the Warriors. The body moved and yet it seemed to stay still. The slashing sword the Guardian carried moved in white blurs though the wielder appeared to stand still! The posture was relaxed and fluid: the movements of a master swordswoman.

A quick bolt of lightning came down on him and instinctively he stabbed his sword into the ground, channeling the energy into the earth. The blast was intense, but the old armor of his forefathers held strong even against such powerful magic. Still, he could not continue dodging deadly bolts from the sky and hope to form any offensive attack, this way he could partially ignore the lightning and focus on a newly formed strategy.

Arrows of fire from his front made him stumble back in a bent line, his sword dragging along in the dirt. Ice shards from the back forced him forward in a mirrored line. A pressing wind attempted to slam him into earthen spikes springing from the ground. Dranus relied on generations of instinct and moved with the slightest alterations of his form, not fighting the wind as it passed over his bowed back. He used the extra force to dive over the bed of spikes and rolled forward towards the Guardian.

Lifting the Sword of Righted Guard from the ground he stabbed and sliced with stunning efficiency. But the Guardian made the gentlest movements with the boy's body so that his strikes were always close but never found a hold, the mirages might as well have been invisible.

A bemused smile was stuck to the Guardian's face; she mocked him. An enraged downward strike with both of his hands had Dranus slicing through thin air, the tip of his sword cracking against the ground where the Guardian had been.

He turned and sprinted in an arc away from the bronze gate, anticipating another elemental barrage. He came face to face with a massive, raised wall of earth which threated to crush him where he stood. It was far too wide for him to get around. His mind was sharp and came to understand the world in a different light as suddenly as the slab fell. With the palm of his hand, he smacked the solid earth. A small passage turned soft and fell away from the hard rock. The rest fell harmlessly about him on all sides as he ducked into the small hole he had made. He could not control the earth, but he could alter its properties as he had done with the water at the Castle Beneath the Waves!

Quickly he sliced his sword back into the dirt and continued on his course, cringing as more electric energy pulsed through him and into the ground. Tall flames erupted in a circle around him, the inferno amplified by the heat of the Day Season. He did not stop; he only held his armored hand over his face and charged through the flames. The fire licked at his exposed face, but his armor held most of the heat at bay. If she could encircle him in flame, she could create a field of flame with him at the center. He had to remember that this Guardian had been of the same era as The Ultimate and the founding of Varz. Those with power gained cruelty and those who were cruel gained power. This apparently applied to The Guardian as well.

She was enjoying this far too much.

His armor must repel some of the concentrated magic or at least dissipate it, but it was still concerning that the full might that The Ultimate had described did not immediately smite him. Perhaps inhabiting this boy's body restricted her power, even with the Devil's Eyes!

Dranus continued his arc, his sword still scarring the dirt.

With rapid movements of his eyes, he stared back at where he began the fight. Then from all directions came projectiles of every element like a closing noose. With a valiant cry the king stopped and stabbed his sword into the ground. He pressed outward with both hands and a cylindrical barrier of glowing green held around him. He held more with his mind than with his hands against the force of the elements until they lost their intense momentum.

The Guardian blinked from place to place with the power of the Sun, always floating above him and looking down with a soft smile of secret pleasure.

The earth lurched once again and flung the king into the air only to be slammed back onto the ground by a vengeful gust. He had lost his breath but could not stop, pure desperation drove him to continue. He rolled along the ground to dodge several vicious cracks of lightning and leapt to his feet with an unnaturally strong push at the ground, searching frantically for his mark in the sand. Again, he planted the tip of his blade into the dirt where it had stopped and completed his semi-circle with everything he had left.

The Guardian paused again in front of Dranus, her back to the bronze gate. Wreathed in the radiant light of the sun her boyish grin had changed to a frown.

"You still fight?" She asked from a place ten feet in the air.

Dranus did not reply. He was down on one knee breathing heavily and trying to regain some strength.

"Don't believe that Stone will help you like it did Baklar. I will not be felled by the same cowardly trick again.

Dranus's energy waned, and his pace slackened as he charged forward. He knew that he could not keep running and dodging like this forever. His body ached from blunted blows and his face stung from burns; his limbs were numb from the static charges that flowed through him.

He stopped a measured distance from the Guardian, trying to catch his breath. Just a little further....

Suddenly, the winds surged all around him and cut his face like razors. He brought his arms up to guard but as he did the furious gusts ceased.

He looked around, puzzled, before noticing that all of his work had been for nothing. The rune he was drawing...The Ultimate's last gift and his final hope against the Guardian, had been scattered by the powerful winds.

"Don't think you can draw a rune beneath my nose and I won't notice," she said with apparent disgust. "You are just a mortal; I am *made* of magic!"

When he looked up, he was surrounded by a bubble of floating water that engulfed him and drenched him through. He held his breath as best he could, but his suffering was not yet finished.

A thunderous crack sounded, and a web of lightning stabbed the water.

Dranus's scream was muted in the water, his eyes wide, the intense pain of every nerve in his body being overloaded by electricity was unlike anything he had ever experienced.

He was dying.

The bubble dropped him, sputtering, gasping for breath into a strong gust that threw him like a rag doll over the dirt. His mind was afire with despair even as his senses were starting to fade. His last gambit had failed. Without the rune to channel the Stone's power, he would never get close enough to use it.

The Guardian's laugh was callous and cruel. "You are resilient King of Varz! Baklar would be proud of you!" A final consolation for the dying king.

He stumbled through the dirt with sword in hand until a claw of rock emerged from beside him and with a cacophonous creak of bending metal it crushed his sword arm, armor and all.

He screamed even as his armor reflexively dulled the pain, but the Sword of Righted Guard had fallen.

All he could do was wait for the finishing....

"Giving up already, master?" the familiar but almost forgotten voice of the Book of Fate's Desire echoed from within his chest plate. Suddenly it was in his remaining good hand.

There was still a way.

He flung himself over with the Book beneath him, its pages open and blank. As much as he had disdained the thought of his Fate being controlled by the sorcerous tome, it was ironically now up to the Book's whims of cooperation if he lived or died.

If he was victorious or not.

Complete control or total collapse.

"At least give me a clean death by your own blade!" Dranus shouted in a challenge.

In a burst of sunlight, the Guardian appeared several yards away, her crescent sword in hand.

"You think me so foolish?" The Guardian's voice was dry and without humor, just as the sands around them.

The heat from the sun was draining and the stunned silence of his gathered armed forces constantly reminded Dranus of the stakes of this duel. Dranus could smell the sweat from his body and the smell of burnt hair. His tongue was dry and his lips cracked as he spoke.

"Then from above," he croaked.

The Guardian seemed to consider this for a moment. If she truly was like the originators of Varz, she would have cruelty, but ultimately martial honor would compel her to accept this request.

Calculations upon calculations flashed upon the Guardians eyes before she said, "On your hands and knees, then. Head down. Eyes closed."

Eyes closed.

Varz sorcery was channeled primarily through the eyes. Could he do it sightlessly?

Dranus's pride roared in defiance as he slowly, painfully, prostrated himself in front of the Guardian, the Book of Fate's Desire just beneath him, the Stone at his waist.

It was the subtle sorcery restricted to the use of Varz monarchs that altered the smallest patch of air above him, hiding the hand that unstrung the Stone and let it fall atop the pages of the Book. Then, he closed his eyes.

Immediately after his eyes had closed, he felt the strong updrafts that no-doubt kept the Guardian suspended in the air above him.

He could not see if the rune had appeared on the Book's pages. It knew what he was planning, they had practiced this spell together many times and the rustling words it spoke before had to be aimed at reminding him of this.

The Book decided who fell this day.

"It's time, King of Varz." She said solemnly. "And let this be a warning to all you of Varz. Rise again and I will return to put you back in the ground!" Her words projected with sorcery to every man and woman of the standing Varz army. Even if they had wanted to interfere, they were every one of them frightened to their cores.

While the Guardian threatened his folk, Dranus let his consciousness flourish.

Swimming through oceans of self-deceit, flying through skies filled with clouds of ill logic, sprinting through forests in which every blade of grass represented a possible reality went his sorcerer's soul. Through all the loops and cutbacks of reasoning and with all the trappings of ancient philosophies it sought a single answer. There was an endless plane of truths and falsehoods surrounding him in every direction. Perpendicular to this plane was where sorcery lived.

In this final understanding of bygone sorcery Dranus felt for a moment that he glimpsed the entirety of the universe dancing around him in perfect balance. He saw for a brief moment two glowing strands of essence in opposition.

Then he was back from his thousand-year journey through magic and in the shadow of the Guardian once more.

Had it worked?

No light came from beneath him that he could sense. The Book was still. The Guardian was still. Everything was still.

The Stone of Pyrán's Plight stood straight up beneath him, its oblong point pressing him up with uncounterable force.

Dranus opened his eyes just in time to see the Stone spin and come alive.

A wave of energy erupted from beneath him as the veins of color representing the former Warriors' powers detached from the stone in long, grasping vines. The vines changed color faster than he could perceive but they moved implacably upward. A single multi-colored vine snatched the sword falling to end the king's life and crushed it back into dirt.

Dranus felt the rubble fall on his back and he rolled over to watch the mayhem.

Sunlight bled from the Guardian towards the golden vine as she tried to blink away. The white and black whips grabbed at her ankles and wrapped themselves several times around her vessel's legs. Blue and green vines like a mountain ridge or a raging river grasped an arm each. A violet arm reached up over her head and split into tens of fingers, grasping at some invisible barrier surrounding the fiercely gnashing Guardian. It pressed and pressed until the intangible substance broke and the purple tendrils encircled the Guardian's head.

The Guardian's cry was one of sound beyond sound. The voice of every descendant of this legendary warrior screamed in existential grief at the same time. The inharmonious blending threatened the very existence of their world.

But the Stone had already begun its work, sapping power from the Guardian until each tendril bled with crimson. Eventually, the hungry hands of the spell were satiated and they withdrew languidly like a hound made weary with a feast.

The ensuing silence was broken by the heavy thud of an armored body falling to the earth and the bone-breaking crack that must come with such a fall.

Dranus lay next to the Stone, now pulsing with a vein of red completing the pattern on its surface. He couldn't even raise his head to look and see if the body that had fallen still moved. He heard nothing, but that was not a guarantee with sorcery.

Both sets of onlookers were still silent, waiting for one of the two fallen to rise and claim victory.

Only Dranus knew that it was over already.

The Book knew, too.

With a splitting sensation and dizzying whirl in his head, he used the last bit of sorcery he dared summon to heal himself very slightly.

It was enough to stand and to grasp the Stone on his way up.

Murmurs broke from the Varz ranks with excitement that furthered into encouraging cheers.

Dranus stumbled and limped to the fallen body, the Stone outstretched before him just in case, his other arm limp at his side.

The young boy that had been the Warrior of Fire stared blankly; his head angled awkwardly.

Dead from the impact.

He wanted to laugh in raucous glee but the best he could emit was a hoarse chuckle. He raised the Stone in the air triumphantly and turned to his forces which immediately exploded with cheers and shouts and the clanking of armor on shields.

Amid the fanfare, Dranus returned to where the Book of Fate's Desire lay open in the sand. His old friend came through for him in the end.

He stopped and smirked when he saw what page it had landed on. It was one of the very first pages he had ever seen in the Book.

There, the words "I will conquer the Five Realms" were ceremoniously crossed through. Like hundreds before his, Dranus's Fate had been written in the magical pages of the Book and thus came to be.

Like hundreds before his, save one.

Dranus leaned over to pick up the Book, his joints aching and his lungs heaving.

He tucked it safely away in his chest plate again, patted the plate fondly where the Book would be, and collapsed to the ground.

# Chapter 37
## What Fate Desires

" **W**hat does Fate desire?"

The year following the duel with the Warrior of Fire was as simple as nature. Although Dranus did not personally enter Myrendel after the duel, the fall of the last Warrior of Pyrán signaled the end of resistance from the great city. When Armodus met with the Superior of the city, it wasn't clear to him whether the city surrendered as were the terms of the duel or if they simply hoped to avoid more inevitable death. And though some ancient part of all Varz soldiers lamented that they had so few chances to battle, King Dranus was set on not repeating the shortcomings of his ancestors.

Where countless monarchs before him had become apathetic in the cradle of peace, Dranus had great plans to maintain the prosperity of his nation without the need for constant violence. The single beneficial thing that had come from their centuries of detached living was the advancement of technology and its blending with sorcery. In the height of new breath in their culture, it was the time for the people of Varz to create. They would create to forge a unified continent and a united military. And when they reached the peak of their power, they could always set their sails to the West and the North to satisfy their warrior's blood.

After recovering from the duel with the Guardian, Dranus went immediately to sacred Pyrán. He sat with The Ultimate and received his congratulations, curt as they were. Something was amiss in the eyes of the First King. He was, of course, proud of his favored son, but he did not seem completely satisfied. The old king could not sit still and even as Dranus retold his harrowing tale to The Ultimate, the man never let his eyes stray from the pages of the Book of Fate's Desire. In the moments where Dranus could glimpse the words in the Book, he saw the countless pages of Fates transcribed and crossed through. In a moment of great pressure, in which The Ultimate donned the crimson guise of a superior sorcerer, Baklar looked to the book, looked towards the room above him, and then stared hard at Dranus.

When Dranus asked for an explanation of his king's odd behaviors, Baklar blatantly ignored him, whispering 'a page is missing' to himself but at a volume that Dranus could easily hear.

His stay was brief, and he was given no new lessons, spells, or magical items. When he made to leave, he was given instructions never to return to Pyrán unless bade by The Ultimate, himself. As a final gesture, or perhaps test, Baklar posed a final question with sadness in his eyes:

"What does Fate desire?"

In Varz, King Dranus reviewed treatises and books on governing an expansive empire. His doing so as a young heir had been a matter of course as none had really expected that the empire would grow much in their lifetime. Thus, he read through the near limitless source of knowledge that the Book of Fate's Desire provided and focused on the works of the Western leaders, whose empires were known for their longevity. He studied how he might sustain such a large area and distribute advancements, how he might avoid rebellion from subjugated peoples, and how he might keep his power secure with his new subjects.

He even considered attempting to persuade The Ultimate to release the constraints on sorcery to convert the Lessers into true citizens of Varz over time, starting with the most fundamental of aspects. This was, he concluded, a request he could not make without jeopardizing his standing with a powerful ally. For the time being, there would be a clear separation of conquerors and conquered; the Varz herders would let the little sheep have their visions of freedom, but if they moved out of line they would be corrected swiftly. Still, the end goal was a united empire of Varz. A Varz strong enough in numbers to resist the empires of the West should they try to take advantage of the turmoil and one gracious enough to accept the half-formed tribes of the North. Perhaps a few generations down the line his progeny might reintroduce magic into the Five Realms but not until his new empire was whole in spirit.

His plate was ever full with quandaries and conundrums of

politics, economics, or civics. And yet, when his mind wandered from boring meetings and impromptu lectures, it went implacably to the mysterious words of The Ultimate:

"What does Fate desire?"

Dranus and Raven were wed in Varz a few months after his ultimate victory and the union was spoken of in all corners of the world. The message that accompanied the news was simple: even one born a Lesser could elevate themselves to the highest station if they only accepted the rule of Varz. The less simple message intimated the prowess of the couple as legends and myths of their deeds spread through tavern halls, mess decks, and prison cells.

To Dranus's outright glee, the strategic brilliance of their marriage was among the less important reasons they had married so soon.

The two were deeply in love. They spent every waking minute together that they could manage and as Raven developed as a sorcerer, they even made time in their dreams for one another.

Dranus managed his new empire while Raven learned all that was necessary to fill her role as Wife to the King. In this position, *she* was next in line to fill in as acting ruler when Dranus was away, instead of the various members of the War Council. What she could learn, she learned quickly and with outstanding aptitude. What she could only experience, she did at her husband's side with martial ardor.

Raven was truly becoming a model woman of Varz. She continued to hone her skills in fighting as well as more practical sorcerous arts. She took to the traditions, customs, and brews of Varz with zeal. Every day she became more and more the woman Dranus had seen that she could become when he had spoken with her as his captive. Even in the limitless landscape of Dranus's imagination he could not conceive of a woman he could love more.

Several months after their marriage, the couple announced the news that an heir had been conceived! Dranus was unendingly curious at what an heir with separate lines of ancestry leading back to the The Ultimate might be capable of. Their child would be greater in blood than any Varz monarch in recent history.

Dranus awoke energized and slept with content.

And yet, with every smile that he shared with his beloved, every thought of his bright future with her and his child came a familiar echo in the voice of a thousand years:

"What does Fate desire?"

The former capitals of the Lesser Realms had all been transformed into Varz cities in a shift of the wind. Varz technicians and Lesser workers came together to create massive libraries, exquisite schools, and spectacular arenas for entertainment. Forges and quarries sprouted like spring flowers to meet demand and a few critical laws kept trade fair between realms, including Varz. By these projects and many more the Varz Empire flourished, and the seeds of cohabitation were planted.

Still, the people of Varz simply could not accept such a rapid change of perspective. Where Dranus saw new citizens of Varz, others saw tools at best and slaves at worst. While discriminant violence and human trafficking was strictly punished, he could hardly hope to prevent these completely. Cities were still segregated in great lengths, with many a Varz noble laying unequivocal claim to the nicer homes in the cities. However, every now and then there were those few who sought cohesion actively and some of the smaller communities had even chosen desegregation. Those struggling to be accepted as new Varz citizens and those struggling to be accepted as old citizens of a new empire flocked to places like these where real progress was being made. Dranus funneled resources to these havens when he could, baring whatever silent contempt his people may have. At their core, even if the people of Varz did not agree with specific decisions, they trusted that the king had the best interests of Varz at heart. After all, how could they question their great reclaimer?

As time proceeded, there were those new citizens who, like Raven, found themselves curiously confused at the lack of barbarism and brutality in the ways of Varz. Their knowledge and tastes, while somewhat bizarre, were refined and intellectual. Their technology as well as their schools of thought were marvels of science and sorcery alike. It was in the kinship of curious minds deep in the halls of newly founded Dens that the bonds forged were tempered.

This did not mean that the conquered folk had forgotten the heinous crimes committed during the war. On the contrary, there were countless resistance movements that manifested from places as large as the capital city of Myrendel to the smallest of oasis villages in Urhyll. Dranus sought to entice the people he had conquered, but he was still a King of Varz.

And the King of Varz did not tolerate such disrespect. He moved to destroy the larger movements in person, making examples of each faction that rebelled. To do otherwise would be to welcome further uprise.

Yet with every resistance group vanquished, every new symbol of peace erected, and every Lesser heart which he swayed called that singularly unanswered question to mind:

"What does Fate desire?"

He could hear it in his mind, day in and day out, echoing like the constant patter of dripping water in a cave. He heard the question in his dreams where he gave it form and chased it through eons of contemplation. He considered every word, every possible meaning, and every improbable interpretation. He gave it every bit of thought that he could muster but could reach no grand conclusion; each answer fell short. It drove him to consider, as he had done nearly every day since acquiring the Book of Fate's Desire, whether he had used the Book to his ends or vice versa. Was that The Ultimate's purpose behind his final query? To show him that he was a mere pawn in the idle games Fate played? That he had done nothing so impressive on his own? Or perhaps to prove that it was Dranus's will which had conquered the desires of Fate.

This was the last great task posed to him by The Ultimate. While he considered the tantalizing ease with which the Book, which bore the namesake of the question, might answer such a question, he refrained in hopes that he might discover the knowledge on his own and prove his worth.

As his mind became ever more lost in the infinite paths of the question, Dranus decided to travel the empire, visiting all of the areas that he then controlled. He scoured his lands both to understand every strength and weakness of his defenses and to search for an answer. While he was gone Raven assumed day to day control of the Obsidian Throne, though it was the likes of Ven and Armodus that guided her voice. It was a matter of great fortune that

Raven was fit by blood to lead the nation so that her word went unquestioned in Varz.

While on his travels he posed the question to every new philosophy or frame of mind that he came across: "What does Fate desire?"

Every time he got a different answer. Every time it felt incomplete.

He felt as though he was falling further and further from the truth with every thought, as if he were now reasoning in reverse!

Finally, he set to return to Varz from Urhyll in the east, stopping briefly to admire the Castle Surrounded by Stone once more and to pay homage to King Vulcan. He had hoped to rouse the dead king for guidance, but the old bones never moved again. Dranus raised the Sword of Righted Guard and thanked King Vulcan the Rock for all he had given him.

One afternoon when the sun was high and the smell of maple wafted on a lazy breeze, Dranus found himself camped early in a small valley swimming with dense brush. He set up his tent and tied his horse near a small shimmering lake so that his mount could drink to its heart's content. The King of Varz sat peacefully near where the waves lapped quietly against the shore. A single cloud traipsed in front of the sun, casting a cool shadow and reminding Dranus that the Dawn Season had not quite arrived yet. Still, it was the perfect place for him to rest his weary body, let his troubled mind rest, and for him to avoid his kingly responsibilities for just one more day.

Although he had come to appreciate the freedom and novelty of travel during his journey to conquer the Four Realms, he yearned for his wife's gentle touch. In his secret heart he wished he could step down in favor of Raven becoming queen so that he could engage with his new kingdom personally and see the world, but centuries of Varz tradition would not allow for more than one of the citizenry to hold the forbidden knowledge of a monarch. His people would not overlook such an integral aspect of their sorcerous hierarchy, especially not while they simultaneously struggled to accept Lesser Folk into their proud culture.

As he sat, the South Star, now a mere ball of red fire in the sky with no army to summon, fell beyond the horizon, casting crimson flames on the late afternoon skyscape. Finally, with a sigh, he stood and adjusted the Sword of Righted Guard in its scabbard at his hip as well as the satchel that held the Stone of Pyrán's Plight. The thing still pulsed color through the pouch's fabric in every shade of its namesake warriors.

With a tinge of reticence, he paced about his camp. His peace was still disturbed by that itch at the base of his skull, beneath the skin where he could not scratch it.

Finally, he came to stand over the Book of Fate's Desire.

A sound in the brush caught his attention momentarily before he turned back to the Book; rodents or some other pest no doubt.

With quiet compliance, Dranus picked the tome up and walked back to the lakeside. He could no longer resist, though he feared that the Book would simply dodge the question or refuse to answer it altogether.

"Tell me Book," he began.

The book seemed to perk up as if caught be a gust of wind.

"You must know...what does Fate desire?"

"What does Fate desire?" The book repeated. It was silent for but a brief second as it appeared to need no time in considering this question.

"That, master, is indeterminable and ever-changing. Fate desires all things and nothing at all. That which Fate desires is constantly evolving and adapting to the times, the conditions, and to the needs of the world. It does not seek that which It desires actively yet It always desires something. What Fate desires, King Dranus, I can never know the whole, as I am but a tool manipulated by Fate and mankind alike." The Book seemed to grow heavy though it may have just been the king's imagination. "But this is not the answer that you seek."

The answer was complex, though it suffered in specificity, and was nothing like what he had expected. It was possibly the most direct answer he had ever gotten from the sorcerous tome. However, it was not the answer that he sought, and he knew so even before the Book declared it. Suddenly, months upon months of frustration held by meager supports of self-delusion collapsed.

But unlike his previous life, who would have seen nothing left of value in the ruins, King Dranus took stock of all that was good in his life.

"Why should I care what Fate desires?! I have everything that I

411

never knew I could hope to dream for!" He shouted not at the book or at the lake, but to Fate, Itself. "I have taken a life of wretchedness into my own hands and achieved what only the sum of *generations* before me have achieved! I have found love! I have discovered passion! I have brought my people back from the brink of destitution to the peak of their potential! I have conquered a continent and in a year, no less! I have defeated prophecy! With these hands I defeated those mighty Warriors of Pyrán!" Somehow, saying all of these things out loud, even shouting them into the open sky, made them more real to him. He felt the levity of each and every accomplishment, personal or societal, lift away the frustration of a single unanswered question.

"What more could Fate desire of me?! No, it is time for Fate to come into my desires!"

He thought of himself such a short time ago and what a poor, lazy excuse for a living soul he had been and then considered what he had become! In a jubilant expression of victory, he raised his arms and regarded the sky, breathing in the fresh air and laughing heartily as he had come to do regularly. The sun was so warm on his skin!

Marveling at the wonder of his success, Dranus did not hear the quiet crunch of pressed grass behind him.

"I am king to a vast empire! I am unquestioned, unchallenged, and *loved* by the loyal people of Varz! I wield sorcerous might to match any of those of legend!" A prickling sensation covered his scalp, and he stood up straighter, intoxicated by the sudden revelation.

His joy was so magnificent that it extinguished the warning given to him by his ancestor King Vulcan. It overwhelmed him so that he did not notice the tugging sensation of his sword being drawn from his hip.

"I am a God among the mere men of this world! Anything I desire is mine to take!"

It was a sharp, frigid sensation that bit through his chest like frozen winds through a hollow. With such adrenaline and glee flowing through his body, he couldn't quite comprehend the feeling at first.

Lowering his arms, his sorcerous gaze came to rest on the pointed tip of the Sword of Righted Guard bathed in a smooth sheen of crimson poking out from his chest. Stunned, he glared at the thing as he might at a relentless fly. He hardly felt anything more than a slight sensation and a certain difficulty of breath.

Dranus's body grew stiff, and he fell to his side, hitting the ground with a cry of pain and a thud. The Book of Fate's Desire fell next to him and fluttered its pages. Dranus struggled to look up, grasping at the tip of the sword in his chest, his mind too fogged by pain to think of sorcery. Standing over the king was the final piece of a forgotten puzzle. Looking down at him with black sorcerer's eyes and short golden hair was the figure of would-be justice and the herald of Dranus's ascent.

Deleron Kaxus, son of Anon, stood over the fallen King of Varz with a wide grin on his lips. He had let the Sword of Righted Guard drop with its victim, but on his left arm was the peculiar shield that he had carried in his first attempt to slay the Varz monarch: the Shield of Second Life. Only then did Dranus see the telltale markings of the shield that had been covered by that crude bronze plating.

Young Kaxus chuckled bemusedly at the bleeding body of his former king.

"And the same will happen to you, King Dranus." He mocked the king in the haughty way he held himself, speaking as if to imitate the words Dranus had spoken when their roles were reversed.

The Book of Fate's Desire had settled on a familiar page. Near the bottom of the list the words "I will kill King Dranus" were gradually being covered by crossing lines.

Dranus's vision was starting to blur, the pain dulling with his consciousness.

Deleron Kaxus, would-be usurper, the beginning and end of Dranus's journey, bent over and picked up the Book laying in the mud and wiped it clean.

"I did as you said, I waited for your signal. It took him two years to drop his guard where I could reach him, but it was two years of wait well worth it!" He praised the Book as he might praise a pet that could sound off on command.

"And that is not all, master Kaxus! He holds the Stone of Pyrán's Plight fully imbued with the powers of the Warriors of Pyrán! Take it and you may even gain their powers!" The Book was full of excitement, speaking hastily and without restraint.

In his fading consciousness Dranus cursed that terrible thing, that which had seen him rise only to fall when he had everything! What

413

cruel desires must Fate have! But he had no strength to react nor to consider the sinister tone the Book had taken on.

"Excellent! My victory will be compounded one-hundredfold with this!" And so, the unknowing boy of Varz, proud and exultant, reached down to take the pouch which held the Stone of his ancestor. He loosed the strings and gawked at the swirling colors, feeling the undulating waves of power it emitted. He flipped the bag, anxiously awaiting the power which he knew would come from the very first touch of the stone!

When it touched his flesh, the thing greedily drew out his life force and tucked it away in the cracks and crevices in the rock. Thus, the lifeless body of Deleron Kaxus, twice confident, twice felled, collapsed next to that of King Dranus.

"Unfortunately, I may have failed to explain that only a direct descendant of Baklar may hold the Stone...." The cursed tome laughed terribly, a vicious laugh that was like the sound of pages torn in great anger.

"Book!" Dranus coughed out his own blood as the word came from his lips. "Tell me! Was I your tool from the very beginning?" He wept then, forced to accept his death, the loss of everything he had gained...the loss of Raven...his child...and the loss of his kingdom.

"No, King Dranus. You did not let me finish before. The answer that you have sought is: It is as He wills it." The tone of the Book softened as it seemed to consider the king once more from its undignified place in the mud.

"As who wills it?" Every word was like knives in his chest now, the will of his powerful thoughts the only thing keeping him conscious before his death.

"He is the Writer of Fate, the one who weaves the threads of this world." It paused. "He sends his regards."

Dranus could not comprehend the meaning of such concepts anymore. It was as if every bit of his knowledge seeped from his mind like blood let from his body.

There was only one thing left.

"Deleron Kaxus was a pawn, Dranus, a 'tool' if you'd like to call it that. He was meant to reach a particular end; in this, Fate desired your death. But you were a unique master. Like so few before you, you were able to bend Fate to your bidding and distort the intended order of things. I may have provided you with the weapons and the information, but all that you accomplished was the actualization of your own desires and will. In my entire existence I have rarely seen a soul stronger than yours. Yours was greater even than Baklar's, though his will remains unmatched. You should be proud of the life you lived, even if it was just a short two years..." the Book trailed off.

With every drop of blood that spilled from the king's body his magic weakened until the Book was silent, unmoved by his sorcerous workings.

He felt cold and weak, but he was proud. To learn, at the end, that he was master of his own Fate was some consolation. But all that he left behind...he lamented he had so little time to spend in peace and appreciation.

The world was truly unjust to take so much from him, but then, he could hardly be bothered with that now.

Wearing a sardonic smile on his lips, King Dranus of Varz slouched into the mud and stared without focus at a spot in space before him. He breathed a long, shuttering breath as black sorcerous eyes fell for a moment on the Shield of Second Life...and then closed.

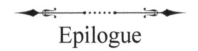

# Epilogue

Raven's coronation was the worst day of her life.

The day started early; the moment the sun broke over the walls of Varz she took her first step outside the castle. A quiet retinue of royal guards, staff, and what members of the Council that could attend on such short notice led her through the city.

A Varz coronation was all about transition. Fresh on the heels of becoming a full-fledged member of Varz society, she went from citizen to monarch, student to master, and protectorate to protector.

A parade through every major thoroughfare of the city would mark this transition, having the new monarch walk in stride with others for the very last time before they would become the sole leader of their people. They would see everything that was now theirs to protect, and they would be cheered on by all, given the full confidence of the city at large.

Unfortunately, that day was not a normal coronation.

Without so much as a blink, Raven willed her running violet makeup back to shape around her eyes. Ven had given her a brew meant to stop the weeping, but it only helped from time to time, in the softest of memory's harsh embraces. With every step she took her lips quivered and her heavily robed body shivered.

The day-long trip around the city barely registered in her mind. It was a blur of architectural wonders, grim expressions, and cruel condolences.

As the sun was setting, they returned to the castle in silence.

Raven had long since given up control over her body. She was nothing more than an automaton of shifting gears following a predetermined set of actions. She did not smile; she could not smile.

After seeing Dranus's face in the crowd for the tenth time, she'd willed her mind elsewhere. Even there in the mental abyss she had created within herself she could not escape the pain and suffering of knowledge she should never have.

Her first seating on the Obsidian Throne was met with a few

scattered bouts of applause that were almost instantly absorbed into the black hole of silence that followed the new Queen of Varz. It was far from the first time a coronation had to come so soon after the previous monarch's death, but such a thing had not occurred in many generations. They were, after all, still technically in wartime. Their mobile forces could not go without a commander-in-chief for as long as a normal mourning period.

The droning of announcements that accompanied the more formal parts of her coronation allowed her to disassociate further into the memory of that day just one month prior.

The Council had become worried at the king's long absence. Dranus was rarely, if ever, late. In fact, it was his curious ability to arrive precisely when needed that had kept them from acting sooner. Raven and many others had dismissed this anomaly as some sort of secret mission or well-deserved vacation, though Raven doubted he would take such a long leave without her.

A report had finally reached Varz from a small village where an old man had found what appeared to be abandoned trappings of the king's camp.

Ven insisted that Raven stay and let outriders from the Mounted Forces, who were used to extreme exertion on a moment's notice, investigate. Raven was pregnant; she had to consider the health of her unborn child!

Regardless, she could not be kept.

She remembered being told that riding horseback could kill the infant and then setting forth on foot.

She'd started slow, only about as fast as a horse at a canter, but as her imagination shaped worse and worse depictions of her dead husband her pace increased. Somewhere along the way she had forgotten to have limits on how quickly she could run. Time would not permit her to take her leisure, not with uncertainty on all sides. So she gave Time nothing in return.

Quietly, almost thoughtlessly, something deep in her blood awakened and her sorcery began to break comprehension. By midday she had reached the small town where the report came from...a two-day ride by horse.

She was given directions to the reported location and was there almost before she could even complete her plans to go.

Raven broke through thick brush in a cloud of dust, covered in loose shrubs, dirt, and insect corpses. Her heart was beating far faster than it should be capable of and her breathing struggled to catch up with rapid shallow breaths. She grew lightheaded again from the rush of oxygen, her limbs going numb for a few moments as she struggled to maintain consciousness.

The scent of the lake was a strong deterrent from collapsing into slick mud. It was refreshing in a way, too, though not enough for her to quickly recover from her sorcerous exertions.

Finally, the world snapped sharply back into focus and her body normalized with some effort.

She had little to go off of in terms of details. The lake was rather large and thick brush surrounded it on a full half of its circumference.

Raven breathed in deeply several times and tried to shift her vision as Dranus had taught her, but to no avail. She would have to do this the old way, with careful examination and thoroughness.

The next hour or so she spent circling the lake, pushing her way through thick brush to make sure she missed nothing. By the time the South Star set she was covered in cuts from thorns and branches, burrs hung on every loose piece of cloth on her body, and she'd twisted her ankle in the mud at least twice.

None of these things bothered her.

She could feel Dranus's presence nearby. She didn't know how but she could just sense it as she got closer and closer to the assumed site mentioned in the report.

Finally, she broke into a small cove-like clearing where a tent bearing the royal symbol of Varz was still set, though it had clearly been rummaged through by wild animals and looters alike. Everything else looked as though it had been frozen in time, untouched since the moment it was found. A downed trunk with a hatchet still stuck in its bark, the black remains of a fire, even a lazily grazing horse tied firmly to a stake in the ground.

She'd approached the horse before seeing the blood....

Raven was ripped back into her own space and time screaming from a searing pain on her cheek.

The red-hot prongs of the royal symbol were being pulled away from her face and her entire body was afire with pain as she writhed in the solid black stone seat of Varz power.

As much as it was taboo for another to interfere in this ceremony, Ven could not help but cast a bit of respite at the girl and soon Raven's mind became unmuddled enough to realize what was happening.

She pressed a hand over the raw skin of her cheek and pulled the heat out, pressing the same burning palm into the cool obsidian rock where it dissipated quickly.

Those present for this part of the ceremony looked at her in confusion; apparently she had agreed that she was ready for the marking that all monarchs of Varz shared in her absent mind. However, she hadn't actually registered that she should prepare herself for the agony that was coming.

Even after the burning had stopped and just the sensation of torn flesh remained, she faded in and out of awareness of what was happening around her. The ceremony continued, giving wide berths for breaches in tradition since Raven had no knowledge of these traditions and was clearly traumatized from the loss of her husband so soon after cementing their love and even conceiving a child together.

Raven slipped a shaking hand between thick dark robes to feel the cloth against her swollen stomach. Every day she had felt a joy radiating from her inner garden but on that day, she felt nothing. Her child mourned just as she did, she was sure.

Walking in full ceremonial garb was difficult enough normally, with a child it was purely nonsensical, but she did it anyway.

The ceremony would be over soon. There was only one final thing for her to embrace as the new reigning monarch of Varz.

The scent of stone and mortar gave way to living mahogany as Raven and Ven entered a secret section of the castle. Of all the people ever to set foot in Varz castle, only those known as monarch or commander of the Mage Corps had ever even known how to find the King's Library, which housed the Forbidden Texts of Varz history, sorcery, and secrets.

When Ven left, Raven was forced to stand alone in front of the massive living doors without the slightest inclination of how to get inside. It was her right, as the new Queen of Varz, to enter and yet nobody living, at least in the natural sense, knew how to do so.

The passing of minutes with her aching palm feeling the grain of the ancient wooden doors gave way to hours with her naked back against the door. Raven hadn't a clue when she'd shed her robes to feel the warmth of her bare stomach. She couldn't think straight. She hadn't even tried anything other than merely touching the door.

What time was it?

This was her last task, certainly her royal retinue would be waiting for her to reappear with confirmation that she'd been able to enter.

Tired like a summer storm she pressed her back against the door and shimmied her way up to her feet.

She yelped in angry pain as a sliver of the door slid into her skin and drew blood.

Falling back to her rear, she spun onto all fours and screamed fiercely at the door as if it were a wandering predator and she was its intended prey, warning it that she was no one's prey.

Then, with a sigh from the aged wood, the doors swung inward.

Suddenly aware, she dashed into the chamber, picking up her robes on the way.

In a final bit of desperation, she went through every room in the King's Library searching for a sign of Dranus. She knew he couldn't really be dead. He was hiding. Where else could he hide where only she could find him?

When it was painfully clear that she was alone in the great library, she carefully went over every book or parchment that was not obviously in its appropriate place. In a flurry she caught glimpses of what Dranus had been searching for before leaving on his last trip. Many of the scripts were in languages she had yet to learn but they all prominently featured a word that went beyond translation: Fate.

That heinous curse The Ultimate had placed on Dranus the last time they met!

He had still been chasing that illusion! But then what had caused his death?

Had he found it?

The way things were scattered about in frustration told her that if he had, it had not been here. But then, when he had no success, he had still been with her. Being unable to discover the answer to the ancient king's riddle had left Dranus without any notable consequence...so then it stood to reason that if he *had* figured it out, something would change.

Something that put him in danger? Perhaps from The Ultimate, himself?

Or something even greater?

If the people of Varz believed that Death had an identifiable physical form, what other forces might have agents that could interact on the same plane as humans?

She knew that in future years of her rule, people would call her insane or unstable. But just as she had instinctively felt that Dranus was near the day she found the site of his 'death,' she could sense that her husband was still out there and that he needed her help. It was the only thing that kept consistent with everything she'd seen.

With steeled resolve, Raven locked herself in the King's Library for days trying to figure out what her husband had discovered.

Every time that sleep overwhelmed her she saw a still image of what she'd seen, forever burned into her mind like the slanted V on her cheek: of a Varz corpse with no wounds, weapons, or armor to speak of, the signs of fatal bleeding several feet away with no apparent source, and the imprint of a wrinkled book in the mud.

# About the Author

Ryan Hampton is a Psychologist and Neuroscientist who studies culture and emotions. Ryan is an avid consumer of stories across genres, platforms, and history and takes inspiration from experiences in world cultures. Ryan's favorite author is Michael Moorcock and he draws inspiration for the dark and strange from such works as Elric of Melniboné and The Chronicles of Corum. Ryan's take on classic fantasy focuses on mature, emotion-accurate characters and relationships, imaginative and innovative settings, and classic head-turning plot twists! In *The Book of Fate's Desire*, he explores themes of personal growth and the struggle against destiny while reversing traditional tropes to be experienced from the villain's perspective. *The Book of Fate's Desire* is the first of the *Books of Fate* Trilogy and is Ryan's first fantasy novel.

Printed in the USA
CPSIA information can be obtained
at www.ICGtesting.com
LVHW090745011023
759464LV00104B/606